An Elusive Sanctuary
Quest for the Golden Key

Also by Charles Humphrey Muller:

Novels:

Spirit of Ecstasy by 'Carolyn Charles' (with Carolyn Muller)

Rapture at Sea (with Carolyn Muller)

Laura's Secret (with Elsie MacMillan)

The Cage and the Cross

A Twist in Time

Wheel of Destiny

Non-Fiction:

Waipori Reflections: Contemplations in Three Locations

Bragleenbeg Reflections

Touches by Angels: Testimonies of Christian Power

The Christian Teachings of Charles Kingsley

Have Anything You Really Want: A Christian Testimony

An Elusive Sanctuary
Quest for the Golden Key

Charles Humphrey Muller

DIADEM BOOKS

An Elusive Sanctuary:
Quest for the Golden Key

Published by Diadem Books

For information, please contact:

Diadem Books
16 Lethen View
Tullibody
Alloa
FK10 2GE UK

www.diadembooks.com

Cover painting of Jedburgh Abbey by Joanne Muller

ISBN: 13: 978-1908026606
ISBN: 10:190802660X

The First Insight in *The Celestine Prophecy* tends to capture our attention and fire our imagination because it taps into what our mythic reality has always taught—that there is a Golden Key, a magical stranger, a meaningful dream, or an unexpected clue that appears to guide us effortlessly to the treasure or opportunity that we seek.

—James Redfield & Carol Adrienne: *The Celestine Prophecy: An Experiential Guide*

CHAPTER 1

Jedburgh 1988

THE ABBEY loomed large and square through the snowstorm. The square tower, the rectangular body of the transept, gave an impression of solidity, in spite of the squalls of snow that drifted by, almost obscuring the details—the terraced rows of interlocking arches, the pitched gables, roofless, the rosette window in the raised prow at the far end. It was like a great ocean liner, stranded, majestic in ruined splendour. The curtains of sleet drifted and swirled.

Harry shivered. He felt dislocated, lost and confused.

The rectangular chunk of the removal van blocked half the road, parked alongside the hotel he had bought. Huddled figures struggled under boxes and beds. In the courtyard workmen banged and hammered, erecting two garden sheds to create storage space for his displaced belongings—the books and paraphernalia of an academic life he would never resume. Snow built up on the roofs as soon as they were nailed in place.

'What the hell have I done?' Harry asked himself.

He had lost hold of his career. He had changed course. Never again would he enjoy the status of a professor. He looked at his hotel.

A gabled Victorian building, perched close to the bank that dropped steeply to the river Jed below, was his new venture, his new attempt at stability. This was a far cry from the prosaic damp-stained university building that resembled an office block where he had lectured to students about Dickens and existentialism, and a far cry from the milling traffic that surged continuously past his Crystal Palace home. Here the rushing London traffic, the rattling to and fro on the Northern Line, was stilled by the steadily falling snow, the wind stinging his face with cold.

But this move to Scotland was a dream conceived five years before, in a cottage at the head of Scammerdale Loch near Oban. The romanticism of that setting, amidst snow-peppered hills and an azure-blue loch seemed to offer a romantic escape from his prosaic life in London—a life of committee and faculty meetings weighed down by the personal anxiety of his wife's mounting debts. The embarrassment of those debts, of her increasing tendency to borrow money behind his back from his colleagues, and the final reminders arising from her addiction to shopping sprees on newly-opened accounts and credit cards, made his London life too painful to bear. He had let go, eventually, when the death of his father in Dulwich left him with sufficient capital to pay all debts and, with the help of a commercial mortgage, buy a small hotel. And here he was. Could he survive here? Would he find fulfilment, here, serving eggs and bacon overshadowed by the ruins of a twelfth-century Augustinian abbey?

He slept badly that night, waking often to fret over what he had done. What made it worse was the cold and the smell of damp in the small coffin-shaped room the sale particulars had described as 'the snug owners' bedroom.' Tiny mushrooms were sprouting in one spot, where the wall met the ceiling. He was not yet forty and never again would enjoy the prestige of being called professor by nervous students, or enjoy the kudos of a new publication, or the respect of staff when he called a meeting. On the other hand, he told himself, never again would he have to mark mounds of papers, set exams, observe deadlines, attend faculty or senate meetings; above all, never again would he have to suck up to the Dean, or fall so readily into the pattern of dancing around and patting academic egos, like a butterfly flapping around dim electric lights. He was cold and frightened, but academic posturing was a thing of the past. In this new world academic degrees, publications, and colleagues' bloated egos didn't matter. They no longer existed.

What mattered was cashflow. Hard cash. He looked at Anne who slept soundly, like a child. So much depended on Anne, he thought. Would she be able to control her impulses to spend lavishly in this new environment? He would have to watch the accounts like a hawk. No longer would there be the comfort of a secure salary, however limited. In London they were always scraping the bottom of the barrel, each month, even with the London allowance tacked onto his salary. But at least there was a barrel to scrape.

The next few days in March Harry stood in the dining-room window, looking at the changing light on the Abbey. The electric storage heaters, dinosaurs of an earlier age when electricity was affordable, only produced a modicum of warmth in the public rooms with their high Victorian ceilings. There were no guests and Harry spoke aloud, disgruntledly: 'This is not a viable business!'

But at least, as Anne said, they were in Scotland. They had made a break with an unhappy past and this was a new beginning where they would be equally yoked as a husband-and-wife team. He focused his eyes on the Abbey. The weather was calm, for once, and the Abbey stood out sharply against the pale blue of the sky. Snow, like icing on a cake, softened the broken surfaces of the ruined arches. Harry listened to the continuous surge of the water as it frothed below, in the Jed. Their first guests, an American couple, had stayed the night before and at breakfast had sat in the window seat. 'What's that old church?' the old man had whined, looking at the Abbey disapprovingly. 'Why don't they fix it up?'

Later he drew on his coat and walked down to the Abbey. The sun was warm on his face and his breath hung white in the cold air. He sat on a bench and looked across the river at the parallel terraces of arches. He felt warm and comfortable in the sunshine and counted the arches. Thirty-six on the middle level, each uniting two smaller arches. A smaller row of nine arches surmounted these. The solid square of the tower was slit by one long window facing the void where the roof had been; the side nearest to Harry had three long window slits overlooking the huge broken arch where the east wing had been. The entire structure was majestic, like a huge machine or engine designed to be driven by prayer. Some of the stairways were exposed, like old conduits, where monks shrouded by cowls had made their way to different levels. He could see the steep steps curving and disappearing into black holes.

He got up and crossed the bridge that bore the cars into Jedburgh and made his way up the steps of the war memorial. Now he was on the same level as the nave and looked down the aisle, the main body of the Abbey. This was the best view.

Awe touched his nerves. On either side the row of high pillars, the parallel lines of shadows and light, the high vaulted arches, one after the other, sucked his soul into an infinity of vision. Cowled figures, rows and rows of them, filled the expanse, the slanting sunbeams catching their hoods, one by one, as they moved, heads bowed. A deep resonance, barely audible, subliminal, vibrated just below the threshold of his hearing. Was it a distant Gregorian chant, or an electric surge from some unknown source? His eyes rose to the circular window in the pitched gable, the white light resolving into rainbow colours. He counted the segments—twelve shafts of corpuscular rays, coalescing in a beam of white light that grew brighter as he looked. Brighter...

'Aye, it will suck ye in!' said a voice behind him. 'Dinna' look ta hard.'

The light dimmed and the window was nothing more than segments of old stone. He dropped his gaze and again the shafts of light fell on the open and empty space of the transept. He turned.

A tall figure, slightly stooped, stood there. The black hood of a duffel coat enveloped a young man's face, like a cowl. His long, lugubrious face smiled at him. 'It's a canny sight. But dinna' look ta long.'

CHAPTER 2

Thomas Cranston

'AYE, IT'LL SUCK YE IN if ye luik ta hard,' said the lugubrious figure with a wry smile. 'Just the way I was sucked oot ta hier.' He swept his long arm towards the City Hall and other stone houses of Jedburgh. 'Sa noo I'm trapped hier.'

'You're trapped in Jedburgh?' Harry laughed politely. 'I suppose in a sense I am too.'

The newcomer introduced himself as Thomas Cranston and it seemed he had been in Jedburgh a long time. It took some time for Harry's ears to accustom themselves to Thomas's speech, which partook strongly of the local colour and dialect. Harry returned to the hotel and found he couldn't shake Thomas who slouched behind him, and politeness made him slow down his walk to allow his companion to slouch next to him. Thomas was tall and slightly bent, the duffel coat with its hood still giving him the uncanny appearance of a monk.

Thomas prattled on about being a gardener in the Abbey's cloister garden where he tended various herbs, many of which were remedies for ailments. There was sweet camomile which reduced swellings and inflammation, wormwood that expelled worms and aided digestion, or skullcap for headaches and nervous disorders.

'Really?' Harry nodded, only half listening. It was becoming increasingly evident that Thomas wasn't quite in his right mind, or that half his mind existed in some other dimension.

'Aye,' Thomas droned on. 'There be herbal concoctions, like, fer fleshly loost, fer immoderate laughing, forgetfulness and the alder leaves bathed in nicht dew will put an end ta excessive crying.' He laughed. 'You name it, the herbs are there for whativer ails thee.'

'Will you come in a for a cup of tea?' invited Harry as they drew level with the hotel.

'Aye, that's verra kind.' Thomas inclined his head, critically eyeing the front of the gabled building. 'Aye, ye'll be needing some painting hier. The wood in the door needs some paint, like. I can do that fer ye.' And he surveyed the overgrown garden that fell in terraces towards the river. 'An the garden needs trimmin', like. Ye'll be needin' a gardener, I was thinkin'. I can do that forra while.'

They entered the hotel, opening the doorway to the little private lounge at the back. Thomas slouched in and stuck out a long thin hand to Anne who was arranging some miniature vintage cars in a display cabinet. She looked up, surprised at the sight of the tall lanky figure.

'Aye,' said Thomas, picking up one of the little cars and without hesitation launching into a detailed explanation of how the internal combustion engine worked. 'When the cylinder cooms oop, ken, a wee spark ignites the petrol and the compressed air that gits verra hot explodes, like, and ...'

'This is my wife, Anne,' smiled Harry. He winked at Anne. 'I found Tom at the Abbey. Apparently he's from the twelfth century and works in the Abbey garden.'

'In the cloister garden,' explained Thomas, taking her hand briefly. 'I can get ye some Roman wormwood fir puir digestion and fir keepin' moths from clothing, yer only ta ask. An' some spurge forra that rash on yer neck, like.'

Anne placed a podgy hand lightly on her neck which was still a little flushed from standing over a hot stove. She smiled uncertainly. 'Thank you,' she said bemusedly. She was a dumpy woman with straight blonde hair tied up in a ponytail by means of an elastic band, the strands constantly escaping and floating in disarray around her face. Once she had captivated Harry with her bright blue eyes and nymph-like beauty, when she was sixteen. It took a stretch of the imagination, now, to recall her once sylph-like figure to memory—when he used to skulk into the back of her mother's house and ravish her on the cold hard kitchen floor. 'Shall I bring you some tea?' she asked, looking up at Thomas who's lanky figure was now bereft of the coat.

'That's kind of ye,' bowed Thomas. 'An a wee bit a' cake, like.'

Fortunately there was some leftovers from a recent chocolate cake. Thomas munched and sipped his tea at the same time, explaining with a full mouth how to bake a carrot cake, and how flour is milled. It seemed he was endowed with a detailed knowledge of everything, on every subject that might be found in Arthur Mee's Children's Encyclopaedia. It was his habit to launch into detailed explanations about how things worked at the slightest provocation, regardless of whether the knowledge was invited or already known to the recipient of the information.

'Are there any others like yourself in Jedburgh?' asked Harry, sipping his tea.

'In Jedworth? Aye, twee or three,' he nodded contemplatively. 'There's Matilda from the infirmary, like. A bonny lass in her day, when she was first sucked through. She were the beauty of Jedworth, see, but iver since her child died she was gone in the heed, like, and wanders aboot. Ye'll surely see her a-wanderin' atween her hoos and the toon. She wanders all the day noo.' He bit off some more cake and sipped some more tea. 'Ye know what I'm thinkin'?' he said ruminatively. 'I thinkin' she still pines fer her first love Quentin, whose a canon in the Abbey, like. But he being a priest, like, she canna' have him, see? He is bound by vows of poverty and chastity.'

'A cannon?' asked Anne with a harsh laugh. 'But the Abbey is a ruin now!'

'Aye, it's a ruin now, ken? Just like puir Matilda's become a ruin, like.' He munched his cake, casually unaware of the illogicality of his information. 'Then there's Abbot John. Ye'll see him wanderin' aboot enough, too, I'll be thinkin'! Ye canna mistake him fer he has a baldy heed, like. He still luiks for his auld place and leeks a dram too much, wheniver he can get it. Ye see, I am much righter in the heed than those twee, and I've read much of the modern times. I'm niver so beheend the teems as they and niver so trapped as they be, see?'

Anne, who wasn't in the direct line of Thomas's vision, grimaced at Harry and twirled her forefinger round her ear, as if to say 'What have we here!'

It was clear that Thomas wasn't going to leave without being asked to, and Harry was too polite to throw him out. After Thomas gave a lengthy explanation of the principle whereby a telescope enlarged images by bending and focusing light rays, Harry quickly suggested that a walk would do him good—before the next explanation offered itself to Thomas's analytically pedestrian mind.

'I need a walk myself,' Harry said casually. 'I'll choose a route past your house so you can show me where you live.'

Thomas accepted the ploy and allowed Harry to steer him out of the front door while he pulled on his duffel coat. 'I can paint the ceiling fer ye,' Thomas said as Harry closed the door behind him. 'Do ye ken, pink paint is made by bringing tagither the pigmentation of white and red paint? There's a canny machine that blends...'

When they reached Thomas's council flat, Harry went inside for a moment and was amazed to see an easel with the large canvas of a painting of Jedburgh Abbey. It was magnificent, though clearly not yet completed with tubes of oil paints lying scattered on a table.

'You're an artist!' exclaimed Harry. 'Thomas, this is magnificent.'

'Aye,' said Thomas, touching a corner delicately to see how the drying was coming along. 'Ye see hier, this is the chapter hoos where Abbot John was accused of loost fer a young cannon.' He gave a little giggle. 'That was the week afore he were sucked oot.'

Harry was quite spellbound and barely heard the nonsense about Abbot John. 'But how did you know how the Abbey looked before it became a ruin? It must have looked like this in 1500.'

Thomas shook his head. 'Afore then. 1285, afore Eddie began ta tear it doon!'

'Eddie?'

'Aye!' he nodded, removing his duffel coat. 'Edward the first, ken. The hammer of the Scots.'

CHAPTER 3

Toil and Trouble

THE DAFFODILS were standing to attention like smartly dressed soldiers as a mark of the beginning of the season. Guests began to filter in, many of them Americans who chose the early part of the season because of its cheapness. Harry imagined that six en suite bedrooms would provide a sufficient turnover to show a reasonable profit, but was dismayed by the onslaught of the overheads. While most of these, like rates, water, refuse collection and electricity, were expected and taken into account in his original cashflow projections, he was dismayed to find how much he had underestimated them.

'*Everyone* wants our money!' he exclaimed to Anne one morning when he opened the post. The electricity bill amounted to a mammoth sum exceeding £500 a quarter, while the crippling mortgage and insurance amounted to over £700 a month. Furthermore, the other on-going costs including supplies from the cash and carry and butcher mopped up any money that might have been left by the end of the month. There were the costs arising from being a member of the Scottish Tourist Board: grading costs, membership fees, and minimal advertising costs amounting to well over £2000 a year. And then there was the constant onslaught of telesales, trying to sell anything from advertising space to laundry equipment.

'At least,' said Harry, raking his fingers through his hair, 'they can't get at me when I'm in the grave! No matter how shrewd and persistent the advertising telesales people are, in death I'll have the ultimate sales resistance!'

Poor Anne! She had little resistance to sales persons, and she was well aware of the high demands of the Tourist Board for quality. The grading officer was quick to point out that certain chairs and dining room equipment were 'looking tired,' not to mention to multitude of nooks and crannies in need of refurbishment. 'Obviously your grading of three-crowns commended is teetering, and you'll have to retile the bathrooms.'

Spend, spend, spend! Harry and Anne had to deliver what the Tourist Board's crowns promised, including warmth of welcome. It was their obligatory smiles—sometimes genuine, often fixed—which greeted the tourists at the door. Because of the exhaustion from trying to do all the work themselves they employed two part-time cleaners, which meant wages, tax and national insurance to think of. And there were other considerations such as fire regulations, food hygiene and bookkeeping. The accountant's bill alone amounted to a thousand pounds a year. If there were any profits they needed to be sunk back into the business in on-going refurbishment or repairs: the plumbing as well as the roof frequently leaked and needed constant costly attention.

'People are demanding higher and higher standards,' complained Anne towards the end of the season. She looked weary and crestfallen, her blonde hair hanging lifelessly down her cheeks that had become ruddy with work. 'It's so difficult to keep up. Each year we'll have to do up a room, or do some major refurbishment. The dining room carpet and the carpet in no.4 bedroom needs replacing.'

'And it's like a damn prison!' complained Harry. 'Our time's never our own. We can never go out together in case the phone rings. And one of us is constantly hopping to the ring of the phone or the doorbell. We have to be up before dawn to serve breakfasts, and by the time the evening dinners are finished and we've washed up it's midnight. It's *always* the same. I hate this damn place!'

'But surely it's better than the university?' Anne said, grabbing a quick cup of tea. 'You said yourself you hated marking papers and going to faculty meetings. You also said you hated commuting, driving through the dark and traffic and then spending an hour on the Northern Line. Would you rather go back to that?'

'No, dammit, I wouldn't.' He shrugged. He put down his tea which had already gone cold because he was interrupted by a guest who didn't understand how the bedroom television worked. 'But this place is beginning to get to me, too. I know that most of our guests are super and very polite. But there are more and more who think they're booking into a five-star hotel. You can't deny that because of the grading system they're expecting the same facilities and quality they'd get at a big plush hotel. And they expect personalised service! So what happens? They're only paying a fraction of the price but they find the room's too small. Or the soap's not individually wrapped. Or there are bath towels instead of bath sheets. The Tourist Board is breeding a soft society. Even the nice English guests are becoming aggressive consumers like the overweight Americans. To meet this level of pampering at competitive B&B prices means no profit at all at the end of the day! I tell you, the Tourist Boards are killing off the B&B trade. And that includes guest houses and small hotels like ourselves. It's a constant strain, financial and nervous, to keep these people happy.'

'But we *are* succeeding,' insisted Anne. 'We've already had a number of guests coming back. In fact, I'd say that 30% of our trade is repeat trade already.'

'Yes, granted,' sighed Harry. 'It's the lunatic fringe that's getting me down. Every time I open the door and smile warmly I know there's a ten percent probability I'll get a kick in the teeth. Some of them can barely manage to smile. In fact, many don't— they just glare and expect me to grovel to their pride. And to think I have a doctorate and was once a university professor!'

'So it's *your* pride getting in the way, just as theirs does!'

'Well, at least *I* smile and grovel!' He shook his head. 'It all takes its toll. And look how many people arrive around midnight, many hours after they said they'd arrive. And that's after we've turned God knows how many people away who wanted the room. Or they don't turn up at all and we might have let the room many times' over. And do you remember when I had to get up at 3 a.m. for Mr Zaponi who wanted a bottle opener? And then he and his drunk friends expected me to serve them drinks from the bar! *And* he demanded breakfast at 5.30 because he had a plane to catch in Edinburgh! Or that stupid Frenchman who checked in at 4 p.m., was told that breakfast was between eight and nine, went to sleep and woke up at 8 p.m. demanding breakfast! And then he had to glare at me as though it was my fault he'd lost—or regained—eight hours. Fucking hell, I can't take some of these people much longer!'

Anne broke into raucous laughter—laughter that grated on Harry's nerves. She had lost all the feminine glamour she had when she was a nymph with a slim little waist and a mischievous smile. He used to be crazy for her lithe lily-white body, covering it with kisses and shuddering with delicious orgasms as he spasmed into her during those many illicit meetings on the single bed of her bedroom. His eyes surveyed her now, squat and fat, tugging at her lower lip, her stumpy legs wide apart on the settee, like a man's.

'That Frenchman was just a joke,' she said as she bit into a jam donut. 'It's that bloody Emslie woman that really got to me! Complaining that her radio didn't work because it wasn't plugged in! I went up to her room, plugged it in for her, tuned into her station, and she *still* wrote to the Tourist Board saying the radio didn't work!'

'And the toilet seat protested under her weight, remember, so she blamed us! And her bedside light blew when she switched it on. So she wrote to complain that nothing worked! And then at breakfast she couldn't bring herself to speak to me. "Would you like a full Scottish breakfast, madam? Bacon, eggs, sausage, tomato and haggis?" All she could do was purse her bloody lips. Her mouth looked like a post office slit. She sat there in the window, overlooking the Abbey, one of the most delightful views in the country, looking squat and grumpy, like a frog. "Tea or coffee?" I urged politely, smiling, wanting to kick in her bloody teeth. What does she do? Just purse her bloody lips again. I suppose I was supposed to grovel on my knees and apologise for my existence and offer her a thousand bloody pounds for the honour of having her gracious almighty frogginess stay with us. *Fuck*!' Harry was becoming quite heated at the memory. 'Shit! And that wasn't *half* as bad as that bitch that wrote to complain about a few drawing pins holding down the wallpaper! God, the drawing pins—about five—were only there to keep the paper in place while it was drying! It's beyond belief! The drawing pins being there in the corner of the room kept her awake all night! Fucking bitch!' Harry spoke in a high-pitched affected voice, quoting the woman's letter from memory: '"I'm afraid I will not be able to recommend your establishment to anyone else!" As if I'd want any of *her* friends staying here!'

'I still think the worst guest so far was that Australian, Mr Slater!' Anne snorted. 'Complaining in the morning that we didn't have fly-screens and that a bee had got in and kept his girlfriend awake all night!'

Harry shook his head. 'What was worse was that he spent the night drawing up a long list of totally irrelevant complaints: the bed was too hard (though others have found it too soft), the water in the pipes made a noise, the bed linen didn't match the curtains, and ... and...' He shook his head. 'I can't remember the other complaints. The list was two pages long. But what got to me was the way the fucking shit leant his head on his hand at breakfast and groaned while I had to serve him bacon and eggs and *smile*! I wanted to smash the bloody plate over his head!'

'He expected me to waive his bill, remember?'

Harry nodded. 'And because you didn't he wrote to the bloody Tourist Board. It's a forum for bloody complaints, that's what it is. They even *encourage* people to complain, calling it quality control. But who's in the front line of attack? *We* are!'

Anne appeared to be keeping her personal spending habits in abeyance throughout the busy months of the season. There was sufficient need to make legitimate purchases for the hotel in July and August when the flow of tourists passing through to Edinburgh and the Highlands beyond ensured a near 100% occupancy level. The phone kept ringing and bookings were filling the rooms nicely. Guests frequently admired the breathtaking panoramic view across the river of the Abbey as the blue summer skies bathed the stones in a warm golden light. It seemed a good little business after all and in spite of the exhaustion from serving breakfasts and meals, there was a new light at the end of the tunnel.

They employed a new cleaner almost full-time. Rosemary was a frowzy middle-aged spinster of a nervous disposition. She was also a medium in her spare time and detected the ghosts of George and Percy who seemed to inhabit bedroom number one. They were mischievous ghosts, she said, which possibly explained why the toilet seat in the bathroom of Room 1 kept shifting off its hinges, and why the Yale lock kept sticking. They meant no harm, Rosemary explained with a nervous laugh. They were simply trying to get her attention because of a need to rise to the next level. Apparently some human intervention by a Christian believer was required, in the form of prayers, for such a move to be made possible in the ethereal world. One day Harry detected the lingering smell of a pipe in Room 1 and Rosemary explained it was George who, in his spirit existence, smoked a meerschaum pipe.

'Do these spirits actually speak to you, Rosemary?' Harry asked.

'Aye, they do!' she tittered with a nervous smile. 'I hear their voices in my head. This morning George said he was *that* worried about you. He said you were becoming very tired and dissipated.'

'Dissipated?'

'Yes,' she smiled quickly. 'I do not know what the word means, but that was the word I heard. I suppose it means you're working too hard. George was worried for you.'

'That's nice of him,' said Harry with a wry smile. 'Give him my compliments. Tell him he's welcome to consult my Oxford English Dictionary, too.'

'No need,' she said with a nervous twitch in he left eye. 'He knows.'

It was in August that Veronica, a widow who ran a B&B establishment down the road, visited Anne. Veronica was a taller and more sophisticated version of Anne with hair drawn back in a bun rather than a straggly pony tail. She came to visit with a smart velvet cloth which she proceeded to unroll on the carpet. Myriads of star-studded jewels twinkled like diamonds, each attached to the velvet roll by means of a small pocket.

'These are just some of the products of Selecon,' she explained. 'Selecon is the leading manufacturer of costume jewellery. None of it is available in the shops because the distribution is through network marketing. It's absolutely sweeping the country. Each distributor is his or her own boss and operates at various levels. The higher your level, the higher your retail discount is. Once you've reached the fourth level the income generated from royalties alone will be in excess of £20,000 a year!'

Anne was captivated and Veronica signed her up as a level-1 distributor that very day. What could be better than to sell jewellery to the guests who were a kind of captive audience for your sales pitch? 'By buying a certain quantity of jewellery in advance you can buy yourself into level 2 directly, or even higher. It makes sense when you think of the fantastic retail discounts. You get 30% at level 3!'

So Anne became a level-3 distributor with a glass cabinet full of jewellery she had purchased in advance. Harry wasn't sure how she managed to pay for it all but she assured him the cashflow that month had been excellent. The cabinet glistened with little diamond-studded cats, diamond-studded lizards and even diamond-encrusted frogs. Of course, they weren't *real* diamonds, but they looked as good and sparkled just the same. She had more than three hundred items. At the end of August she had sold two—one frog and one ruby ring.

The season petered out by the end of September and Anne was called away urgently by the sudden illness of her stepfather. This meant a bus journey all the way to Streatham. She would be away for at least a week and in the meantime Harry pressed Rosemary into cooking the eggs and bacon for the guests. Rosemary became flustered and kept breaking the eggs and got the orders confused. Harry had to take over and broke the eggs into the frying pan with fewer casualties and apologised to the patient guests: 'I'm sorry,' he said, 'but my cook's gone bezerk.'

'Oh, that's fine, don't *worry!*' a plump rosy-faced woman smiled up at him. 'We've plenty of time.'

Eventually Rosemary got the hang of things a little more and handed the plates to him with less trembling and less nervous laughter and apologies.

It was during this time of Anne's absence that Harry received an urgent letter from the bank manager. 'Would you please contact me as soon as possible so we can discuss your account.'

It was a Saturday when Harry received the letter so he had to wait until Monday before he could get to the bank. But he *knew* something was drastically wrong. Fortunately it was a quiet period and there were no guests. He knew the bank manager's letter had to have something to do with Anne and he was aware that she had a drawer in her desk that she always kept carefully locked. He had noticed for some time that she had always rushed to intercept the post before he had access to the daily pile. Most of the stuff he waded through was 'junk mail'—business opportunities, chain letters and letters from journals urging him to advertise with them. Anne wasn't due to return for a week yet. He wriggled the locked drawer but it was firmly locked. He felt a wave of alarm and anxiety. He *had* to find out what was in that drawer before he saw the bank manager on Monday.

CHAPTER 4

Tightening the Screw

HARRY went into one of the garden sheds used for storage and found a screwdriver. When he returned to the house he pulled Anne's little desk away from the wall. It was the same desk she had used as a schoolgirl and she treasured it with a sentimental value. Harry had always respected it as her private domain and it felt like a violation when he unscrewed the back panel from the desk. Once the panel was removed he found it easy to slide his hand into the space above the locked drawer and pull out its contents.

There were about five letters from the bank, all addressed to him. His fingers trembled as he opened them, his heart in his mouth. They were all the same, all from the bank manager asking him to come in urgently in order to discuss his account. His stomach knotted up with anxiety and felt he wanted to be sick. He knew instinctively that something of Anne's old problem had reared its head again. It was near the end of the season and his business account should be at least five thousand pounds in credit—the amount he needed to get through the winter months, for the hotel was a seasonal business, operative only during the summer when the tourists were about.

Somehow Anne had managed to find access to the business account which was in his name only. He had taken that precaution, understanding the nature of her problem with money. Apart from the Selecon marketing franchise she had joined, he had authorised all the spending for the hotel though he had always referred to her opinion.

He got out the latest cheque book from his own desk and examined it. Apart from being much thinner than he imagined, there seemed to be no problem with it. Then he looked at the back of the cheque book and a slip of torn paper very close to the binding caught his eye. He examined it closely, then realised with a cold touch on his spine that at least ten cheques had been carefully torn out from the back with their counterfoils.

There was no telling how much money Anne had withdrawn from the business account. He prayed that there would be enough left to get them through the winter months.

It was agony waiting for Monday. He resisted the temptation to phone Anne and question her about the bank's letters she had hidden. She would simply weave a network of lies. He knew what she was like. When he had found out about all those different accounts in London she had said they were just an aberration of her youth, a fling that wouldn't be repeated.

'Have you any other accounts I don't know about?'

'Of course not,' she had said, looking him squarely in the eye.

'Do you swear?'

'God, what do I have to do to make you believe me!' she had snorted, staring at him with wounded eyes. Then her look softened and she came up to him, put her arms round his neck. Her blue eyes filled with tears. 'I promise you, darling. There are no more accounts.'

The next morning while she was out three more accounts— from the bottle store, a fashion store, and a departmental store arrived, all in red and threatening legal action.

Anne was the only person he knew who could lie sincerely. She was the only person he knew who could lie while looking you straight in the eye.

He felt drained of hope. On Sunday night only one room was let so thankfully there were only two guests requiring breakfast in the morning. When Rosemary arrived Harry left her alone in the invisible company of George and Percy while he went down to the High Street and paced in front of the bank, waiting for the doors to open.

The bank manager was a fatherly figure, a lean man like himself but with a little Hitler moustache above his upper lip. His eyes were soft and understanding. He asked a staff member for a printout of Harry's business account which showed that he was £4560.89 overdrawn.

'You should have asked us if you needed overdraft facilities,' said Mr Morgan kindly and with just a trace of a Welsh accent.

Harry shook his head. 'I should be over £5000 in *credit*. May I see all the cheques, please?'

Mr Morgan picked up his phone and asked for all the cheques to be brought in.

It took more than half an hour for Harry to sift through the cheques and identify the ones with his forged signature. Unfortunately he had an easy signature for Anne to forge. Most of the forged cheques were made payable to Selecon Enterprises, though many were for cash withdrawals.

'I'm afraid these are all forged cheques,' Harry said, sliding a thick pile towards Mr Morgan. 'They should not have been paid out.'

The Manager examined the cheques. 'You must admit the signature is very close. I can't really blame my staff for honouring them. But yes,' he looked up at Harry with soft eyes, 'we will naturally credit your account with these amounts—but...' He smiled sadly at Harry.

'But?'

'But, it means, of course, that we will have to take legal proceedings against your wife. Do you really want that?'

Harry hung his head. When he looked up his eyes were red-rimmed. 'Yes. I'm going to file for a divorce.'

Mr Morgan's manner was gentle but sure. 'Wait until she returns from London. Talk to her first, then come back to me. There is another solution, you know.'

'Solution?'

Mr Morgan nodded. 'This debt, plus the amount you need for the winter, can be added to your mortgage. Fortunately your mortgage is with us, and there is still sufficient equity in the value of your hotel to cover the amount you require.' He took a sip from the cup of tea his secretary had brought him. 'Or you can distribute the debt between a smaller increase of the mortgage and an overdraft, provided you can meet the minimum payments through the winter.'

Harry picked up his own cup of tea but it had gone cold. He put the cup down and smiled sadly. 'I'll wait then, until she returns on Wednesday. But I've had enough, I fear. I don't want to go on with the same old problem.'

'Just wait and see,' Mr Morgan smiled. 'On your way out tell my secretary to make a new appointment for Thursday.

'That's most kind of you, Mr Morgan.' Harry stood up.

'Not at all,' Mr Morgan smiled up at him. 'I'm just doing my job. We're here to help small businesses, not to crush them.'

He plodded back to the hotel with a heavy heart. If only, if only there was an escape from the trap of this life, he thought. He saw the Abbey loom in the autumn mists and the jagged walls, the Gothic arches on rows of columns, seemed to offer an escape. He thought of Thomas and his herbal cures from the twelfth century. If only he could provide a cure from depression. Or show him how to be 'sucked in' by the Abbey, through its time gateway! To know Thomas was to know madness. And Thomas believed he was trapped here, too, or surely he would allow himself to be sucked back by the Abbey. Or did he prefer ghosting about modern Jedworth, living on social security and growing the old herbs in his council-house garden? As he walked towards the underpass that would take him to the other side of the A68 he saw Matilda approaching. She wore her usual dirty woollen coat and flat slippers. Her grey hair that was once blonde fell lifelessly around her shoulders, and as she drew close he saw the stiff hairs that sprouted from her chin and upper lip. She barely glanced at him with her watery blue eyes as she chugged past, breathing asthmatically. She gave a faint smile of recognition and walked on, her right hand held waist-high with forefinger jabbing the air, as if constantly making a point. Before he emerged from the underpass he looked back and saw she had squatted down, releasing a stream of steaming urine from under her seedy coat.

He plodded on, shaking his head. He had come here to join these displaced persons. He stopped at a corner shop and rented a video—something to take his mind off the bleak reality of his life. As he struggled up the steep street lined with bleak terraced houses he saw the other displaced person strolling towards him. It was the man Thomas called the Abbot, though to Harry he resembled a bank manager. He had a bald head with hair sprouting round the temples. He was portly and wore a smart tweed jacket and walked with a air of stern authority. He gave Harry the usual curt nod as he walked by, his arms swinging purposefully. In his mind Harry called him Mr Walker for, like Matilda, he was constantly walking. Whenever Harry walked into town he was almost certain to see one or both of them—the Abbot or Matilda. He knew that Matilda walked into town and turned back as soon as she reached the High Street. The minute she reached the front door of her council house, high up on a hill, she would turn round and retrace her steps to the High Street. She usually relieved herself in the underpass where the local yobs had filled the walls with graffiti—the names of girls and crude drawings of grotesque genitals.

When he returned to the hotel Rosemary had finished cleaning and tidying up the room the guests had occupied the previous night.

'Did George and Percy have anything to report?' he asked her, trying to make polite conversation.

She looked sadly at him. 'Just a warning to you,' she simpered. She glanced about her nervously, rapidly, as if not wanting to be overheard. 'George said you're becoming more dissipated and weary. You must take care, Mr Denton.'

He sighed. 'Thank you, Rosemary. I'll be fine.'

When she was gone Harry slotted the video he had rented into the VCR machine. It was a Playboy video and showed a series a of glamorous young women in misty settings and in various states of undress. He messaged his mind with the glamorous images which he found enchanting. There was one young women he particularly liked, wrapped in transparent silk which flowed as she swung to and fro on a swing in the morning mist. It wasn't her quivering breasts, satin soft and nubile, so much as her enchantingly innocent blue eyes that drew his attention. He swallowed a double scotch as he watched and longed to be sucked out of his life in the hotel and his unglamorous life with Anne.

Anne had become so stocky and prosaic, apart from her financial weaknesses. She never wore makeup and if she washed her hair, she never bothered to do anything with it unless it was to twirl it back in an elastic band left by the postman. When she ate she smacked her lips, and when she sat down she spread her knees in masculine fashion, one elbow on a knee, her wrist supporting her chin. He remembered watching her one evening, sitting like that watching the television. What was she plotting against him, he had wondered? It was as though another person possessed her. Her stepmother had once told him that she was divided against herself. When he had married her she was such a pretty little thing and he had adored her. And now he searched his heart and knew that he no longer loved her.

When he went to bed that night he picked up a book to read and a sheet of paper fell out. It was an old poem in free verse he had penned while he still worked at the university. He read it and it was nauseatingly familiar:

> *Unless this account is paid in full*
> *within 31 days*
> *legal proceedings will be taken against*
> *me*
> *We refer to your letter of the 7th instant and attached*
> *hereto*
> *find a copy of the application your wife made to open*
> *an account*
> *We trust that you find this in order*
> *Do you have any more?*
> *No*
> *Think hard*
> *No, I swear*
> *I can't face the unknown*
> *Darling, can't you understand, this time*
> *I'm telling you the*
> *truth*
> *You said that last week,*
> *month*
> *year*
> *the last five years*
> *Notice is hereby given*
> *that any debts*
> *incurred*
> *She left a suicide note*
> *again*

Every time there was a row she would disappear for a time with a suicide note left somewhere. It was a tedious ordeal, contacting the police and waiting for news.

Harry didn't leave suicide notes. He merely contemplated and fantasised about suicide. It was one of his ways of escape. He went for long walks in the country, thinking that before he returned home he would step in front of a fast-moving truck. But every time he saw a truck approaching, though he held his breath and his heart pounded madly, he never had the courage to jump. His neighbour had had the courage to kill himself the previous month with a nail gun. He admired his courage. He nursed his depression by taking long walks through the cemetery, standing a long time over his neighbour's fresh grave. He thought of his body down there, still fresh and intact, but with the hole in his head. Andrew—for that was his name—was blissfully unconscious of misery and beyond the reach of depression and disappointment. Harry envied him his peace. But then, he thought in consolation, it was just a matter of time before we all enjoyed that peace, that blissful cessation of consciousness. Praise God, he thought, for our mortality.

Just as he was drifting off to sleep the shrill sound of the front doorbell jerked him back into full consciousness. He put on his gown and stumbled to the front door. A young couple huddled there, wanting a room. He showed them to a double room and returned to his bed.

In the morning he served the couple breakfast. The young girl couldn't have been more than twenty. She had the sweetest smile he'd ever seen. She sat there, slender and slight, her long wavy silken red hair framing her sweet fragile face, her crystal blue eyes brightening with each look he stole from her. He looked for every excuse to speak to her, to ask her if she wanted more tea or more toast—to smile at her merely to see that sweetness, that response of honeydew that came unhesitatingly and readily to each of his smiles or glances.

The pain of the gulf between them, of her everlasting unattainability, put him into a new dimension of ecstatic hell. When she was gone he sat where she had sat, his hands between his head, the depression deeper than he had ever known. When he got up with a sigh to clear the table, he took up the cup from which she had drunk. There was still a pool of cold milkless tea at the bottom, and without premeditation he put it to his lips, touching the cup where her lips had touched, tasting the cold sweetness of the tea. It was the closest he would ever come to heaven.

CHAPTER 5

Autumn

THE DAY BEFORE Anne was due to return Harry took a long walk by the Jed River. His eyes were drawn across the rich blanket of Sycamore trees that lined the bank that reached up to his hotel, the silver underside of the leaves twinkling as the breeze alternately caressed and ruffled them. The sea of green was variegated with the small corrugated leaves of an occasional elm and the smaller spiky leaves of an Elder or Ash. In the undulating park to his left a large Beech dominated the scene with its mass of waving green foliage while the surrounding cherry trees, neat and compact, paid homage in a tight circle. The Arcadian parkland scene was a tribute to the new tourist industry that had long since replaced the redbrick mills and chimney stacks of the old rayon factories, the rubble of which still lay embedded beneath the neatly contoured and grassed mounds. His eyes lifted up the steep bank to his hotel, stocky and square behind the Victorian gables, bedecked in ivy that softened the harsh angles and buff plaster of the building.

He sat down on a bench overlooking the old packhorse bridge that spanned the rippling Jed in twin-stone arches. The delicate silver trunks of two birch trees reared up behind him, the olive-green leaves sighing above him as the breeze gusted gently. As he watched he saw the top-half of Matilda chuffing along over the arched bridge, on one of her shuttle-journeys to the town. Her seedy rust-coloured, dirt-stained coat looked more dishevelled than usual, her finger jabbing as she pontificated to an unseen companion.

It put him in mind of Anne. The straight lacklustre hair, had it not been grey, could have been Anne's. Thomas and others in the town told him that she was the 'beauty of the toon' in her day, with her blue eyes, slim figure and long blonde locks. It must have been shortly after she was 'sucked through,' as

Thomas put it. Thomas's story was, of course, mythological, but many other townsfolk confirmed how pretty she was before she bore a child that died in infancy. Since then she was 'gone in the heed' and eked out her life perambulating ceaselessly between her council house and the High Street.

There must have been a moment when the change took place. Matilda's change from town beauty to old hag wasn't instant, of course, but there must have been a moment when the old spark died and the new lacklustre soul took root. It made Harry wonder about the precise moment when the change took place in Anne. But the seed of her downward spiral might have been already present when he fell in love with her. She had been a pretty schoolgirl with frizzy blonde hair and a lithe figure that ran into his arms. Then one windy summer evening on the porch of her stepmother's home she cried and told him he should forget her.

'What's the matter, Anne? Why shouldn't I love you?'

She looked into the distance where a light appeared and reappeared as a tree was tossed by the wind. 'Because I'm a thief!' she said melodramatically.

'Whatever makes you say that!'

'Because I stole my school fees,' she said, sniffing. 'Last year mother gave me the money in an envelope to give to the secretary at school. Instead, I took it into town and spent it.'

'You what!' he laughed, capturing her in his arms and squeezing her. 'One mistake doesn't make you a thief, you silly creature!' And he covered her in kisses. She melted into his arms and he picked her up and carried her light frame into the dark garden where he slipped off her pants and made love to her vigorously. He poured his adoration into her, coming into her in such powerful jets of love that she cried for joy.

But she *had* warned him and he had chosen to ignore that warning.

He had compounded his error. She had been the first girl he had ever made love to, and the memory of the easy way his exploring finger had slipped into the secret damp crevice between her slim thighs was forever enchanting. He was a first-year university student and she a provocative schoolgirl and she engineered multiple opportunities for his clandestine visits. He

32

protested in vain that they should wait until she left school before developing their relationship, but she would have none of it and he was putty in her hands. It was as though she had cast a spell over him and he couldn't shake off his infatuation which was like a constant itch needing to be scratched. Her longing face, her brilliant blue eyes and turned up nose and sultry lips, were constantly before him, during lectures and when he lay down to sleep. He developed a deep hunger for her lithe porcelain body, her little buds of white breasts crested with taut pink nipples, her sleek milk-white limbs that so readily slid over him and entwined his soul.

During one brief clandestine encounter after school she urged him to spend the night in her bedroom.

'Wait till mum and dad are asleep, usually after 11 p.m.,' she whispered urgently. 'I want you in my bed—all night long!'

'You're mad!' he laughed nervously.

'Please, boy.' She always called him 'boy.'

She was crazy, he thought, his heart beating wildly. But he did it, nevertheless. Late in the night he felt his way across the unlit lawn. He fell heavily over an abandoned wheelbarrow and jarred his knee painfully. But he limped to the porch where she was waiting, sliding out of the dark to take his hesitant hand and pull him in. They edged down the long passage to her bedroom, their backs to the wall to avoid treading on the creaky floorboards in the middle of the passage. When they reached her dark bedroom he was trembling and short of breath. But he pulled off his clothes and slid into her narrow bed, clasping her warm lithe naked body that instantly wrapped round him. 'You're the nicest boy in the whole world,' she whispered and her responsive body was hungry like a ravenous vixen. He must have made love to her three or four times that night, coming every time with the illicit excitement. Every time her young thighs opened and gave him immediate admission, tightening around him until he spasmed with relief and exhaustion. The room was adjacent to her stepmother's and the wonder is that their whispered endearments and vigorous, sharp lovemaking wasn't overheard. When Harry sneaked out in the small hours of the morning it was with welcome relief and guilty satisfaction.

It couldn't last, of course. Eventually his love notes to her were discovered by her stepmother, a strict fundamentalist churchwoman and a teacher. 'In the Old Testament you would be stoned to death!' she shouted at Harry, shaking a bony finger. She forbade him all further admission to her home. The meetings continued in secret, of course, but when Harry graduated he enrolled for a Master's degree at the University College of Wales to place himself beyond the reach of temptation. But when Anne turned eighteen she nagged her stepmother to death until she caved in and told her she could marry her damn Harry and get out of her sight forever.

Harry couldn't believe his luck when Anne phoned and said her stepmother had agreed to let them marry. It would have to be in a registry office and as soon as possible, before her stepmother changed her mind.

Harry drove down in great excitement in his battered Mini and when he reached Anne she had changed her mind. She was alone in the house so there was no-one present to make her behave like a stranger. She was morose and glared at him and told him to go away—she never wanted to see him again.

'Anne, for *God's* sake, what's happened to you? I drove down through the night. I'm *here*, darling. Why can't we get married now?'

'I don't want you. Please go away.' She glared at him, then turned her back to him.

'Just who is making you say this? Darling, I love you so much.' His voice broke and he had to swallow to ease his throat. 'Anne, don't do this to me,' he whispered. He came up to her and put his arms round her.

She swung round and pushed him away. 'Go away!' Her eyes burned with hatred and rebuttal.

The anger welled up inside him and he slapped her face hard.

She bit her lip and tried to slap him back but he held her wrist in a vicelike grip. Her eyes bored into him.

'Anne, I...I'm so sorry. I was trying to slap sense into you. Give me the old Anne back. The Anne I love.'

He released her and she spat the words at him. 'Go! Get out of my life!'

It was an absurd thought, now, but Harry felt those were the last words spoken to him by the real Anne—the beautiful young girl he loved and trusted. Perhaps she loved him so much she was trying to force him to go, to get away before the new entity—the impostor soul who looked like Anne but wasn't Anne—took over.

He gave in and returned, crestfallen and heartbroken, to his parents' home in Dulwich. He spent the day crying in agony to God, imploring him to change Anne's heart. In the morning he had packed again and was about to drive back to Aberystwyth when the phone rang. He lifted the receiver and Anne's voice spoke to him: 'Hello darling,' she said, as if nothing had happened.

'Anne! My God, Anne, you said darling!'

'Of course, boy,' she said sweetly. 'Aren't we going to get married? Mummy says we can. Thank God you slapped me. It brought me back to my senses.'

Two elders of the church visited Harry at his parents' home. They were young and businesslike and spoke with a sense of grave duty. The taller of the two was emaciated and wore wire-rimmed glasses and was the one who did all the talking. 'We understand that you and Anne have already consummated your marriage?'

'Well..., yes,' said Harry awkwardly.

The smaller of the two men, dressed in a natty suit, scribbled in a notebook.

'Was this before her eighteenth birthday?'

'We were friends before then, yes,' Harry nodded, smiling thinly.

The taller man fixed his wire-rimmed eyes on Harry. His manner was gentle but firm. 'Did you have sexual intercourse?' The smaller man looked at Harry, his hand poised above the notebook.

Harry stared back at them and swallowed. 'Yes,' he said, gritting his teeth.

The smaller man wrote vigorously in the notebook.

The taller man sighed. 'It's imperative that your marriage takes place as soon as possible. Can you support Anne?'

Harry smiled thinly. 'I have a student grant. My MA thesis should be finished this year.'

The man grimaced. 'Get a job, man! Get a job.'

Those two elders were working in a bank at the time, Harry recalled. Later they became lecturers at a university and contacted him, when he was a Professor, for help in preparing their lectures. He was expected to help as one who served the same Lord. They were all brethren in Christ. In time their own marriages broke up.

Harry stood up and gazed into the running waters of the Jed. As he watched, the dark body of a fish made its way rapidly upstream, darting swiftly above the cobblestones in its translucent medium. How life changes us all as we swim upstream, he thought. We're all locked into a predetermined cycle of life. Even in the twelfth century trout and salmon were making their way up this same river, looking for a place to spawn and die in the shadow of the Abbey.

At first they seemed blissfully happy. Anne got a job in a bank while Harry completed his master's degree. Then they moved back to London where he got a teaching post at a secondary modern school in Surrey, registering for part-time research towards a PhD at Birkbeck College. Anne got another job at the Natwest Bank in Victoria. Their income was enough to allow for a small one-bedroomed flat in the attic of an old Victorian house in East Dulwich. Anne began to put on weight rapidly, filling her miniskirts voluminously with her sturdy thighs. Because her stature was small the fat became obvious. During one hot summer she was inclined to remove all her clothing in the hot uninsulated attic flat while watching television. Perhaps she thought she was being provocatively sexy, flaunting her nakedness for Harry's delight, but he found her squat fatness and thick torso repugnant. When she smiled her once fragile face was wreathed in double chins, and her girlish giggles transmuted into raucous laughter. Her unfeminine posture dated from that time, legs apart, double chins resting on a stocky arm supported by a fat apple-pie knee. The image became so fixed in Harry's mind that he began to drop into Soho strip clubs on his way home from university late at night. He loved sleek pristine feminine forms and watched, spellbound, as one young housewife (for most of them were housewives earning an extra penny) swung sweetly from a swing, her firm breasts quivering provocatively from a slim torso. Her smile was sweet and unencumbered by double chins.

Apart from his visitations to strip clubs his fidelity to Anne had been absolute. His lovemaking, though, became quick and perfunctory, and he found that recalling to mind the images of the sweet feminine forms in the strip clubs at the right moment sometimes aided his struggling orgasms before he collapsed, panting, by her side.

Anne came home with loads of official papers and forms from the bank.

'Those look terribly official. Are you sure you should be bringing them home?'

'Oh, they're just stuff to throw away,' she said with a shrug.

The following week her eyes shone with interesting information. Penny, a work mate, wasn't able to keep abreast with her filing so she stuffed the overflow material into her locker. She had a telling off from the manager. On another occasion she came home in tears. It was Friday and she had just been paid—but her purse had been stolen on the bus. Later she was asked to do some baby-sitting for some friends and when she left the couple had given her mounds of unwanted clothes, including a new coat. The following week Peter, the husband, phoned Harry and said they no longer wished to have anything to do with either of them.

'No, I'm not willing to discuss it,' Peter said mysteriously but firmly. 'Anne can keep the clothes but she's not to come here anymore. We're withdrawing our friendship from both of you. Goodbye.' And the phone went dead.

Harry never did find out what it was about and Anne said she was flabbergasted.

Before long she came home with more interesting news from the bank. 'Penny stole three hundred pounds from one of the safes!'

The following week Anne was dismissed from the bank on suspicion of having stolen money from one of the safes.

Harry was enraged and went to see the manager who merely shook his head sadly at him. 'We've given her so many chances. Now I've washed my hands of her. I'm sorry.'

Harry protested. 'She said a girl called Penny stole from the safe!'

The manager shook his head and smiled indulgently. 'She was referring to herself. We have no Penny working here.'

When he reported this to Anne she cried. 'I was trying to save you the embarrassment,' she sobbed. 'The truth is the manager made a pass at me and I pushed him away. So he sacked me to cover his tracks. I *hate* him!'

Yes, the signs were there already, Harry thought, sedately following the riverbank towards the Abbey. Their joint bank account always seemed to have less than he expected. Then there was the time she stayed out all night, working as a television salesperson. He was distraught with anxiety and when she came home the next day and calmly told him she had to stay overnight at an hotel because of a late sales meeting he lashed out and hit her. She was shocked though unharmed. But Harry had broken his wrist and had to have his hand in plaster for the next month. He had taken up a post at the university by this time and his colleagues asked him what had happened.

'I hit my wife,' he explained sadly.

They laughed. 'Oh, so *don't* tell us what really happened then!'

But they believed him after she began to approach *them* for money. 'Harry is cruel and unkind to me, and I'm too frightened to ask him for a loan,' she explained tearfully. Some of them were sympathetic but when they weren't repaid after six months they approached Harry for the money.

What she did with the money or the goods bought on account Harry never discovered. One of his colleagues suggested she had a second establishment somewhere.

'You mean, like a flat? A second, or a secret life?'

'Precisely.'

But there never was any evidence of another establishment or a secret life. Only the secret life she lived in her head. As they drew apart they made love less and Harry's visits to the Soho

38

strip clubs became more frequent. His moments of escape had become a matter of routine.

The hotel might have offered a new beginning. But that hope was a forlorn one now. Someone had once said to him that a leopard never changed its spots.

When he went through the underpass under the A68 the Abbey with its stocky bell tower loomed above him. Thomas in his duffel coat slouched to his side, his long face smiling dolefully as Harry made his way along the riverbank below the Abbey.

'Aye,' nodded Thomas. 'Ye can see the latrine block or reredorter from hier, or at least the foundations where it was.' He pointed across the river. 'The water from the river was channelled, ye ken, through a drain so it flushed awa' the muck.'

'You know a lot about the Abbey, Thomas.'

He nodded. 'I ken, I ken! It were part o' ma leef, ken?'

'Don't you miss it?' Harry smiled at his own acceptance of the illusion. 'I mean, don't you ever want to go back. Was it 1285 you said? Surely there were people then that miss...,' He paused and smiled at his error. 'That missed you.'

'I will no' gang back!' he said, almost fiercely.

'Why not? What do you fear?' he prodded gently.

But Thomas merely shook his head. 'I'll no' gang back.'

'But I thought you were trapped here, that you couldn't go back anyhow?'

Thomas was silent and slouched back towards the bridge, in the direction of the hotel. Harry turned up the street towards the knave of the Abbey, not wanting to return to the hotel in the company of Thomas since then it would be so difficult to make him go home. Thomas slouched next to him, unwilling to leave him yet unwilling to approach the Abbey more closely.

Harry climbed up the steps past the War Memorial and once again peered in at the eastern limb of the church which housed the canon's stalls and high alter. The eye was naturally drawn to the arcade and gallery stages that were enveloped by arches on giant cylindrical columns. The impressive structure breathed a sense of power that reverberated subliminally in Harry's mind, drawing it into the depths of its mystery.

'Dinna luik ta hard!' protested Thomas who hung back behind him.

Harry's eyes followed the flight of stone steps that wound upwards to the gallery above and then disappeared abruptly. He inhibited a strong desire to mount and follow the steps, though they weren't accessible from his position. He would have to go through the visitor's centre and pay the admission fee first.

'What have you escaped from, Thomas?' Harry prodded gently. 'Has someone in the past been unkind to you?'

'I'll have no' meer ta do wi' the Black Canon!' he said fiercely. 'He's no guid father to me! He's no' father of mine, I tell ye! I will no' gang back there. Come away the noo!'

'What's he done to you, Thomas?' Harry began to see the light. 'What's your father done to you?'

'He's no' father of mine!' he protested vehemently, and turned away. It was the first time Thomas had voluntarily left him.

On his way back to the hotel Harry passed the bank manager again—or, at least, the Abbot. The man gave him a precursory nod and glared ahead of him. Harry was puzzled. It was what the government called 'care in the community,' he supposed. At least the displaced persons of Jedworth were harmless enough. And there were only three—or four, counting himself.

CHAPTER 6

Ladder

HARRY put himself to sleep the night before Anne's return from London by imagining he was climbing up the flight of steps that wound upwards in the Abbey. They were interminable and went on and on, but eventually they took him through a dark archway. In the black darkness beyond the arch he could just make out the lower rungs of a ladder. He mounted the ladder and pulled himself upwards. Perhaps he was trying to pull himself out of his dark depression, nearer to the uplifting power of God. He had made up his mind to escape his unhappy marriage with Anne and knew that the next day he must face the awful first steps of the break-up. The depression weighed him down and he pulled the harder on the ladder, drawing himself up the next rung. He went up and up, but there was no end in sight. The ladder was enveloped by permanent darkness, suspended in space, and he kept climbing. Up, and up and up. He looked up but there was no sign of light. But he kept moving, up, and up and up.

He met Anne off the National Express coach on its way to Edinburgh. She seemed pleased to see him and chatted brightly of her stepfather whose health had improved. Her stepfather was paralysed from the waist down and was wheelchair bound. He was totally dependent on Anne's stepmother who ruled him with a rod of iron. Harry had often entertained the notion that it was her cruel treatment of him that made his nerves fail and cause his legs to collapse under him one day. She had been cruel to Anne, after all, frequently beating her with an umbrella or length of electric cord. At least, so Anne had said. Harry thought of her as the wicked witch and when he had confronted her one day with her cruel treatment of Anne, she had turned on him, glaring. She had said icily: 'What you don't understand, Harry, is that Anne has been a very difficult child! And I'll thank you to mind your own business.'

When Harry finally married her and took her away, it was like rescuing the pretty princess from the cruel ugly witch. When the woman at the registry office had stamped the marriage certificate, she did so with a vindictive thump: 'There!' she exclaimed, bringing the rubber stamp down hard onto the paper, 'She can't change her mind now!'

And they were so excited, driving out of London in the mini after the clinical little ceremony. Anne was so excited and happy that she dropped a fleck of burning ash from her cigarette onto her stocking and burnt a hole in it. For a time life was full of laughter and joy. They stopped at a little hotel in Wrexham for their honeymoon night, desperate to make love though Harry had forgotten to bring any condoms. So he entered her slowly and deliciously, careful not to come before withdrawing and spilling his seed onto the bedsheet. It was almost as delicious as the time he ravished her in her stepmother's kitchen, withdrawing at the last minute and spilling his seed on the hard cold floor as, still gazing into her smiling eyes, he throbbed with ecstasy relieved.

Harry told her how Rosemary went berserk over the eggs that broke and she laughed raucously as they entered the front door of the hotel. She slumped down on the settee and spread her legs wide.

'I'll bring you some tea,' he said.

'Thanks, boy,' she smiled. 'Did you miss me?'

'I certainly did,' he said, walking into the kitchen. He poured out the tea and placed it on a tray with the opened collection of letters from the bank manager. He caught sight of his lean weary face in the mirror stuck on the cupboard. The creased lines of his face were like an unmade bed, and his weary grey eyes stared accusingly back at him.

'I hate you, you bloody fuck!' he hissed at his reflection, and took the tray to Anne who had oozed more comfortably into the settee.

He set the tray on a coffee table next to her and sat down opposite her. He watched her pick up the cup and take a sip. 'What's this?' she asked innocently, picking up one of the bank manager's letters.

'Just some post that arrived in your absence.'

She studied the letter in her hand, then picked up another. She put down her cup, still holding the letter. Then she let her head slump forward as though she were a puppet and a vital string had been cut. The silence hung between them.

'I tried to warn you,' she said at length, addressing the carpet.

'About what?' he asked, keeping his voice calm.

'About all that spending. The retiling and the dining room refurbishments.' She was still addressing the carpet, averting her eyes.

'We had to do those, if we wanted to keep our grading of three crowns. And according to my bookkeeping the money was in the bank.'

She didn't reply and the silence built up between them.

'Do you know how much we're overdrawn?' he asked, gritting his teeth. He could feel the anger welling up inside him. She sat there like a bloated frog hanging her head.

'Five bloody fucking thousand pounds!' he screamed, losing control.

She lifted her eyes to him like a wounded animal. Her injured innocence made his anger and frustration boil over.

'Fuck you, Anne! You don't have any conception of the value of money at all, do you! So you just ...' He drew breath, his heart thumping wildly. 'So you just tore cheques out of the back of the business cheque book and forged my signature!'

She looked at him with smouldering hurt or hatred, he couldn't tell which.

'Fuck you, Anne! You're a bloody, fucking bitch!'

He flung out of the house, forgetting to pick up his coat. He wanted to get away from her wounded eyes and from his own anger. 'Fuck, fuck, fuck!' he swore as he stomped up the hill and into a park that overlooked the Abbey and the town.

He walked up the path that led under a row of towering Horse Chestnut trees heavy with conkers or 'sheggies' as the local children called them. He picked up a handful of conkers from the gravel path and carried them in his fist. The leaves were in heaps of red, piled up like snow drifts against a long wooden fence. He kicked the leaves that sprayed out ahead of him as he walked. When he reached the crest of the hill there was a bench that gave him a God's-eye view of the ruined Abbey. He flung the conkers at the Abbey but they bounced impotently on the green lawn that sloped steeply downwards. He was dimly aware of the traffic noise below on the A68 that sliced past the Abbey at the bottom of the valley.

His life with Anne was full of broken expectations and hopes, like the Abbey's broken arches ruined deliberately by the soldiers invading from England. Somehow it was Anne that methodically ruined, and who was continuing to ruin the life they had hoped to build together. The enemy was within and dwelt with them. As the witch, Anne's stepmother said, she was divided against herself—and great was the destruction that ensued. He looked at the rows of pointed Gothic arches and gallery tiers balanced on fluted pillars and the ruined walls, broken and jagged and torn apart, and saw the metaphor for every broken marriage. One spent a lifetime building dreams of romance and glory, only to tear them down with indiscriminate violence. He saw Anne's wounded eyes again and felt immense pain under the weight of guilt. Every time they fought his words brought down more edifices of hope. Yet somehow, every time, more out of pity than love and in honour of the memory of the sweet nymph he once loved, he restored or tried to restore peace and hope and begin anew. But how long could he build on the collapsed walls of former dreams?

He got up and walked back to the hotel. No, he thought, this time he had to start anew. He had lost his will to try and mend the widening rift between him and Anne. The wind rustled the leaves above him and a spray of rust-coloured leaves filtered down around him. They crunched underfoot and as he descended the hill he saw the Abbot who, he noticed, was beginning to look dissipated, unshaven and his tweed jacket hanging loosely on him. He barely nodded at Harry, his eyes stern before him as he marched on, swinging his arms.

Someone—was it Thomas?—had told him that the Abbot had taken to drinking heavily. Perhaps that's why he was looking dissipated, he thought.

When he entered the hotel Anne flung her arms around him. Before he could protest her mouth was on his lips. Then she drew back to look tearfully into his eyes. 'Sorry, boy. I'm so sorry. It won't happen again. It was that woman pressing for money all the time for the jewellery. And... and...' She sobbed, the tears running out of her eyes and down her cheeks. 'I'm not a bitch. I've always been faithful to you.' Then she kissed him again and Harry didn't have the heart to push her away.

'Come!' she said, drawing back again and pulling him towards the bedroom. 'Make love to me, boy.'

She always did this, he thought. She always used sex to make up and diffuse his anger. 'I want you, I want you,' she pleaded. 'I need you and I love you so much.' It was the voice of the old Anne, the nymph that first infatuated him with her blue eyes and lily white body.

He allowed himself to be drawn up to the bedroom like a sacrifice. When she drew up her legs and splayed her fat white thighs he entered her easily, ramming down into her with a fury of passion, like a suicide flinging himself from a great height. He looked down at her, seeing her lack lustre hair drawn back for convenience, her splodgy breasts quivering like jelly every time he thumped into her. As he thrust he felt his desire wane. He tried to recall the sweet provocative nymph he ravished on the kitchen floor, but the image retreated before the bouncing and fawning Dunloppillo that quaked beneath him. It was like fucking Miss Piggy. Then he closed his eyes and conjured up the image of a slim dark-haired enchantress swinging through veils of silk. The image transmuted into the sweet smile of the little redhead with her crystal blue eyes and he felt the first flurry of an orgasm like a touch of sweetness. He unbuttoned the silk blouse of the redhead who continued to smile sweetly, seeing her pert breasts pointed at him with bewitching urgency. He bent down and kissed her sweet lips and his orgasm rose suddenly, crested and released him as he collapsed by Anne's side, panting and weeping.

Anne was bending over him and cooing to him like a doting mother, lisping with tenderness. 'Whath's the mather, my boy, eh?' She ran her stumpy fingers through his hair that was damp from the effort of the loveless union. 'Let Anne make it bether, my boy.' She kissed him. 'You're the betht boy in the whole wide world.'

After Anne fell asleep that night she slept like a child. She always slept deeply and peacefully, her mind permanently insulated against financial anxieties.

But Harry tossed and turned. He knew he would give in and take the bank manager's offer of a higher mortgage. It was the old story. The burden of guilt was too much to break out of the marriage. He was trapped in the marriage like Thomas was trapped in Jedburgh. Or had Thomas in reality escaped the old Jedworth? Either way, it was a worthless existence. He got up and went downstairs and helped himself to a malt whisky from the bar. He forced at least three double tots down his throat and took five aspirins for good measure. Then he crawled into a sleeping bag on the hard floor of the private lounge. He tucked a cushion under his head and thought again of the stone steps and the ladder. As he climbed up, lifting himself from rung to rung in the dark, his mind began to reach out and rotate, like a searchlight or radar beam, wondering where he could find a soulmate. His brain swirled and swung with the searching beam. Was there a blip anywhere as the beam passed round the world in a widening arc? Could there really be a woman of his dreams? How far would he have to search? In Jedburgh? In Scotland? In the United Kingdom? Or further afield, much further, beyond the surf-washed shores of Britain? Could a girl with the tender sweetness he saw in the redhead, or the bewitching smiling eyes of the brunette on the swing, exist anywhere? Could she exist for him?

His brain swirled and rotated in the stretched balloon of his skull as it lost consciousness.

CHAPTER 7

Indian Summer

FOR THE TIME BEING the only way out was to cave in to the demands of money and accept the higher mortgage from the bank. With the winter months stretching ahead there would be less cashflow, but also fewer reasons and less opportunities for Anne to spend. It was the memory of the young girl he had once loved that bound Harry to her—through his pity for the woman she had become. Seeing her change for the worse was like a living bereavement and he blamed himself since her deterioration in appearance and integrity had taken place under his care. It was like seeing one's partner's personality retreat and disappear, like the once loving wife or husband afflicted with Alzheimer's disease and the former bright personality disappearing from view. But the retreat of the alert bewitching Anne with frizzy hair that bounced on slim shoulders into the enveloping sloth of a pontificating Michelin woman with spare tyres was a gradual process. There was a sense of inevitability about her personality collapse, the old Anne he loved still lingering on, insecure, flicking out a hand towards his, constantly seeking some reassuring contact. But she wore no make-up, barely ever brushed her straight lacklustre hair, and went around in a frumpy waistless dress with a loose-fitting brown smock, pontificating about those insecure women who felt the need to impress by painting their faces. Apart from wandering Matilda she must be the most unglamorous woman in Jedburgh, Harry thought bitterly. When she went out into the growing coldness of the air she wrapped herself in an unbecoming anorak that made her look like a stout Eskimo. But he didn't have the heart to criticise her appearance, assuming it was an outward and superficial condition she couldn't really help, like cancer. He also learnt to live with her abiding untidiness, clothes strewn over banisters, spilling out of cupboards and shoes abandoned in the middle of the floor where he either tripped over them or kicked them out of the way. The used sanitary towels stuffed in drawers and bedside cupboards seemed a part of normal existence and he was always careful to replace them where he came across them in the process of searching for a lost article.

It was during one of those calm Autumn mornings that formed a little Indian summer at the end of the season when a new influence filtered into Harry's life. He was giving the terraced lawn below the front of the hotel its last mowing before stowing away the mower for the season. The Abbey appeared closer though shrouded in mist, the square bell tower looming solidly out of the opaque misty air. The burgeoning Horse Chestnut trees that clustered close to the Abbey were amorphous grey shapes in the mist. The electric hum of the mower was loud in his ears when he sensed a movement above him.

He turned in time to see the slight figure of a young woman in a white dress. She came fluttering down the stone steps towards him like a butterfly. It was an enchanting image and one which he would never forget. She had jet black hair, biting blue eyes and a delicate oval face like a Dresden doll. Even her body was delicate, almost fragile, with a tiny waist. Harry relaxed his grip on the lawnmower so that it switched off automatically, and into the suddenly still air her voice was crisp and musical like the tinkling of crystal bells.

She had to repeat her question for he was mesmerised by her ethereal beauty. 'Are you the owner?' Her wonderful shy smile, full of delight and innocent simplicity, was enchanting.

'Why..., yes,' he replied hesitantly, giving her a nervous smile. Her beauty was intimidating. She must be a model or an actress, he thought. Somebody famous. One only saw girls like her on TV or the cinema.

She flashed an engaging smile. 'I'm looking for accommodation. For my husband and myself. Do you have a room at a special rate for a long-term stay? About two or three months?'

He blinked and swallowed for his tongue was dry, his mind wiped clear of thought. He made an effort and focused his mind. 'Yes, certainly—as long as you like!'

'Oh, good!'

'Would you like some tea?' he heard himself say. It was fitting to offer a princess more than a room.

'That would be super!' Her blue eyes flicked another soul-freezing smile at him. It was such a stunning combination, Harry thought—the bright blue eyes and the jet black hair.

His heart was in his mouth as he led the way up the steps and into the front lounge of the hotel. Please make her stay, he prayed involuntarily to whatever deity might be listening. God, he would pay *her* to stay, he thought.

He invited her to take a seat and dashed into the kitchen to find Anne. 'There's somebody here wanting a room for two or three months!' he said breathlessly. 'I'll just make her some tea and take in some biscuits.' While the kettle boiled and Anne gaped he rushed out with the biscuits. He lavished attention on her, stumbling over his words and laughing awkwardly, hoping she wouldn't see how flushed and delighted he was. Anne came in with the tea and slumped down, knees apart, and pontificated about the terrible vulgarity of Jedburgh while the young woman's cosy tinkle of laughter filled the silences.

'What brings you to the Borders?' Anne asked, pursing her lips. 'It's such a drab sort of place. So isolated from the bright lights and decent shops.'

'I thought it was *super*,' the young woman's laughter tinkled. 'I love the countryside. There are so many shades of green and the hills are delightful.' She took a delicate sip of her tea, her little finger stretched outwards. 'But it's Max's job that brings us here. He's a sales executive for Fenetre Windows. And we need to find a place to stay while we house search. We don't want to rush into a purchase, do you know what I mean? Any of the Border towns might do—Kelso, even Galashiels. Max's head office is in Edinburgh, but the whole of the Borders will be his territory.'

Anne snorted. 'I should think Hawick was the best choice. At least they've got a few decent shops.'

'Oh, but Jedburgh's much prettier,' objected Harry. 'And it would be a better base, I should think.' He sought out her pretty blue eyes and his heart missed a beat when she smiled back at him. A princess like her was automatically out of his reach so he wasn't put out to hear about Max. If anything, he was grateful to

Max for introducing such an object of beauty into the area. It was enough to bask in the shadow of her effervescence. His soul was starved of glamour and drank in her presence, like the parched soil of a desert in the first rains of the season.

'Jedburgh's a vulgar place!' Anne pulled a face, having forgotten to sugar her tea. 'The hooligans carry on and swear four-letter words outside the hotel on Friday nights. The High Street and the bus terminus are noisy with drunks. The village idiot thinks he came through a time gate from the twelfth century and constantly calls to see Harry. And there's a mad old woman that urinates on the pavement.' She rapped out the phrases urgently, perhaps sensing something unhealthy in Harry's fawning attention.

'Oh dear,' said the princess, crestfallen.

'Not at all!' objected Harry, wishing Anne would go away. 'It only happens occasionally—the drinking, I mean, and in *all* the Border towns, not just Jedburgh.' He searched out the blue eyes and drank in their startling sincerity. 'We can give you the family room that faces the Abbey, away from the street. It has a magnificently elevated aspect over the river, and the Abbey's floodlit at night. It's a spectacular view!'

'That's a *family* room!' Anne looked daggers at Harry, curling her lip. 'We'd have to charge the full family tariff.'

'Of *course* not!' Harry added quickly. 'For a long stay we would...' He came to a rapid decision. 'We would only charge half the normal low season tariff—for a double room.' He was well aware that the hotel would be practically empty during the winter season. Anything was better than nothing—and to have *her* stay would be manna from heaven!

'Can I see the room?' the princess beamed. 'It sounds *super*.'

He loved the way she said 'super' with a musical lilt that extended the first syllable. God, she was such a super looking creature, he thought. The word came to epitomise her for him.

Harry stood up. 'I'll show you the room.' When she stood up be put out his hand to her. 'My name's Harry Denton, by the way, and this is Anne.'

She placed her small hand in his. Her touch was delicate and sent shivers down his spine.

'Mine's Eleanor.' She flashed that blue-eyed smile again that froze him into petrified ecstasy. He held her hand a little too long and she pulled it away with a gentle pressure. 'I'll just see the room and report back to Max. If it seems okay he'll come and check it out on Monday.'

Her vocabulary was delightfully girlish, he thought. When she entered the large en suite bedroom with its panoramic view of the Abbey she gasped. 'Oh, this is brilliant! What did you say the tariff was?'

When she left Harry was on Cloud Nine. He was barely aware of Anne's embittered remarks about the plastic appearance of the inane girl. 'You'd think she was a Barbie doll,' she said sourly. 'All dressed up in a flouncy dress with gold bangles and a gold necklace. You'd think she was going to a party!'

Harry hadn't even noticed the gold jewellery. It was the smiling blue eyes that still infested his mind like a delicious parasite. 'But you have gold jewellery, too,' he pointed out. 'All that Selecon stuff.' He looked at the little cabinet which was still stuffed with the costume jewellery. 'You never wear any yourself, Anne.'

She snorted. 'I only bought the stuff as an investment—as a business. To sell to empty-minded little imbeciles like her.' She nodded her head towards the south, supposing that was the direction from which Eleanor had emerged.

'I thought she was quite nice, actually,' he smiled weakly.

'You *would*!' she pursed her lips. 'Men are so easily taken in by inane girls. I gave you more credit, Harry. I'd have thought you'd have seen through her right away.'

He frowned. 'Well, I suppose she was rather flippant. It's true, you can't judge a book by its cover. Still, if she—if they—take the room, it will be a nice bit of income through the winter months.'

She gave a raucous laugh. 'What about the heating? At the price *you* offered we'll hardly make a profit.' She shook her head. 'I'm not looking forward to simpering to the likes of her for three months!'

Harry thought what a welcome relief it would be to simper to her rather than to frog-like guests who couldn't plug in the radio and couldn't manage even a glimmer of a smile. What a relief she would be after the sour Americans who insisted on just the right temperature of the water in the shower, and the Australian who complained about the absence of fly screens. He looked forward to Monday with a fervour that surprised even himself. It was quite possible, of course, that she wouldn't come back. It happened so often—a wife or husband would come in while the spouse waited in the car. He or she would look round, see the room, ask about the tariff, then say he (or she) 'would just discuss it with my husband/wife and be back in a moment.' Invariably he never saw them again. It was the price, usually, that put them off—but at least he was satisfied that he had offered Eleanor a more than reasonable tariff.

Harry was more than usually attentive to the doorbell on Monday. He was in a state of nervous excitement and jumped every time it rang. First it was the butcher with a packet of bacon. Then it was someone asking about the price of rooms for a wedding party in the spring. Then it was Eleanor, looking heavenly in a sky-blue suit that matched her eyes. Her husband's face loomed behind her, wreathed in smiles.

Harry showed them into the lounge, breathlessly talking and welcoming them and calling Anne for some tea and biscuits. He fawned around Max as was fitting to one who owned the pearl of great price.

Max wore a double-breasted suit which was well cut to fit round his stocky but portly frame. It wasn't his thinning dark hair so much as his bruised, overworked eyes that drew Harry's attention. They were exhausted-looking eyes with sagging bruised pouches. His dark Panda eyes were constantly busy, observing, noticing everything, missing nothing, yet fixing Harry in the eye when he spoke.

'What is your dream, Harry?'

The question surprised him and he laughed nervously. 'I'd need time to think about that. You mean, if I won the lottery or something?'

Max nodded, eyeing him steadily. 'Perhaps you've thought of a new Mercedes? There's a new S-class model, you know, that's built so securely that even the door clicks shut by itself if you've forgotten to close it properly.' He grinned with half-closed eyes. 'A very satisfying click.' He snapped his chubby fingers.

'That would be nice, I suppose.' He was aware of Eleanor's smiling eyes on him. They were so sweet, so enticing and engaging. He smiled back at her, nervously.

'Come on, Harry,' Max urged gently. 'There must be something you want. What do you want most in the entire world?'

The thought shot into his mind before he could stop it: to fuck your wife, Max. His eyes flicked away from the dark magnetic eyes of Max to the dreamy gaze of Eleanor's crystal blue eyes that still smiled bewitchingly. Oh God, he thought, you're so absolutely adorable! Max must be the happiest and most blessed man in the world. To be in bed with you, you divine creature, to encircle your tiny waist and kiss your cupie-doll lips and lose oneself in those eyes must be heaven itself. God, I would give my soul for someone like you!

He looked back at Max, blushing. He scraped his hand through his unruly hair and took a deep breath. 'I dunno, Max ... to escape this place, I guess.'

'Escape?' Max smiled quizzically.

'Yes,' he sighed. 'Not to have to get up each morning to serve breakfasts. To be free. To do something I enjoy.' He laughed. 'To sail away. Live on an island. Get away from people.'

Max smiled triumphantly. 'I've got a business that can give you all of that. All the free time you want.' Just then Anne came in with the tea and biscuits. 'Sit down, my dear!' he said, patting the seat next to him. 'We want to talk to you too.'

Anne eyed him suspiciously but lowered herself into a seat opposite him and for once didn't allow her knees to sag in opposite directions. 'Have you seen the room?' she asked, creasing her brow. 'There's a double room that's cosier and warmer than the family room.'

'What is your dream, my dear?' He threw the question at her. 'A mansion twice this size? A second home in the Lake District? A shopping trip to New York? A world cruise?'

Something he said hit home and she bit her lip, looking at him steadily. 'What's the catch?' she said, narrowing her eyes.

'No catch.' He smiled beguilingly. 'You can have anything you want. All you need is the right vehicle.'

'Vehicle?' smiled Harry.

'Sure.' Max smiled magnanimously, yet smugly, at Harry, leaning back in his chair. 'Look at me, Harry. Have you ever seen an uglier bastard?' He held his grin and his bruised eyes drilled into Harry's. 'Let's face it, Harry. If an ugly bastard like me can land a pretty bird like Eleanor, imagine what you can achieve. All you need is to believe in yourself—and have the right vehicle.'

CHAPTER 8

Extended Family

ELEANOR smiled back at Harry in a shy acknowledgement of Max's compliment, then smiled at Anne and spoke in her musical voice: 'Perhaps you'd like Max to show you the Speedway business plan? You look like a sophisticated businesswoman who knows where she's going! You'll like this plan, Anne. I couldn't sleep all night the first time I'd seen it!'

Anne shrugged her shoulders. 'I'm not really bothered.'

Anne transferred her smiling gaze to Harry. 'What about you, Harry? It only takes five minutes.'

'Sure!' Harry nodded. He would be happy to be shown anything provided it kept Eleanor there, in touching distance, where he could enjoy the close proximity of her smile with her sharp eyes and her pale complexion as thin and delicate as a piece of paper. It was an aesthetic experience that warmed and paralysed him with a sense of illicit pleasure.

Max went out to his car and in no time had a white board propped up on a tripod, as though he were about to address a meeting. He grasped a black felt-tipped pen in one hand and a silver pointer in the other. He cleared his throat and began importantly: 'If you wanted to go from London to Rome and you needed to be there in two hours, would you go by train or aeroplane?' He cleared his throat again and drew two circles, linking them with an arrow. The pen squeaked on the board. 'You would choose the right vehicle that could get you where you want to go in the amount of time that you want to get there. The right choice of business vehicle is just as important. By putting your efforts into the right choice of vehicle and having a dream or goal to strive for, we have a realistic formula for success.' Max drew three more circles on the board and linked them with plus signs, and wrote the words 'Dream', 'Work' and 'Vehicle' in each of the circles. Then with some final squeaks of the pen he put down an equal sign followed by the word 'Success.'

Anne yawned. 'You haven't seen the room yet, Max.'

'All in good time,' Max waved her interruption away and changed his posture, stepping on a floorboard that creaked loudly. 'Now we get to the exciting bit.' He drew more circles on the board. They looked like an inverted bunch of grapes. He spoke of lines of production, of uplines and downlines. Every time he made a significant point he stepped forward and made the floorboard creak. 'So you see,' he said with practised enthusiasm, 'from the royalties cascading down from all the people you introduced and from all the people *they* introduced, you'll be netting an income of over £45,000 a year—simply through the principle of duplication! No other business can bring you that kind of money for so little effort and time! And that's just the *beginning*!' The floorboard groaned louder than ever.

'It's like Selecon,' said Anne wearily. 'We tried that already.'

'Yes, but I can see where this concept goes a lot further,' Harry replied quickly, smiling at Eleanor whose cheeks dimpled as she returned the smile. He hadn't noticed the dimples before and thought how exquisite they were.

'That's right, Harry,' she said musically. 'This is a business that involves the distribution of goods and services from a wide range, household, personal care, cosmetics, gift lines to phones and electrical goods. And you're supplying products *direct* to the consumer. Do you know what I mean?' She smiled sweetly. 'It means starting up without the overhead costs of traditional marketing.'

'Right!' Max slapped the board with his pointer stick that telescoped outwards like an aerial. 'You're not paying for supermarket car parks! It's like a club where everyone agrees to cut out the supermarkets and shops and sell to one another. You keep the profits in the family and, of course, you're always your own best customer!'

'Right.' Eleanor went on softly. 'We're a family—do you know what I mean?' She smiled. 'Your upline looks after you and they're always at hand if you need help.' Her cosy tinkle of laughter filled the room. 'It's such fun to wash up! Just think, each time you wash up using Speedway products you're actually making money. Every time you brush your teeth with Speedway toothpaste you're saving money! Do you know what I mean?'

Harry nodded. 'And where would I buy my washing-up liquid, or my toothpaste from?' he asked, though he knew the answer.

'From your upline, of course.' Eleanor's cheeks dimpled again. 'That would mean *me*—and Max.'

'Is that right?' Harry smiled at her. He longed to reach out and touch her neat wispy hair, to let his hand trail down the fine cheek, to stroke and hold her perfect little neck.

Max tapped the board again, indicating another bundle of grapes. 'And you, of course, would be selling direct to your downline.'

Harry nodded. His heart lurched when he turned and saw Eleanor's intense blue eyes still on him. 'It sounds marvellous,' he heard himself say, and was aware of a grunt from Anne.

'Networking will save you time, Harry,' she lilted on. 'Do you know what I mean? Speedway eliminates buying from shops. There's no retail side. It provides wholesale products to every man in the street! As I said, we work as a family. Chuck Halliday—he's the U.K. Speedway Chairman—sent us so much material and wouldn't accept a *penny*. We're a family, he said. The support you get is super. He even advises university research groups on health and hygiene products. Chuck says the company has been established for seventy years—and they've been networking for fifteen years.' She hesitated and furrowed her brow, then shook her head and swept back her fringe in a smooth easy wave. 'No, I tell a lie! They've been networking for *seventeen* years. It's the most explosive networking company in the States. There's been a tidal wave of growth. Two million new members in only two years! Now it's a billion-dollar company. You can't go wrong, Harry. Do you know what I mean?' Her smile was patently sincere.

'And if I need help, you're always at hand?' Harry looked at her, still lost in her blue eyes.

'Of course,' she said quietly, her cheeks dimpling again. When she put out her hand and touched his hand lightly, his heart seemed literally to leap up towards his throat.

'So what do I do next?' he said hoarsely, grinning at her. It was like a seduction and he was a willing victim.

'As luck would have it, Harry,' Max purred, 'I have a starter kit with me. For an investment of a mere £70 it must be the best value in the world for an established business with a proven track record!'

Max returned to his car and brought in a box. It contained a selection of Speedway products with folders full of promotional material and what looked like a little black bible. The 'bible' was the 'plan' with stiff coloured sheets that would help Harry explain the concept to his friends and acquaintances. Anne scowled and Eleanor beamed when Harry took out his chequebook and gave Max a cheque for £70.

'There's a Speedway Convention in Edinburgh next month, isn't there, Max?' Eleanor smiled up at her husband who was standing at the reception desk filling out the paperwork for Harry's membership. 'Chuck Halliday as well as a Diamond from America will be speaking.'

'What's a Diamond?' asked Harry.

'A millionaire.' Eleanor smiled sweetly at him. 'There'll be lots of Diamonds at the Convention. The American will be talking about Fast-track—a method of getting into networking quickly.' Her frown made her face pucker up like a pixie. 'It's not fair. The Golden Silvers and the Rubies get in free and they have the most money and can easily afford the costs. Do you know what I mean?' Her laughter tinkled again. 'It costs £170 per night which includes accommodation. But we'll just take the daytime tickets at £30 each.'

Max nodded and took out a book of tickets. He smiled at Harry. 'Now, Harry, as a shrewd businessman you know the value of saving money, don't you? So you're going to take the discounted tickets by buying them now, aren't you? That means getting them for £25 each instead of £30. How many should I put you down for?'

Harry swallowed. 'When is the Convention?'

'Oh, you really need to be there. It's on the 2nd and 3rd of next month.'

Harry felt things were getting out of hand. Anne was scowling at him and shaking her head. Her knees had sagged apart and she had her arms folded like a barrier across her chest.

'Well, I'm not sure that would be a suitable time,' Harry said. 'We might be tied up at the hotel.'

'Well, let me put it this way, Harry,' Max smiled blandly at him, leaning back and placing a hand in his pocket. 'If you were given a choice of driving fifty miles and attending a meeting for an hour in order to be paid ten thousand pounds, or of staying at home to earn fifty pounds, which would you choose?'

Eleanor's cheeks dimpled at him. 'You can come with us, since we'll be going anyway, Harry.' The touch of her hand on his was featherlight.

Harry looked at her. Her blue eyes seemed to suck in his soul. 'I'll come with you, of course,' he said softly, once again taking out his chequebook.

'You can count me out!' Anne rattled the cups back into the tray and stood up. 'I don't know if you want to see the room. I'll leave it to Harry.' She glared at Harry and walked out with a peremptory swagger. The crockery rattled on the tray as she walked.

Harry led Max and Eleanor up to the family en suite bedroom that overlooked the town and Abbey. Eleanor walked to the window and was framed by the long white curtains. The light shone behind her and flowed around her so that her slight, fairy-like frame looked ethereal and transfigured. Max in his double-breasted suit was like a well-dressed bull-frog beside her.

'What's that old church?' enquired Max, gazing hungrily yet wearily at the Abbey. 'Do you think it's likely to be restored? Fenetre-Windows would give them a hefty discount.'

'You'd have to take that up with Historic Scotland,' smiled Harry. 'I can put you in touch with the custodian, if you like, but I expect they find the Abbey has more value as a ruin. It's our main tourist attraction, you know.'

'Pity.' He pursed his lips.

'Max, isn't this room *super!*' enthused Eleanor. 'It's so big and airy. And the view!' She gazed at the Abbey. 'Did you say it's floodlit at night?'

'Yes, and the Castle Goal.' He stood close behind her—as close as he dared. Her perfume was sweet and herbal. She was at least five inches shorter than him. If he bent over he could nibble her delicate ear.

'Well, its super!' She turned her head round and smiled up at him, making his heart twist with agony.

Max had moved towards the front window that overlooked the terraced garden. He ran his hands along the wooden sill. 'You should think of replacing these windows, you know,' he said ruminatively. 'They're old and you're losing a lot of heat through the single panes. Are all your windows like this, Harry?'

'I'm afraid so,' he said uneasily. 'The building's a bit run down. It'll take a few years to refurbish properly. I want to put in central heating first.'

Max shook his head disconsolately. 'No point when you'll lose the heat through these windows. You should let me have a survey done for you, Harry. No cost to you at all and with my clout I can give you a whacking discount. And you'll have triple-glazing set in cellular uPVC frames. The sealed compartments will prevent any transmission of heat. Our product is the best on the market.'

'That's kind of you, Max.'

'Not at all, Harry. Fenetre-Windows is my day-job, you might say, but being a member of Speedway makes you family now. I'll see you right!'

'Why don't you do Speedway full-time?' Harry smiled. 'You could become a Diamond.'

'Oh, I will, I *will*!' Max's Panda eyes brightened. 'As soon as we reach Golden Silver status we'll drop the crutch! You too, Harry. As soon as you reach Golden Silver you can close the hotel!'

'That would be heaven,' Harry smiled at Eleanor whose eyes smiled back sympathetically. 'The hotel's a frustrating business. It's like a prison.'

Max nodded. 'We all need a crutch or cash-cow, Harry. Wait till the convention. You'll be on the fast track out of here soon.'

'Are you aiming for Diamond?'

'Of *course*,' Max smiled. 'Before I'm fifty!'

Harry wondered how old Eleanor was. She barely looked thirty, though on close inspection he could see the faintest trace of crow's feet at the corners of her eyes. But those were probably from smiling and gave her character. 'What do you think of the room then, Eleanor? Will it do?'

Her eyes crinkled and her cheeks dimpled. 'I think it's super!' She looked at Max. 'Don't we, darling?'

Max and Eleanor left with a promise to return in two days ('We have to give notice to the Royal first and organise our things, do you know what I mean?'). Eleanor smiled back at him as he waved them off. He found Anne sitting in the window seat overlooking the Abbey in their private sitting room. Smoke spiralled from a cigarette between her fingers.

'Did they take the room then?' she asked, still studying the Abbey.

'They're moving in as soon as they give notice to the Royal in St Boswells.'

'So what's wrong with the Royal?' Her tone was disgruntled.

'A noisy pub. And they weren't offered a discounted long-term rate. It's quite a lucky booking for us, really.'

She turned accusing eyes on him. 'So now you're a member of Speedway? Yet you yelled at me for joining Selecon. It's okay for *you* to throw money away.'

He bit his lip, guilt stirring the pit of his stomach. 'This is different. Speedway deals in products across the board. Even we can use the products for the hotel and save money. And, as Eleanor said, it operates like a close-knit family.'

She snorted. 'Eleanor's an inane simpleton.' She added in a high-pitched squeak: *'Do you know what I mean?'* She flicked the ash from her cigarette into a flower pot on the window sill. 'I can't stand her simpering little voice, like a little girl. Most of what she said was put on—you never see her real self! She assumes you're stupid.' She screwed up her face into a parody of a sweet smile. *'You look like a sophisticated businesswoman who knows where she's going!'* she squeaked again in mock imitation of the voice that was music in Harry's ears. 'God, she's so *patronising* and insincere! It's nauseating. How could you be taken in by those people! And especially after Selecon! You surprise me, Boy. You really do. And look what you paid for that bloody junk. Seventy bloody pounds! I hope you had the sense to refuse that ticket. God, they're so transparent with their sales talk.' She squashed the cigarette butt into the soil at the base of the plant. 'God, that woman's so *pathetic!* And ... and...' She sniffed, biting her lip. 'If I didn't know better, Harry, I'd have said you were positively drooling over her!'

CHAPTER 9

Posture

WHEN HARRY EMERGED from the hotel, smartly dressed in a suit for the Speedway Convention, he was surprised to find Eleanor in deep conversation with Thomas, who slouched beside her in his duffel coat. Because she was so much shorter, Thomas was bent over more than usual and listening intently. What stopped him in his tracks was the striking contrast between Thomas in his rainswept coat and creased trousers and Eleanor who was elegantly attired in a short sophisticated velour dress with scoop neckline and long sleeves. Her immaculate and slick hairstyle in a shiny helmet bob with wispy fringes spoke of minute attention to personal grooming. Thomas, on the other hand, had dishevelled strands peeping from the cowl of his coat, his hands in pockets well-greased from frequent use and lack of laundering.

Eleanor's eyes turned towards Harry and shone with animation. 'Harry, have you met Thomas? He's a mine of information! Did you know that he's connected with the Abbey and cultivates herbs?'

Harry nodded, smiling. 'Thomas is an expert on the herbs cultivated by the old canons. He's from the twelfth century, you know. There was a time gate.'

'Oh, really,' she said, frowning prettily at Thomas. 'That's fascinating, Thomas. Have you always cultivated herbs? Speedway has a well-developed and researched range of health products based on some of the old alternative medicines. But Chuck Halliday stresses that nutritional health, for Speedway, always comes first—do you know what I mean?' She smiled at Harry. 'I was telling Thomas that networking is the only means of distributing the herbal products. They're not available from shops.'

'Aye,' nodded Thomas with his long lugubrious face. 'The brethren are self-sufficient in everything, like, and niver went ta the shops. They were like a family, like, when it came ta giving one another the herbs. They grew flooers fur the alters, tatties, fruit and pot herbs for the table, an' medicine herbs fur the infirmary, like. Yarrow an' evening primrose stopped the fevers, the itch of fleshly loost and cancer asweel. Spurge an' wormwood were best fur constipation, like.'

Eleanor nodded. 'Speedway is like a family, too. I was telling Harry that the other day, wasn't I, Harry? Your upline's always there when you need help. And they probably have all the herbal remedies you mention.' She lifted her little hand and ticked off some items on her fingers. 'When my aunt felt really poorly, I gave her Milk Thistle; within eight hours she had normal bowel movement. From that day she improved in leaps and bounds.' She lifted a second finger. 'I introduced Slippery Elm Bark to build her up. It also coats the entire digestive tract.' She raised more fingers. 'Then, one at a time, I gave her vitamins C, E, Beta Carotene and Selenium in high doses. These are anti-oxidants. They help fight the free radicals that cause cancer and all other diseases.' She smiled sweetly at Thomas. 'You know, all your herbs and vitamins can be provided in concentrated form from Speedway. There's no need to live in the past. Why not have the benefit of modern research and patents, is what I say. You could do a lot worse by networking with us and being part of our family, do you know what I mean?'

'Aye, the family's the thing,' Thomas nodded lugubriously. 'But niver have anything ta do with the black canon. He ...'

At that moment Max shot out of the front door importantly with his briefcase. He scowled when he saw his immaculate wife with Thomas and looked quizzically at Harry, raising his eyebrows. 'We'll be late. Come, come,' he said hastily. He aimed his key at his blue BMW and the automatic locking sprang open. 'I like to be early. I need to see Chuck Halliday before the meeting.' He was dressed as for a business meeting in his double-breasted suit and his eyes had a hunted look. The engine sprang into life and Eleanor got quickly into the passenger seat while Harry scrambled into the back. The car whined as it reversed, shooting past the surprised and still slouching Thomas, swinging into the main street.

'I don't like to see you talking to riffraff, snookums,' Max said curtly, engaging first gear. 'It's not good for the business.'

'He was ever so knowledgeable!' Eleanor protested crossly. 'I know he looked—well, tatty. But does that mean we should ignore his dignity? I believe every human being should be respected for his dignity!'

'Calm down, you silly moo,' Max laughed. 'I was only thinking of the business.' At the T-junction he swung the car into the traffic of the A68 and Harry felt himself pushed back into the padded seat as the car accelerated rapidly.

'I was impressed, actually,' Harry chuckled, his heart genuinely warmed by Eleanor's response. He had an irrational impulse to hug her, easily inhibited by his seat belt and the authoritarian presence of Max in control at the wheel. 'He really *is* quite knowledgeable, like a walking encyclopaedia. He's unemployed, so maybe he could do networking.'

'Forget it, Harry,' Max tossed his reply from the driver's seat. 'He has poor posture. You'll see what I mean tonight. Chuck Halliday's talk's on posture.'

After crossing the Fourth Road Bridge parking was achieved with difficulty since the hotel where the Convention was being held was surrounded by cars cluttered everywhere, parked two-abreast on the pavements and spilling out of the car parks. At the front of the hotel a huge brand new Bentley gleamed in racing green. 'That's Chuck Halliday's car,' whispered Eleanor in awe. The foyer, the public rooms and the bars were awash with people, milling like ants, shouting and cracking jokes, and Harry had to turn sideways to press through them towards the lecture hall. Tables were drawn together near the doorway with peroxide blondes taking tickets, money amassed in boxes. Max strode purposefully towards the raised dais, looking for Chuck Halliday and waving to other figures in double-breasted suits. Harry realised all the men were wearing suits, the women dressed fashionably in two-piece suits or evening dresses as though for church or a gala evening. Almost all the men and some of the women clutched little black bibles which Harry realised weren't bibles at all but copies of the business plan. It was like the reunion of a great fundamentalist church on the eve of the parousia.

'Max is involved in the ushering,' Eleanor explained. 'We can take a seat near the front in the meantime, while we can!' She led the way to a row of empty seats behind some smartly-dressed people. A conversational buzz filled the room. As they sat down the woman in front swung round and stretched an arm ringing with bangles towards Eleanor.

'Eleanor!' she beamed. Her face was wreathed in smiles and rich auburn curls. Her husband, who looked like a bank manager, turned round with a supercilious grin. 'We've just returned from the Bahamas!' the woman gushed. 'We didn't see you this time!'

'The Bahamas? That's *super*!' trilled Eleanor with genuine sincerity, touching her hand. 'Sandra, this is Harry. He's a new member. This is Frank, Harry. They're new ruby distributors. Rubies and Emeralds went to the Bahamas in June.'

'Hi, Harry!' Sandra beamed. 'You see all these people! So now you *know* the business works!' She looked excitedly back to Eleanor. 'Eleanor, we went from 9% in August last year to Ruby in May this year! We'll soon have our dream!'

'What's that?' smiled Harry.

Frank smirked with satisfaction. 'A castle in the highlands.'

'Oh, that's *super*!' thrilled Eleanor, touching Sandra's hand again. 'Good on you!'

'Hello Eleanor!' enthused a bald-headed man in a grey suit. His eyes slanted downwards at the outer edges and almost disappeared as puffy pouches rose upwards in a beaming smile. 'Just back from Florida? I thought I saw Max in the convention there!'

'Haloo Renton!' Eleanor sang in her musical voice. 'You're looking super! No, I didn't go with Max this time. Did you and Karen have a good time?'

'The best! The best!' He smiled enquiringly at Harry.

'Harry's a new member, Renton. He owns the hotel we're staying at.' She smiled up at him, then looked at Harry. 'Renton's an Emerald Distributor.'

'Emerald *Direct*!' corrected Renton, leaning over further and grasping Harry's hand. 'You'll soon learn to make things happen, Harry! The business is your opportunity. For Karen and I it's been the road to freedom and the future.'

'So what next, Renton?' Sandra gushed from the seat in front.

'Diamond! Diamond, I trust, Sandra!' he laughed generously and moved away.

'He's such a nice man,' Eleanor confided to Harry. 'So gentle and sincere. He just gets on quietly with the job and radiates confidence.'

'Wonderful,' smiled Harry, feeling suddenly depressed. He found that he was instinctively recoiling from the flamboyant display of wealth and confidence and couldn't understand why. Perhaps it was because he always felt shy and retiring in large gatherings. Somehow he couldn't see himself grasping hands and flaunting confidence in a double-breasted suit. Somehow it enhanced the social distance between himself and Eleanor who so glibly rubbed shoulders with these globe-trotting icons of success. It was like being back in academia where all the senior lecturers and professors were acutely aware of their rank and status. It was like an ego parade, but much more suave and glib than an academic parade.

The hubbub of greetings and camaraderie-exchanges suddenly died down when a portly man in a navy suit strode easily down the aisle to the front. The auditorium broke into applause and the whole assembly to a man stood up, still applauding.

The man had a dome-shaped head that shone with the reflected lights of the auditorium. A lean grey-haired man smiled benignly and held up his hands. The clapping reduced to a discrete spattering of applause before silence reigned. The man lowered his hands to indicate that everyone should be seated.

'Chuck Halliday needs no introduction, I see!' the grey-haired man beamed.

Thick velvet curtains stirred to the right to reveal the hunted bruised eyes of Max surveying the scene. The curtains closed and in a moment parted elsewhere, the same bruised eyes staring importantly at the crowd. He was in his element, Harry realised, ghosting quietly behind the scenes close to the man he wanted to emulate. All eyes focused on the bald-headed man who grasped the microphone. He smiled and a new wave of whistling and shouting and applause broke out. He held out his hand amiably and the silence filtered back into place.

Harry leaned over and whispered to Eleanor. 'Why'd everyone stand up when he came in?'

'Shhh,' she responded, placing a finger on her delicate lips. 'He's a double diamond.'

Harry nodded. It referred to his wealth, he supposed. It was like the Temple of Mammon. He waited with baited breath to see what pearls of wisdom would first fall from the lips of the multimillionaire.

Chuck Halliday cleared his throat and spoke with a hint of an American accent. 'If you haven't got a pen and paper, beg, borrow or steal—but *get* some.'

There was a shuffling throughout the auditorium.

'Don't ever come to a function without pen and paper,' he said calmly, the megaphone transmitting his quiet words to every ear. 'Or you'll never remember them at home. Now write down the following letters.' He spoke softly and unhurriedly and spelt out the letters: 'P.O.S.T.U.R.E.' He chuckled and there was a *frisson* of excitement, a rustling in the auditorium as everyone chuckled in return.

His delivery was like a casual talk. 'It's not *what* you say, it's how you *feel* and what your *attitude* is,' he chatted on. 'That's what I want to talk about.' He smiled benignly at everyone and everyone smiled back. 'How would your dog react if you shouted "You good dog!" in an angry voice? In a nutshell, that's posture. Don't try to logic it out, like a bank manager with graphs.' He laughed and everyone laughed. 'Bank manager's always want cashflow forecasts. God knows why because the banks have plenty of cash anyway.' More laughter. He shook his head. 'No, you don't learn this business naturally. Ask yourselves this: who, before they got into this business, went around shaking everyone's hand, smiling a lot, or went around commending people, building them up?' He shook his head and chuckled. 'I've never read that anyone has given birth to a Speedway distributor!' Laughter again. 'No, it doesn't happen naturally—it's something you learn. You need to learn that you lose people with bad posture.'

Harry leaned back to relieve a slight ache in his back. He glanced across at Eleanor and saw that she was one of the few who wasn't scribbling furiously. Her delicate little hand rested on her lap, only inches from his own. He moved his fingers casually and closed the gap to within less than an inch. It was a daring act and it made his heart lurch pleasantly into his throat. It made the hairs on his fingers lift and stir, as though aware of a synapse of electricity that began to flow between the two hands. It was a delicious and comforting sensation.

Chuck Halliday was saying how everyone needed to compile a list of up to 150 names—of friends and acquaintances who they could invite to a meeting. 'Right at this stage your posture begins to show.'

Harry slid his eyes sideways and realised that by squinting down Eleanor's dress he could clearly make out the firm swellings of her breasts, like two firm apples. He glanced up at her face and saw that she was listening to Chuck Halliday with rapt attention. He allowed his eyes to drop back to her cleavage and drank in the sight of her breasts with a more relaxed enjoyment. They were like porcelain, the texture like silk. She wore a black lace bra with a little white bow just adjacent to the little valley of the cleavage. He yearned to dip in his fingers and drink in the soft texture with his fingertips until a stirring within his groin made him draw his eyes away sharply.

He concentrated on the speaker's words. 'You must talk to people at your own level, or above! At your own *attitude* level. If you sponsor people that look up to you your business will surely go down.'

But Harry's stirring erection had no intention of going down. He concentrated on the bald dome of the speaker and on his protruding paunch, but nothing would stop the upward movement. He moved his left hand with the piece of paper so that it covered his groin, not wanting to sacrifice the synaptic gap occasioned by his right hand being so close to Eleanor's. He breathed deeply and tried to follow the thread of Chuck Halliday's narrative. 'A consultant surgeon would feel comfortable talking to other doctors. Does he talk to nurses?' A flurry of laughter swept through the auditorium. 'So! Staff nurses talk to trainee nurses! The trainee nurses talk to sick patients.'

He chuckled. 'You know what they say: roll over, I've got something for you!' The laughter broke out in full force. 'And who do the sick patients talk to? Why, there's only one step down from there, you see! They talk to the people in the morgue!'

Laughter filled the auditorium and Harry sighed with relief, sensing the erection had lost its independent life. He dared to look down again but his eyes were drawn like a magnet to Eleanor's trim little thighs that curved sensuously out of her short black dress. She wore stockings which nevertheless revealed the perfect curves of the thighs, her sculptured knees and the carves below. His erection returned with a vengeance and bent painfully against his trousers, just as Eleanor's laughter tinkled in unison with everyone else's. She swung her face towards Harry, her laughing eyes seeking out his own. He laughed with her, red faced and awkwardly, feeling the flush of his illicit lust melt over him like hot wax.

Chuck went on to talk about the importance of the curiosity approach. 'Listen, this information is worth a fortune,' he said. 'We are looking for *lookers*. So don't try to convince knuckleheads. Make *them* choose *you*! It's like feeding pigeons. You don't try to force food down a pigeon's throat. You tempt the whole flock by scattering a few seeds! And it's your *posture* that catches them. Your posture must say "I don't need you." Make them chase you! Drop a few hints. Really sharp people won't let you go without wanting to know more. And it's the sharp people we want!'

Harry shifted his position to ease his discomfort and his hand came suddenly into contact with Eleanor's. It shot his heart into his throat which was already dry from the excitement. She turned her rapt eyes from the speaker and smiled sweetly and indulgently at him. Her eyes, blue and intense, lingered just long enough for him to fall in love. She whispered something he couldn't hear and turned her eyes back to the speaker. Her delicate small finger was still against his, the contact so featherlight that he was only aware of it through the electric surge that seemed to flow from her. He almost stopped breathing.

When he looked up it was into the bruised eyes of her husband, staring dolefully at him from between the velvet curtains. Harry's heart stopped for a moment and he released his breath slowly, scooping in the next breath under tight control while pretending to be absorbed by the speaker's words. He nodded fervently to show his agreement with whatever he was saying. 'Always try to be in a hurry when you lend people a tape about the business,' Chuck was saying. 'And tell them you want it back in 24-hours!'

When he shifted his eyes he found Max had moved on to a different vantage point and was looking at Chuck, not him. Harry breathed more slowly and felt Eleanor's little finger scrape subliminally but deliciously against his. He glanced down and once again took in her pretty knees and slightly swelling thighs. God, he thought, Max was a lucky bastard. Just then Eleanor's hand snapped away and clapped with everyone else who whistled and screamed wildly in a frenzy of applause. Harry joined the clapping, smiling at Eleanor who smiled in return, sweetly and innocently.

'That was *super*, wasn't it, Harry?' she asked in musical tones above the clapping. 'It's true what he says. People don't want to get into business with you if they think you need them. You really have to be committed and believe in yourself, do you know what I mean?'

'Sure,' he nodded, swallowing. 'It's just a matter of having the courage to take the plunge, though, isn't it?' He smiled. 'I've always been a bit shy, you know. Like the Kamikaze pilot on his fifth mission who says "This time I will do it!"' He gave a little laugh. 'I'm not used to ...' He glanced at her hand and wished he'd had the courage to hold it, but knew that was forever impossible. 'I'm not used to taking risks.'

'You just need a push, Harry.' Her smile was sympathetic. 'Even Eagles need a push out of the nest so they can learn to fly, you know what I mean?'

Harry sighed. 'Sure.' But she belonged to another eagle's nest, he thought disconsolately. No amount of courage or pushing would help. Besides, he was tied to Anne, and she was a dodo if ever there was one. 'But where do I fly to?' he smiled. 'All the best perches are taken.'

She placed her hand lightly on his, unaware of the thrilling effect on him. 'Oh Harry, you *must* have a heart's desire. You can soar towards it by rising above your doubts, do you know what I mean? Just *go* for it, Harry! And you can depend on my help.' She gave his hand a little squeeze that brought tears to his eyes.

'Thank you, Eleanor.' He smiled sadly. 'But you can't teach an old dog new tricks, you know.'

'Oh yes, you can!' she said cooingly. 'You wait and see. This business will give you a new lease of life.'

The next speaker was a young American who took the microphone by storm. Everyone was electrified to attention by his evangelical fervour. He clutched the microphone by its throat and shouted. 'When you married you made a promise to that awesome woman sitting beside you!' he yelled. 'And what did you do, my friend? You sat night after night on a couch watching TV! Let me tell you, my friend, I had a fifty-thousand dollar couch like that five years ago! It was a fifty-thousand-dollar couch because that was the amount I was losing by sitting on it! One day I looked at this awesome woman!' He pointed to the painted Barbie-doll who sat primly on the dais next to him. She simpered at the audience and fiddled self-consciously with her hair. 'I looked at myself and said, "What are you doing for this awesome woman!" I had been a sleeping member of Speedway for five wasted years, and then, and then one night I got off my couch! Do *you* have one of those fifty-thousand dollar-couches at home, my friends?' He pointed fervently at the audience. 'Do *you*?' He pointed in a different direction. 'Do *you*?' He pointed at Harry who lowered his profile fractionally. 'Well, let me tell you this, my friends! That night I turned my life upside down! I took the plan and showed it to five people! The next week I showed it to a meeting of sixty people!' At this point his delivery went ballistic. He pointed to his wife and shouted: 'I made this awesome woman the wife of a millionaire! And I did it, just as YOU can!' Then he screamed into the microphone and the roof reverberated. 'YOU CAN DO IT TOO! DO IT FOR THE SAKE OF THAT AWESOME WOMAN NEXT TO YOU!'

Harry glanced self-consciously at Eleanor, but her face was turned towards the speaker. His heart was beating uncontrollably and he took a deep breath. The only woman he had made marriage vows to was asleep in bed, probably snoring. At that moment he didn't think of her as awesome, and she wasn't the drop-dead gorgeous creature next to him.

Then the speaker did a surprising thing. Once more he shouted into the microphone: '*YOU* CAN DO IT!' Then he left the dais and the microphone and walked about the audience, shouting '*You* can do it!' to individual people. He stood in front of a young girl and shouted, placing his hand on her shoulder: '*You* can do it!' He moved to the next person, a stout middle-aged man. '*You* can do it!' He moved onto five or six other victims and Harry wondered uncomfortably if he was going to have a turn too. The man's voice was barely audible without the microphone. Then he returned to the dais and sat next to his prim smiling wife.

The audience rose to its feet in a fury of applause.

CHAPTER 10

Incestuous Infatuation

AFTER THE EVENING'S LECTURES Max sought Harry out and cleared a way through the crowd to where Chuck was holding forth to a group of admiring Pearl and Emerald members. In a lull between questions Max saw his chance and presented Harry like a new trophy, holding his shoulder in a proprietorial grip.

'This is Harry Denton,' growled Max with pride. 'I signed him up last week.'

'Glad to meet you, Harry.' Chuck held his hand loosely, smiling with soft grey eyes.

Harry felt awkward. 'I don't think I've ever met a millionaire before, let alone shake hands with a Double-D.'

Chuck smiled indulgently. 'Oh, I try to keep abreast of things, you know.'

'Max says Speedway is an excellent vehicle to specific dreams.'

'Oh yes, it is,' Chuck said quietly. 'It will take you wherever you want it to take you, Harry. Just fuel it with hard work and conviction. Have you compiled your list of names?'

'No, but I'm working on it.' He smiled at Max. 'Max has asked me for the list and he'll contact all the people.'

'Contact them yourself, Harry, and hold a meeting. Your sponsors must relate to you, not Max.' His eyes drifted away from Harry and someone else caught his eye. 'Excuse me, Harry. Best of luck.' He gave Harry a precursory glance and moved away.

A man in a sleek grey suit strutted up to Max and tapped him on the shoulder with his business plan. 'I want to speak to you about the Leadership Seminar in Malta, Max.' The man's upper lip lifted in an easy smile. 'Should the Emeralds be addressed by their Directs or just one selected Diamond?'

Harry drifted back into the crowd and gravitated towards Eleanor who was daintily helping herself to a cracker with caviar to go with the cocktail she held in her hand. Once again Harry thought she looked like a model, slim and petite, so different from the other women who were lavishly painted and powdered, some with broad-brimmed hats as though dressed for Ascot. She smiled at him, showing a line of brilliant white teeth blemished by a speck of caviar stuck between the perfect front teeth. The voices of the other women floated over him, sounding affected and over-effusive: 'Oh my deah, the weather in Cyprus was so *awfully* atrocious!'

Eleanor, by contrast, looked slight, almost too thin and vulnerable, he thought, and the speck of caviar gave her the look of a young girl who didn't quite belong. She dipped her hand into a plate of salted peanuts and daintily tipped them into her mouth.

'You're hungry,' smiled Harry.

'Yes,' she gurgled through the mouthful of peanuts, giggling. 'We left in a bit of a rush, didn't we? You've caught me pigging out.'

'You hardly weigh anything, I should say. You need feeding up!'

'Oh Harry, I've always had trouble putting on weight. Last year I had an ulcer, you know. But the Speedway mineral supplements have really helped. Speedway is the only company that produces minerals in colloidal form. Max ordered them for me and I've been taking them ever since. They're plant-derived, you know, so they're highly absorbable. And they make the vitamins in the body work.' She smiled engagingly. 'Now I feel really well, and my weight increased from 6 stone 4lbs to 7stone 4lbs! Can you imagine that! I have never been over 7 stone for years!'

'That's wonderful, but I still think you could do with fattening up.' He looked at her tiny waist and marvelled that she could be so fragile and compact. 'Gosh, Eleanor, I think I could sweep you off the ground easily.' He longed to try it and imagined his hand almost all the way round her little waist. He had an incurable ache to touch her. Instead, he rocked on his heels, disciplining his impulses, his hands held firmly behind his back. 'But I'm glad your ulcer's gone, Eleanor. Surely you're not a worrier? You seem to be so—together?'

'Oh, no!' she shook her head, cracking a crisp between her immaculate teeth. 'We all need to work on our posture with positive thinking, Harry, do you know what I mean?' She smiled confidentially and moved closer, brushing against his arm as she stretched out her hand towards a cheese dip, wafting her herbal aroma in front of him. 'Last year I really had to cleanse my own aura and get myself straight. Max engaged a Feng Shui consultant who set out a number of crystals and silver coins around the house—in the hallway and on window sills.' She giggled. 'Mind you, at first when the crystals went out I flipped!'

Harry was confused and smiled quizzically. 'What did you say—shang shoo?'

Her crystalline laugh tinkled musically. 'Feng Shui! It's the Chinese art of living in harmony with your environment. Really, you'll think I'm daft, Harry, but it works. But at first I flipped!'

'Flipped? You mean, stressed-out? I can't imagine you being stressed-out.'

'Oh, but I was! Max agreed, it was the crystals—because of the sudden release of energy. But the energy subsided and before long everything began to work out wonderfully. Things that were broken started to work again. The TV, even the Dehumidifier! We sent it in for repairs and they returned it, saying they couldn't fix it. But when I turned it on it worked perfectly!' She stretched another slither of carrot past him into the cheese dip. 'This dip is super. You should try it.'

Harry became more fascinated than ever. Somehow her preoccupation with what sounded like superstition made her seem more vulnerable, more naive and therefore more accessible. She ranted on, as Anne would say, about inanities, as though she were a mouthpiece for Speedway products. Her almost literal mind fascinated him—the way *she* was fascinated by products and spoke with wonder and conviction, with so much bright-eyed enthusiasm, about detergents, toothpaste and minerals. The same attention given to an altogether different subject like crystals and what sounded like mumbo jumbo made her childlike. This was a new dimension to Eleanor. It gave her a spark of real humanity, a spark that informed her incredible doll-like beauty with vibrant life. It made him feel strangely protective towards her. It was like a new intimacy.

'I didn't realise there was so much power in crystals,' he said, smiling.

'Oh, I won't sleep without a crystal under my pillow,' she confided with a little laugh. 'I'm looking for a Buddha. That, and some wind chimes in your hall can really improve your health, wealth and love-life, Harry.' She smiled sweetly. 'You should put a Buddha in the hallway of your hotel.'

Harry was quite amazed. 'And in my bedroom,' he said, with a little daring. 'I could use a little more luck there.'

Her eyes creased, her laugh a little tinkle like the chimes she spoke of. 'Oh, I can see you and Anne are very happily married, Harry. You're a super couple. I'm sure you're both very good together, do you know what I mean?'

'Like you and Max, I'm sure,' he ventured experimentally.

'Oh, Max is super,' she said, her bright blue eyes twinkling.

When he returned to the hotel that night Harry was aglow with a form of vicarious happiness. The suave talk and display of wealth had depressed him, made him feel excluded, but in the end the sustained proximity to Eleanor had excited him. Apart from being an illicitly erotic evening, he was awash with the warm glow of her presence that persisted like an aura. He snuggled into bed next to the shapeless sleeping heap of Anne and cuddled his pillow, imagining it was Eleanor. He imagined he could feel the delicate wisps of her hair against his cheek as he began to drift off.

Anne's voice was harsh in his ears and shocked him back to alert wakefulness. 'So what was it like, Boy? Have you started on the ladder of success?'

He blinked in the dark. 'What?'

'The meeting,' her voice grated in the dark. 'So what's the next step?'

'I have to make a list of names—of friends and acquaintances, you know the drill.'

'It's no good, boy. We used them for Selecon.'

'I know.'

'So what's the point, then? Why did you bother going to the meeting?'

To be with Eleanor, he thought, staring into the dark. To peek at her cute little thighs and her tits. It was delicious, Anne. You should have been there.

'Are you asleep, Boy?' she said, softening her tone.

He felt the light touch of her fingers on his groin. She found the slit in his pyjamas and insinuated her fingers between his thighs, searching out the erogenous zones around his testicles—a ploy she knew never failed. He stared into the dark, biting his lip. He wanted it to be Eleanor, not her.

When he felt his erection growing, betraying him, he knew he'd have to give way. He closed his eyes and imagined the thin delicate fingers of Eleanor's hand. He conjured up the short black dress spun tightly over her shapely thighs, and saw again the little white bow on her black lace bra, the small breasts like apples. He groaned.

'You've got a muckle een, Boy,' Anne simpered, using the local parlance of the Borders, closing her hand around his urgently erect lust for Eleanor. 'Does it want an itsy-bitsy relief, eh?' She spoke in a childlike voice, as she often did when she wanted sex. 'Does it want an itsy-bitsy visit in my itsy-bitsy honey-patch, eh?'

Harry sighed. 'Sure, Anne.' He turned over and pulled off his pyjama trousers. Anne pushed down her pants and splayed her thighs. When he mounted her she said: 'Yeh, yeh, yeh!' imitating a child on the brink of receiving an ice lolly and chuckled lasciviously.

He entered her with practised ease and shafted rhythmically, keeping himself raised on his arms to minimise close contact. All he was aware of was the soft rippling cocoon of her ample vagina as he thrust and, with eyes closed in the dark, visualised the biting blue eyes of Eleanor. But Anne began to grunt and it shattered the illusion. He felt his erection begin its inevitable collapse and, after forcing himself to maintain the rhythm until he felt her sharp intake of breath, he made himself shudder powerfully in imitation of an orgasm.

'God,' she sighed, as he collapsed by her side, 'I think you should go to Speedway meetings more often, Boy!'

She stretched out her hand and kneaded his hair, like a satisfied cat. He listened to her breathing grow deeper. When she began to snore in long, rasping notes, he got up quietly and trod gingerly down the stairs to the kitchen where he made himself a cup of tea. It was cold in the kitchen and he sat uncomfortably on the straight-backed chair, sipping the hot sweet tea. He thought again of the meeting and Chuck's talk on posture. He wondered if it was true that he could turn his life about through a change of attitude, through a belief and conviction in Speedway as a powerful marketing tool. But the thought of direct selling depressed him. It just wasn't *him*. He was too shy and self-effacing. He knew his few friends wouldn't want to hear, anyway, especially after Anne had already plagued them and exhausted their patience about the cascading wealth from Selecon. Surely there must be some other kind of vehicle? Anyway, he thought bitterly, his only motive for going was to enjoy Eleanor's company. He smiled, remembering her belief in crystals and silver coins. Usually it was Anne or Rosemary who tidied Eleanor's room—which was also Max's room, Harry thought bitterly. If ever he had the chance he'd look out for her crystals—especially the one under the pillow. She'd said she was looking for a Buddha. Perhaps he could buy one for her. He made a mental note to search the antique shops the next morning.

The faint cries of a woman's voice filtered into his consciousness. It was nearly a minute before it dawned on him that it was Eleanor's voice.

He stood up, anxiously. The hotel was dark and empty apart from the hall light. He opened the door that divided his private quarters from the hotel hall and heard her cries more clearly. He held his breath and tiptoed gingerly up the main hotel stairway, around the dimly lit curve in the stairs until he was standing on the wide landing outside her bedroom. It was the only bedroom occupied since the seasonal trade had evaporated. All was silent and he listened intently, holding his breath. God, he thought, what had Max been doing to her?

Then, without warning, she cried out again, with a vigour so fierce it chilled his blood. Her cries came persistently, imploringly, urgently, subsiding in pleading, whimpering tones. There was a brief silence before they broke out afresh, this time rising, escalating in intensity in sustained screams, trilling like an opera singer striking a high, sustained note of ecstasy. There was one brief shout from Max. When her screams stopped the silence was palpable.

Harry had never in his life heard anything like it before. He realised he was sweating, in spite of the cold landing. He wiped a clammy hand across his damp forehead. 'God,' he whispered under his breath, 'Max is a bloody lucky bastard.'

It was impossible to sleep now. He went upstairs and dressed quietly so as not to wake up Anne whose snoring was still quietly audible. He pulled on his coat and walked out into the cold brilliant night air. He followed the yellow streetlights along the pavement of the A68 southwards out of town, past the floodlit Abbey that looked like a wedding cake against the velvet sky. He followed a minor road that led off the A68 artery, and soon found himself plodding silently up a steep hill under the overarching trees that filtered leaves silently upon him as he walked. The darkness was almost total and he put one foot in front of the other cautiously, feeling rather than seeing his way ahead. His heart lurched when someone coughed, and then he realised it was a sheep, the doleful head barely visible through a gap in the hedge. He padded on until he emerged from the dark tunnel of trees and looked up to see the brilliant lights of stars, now clearly visible away from the glare of the streetlights.

He made his way through the wet dew-soaked grass to lean on the cold metal of a farm gate. The rusty metal was damp from condensation. He looked up and studied the stars, clearly seeing the dense clustered arc of the milky way and the three bright points of the dagger in Orion's belt. He stood there for a long time, spellbound in the silent, crisp air. He longed for one of the stars to descend, like a UFO, and sweep him away. There wasn't a human in sight, he thought, and an amiable alien could easily land and abduct him without anyone's knowledge. He yearned with all his heart to be lifted up into the stars. Then he saw that one star was moving, almost undetectably. As he watched he saw that it was moving purposefully, in a steady direction. He wondered if it was a distant satellite catching the light of the sun. But then he detected just the faintest trace of a red light flashing close to it, accompanying it in the same direction, and realised it was an aircraft. It was moving almost imperceptibly to the south. He craned his neck, watching. It must be a flight from Edinburgh to London, he thought. He followed it with his eyes and his heart. Eventually the light merged with the stars near the horizon and then was eclipsed by the dark shapes of the trees.

Suddenly he felt tired enough to drop. The cries of Eleanor's sexual ecstasy were still ringing in his brain but he felt exhausted enough to slump down in the wet grass and seek oblivion. But his feet plodded back, slowly, retracing the way he had come. The hotel was silent like a tomb. After undressing he crawled into his bed next to the still-sleeping Anne, sensing her warmth, and fell asleep directly.

He dreamt he was on board ship, sailing south. It was a reconditioned cargo vessel fitted out for some kind of expedition. There were many chambers or compartments filled with children being taught. There was a wonderful sense of order and camaraderie. The children sat in neat rows, well-behaved and there was a sense of fun and happiness. Harry went from deck to deck, and it was all the same. In one of the classrooms he met one of the teachers, a young woman with short black hair and a relaxed smile. 'Gosh!' exclaimed Harry, smiling at her. 'To think I was sweating over exams in November when you were on the high seas having fun!' She smiled indulgently at him. Then he went on shore across a ramp (for the ship was in port) and came across a lean man with sandy grey hair who ran the show. He spoke of the teacher he had met in glowing terms. 'She's dedicated and thorough, and the children love her,' he smiled. 'She'll grind to a fine flour any mission you set her.'

Harry awoke, and the dream still hung heavily in his mind, seeming real. He thought of the young woman and her ready smile, and the strange words the man had used of her. Then he turned over and fell into a dreamless sleep.

CHAPTER 11

Tantalus

'**S**HE ASSUMES you're bloody stupid!' Anne jerked the contents of the bully-beef tin into the pot on the cooker and stirred in the baked beans with vehement force. 'I think she'd honestly thought I'd never worn a spot of makeup in my life! I wanted to hit her! Look at the way I looked when we came home. Like a painted hag! It was pathetic!'

She poured the mushy mixture over the slices of toast in front of Harry. It steamed and misted his glasses which he removed and wiped with a handkerchief.

Eleanor had taken Anne to a make-up session with a neighbour, using Speedway beauty products. It was a 'party-plan' method of disseminating Speedway products and the business plan. But Anne's disposition had proved incompatible with make-up of any kind and the futile exercise had exasperated her. '*Oh, you look so super*!' Anne squeaked in imitation of Eleanor's voice.

'How did Cynthia take to the make-up?' asked Harry.

'Hah!' she scoffed. 'She's so weather-worn! She just looked colourful, sort of Barbara Cartlandish. We probably all looked like younger versions of Barbara Cartland! She treated me like I was stupid.' She shrugged and sat down to her mush of beans and bully-beef. She attacked it fiercely with knife and fork, as though making a statement. 'I suppose she was playing a game with me. She only hears what she wants to hear. Typical Speedway mentality. She couldn't stop talking—she just rants on and on. The insincerity of it all makes me sick. It's just all hard-sales stuff, that's all. Speedway is like the crystalline entity, sucking the life off the whole planet.' She jabbed a piece of toast with her fork and pushed it around the plate, mopping up the remnants of the grease.

'Crystalline what?' he laughed.

'It's an alien force they have in *Star Trek*. It attacks planets and methodically mows all the life off it. When it's finished with one planet it goes on to the next. Speedway's attacking the Borders at the moment.'

Harry laughed. 'They're attacking the whole country, if you must know. As well as other countries. But the reply to your argument is that it's an enriching process, not an impoverishing one. The idea is to make everyone wealthier.'

'Umph!' she snorted. 'Not in practical terms, I don't think. When people find they've burnt their fingers, like I did with Selecon, they'll get hard of hearing and Speedway will move off to another area. The same thing happened with Swipe in the old pyramid-selling days of the 'sixties.'

He shook his head. 'Well, I believe Eleanor and Max are perfectly sincere, Anne. And I really like them. I've never made any decent friends here, you know that. It's nice to have someone to talk to, at my own level.'

'Well, you can speak for yourself.' She stood up and shovelled Nescafe into two mugs. She poured some boiling water into the cups. 'You can't get out there fast enough to serve them breakfast in the mornings. I'm beginning to think you've got the hots for Eleanor!'

'What a lot of rot!' Harry nearly choked. 'She's so inane. Give me more credit, Anne.'

'Just now you said you liked them?'

'Well...yes, of course,' he said casually. 'Max has an excellent sense of humour.'

'He's very course, if you ask me. If he's not talking about Speedway and double glazing, he's telling rude jokes and leering at me. Or haven't you noticed?'

He looked at her with disbelief. 'I can't say I have, in all honesty. Haven't you noticed how attentive he is to Eleanor, always stroking her hair or pawing her?'

She slapped the mugs on the kitchen table, making the coffee spill out. 'Ever since they came here life has been a strain. She's constantly knocking at the door wanting things. The hairdryer, the iron, curling tongs, even extra coffee sachets. And you jumping up like a jack in the box, smarming all over her. I've never seen you so interested before in crystals and compacts.'

She sniffed. 'You even bought her that silly little bronze Buddha thing. You never buy me things.'

He grinned self-consciously. 'There's a nice nurse's outfit or maid's outfit with a shortie skirt I can get you. With black stockings and garters. I saw it in one of Max's catalogues.'

'No thank you.' She slumped down and drank some of her coffee. 'Obviously that's what you'd like to see Eleanor in, or am I wrong?' Her weary blue eyes surveyed him over the top of her mug. 'I can read you like a book, Boy. Just ask yourself how I must feel, seeing you fawning around her.'

'I'm not fawning!' he protested with rising chagrin. 'All their stuff is packed in boxes, so of course they have to ask for things.' He cleared his throat and took the plunge. 'In fact, I've invited them to dinner tomorrow night. Max works so hard, and Eleanor's just started that new job repping beauty products.'

She sat up, stonefaced. 'You *haven't*? Oh, shit, Harry!'

The next day was Saturday and Anne was out shopping for the evening's supper. Harry waited with baited breath for the sound of Eleanor's canary-yellow VW Golf which she acquired recently for her repping job. It was a diesel and it wasn't long before he heard the distinctive throbbing rattle of its engine as it eased down the steep slope of the little car park. Harry ambled casually into the front sitting room, pretending to tidy up leaflets and brochures, his heart beating rapidly with the anticipation of seeing Eleanor pass through the hallway on her way to her bedroom. When she nudged open the front door with parcels in her arms he sprang to attention.

'Eleanor! Let me help you with those.'

'Halloo!' she cooed in her singsong greeting. 'Thank you, Harry. Come up and let me show you the super little oil burners I found!'

Her little body was smothered in a mock fur-coat and Harry willingly followed her up the stairs, admiring the sleek calves that twinkled enticingly below the hem of her thick coat. Once in her room, which was warm from the heater being turned on all day, she emptied the parcels onto the bed and undid her coat.

'There's a new ethnic shop in Galashiels that specialises in aromatherapy and it has a super range of essentials oils and the dearest little burners and expression dolls.'

She looked so cute, Harry thought, in her neat black bobs and wispy fringe. She pulled off her coat and let it fall across the bed, chatting and smiling all the time. She wore a trim black waistcoat over a frilly blouse, and a tight black skirt with black stockings. 'It's quite warm, isn't it?' she smiled sweetly. Harry didn't mind that he was paying for the heating. It was worth it to have such a petite and fascinating creature like her in his home. She unbuttoned her waistcoat and peeled it off, hanging it carefully in the wardrobe.

'Here you are,' she smiled, picking up a brown paper packet and dipping into it. She removed some fine silk paper from a little object. 'Just look at the delicacy of this little lamp. Can you imagine the soft rosy images it will cast when the candle's lit?'

Harry accepted it gingerly into his fingers, like an offering. It looked fragile and was bulbous to allow for the little candle in the middle. It had a delicate fretwork of spidery gold lines, like a fine web spun round the stained glass ovals that formed rose-coloured petals. The rim of the glass on top was tipped with fine gold.

'It's beautiful, Eleanor,' Harry said with a touch of wonder. He returned it to her hands, feeling the light touch of her fingers as he did so. It was like a kind of communion and he felt transfigured with mystic delight in her presence. He dropped his eyes from her brilliant blue eyes and his heart missed a beat. Both her small breasts, milk-white with pert brown nipples, were clearly visible through the thin fabric of her blouse. He felt deeply honoured that she had so casually allowed him admittance into the privacy of her room where she presented herself thus, so naturally and unselfconsciously, not minding in the least that he should see the full splendour of her delicate breasts. It was in keeping with her childlike simplicity and lack of affectation.

'Thank you, Eleanor,' he said softly, his gaze returning to her smiling eyes.

She held his eyes for a moment, then dipped back into her little brown packet. 'And look,' she said, like a child discovering more wonders. 'Aren't these little oil burners adorable? They have a burning time for one and a half hours, the man said. I brought one for you and Anne.' She placed a tiny terracotta lamp in his hand that was like a miniature teapot with a lid. 'And this is the stand. You see, a little candle fits into the base.' She dipped into the packet again and produced a minute glass bottle. 'This is lavender, one of the essential oils. Just put it in the burner tonight when you go to bed and light the candle, see?' She smiled her sweet smile and giggled. 'You and Anne will have a special night, do you know what I mean?'

It seemed that Eleanor had introduced him to a whole new world. He saw that the room itself was transformed into an Aladdin's cave of wonders, with the little ornaments, potpourri and crystals.

'You're ever so sweet, Eleanor,' he smiled, thrilled.

'You need to relax, Harry. It will help your aura, you'll see.'

'You're very kind, and so sweet,' he repeated. Her presence in front of him, so near, her fragrance so sweet, was like a magnet and he had to exercise strict control not to take her into his arms. His eyes were aware of her pert little breasts and he longed to reach out and touch them. It was almost as though she were inviting him to touch them and he wondered what her reaction would be if he gave way to the impulse. He fought the instinct and smiled. 'I'll have to go down and help Anne with the roast, you know. We're really looking forward to the evening with you and Max.'

'Yes,' she said. 'Anne is so kind, isn't she? I hope she's not going to much trouble. We're easy to please, you know.'

'Oh, she's really looking forward to the evening,' he lied. 'She loves to cook for friends.'

'Oh, she's super, she really is, Harry. You two make a super couple.' She smiled, unwrapping another little parcel. She giggled with delight when she saw the little dolls. 'Oh, these are so sweet! I couldn't resist them. Max will really have a laugh. Look!' She placed the four little figurines on the window sill. They were like little toddlers with squat legs, naked except for caps at rakish angles. Their faces were cheeky. Two were sticking out tongues, and two were grasping tiny erect penises. She giggled. 'They're a little naughty. Max will love them.'

Harry laughed. It was on the tip of his tongue to say he couldn't blame the little chaps being turned on in her presence, but he crushed the thought, turning red. But her showing him the expression dolls was like a new intimacy between them. When he descended the stairs he felt he was floating on air. Her radiance and her intimate manner, so relaxed and natural, had charged him to his very fingertips. When he entered the kitchen Anne was unpacking groceries with a shoulder of beef onto the table. She wore a faded navy smock over a frumpy floral dress that ended just above the knees. Her leather boots were an attempt at fashion, and her podgy knees that peeped between the hem of her dress and the top of her boots were like two pink footballs.

'You've been with Eleanor?' she threw the question casually, her eyes on the groceries.

'Yes,' he replied brightly. 'She had some things to carry.'

The silence stretched between them as she continued unpacking. Then she said, almost under her breath, 'I had to lug these in myself. Maybe I should wear short skirts and makeup, too.'

'Oh, she bought you this!' he said, ignoring her remark, placing the little oil burner on the table. 'She even provided the lavender oil. We'll try it tonight.'

She gave the burner a precursory look, pursing her lips, sweeping some tins into her arms.

Harry smiled. 'It will help us relax, she said.'

She began to pack things into cupboards, slamming the cupboard doors. 'You want to be careful of all that New Age stuff, Boy. It's part of a modern movement. It's all designed to seduce us away from the church. From the Kingdom of God.'

'You don't still believe in all that fundamentalist stuff, do you, Anne?' He asked, surprised. 'I know you were brought up in it. Escaping from it was like an escape from prison, for me.' He looked at her sadly. It was as though she were withdrawing back into an old discarded shell.

'Who knows what the real truth is?' she shrugged. 'But surely the fundamentalists have a better foundation for their beliefs? I mean, there's the bible. The New Age people—well, what have they got? They might as well read palms and tea leaves.'

He smiled thinly. 'Eleanor is hardly a gypsy, Anne. She—and Max, too—are expanding their consciousness. They're not afraid to experiment with life. Life's an adventure. Even in their businesses ...'

'What businesses!' she swung round, scornful. 'Max is stuck in double glazing, in spite of his dreams of being a "Diamond," and Eleanor flits from job to job. She's in Speedway, but she's a rep for other beauty products—and now she's looking for a modelling job! She's a butterfly, Boy. You're taken in so easily by a pretty face.'

He sighed. 'I won't argue with you, Anne. At least they're a welcome diversion from this boring hotel lark.' He walked towards the larder. 'I'll put some wine into the fridge for this evening. It's time we had some fun.' He came back and pecked her on the cheek, then squeezed her shoulders. 'Come on, old thing, relax.'

She put down the tin she still held in one hand and stretched her stubby arms round his neck. He felt the hot tears in her eyes against his cheek. 'I just don't want to lose you, Boy,' she sniffed, speaking in a voice suddenly girlish and desperate. 'I feel I'm losing you and I don't know what to do to keep you.'

'Nonsense, Anne, I'm here,' he said softly. He placed his arms round her wide trunk and patted her on the back, as one would a dog that needed sympathy. 'I'm here, Anne. I'm here.'

Max was in high spirits when he arrived home. He had made a sale of a conservatory to a retired couple in a terraced council house they had recently purchased. It would mean a healthy commission and he announced his success that evening with wreathes of smiles and a bottle of Riesling. Eleanor hung onto his elbow like an extension of his bonhomie, smiling sweetly in a suede stretch dress that left her shoulders, arms and sleek legs bare. An interesting feature of the dress was the full-length zip along the front instead of the back.

Max continued to be expansive at the dinner table. Anne had set the large mahogany family table in the main dining room for the occasion and the old storage heaters were putting out a measurable level of heat. An additional flow of hot air came from the little fan heater that purred in the corner.

'A bum on a sofa a night!' exclaimed Matt, chuckling. 'That's my motto in the double glazing business. Always make sure you have an appointment in at least one homestead each night. And who knows? When you've signed them up, there's always the chance of showing the plan. At least fifty-percent of my double glazing prospects invite me back to see the plan. I always leave one of Chuck's Opportunity tapes and say I'll be back for it in twenty-four hours!'

Eleanor smiled brightly. 'I left an Opportunity tape with one of my beauty customers today. I said you'd follow it up, Max.'

'Good girl, snookums.' He leant over and kissed her. He stroked her hair and beamed back at Harry and Anne. 'She's a good learner. I was telling her, always study your prospect in advance, even before you enter the house.'

'Is that right?' Harry smiled at Eleanor, envying the hand that stroked her hair. He watched the hand trail down her cheek and fondle her bare shoulder. She smiled back at Harry, radiating happiness.

'The point is,' Max rushed on, pouring out the wine, 'is to know your prospect thoroughly—everything you can find out about him. Take in the kind of car he drives. Whether his house is neat and presentable from the outside. Is he untidy at the back? Does he look as though he's house-proud? It tells you how to pitch your sale.' He lifted his glass to them, smiling like a Cheshire cat. 'To the business, Harry. To the business, Anne. Long may it prosper!' He clinked his glass with theirs and took a generous sip, smacking his lips. 'And *always* have an answer. The same applies when you're telling people about the business. Meet their objections every time. If he wriggles out of the sitting room, get him in the kitchen. If he wriggles out of the kitchen, get him in his back passage!' He sniggered. 'Always have an answer. But make sure you hit the right spot. Listen to what he's saying. Maybe he doesn't like the catch on a window. If that's the case, there's no point in rambling on about how wonderful the insulation is, how clever the sealed compartments are.' He shook his head. 'No, if he's niggling about a small thing, he won't be listening to you about the big benefits. Make sure you get at what's worrying him.' He cleared his throat and took a bigger swig from the glass. 'God, Harry, sales divides the rams from the sheep! If you can sell, you've got balls!'

Anne gave a raucous laugh. Harry turned to her, surprised, and saw that she had finished her wine. Her cheeks were flushed, as always happened when she drank. At least, he thought, Anne would be in a better mood and allowed himself another smile at Eleanor. His heart gave a little twist when he saw that her blue eyes were on him, is spite of Max's plump hand that played with her neck.

'Still,' said Max, emptying his glass and topping up his and Anne's glass. 'The sooner I get out of Fenetre the better. We were meeting with the Regional Director in a pub last night and he told me off, the bloody fool, because I broke a glass.'

'You broke a glass?' Harry smiled.

'Yep!' he forked in some of his roast meet and followed it with a sip of Riesling. 'The damn fool couldn't see my reasoning. I was making a point.' He studied Harry with his Panda eyes.

'You were making a point?' Harry smiled again. 'By breaking a glass?'

'That's right! I was perfectly sober and the action was perfectly logical. Everyone notices, so the point went home.'

'What was the point?'

He shrugged. 'That's not the point, Harry. It's the method that counts, you see. How you present something. How many sheep would break a glass to make a point? It's a question of balls, you see.'

'Yes, quite,' Harry nodded.

'Here's to balls!' sniggered Anne, draining her glass for the second time.

'That's my girl!' beamed Max from across the table, his hand fondling Eleanor's little neck.

'I'll get another bottle,' said Harry, standing up. 'I put a Niersteiner in the fridge earlier.'

'Good lad,' beamed Max, turning to his wife. 'So what has snookums been up to today, apart from leaving a tape?'

She smiled up at him. 'I told the shop owner of Beauty Box about Speedway products, though I'm not supposed to talk about other products while repping. But it seemed a good opportunity, do you know what I mean?'

'Sure, snookums.' He winked at Harry who was returning with the new bottle of wine. His hand still automatically stroked his wife's neck while Harry topped up everyone's glasses. 'She's a smart little cookie.' He bent over and nibbled her ear.

She smiled, her cheeks dimpling, her blue eyes on Harry. 'I told her that Chuck Halliday explored fifteen different companies in the States before he joined Speedway because it was definitely the best!'

'You told who, Eleanor?' Harry asked, resuming his seat.

'The woman at Beauty Box. I told her Chuck looked very closely into two companies that interested him at first. One was New Wave. The other was ...' She screwed up her nose thoughtfully. 'I can't remember. It was Wealth Something ...' She shook her head. 'No, I tell a lie! It was ...'

'Never mind, Eleanor,' smiled Harry. Her eyes held his, as though it were a vital point she wanted him to understand. 'I get the point. Obviously he looked into other companies very thoroughly.'

'Yes, well, Speedway was the best because...' Her eyes brightened. 'Oh ye-e-es,' she stretched the word with delight as memory flooded in. 'It was Enrichment Inc! He looked into Enrichment Inc before going on to Speedway. That was it! Anyway, unlike these other companies, I said, with Speedway there's no retailing. Speedway saves you time because it eliminates all that ...'

'Yes, yes, you explained that to them last time, snookums,' Max kissed her cheek. 'She likes to be thorough, does my snookums.' He smiled proudly at Harry who was quite happy to listen to the whole spiel again as long as it meant drinking in those beautiful blue eyes. His gaze dropped slightly to the little bulges of her breasts that were just peeping from the top of her dress. He longed to pull down the zip and make them pop out. Her dress had two straps over her shoulders and there was no sign of bra straps. He presumed she wasn't wearing one and he recalled with a flow of delicious warmth his earlier sight of the two provocative little mounds complete with nipples. It was a treasured memory which he hugged to himself, like a secret vice. He smiled back into her blue eyes in the delicious knowledge that she knew he had seen them. It was like a secret between them.

CHAPTER 12

Bacchus

AFTER DINNER everyone transferred to the lounge where Harry had lit the gas fire and introduced another bottle of Piersporter. Max oozed into the comfortable settee and wrapped a stout arm around Eleanor's delicate shoulders. He had become quite loquacious and twirled a stubby finger around a lock of his wife's hair as he spoke.

'I'm looking forward to the next Speedway Convention in February,' he smiled. 'It's being held in Malta. They're putting us up, in the first instance, in the luxurious Phoenix Hotel in Valletta. From there they're transferring us by helicopter to the five-star Meridien Hotel in Gozo, the other island. You should come, Harry—both of you!' He beamed at Harry and Anne as he settled further back. 'It's free for Emerald Directs, but you could always stay in less expensive self-catering accommodation. You could attend the day seminars.'

'I really don't think we could,' replied Anne, shaking her head. She had made herself more comfortable by tucking in her stout little legs beneath her on her settee. Her tent dress appeared to envelope her whole body. 'We can't really get away from our hotel.'

'But it's in February!' protested Max, his face wreathed in smiles. 'It's during your dead season. Come now, Anne, as a good businesswoman you surely know the value of a good marketing seminar for your forthcoming season! It will set the mood for a positive and motivational year!'

'It would be fun, actually,' put in Harry, smiling at Eleanor whose cheeks dimpled in return. He transferred his smile to Anne. 'We're due for a holiday, anyway.' He grinned at Eleanor, on impulse risking the remark that flashed in his mind: 'And the girls could bathe topless!' The thought of seeing Eleanor's pert little breasts again was exciting and she returned his smile, as if reading his mind.

Max guffawed. 'Not in Malta! It's a Catholic country and they have strict rules about that!' He leaned over with the bottle, refilling everyone's glass. 'But the hotel in Gozo does have a sauna and a masseuse! We could hire a sauna together and I'm sure Harry and I will make excellent masseurs!' He winked at Harry. 'Sensuous massage is something Eleanor and I are into at the moment. I've got a book I should lend you. It's beautifully illustrated.' He leered at Anne. 'I dare you to read it, Anne.'

Anne sniggered and she smiled crookedly at Harry. 'I'm not sure I want Harry ogling the breasts of other delegates' wives! Though I don't mind if you acquired some new techniques, Boy. But then I wouldn't want you to do anything I wouldn't do!'

Harry cringed. He hated her use of her pet name for him in the presence of others, and he particularly disliked the cliché of not doing anything she wouldn't do—a phrase she was particularly fond of trotting out in company.

Max sank his glass of wine and reached for a refill. He laughed. 'At the Speedway Leadership Seminar in Cyprus the hotel manageress told us Speedway people had more fun than other groups.' He winked again at Harry. 'You see, Harry, we know how to relax—and have fun. Speedway is a whole new dimension of fun.'

Eleanor giggled. 'The manageress at that hotel wore a bodystocking. Max nicknamed her Mrs Bodystocking.'

Max grinned, quaffing half his glass of wine. 'You could see right up to her crotch when she sat down. To the seam where the bodystocking was joined!' He laughed. 'That reminds me!'

Eleanor's eyes twinkled as she stretched her smile into a little grimace. 'Here it comes!' she laughed.

'No, no,' Max chuckled. 'This is really good! There was a sweet young thing whose toes curled every time her husband made love to her! He was intrigued by this and one day asked her: "Is it so nice, honey, that it makes your toes curl?" She replied: "No, you twit! You're always in such a hurry that you don't give me time to remove my pantyhose!"' He roared at his own joke, his eyes disappearing as his puffy eyelids and plump cheeks squeezed together. Anne's raucous laughter kept company with his own as it subsided into a rippling chuckle. Eleanor kept her smiling eyes on Harry who grinned politely. She was basking in the tactile attention of Max whose hand stroked her cheek or twirled her hair, as well as in the conscious pleasure of Harry's appreciative appraisal.

Harry's smile broadened self-consciously, seeing her sleek legs thrust forward, her hips sunk in the comfortable settee, her breasts firm and supple under the stretched fabric of the suede dress. Again his eyes were drawn to the two straps of the dress over her delicate shoulders. Again, he longed to pull down the zip between her breasts and make them pop out.

Max basked in the laughter his joke had elicited, though most of the laughter it generated was his own. 'Here's ..' He chuckled, looking at Harry. 'Here's one for you, Harry. You used to teach literature, didn't you? Well, did you ever read the bit in one of Jane Austen's novels—where she wrote "Emma turned sixteen and began to yearn for balls"?' His eyes squeezed shut again as his laughter broke loose in high-pitched staccato peaks. Anne surveyed him quizzically until the penny dropped, when she released a raucous guffaw.

Eleanor smiled indulgently at Harry, as if to say 'What am I going to do with him?' Harry grinned, sipping his wine, succumbing to the agreeable sensation caused partly by the growing numbness in his legs and partly by the dimpled cheeks and blue smiling eyes of Eleanor. It was an altogether delicious combination.

Harry cleared his throat, sensing it was time he made a contribution. He didn't want the evening, with those intense smiling eyes, to lose its impetus. 'I'm not very good at remembering jokes, but there's something I remember a student once wrote.' He crinkled his eyes at Eleanor. 'It was about a passage from one of Jane Austen's novels, again. She wrote: "We can all respond to the fellow feeling in the passage."'

Anne gave a polite guffaw. She'd heard it before. Eleanor continued to smile indulgently.

Max's dark eyes drilled into Harry, digesting his words. Then he put his head back and roared. 'Very good, very good, Harry,' he spluttered, recovering. 'Now...', he chuckled breathlessly, helping himself to more wine and refilling the other glasses, draining the bottle into Anne's glass. 'Have you heard the one about the two nuns on a bicycle?' He burst into renewed chuckling at the anticipation of the punch line. 'You see, the one was giving the other a lift. It was a man's bike with one of those crossbars, and the nun was straddled on the bar. Then the bike bumped over some rough cobblestones. The one said to the other: "Do you usually come this way?" and the other replied: "No, I usually use a carrot!"'

Anne's harsh guffaws punctuated the rippling staccato of Max's laughter which had become high pitched. His eyes reappeared above the dark pouches and he wiped away the tears. He looked at Anne helplessly, appreciative of her response. 'Now...', his chuckling died down to a controllable level. 'Now it's your turn, Anne!'

Anne shook her head, tugging her lower lip. 'It's difficult to match your inventiveness, Max,' she smiled. Harry was pleased by the thought that the influence of the alcohol and the laughter had helped to lift the cloud that had apparently settled on her since Max and Eleanor moved in, and he was thankful. It seemed that a thaw had at last set in. Anne's lip curled with sudden bravado. 'Do you enjoy Laurel and Hardy? I think it would be more fun if they had a wanking competition instead of simply falling about.'

'A *what*!' Max tittered. Harry couldn't believe his ears. But then he knew alcohol could bring out the crude in her.

'Well,' Anne went on with a twisted grin, her arms folded firmly in front of her. 'It would be funnier than falling about, wouldn't it? Laurel would say: "Now *look* what you did! You've come all over me!"' She flicked her eyes rapidly at Max and Harry before dropping them.

Harry smiled, embarrassed. He saw that she was red-faced and that her neck was flushed. Her sense of humour, even under the influence of wine, was stodgy, like her appearance. He transferred his gaze to Eleanor who smiled sweetly. By contrast Eleanor was so petite and decorous, he thought. He was aware of the quiet surge of the gas fire in the lingering moment of surprised silence.

Max chuckled. 'That one's difficult to cap, Anne! But there's the story about the orgy in Olympus. One of the gods introduced himself to a sweet young thing. "I'm Thaw!" he said, and she replied, "Oh, goth, tho am I!" He tittered again, his eyes disappearing momentarily. 'Oh yes, and when the host at the orgy said "Thank you for coming," the sweet young thing replied, "Thank you for having me!"' His stocky body shook with mirth as he turned appreciative eyes on his audience. Harry grinned at Eleanor who crinkled her eyes back at him, and Anne bit her lip in a suppressed smile.

'I think it's time for coffee,' smiled Anne, briefly lifting her averted eyes. 'Before the evening degenerates any further.' She unwound herself from her folded position on the seat and got up.

'I'll come with you,' smiled Eleanor, disentangling herself from Max's arm. 'Once Max gets going, there's no stopping him!' She followed Anne into the kitchen.

Max slipped further back into the settee, grinning conspiratorially at Harry. 'She's quite a cutie, isn't she, Harry? And she really likes Anne, you know. They make a good pair, don't they?'

Harry nodded dubiously. 'Anne thinks Eleanor's lovely,' he lied. 'You're very fortunate, Max, to have such a doting wife.' What he meant was 'such a devastatingly adorable little creature.' He continued: 'She looks radiant in that dress, Max.'

He looked pleased. 'I bought that little number for her today. I think she was wearing it especially for you, Harry.' He grinned. 'She likes being admired and I enjoy seeing her being appreciated. But then all women are like that, aren't they?'

'I guess so.'

'Women like to receive gifts, Harry.' His grin broadened. 'You know, I'll say this for myself, I know how to treat a woman, Harry. It's like a good sales technique. I know how to pamper women. They like to receive things, like lingerie and trinkets.' He winked. 'If you want some great sex, bring home a new pair of frilly knickers, or a lacy bra.' He reached into the inside pocket of his suit and brought out a packet of cigarettes. He offered one to Harry who shook his head, smiling. He flicked one out, talking as he lit it, drawing in the smoke. 'Women are very tactile creatures, too. They like to be touched up.' He blew out a stream of blue smoke. 'God, Harry, I'll tell you this—and I'm not bragging, I'm just stating a fact. I know how to treat a woman. I know how to make them feel good. I know how to make love to a woman.' He drew on his cigarette and smiled with narrowed eyes.

Harry smiled uncertainly. 'You must have a lot of experience, Max.'

'Sure!' He pulled at his cigarette again and contemplated the smoke as it drifted towards the ceiling. Then he fixed his eyes on Harry. 'It's like a good salesman, Harry. You have to build on experience. My God, Harry, I can make a woman scream like a banshee, whatever her social class or education. As I said, it's like being a good sales executive. You have to know how to adapt. The same thing applies when you pleasure a woman. It's like selling. You soon find out if you've got balls!'

'That's great, Max. Eleanor's lucky to have someone like you.'

'Oh, I'm sure you and Anne...' He waved his cigarette, making the blue smoke spiral. Then he chuckled. 'I remember the time Eleanor and I were having it off against the bedroom door in her parents' house. I could see my father-in-law outside mowing the lawn, and Eleanor screamed like a banshee—God, you should hear her scream, Harry!' He grinned crookedly at him. 'Anyway, I could see my father-in-law stop and switch off the mower. He stood there with an ear cocked. I think he thought someone was being murdered!' He grinned with self-satisfaction, chuckling.

'The two of you seem so well matched,' Harry conceded. Like Beauty and the Beast, he thought to himself. 'I mean, she's obviously very happy.'

'Oh, we have an understanding, Harry.' He winked slowly, warming to Harry's appreciative responses. 'It's a give and take relationship.' He pointed the cigarette towards Harry. 'I'll give you an example of how generous and giving she is. When we were staying at her parents' house in Darlington—while her parents were out, of course—she pushed her younger sister Sally into the room, where I was reading. They were both completely naked.'

'Her sister was naked?' Harry was amazed.

97

Max grinned. 'Starkers. And I tell you, she's a real looker, with bigger knockers. Harry, can you imagine the effect on me? You look up, and there's this ravishing creature—*both* of them ravishing, of course, both stark naked and giggling.'

'So what did you do?'

He shrugged, smiling. 'Oh, that was the first of some romps we had. But the point is, it shows the kind of girl Eleanor is. A girl in a thousand.'

'You're sure lucky, Max,' smiled Harry, his stomach registering a twinge of frustration. He picked up his glass and drained the last of the wine. 'Anne and I don't seem to have that kind of relationship.'

'You should go on a nudist holiday together, Harry,' he smiled patronisingly. 'Try to relax with each other, and be relaxed with others.'

'In the nude, you mean?'

He nodded. 'Eleanor and I joined a nudist camp in the summer. We had to go through a series of interviews first to ensure we weren't weirdoes—that we weren't going just to ogle at others or to get up to pranks. Accepting one another's bodies in natural surroundings is a great experience. Eleanor makes a great naturalist. It's right up her street.'

'Sounds like a wonderful idea, Max.' Harry couldn't imagine Anne walking around without clothes in the presence of others. She would be flushed and red faced, and besides, her appearance was no longer nymph-like. He sighed. 'I don't think Anne would agree.' But he couldn't think of anything more delightful than being able to feast his eyes on Eleanor *au naturel.*

'It's a funny thing about clothes,' Max droned on. 'I went into a sauna with a group of men in London. We were there without clothes, of course, and we all got along fine. Everyone was—well, natural, and we chatted and laughed easily. No one was being pretentious, know what I mean? But afterwards, when we were dressed again and going down in the lift, everyone was stiff and uncomfortable. They turned into bank managers and shareholders.'

'So our clothing divides us—gives us artificial identity.'

'Exactly,' he nodded.

'So,' Harry said thoughtfully, 'women would be more natural without clothes, too?'

'Sure,' he crushed the remnants of his cigarette in an ashtray. 'That goes without saying.'

'What about lingerie, then? You were saying how they liked to receive...'

Max laughed outright. 'You've got me there, Harry.' He gave a leering wink. 'Lingerie is garnish. It brings out the femininity of a woman. It's the garment that gapes that turns one on, you know.' He smiled mischievously. 'Look, I've got some lingerie catalogues in my bedroom. There's some naughty numbers—*beautifully* modelled! Shall I fetch them for you?'

'I don't mind, Max,' Harry smiled. 'I dare say Anne would be delighted with a pair of frilly knickers. I know she's not partial to a nurse's outfit.' He laughed.

'Oh, it's not so much the lingerie you want to see,' he said, standing up. 'It's the *models!*' He grinned. 'I'm very susceptible to that sort of thing, you know—glamour models, I mean.'

Max went out and Harry listened to his footsteps on the stairs, wondering how he could be turned on by photographs of models when he had Eleanor with her pristine feminine beauty.

Eleanor was chattering and giggling when she returned with Anne and the coffee. She smiled sweetly at Harry and sat down neatly on the settee with her legs stretched out and drawn together while Anne spread out the cups and poured out the coffee. 'We've been enjoying some girl talk, Harry. Anne is so super to talk to.' She laughed, looking for Max. 'Where's that incorrigible husband of mine?'

'He's gone upstairs to fetch something,' he smiled. 'What have you been nattering about then?'

'Well,' Eleanor prattled on with a giggle. 'I was telling Anne how I started to get giggly when I was having my smear test. I was getting turned on by the doctor's hand.' She smiled at him out of the depth of her sharp blue eyes. 'I just couldn't stop giggling. It was so embarrassing.'

Anne laughed, shaking her head. 'Oh dear, I don't know, Eleanor! You take the cake! I hate internals.'

'Oh, it doesn't take much to make me giggly!' her musical laugh tinkled. 'I can get quite giggly on water, do you know what I mean? The other night I couldn't stop giggling after I woke Max.' Her smile, directed at Harry, was disarmingly innocent. 'I woke up feeling terribly randy and I couldn't wake up Max, he was sleeping so deeply. So I masturbated instead.' She giggled, her cheeks dimpling. 'And when I started to come I yelled and that woke him up.' Her laughter tinkled again. 'And then he was so concerned and attentive, asking me if I had a bad dream, and was I all right! And all I could do was giggle!'

'Good Lord, Eleanor!' Anne's laugh was harsh. She shook her head in amused disbelief. 'That's *terrible*!'

Harry was stunned and delighted at the same time. He laughed, blushing with pleasure and embarrassment. The revelation was like a new intimacy.

'Oh, but it's not terrible, is it?' Eleanor smiled at Harry. 'Masturbation's quite natural. You're not hurting anyone.' She looked towards the door. 'I wonder what's keeping Max?'

'He was fetching a magazine or something, I think,' replied Harry, a little breathlessly.

Eleanor's smile dimpled again. 'I replied to an ad in a contact magazine the other day. It was to a woman looking for a couple. Max keeps on saying he fancies an extra woman in his bed.' She laughed. 'I want to call his bluff, do you know what I mean?'

They heard Max's footsteps coming down the stairs, and he entered, smiling. He gave Harry a couple of rolled-up magazines, winking. 'There you are, Harry. Something for you to digest at your leisure!' He sat down and produced a small black photo-wallet. He opened it and showed a photograph to Harry.

'That's one of Eleanor, Harry!'

Eleanor shrieked, smiling. 'Oh, Max, not *those!*' She giggled.

He laughed. 'No, no, it's just the one of you on the sail-board, snookums!'

Eleanor giggled, sipping her coffee. 'My father wasn't impressed when he saw it! It came up unexpectedly when we were showing the family our holiday pics in Corsica.'

Harry put down his cup of coffee and looked at the photograph. It showed a picture of a young woman on a sail-board. He couldn't make out her face because it was behind the sail. But there was a square window of clear perspex in the sail which perfectly framed Eleanor's uncovered breasts. 'Oh yes, I can see it's you, Eleanor,' he laughed, then turned red, realising her breasts were the only means by which she could be recognised. 'Maybe we should swap intimate pictures of wives,' he said quickly, trying to cover up his *faux pas*.

'Done!' Max grinned cheekily at Anne.

'Let me see!' said Anne, putting down her cup and reaching out for the wallet. She looked and burst out laughing. 'What a picture! How could you tell it's Eleanor, Boy?' She gave him a sidelong glance.

Harry felt hot and cold and laughed awkwardly.

Max came to his rescue. 'She's nearly recognisable now, isn't she, Anne!' He drained his coffee, then leant over and neatly unzipped Eleanor's dress about four inches down, revealing the cleavage all the way between her breasts. 'You see, just like the picture!'

'Max!' Anne shrieked, then laughed.

But Eleanor smiled blandly, unresisting, letting him pull the zip down a touch further. The soft swell of each breast was clearly visible. She smiled broadly at Harry. 'I'm sure Harry's seen breasts before, Max.' She giggled.

Anne's laughter was raucous. 'Well, I think that's the cue for Harry and me to retire to bed!' She got up and held out the photo-wallet to Max. Everyone stood up, Eleanor giggling as she half stumbled against Harry. Max accepted the photo-wallet and impetuously scooped Anne into his arms. 'Good night, Anne. Thanks for a lovely evening!' Then he kissed her, long and hard.

Eleanor looked at them, surprised. 'Oh shit!' she giggled. 'All right, then,' she said, turning to Harry. Her arms snaked round his neck and her lips sought out his. She sighed audibly, as though in a swoon, as his lips melted against hers. They felt soft yet sinewy. Harry couldn't believe it was happening. His hands automatically slipped down and cupped the pert cheeks of her bottom as she melted against him. The contact with her thin liquid lips and lithe limp body was a moment in paradise.

Anne was flushed down to her neck when Max drew away. She stumbled, regaining her balance, standing alone, blinking. Eleanor yielded to the pressure of Max's hand tugging her.

'Come on, snookums. Beddy-byes for us!' he laughed, towing her towards the door as he looked back and winked.

Anne grunted in her attempt at a lascivious laugh. 'Don't do anything *we* wouldn't do!' she shouted after them.

Harry cringed as he surfaced from the happiest moment of his life.

CHAPTER 13

On the Blink

HARRY looked forward to the little oil burner that night, and lit it before Anne came up to bed. The lavender aroma suffused the room, licking into every corner with its sweet smell. It was like an extension of Eleanor's feminine aura. He placed a CD into the little bedroom Hi-fi and the gentle tones of Mozart's *Moonlight Sonata* trickled into the air, blending with the subtle lavender scent. Then he descended the steep narrow stairs into the kitchen on legs that felt too heavy for his body. The wine had left him light-headed with leaden legs.

Anne was making an effort to pack the dirty crockery into the dishwasher.

'Leave that, Anne,' he smiled, seeing her squat little body bent over the open machine. 'You go to bed and I'll take care of this. I'll be up in a moment.'

'Thank you, Boy,' she said, looking up and giggling. 'I'm feeling clapped-out. That wine's made me feel quite heady!' She stood up, leaning against the sink. She wiped the straight strands of her hair off her forehead, watching Harry pack away the dishes. 'God,' she laughed, 'Max is really a card!' She sniggered. 'His jokes are so close to the bone.' She gave a raucous laugh. 'And he gets *away* with it!' She shook her head, and repeated: 'He gets away with it! He's such a cheeky blighter!'

'You seemed to get on well with Eleanor,' he grinned. sitting on his haunches as he packed in the coffee cups. 'She said you're super.'

'Oh,' she laughed, shaking her head, 'She means no harm, I suppose. She can't help being inane.' She gave another laugh. 'God, can you imagine being turned on by a cervical smear test! She must get turned on by anything!'

Harry smiled thinly. 'Max reckons he knows how to make love to a woman. It's his speciality, like sales. He can make anyone scream with ecstasy.' He closed the dishwasher door and pushed the on button. It began to hum electrically. 'It's true, Anne. I heard her. One night when I was sitting down here having coffee.'

'Oh yeah!' she grinned, flicking a sideways glance at him. 'I'd like to put him to the test, just to call his bluff.' She shook her head. 'God, Harry, Eleanor even admitted the screams when she's using her own hand. Max was fast asleep. Just put two and two together, Boy.' She laughed. 'Just because I don't scream doesn't mean I don't enjoy it.'

'Well, you go upstairs, love. I'll join you in a tick.' He smiled, wiping the top of the draining board. 'Who knows, I might put you to the test tonight.'

'That sounds promising, Boy.' She grinned, staggering against the kitchen table as she walked. 'Oh God, I'm pissed!'

He watched her frumpy body disappear into the larder which led to the little upstairs bedroom.

He wondered how serious she was about putting Max to the test. Her statement was obviously a joke, but even so it didn't awaken the slightest twinge of jealousy in him. If anything, it gave him a twist of hope. If she were ever open to Max—and Max seemed prepared to extend his experience anywhere—then, why, he and Eleanor might ...

He dismissed the thought. It was too wild and heady. Might as well wish for the moon, he thought, and he wondered just how old Eleanor was. She could never actually fancy a burnt-out old codger like himself. There must be more than ten—even fifteen—years difference, he thought. And yet there was Max who looked no younger than himself. If anything, he thought, Max looked dissipated. But then *he* was an expert. He knew how to make love to a woman. The only woman Harry had ever had was Anne.

He went into the poky little toilet and shower-room at the end of the passage beyond the larder and brushed his teeth. His face was too lean and long, he thought, his once fair hair almost black. He saw the lines around his eyes. His nose seemed too long and with his sad eyes gave him a lugubrious look. He forced himself to smile but dropped it because it gave him the look of a clown, like Sad Sack trying to smile. *'Fuck* you,' he said to his reflection, and his reflection stuck a tongue out at him, frothing with toothpaste. He washed his face, opening the tap that throbbed and screamed like a pig. *'Fuck* you,' he said, turning off the water and the noise in a single twist.

When he went upstairs and put on his pyjamas, Anne was just settling in, her legs fat and lumpy in her pyjama pants. The music tinkled gently and the lavender smell was pervasive.

'Are you all right, love,' Harry asked, looking at her. She was half sitting on the bed with the bedclothes pulled back. She had a sour look on her face and was contemplating the sheets. She nodded. Just then she was caught in a sudden convulsion and her stomach emptied itself on the sheets. She sat there, squatted on her folded legs, supporting herself on her arms. While she still looked at the mess, dazed, more of it globbed out of her mouth, great splodges of vomit that splattered onto the sheets, spreading out in a yellow ooze speckled with bright red and green undigested bits of salad.

The reek combined sweetly with the lavender and the tinkling piano tones of Mozart.

Anne clapped her hand to her mouth, emerging from her daze, and stumbled out of the room, down the stairs to the toilet where she slumped over the toilet bowl, continuing to retch. Harry bundled up the sheet with its splodgy contents and went down, too, shoving it all into the washing-machine. He found a clean sheet in the linen cupboard and spread it on the bed. Anne's podgy knees seemed to have taken root to the cold tiles of the toilet floor, and Harry had to help her up, help her wash her mouth while the tap squealed, protesting at having once again been troubled. Once Anne was back on the bed she lapsed into unconsciousness, snoring volubly. By this time the CD had run out. Harry lifted the little teapot off its base and blew out the candle that spiralled a slim turbulence of black smoke into the room. He went down and wrapped himself in a blanket, far away from the sickly odour and curled up on the couch in the small private lounge. Eleanor's high-pitched trills of ecstasy filtered through from the bedroom in the main hotel section as his own mind dropped into unconsciousness.

'Max is a lucky bastard,' he thought, as he drifted into sleep.

His head was full of muddled dreams. He was a passenger in a jet fighter, swooping over the skyscrapers of a large city. The cockpit was open, like a convertible, and he felt the wind rush through his hair. It was exhilarating as the plane banked and the buildings below tilted. Then the plane swooped low, flying up a canyon of buildings, skyscrapers on either side, the crowded street below. But the plane went so low that it landed with a rumble and got caught up in the traffic. The plane trundled slowly behind a big truck spewing exhaust fumes. He struggled to get his camera out to photograph the pilot in front, following the truck. 'They'll never believe this at home!' he said. Then the plane was swallowed by a tunnel and he held his breath, trying not to breathe in the stench of the fumes. When he emerged from the tunnel he was no longer in the plane, but standing amongst women in long ragged dresses, all of them clutching large slabs of coal. They were refugees and he was clutching a brittle slab too, but threw it down so that it broke and splattered. A stout and prosperous gentleman stepped forward, saying how he preferred oil-fired central heating to coal, and how he could make any woman of any class scream. Then they all screamed and threw their bits of coal at him.

The dream changed. He was on a holiday island, like Malta. He was with Eleanor, in the courtyard of a big hotel, and she was in his arms, pressed against his body, her honey-sweet lips on his. Then he glanced up and saw the dumpy shape of Anne on a balcony far above, turning away casually, and he realised she must have been watching him. He walked with Eleanor to the lifts inside and while they were waiting for a lift he drew her close again and slipped his hand into her dress that gaped, delicately touching her thigh. 'Oh *look*!' she exclaimed, breaking away, beaming. 'There's Max!'

He awoke with a start, his heart beating wildly. But all was quiet. He staggered, his body still half asleep, to empty his bladder, nearly falling asleep again while sitting on the toilet. But the cold seeped into his bones and he returned to his bed next to Anne who still snored, dead to the world. He lay down, the sickly-sweet smell of her vomit still lingering in the air. He drifted back into sleep.

The next morning Anne went out in the car to the Cash and Carry to shop for the forthcoming New Year short break. They had placed an advertisement in a Glasgow Sunday paper for the New Year period, and bookings were tumbling in. Harry was unpacking the dishwasher when there was a gentle tap on his private door. He opened the door with baited breath, half hoping it would be Eleanor, and his heart lurched with pleasure when he saw her sweet dimpled smile.

'Our telly's on the blink, Harry,' she said, crinkling her eyes. 'We're getting a lot of snow and lines.' Her delicate laugh tinkled and her singsong voice was like music in his ears. 'I'm sorry to be a nuisance. Do you suppose you could look at it or get someone in to fix it?'

'That's okay,' he said slowly, lost in her fierce blue eyes. He thought she must be from an alien planet, to have eyes like that. She certainly wasn't from this world, though she came from Darlington. He took in her dressing gown. 'I'll come up and have a look whenever you're ready.'

'Oh, you can come anytime. I'll be washing my hair in the bathroom. Max has gone out for the day,' she said casually. 'I'll leave the door unlocked. You won't bother me.' Her eyes crinkled and her cheeks dimpled again. 'Thanks, Harry.' And she flitted up the stairs.

His body was aglow with excitement. He went to fetch his little red toolbox and saw that his hand was trembling when he picked it up. He had to take a few deep breaths. It was like time alone with a goddess, though nothing could ever take place between them. It was as though he simply couldn't get her out of his system. The infatuation was driving him crazy. It couldn't be love, he told himself. But he began to entertain crazy dreams where Max was killed in an accident and Anne was abducted by aliens, and Eleanor sought him out for comfort.

He went up to her bedroom and the door opened readily when he turned the handle and pushed against it. He could see that the bathroom door was slightly ajar and he heard the sound of running water. A dress and some underwear were spread out on the neatly-made double bed. Eleanor's distinctive herbal perfume bathed his nostrils and he crept in, sedately, as though into the boudoir of a goddess. He knelt down by the window that faced the Abbey, where the television stood on the wide window sill. He placed his tool-kit on the carpet and drew away the heavy metal luggage rack that was pushed under the window sill. He immediately saw the problem. One of the legs of the luggage rack had been pushed against the aerial which made it come out of its socket where it was plugged into an electric booster. He reached up and switched on the television, and saw the snow and alternating zigzag lines that Eleanor had mentioned. He bent down and pushed in the aerial, and a sharp picture at once filled the screen in brilliant colour and detail. Girls from a band were being interviewed and one was displaying an elegant length of thigh. On impulse he jerked out the aerial again so that the picture reverted to snow and zigzag lines.

His heart was in his mouth as he glanced towards the bathroom. The water had stopped running and he could hear the hum of Eleanor's hairdryer. It was crazy, he thought, breathlessly, but it was a pity to end the session so quickly. It felt so enticingly delicious to be so close to her, and he could easily prolong the moment.

He unplugged the television and began to unscrew the front panel.

He was hyperaware of Eleanor when she emerged from the little bathroom. She smiled sweetly, seeing him kneeling by the television and he allowed himself a quick sideways glance at her, his heart palpitating. She was wrapped in a soft pink towel, her legs white and sleek, her breasts barely concealed by the towel.

'I'm sorry, Eleanor, I should have finished by now. This won't take much longer.' He gave her another quick glance. 'I'm sorry, Eleanor. I better wait outside.'

'Don't be silly,' she smiled, strolling over to the dressing table where she picked up a compact. 'I'm not getting dressed yet. There's no hurry.'

He fiddled dutifully with a screwdriver where the panel had been removed. 'This needs some refocusing, that's all.'

She sat down on the little dressing-table stool. He was aware, without looking, of her delicate knees and the smooth swell of her thighs. The situation was embarrassing though illicitly delicious, and he decided to finish his repairs. He felt self-conscious and guilty.

'I'm afraid we're a little noisy,' she said with a shy giggle, applying some eye liner. 'I don't know if you heard us last night.'

'Not at all,' he laughed, turning red. 'I'm really delighted that you're so happy together—and in my hotel!' He meant it genuinely, and he blushed the more, realising that his words betrayed the fact that he had heard her.

'You're very sweet, Harry,' she smiled. 'You and Anne are a super couple.'

He wished she wouldn't keep bringing Anne into the picture. He replaced the little panel. Then he was aware that she had stood up and he sensed her presence close to him. He dropped back on his haunches and looked up at her. She was holding Max's little black photo-wallet and smiling down at him. Her eyes twinkled.

'I thought I'd show you some of the other photos in Max's collection.' She gave another of her self-conscious giggles. 'Would you like to see them, Harry?'

He looked into her twinkling blue eyes and was aware of her dimples. One of her white naked thighs was almost touching his shoulder. He was terribly aware that if he lifted a hand he could slip it easily up the towel, against her inner thigh. He tried to keep his eyes averted from her thighs, so as not to intrude. His throat constricted with excitement. 'I'd love to see them, if you don't mind,' he smiled shyly.

She handed him a photo. 'That's Max on the double bed in my parents' home,' she giggled.

He looked at it. Max was sitting on the bed with his plump legs tucked under him, naked except for the fluffy toy poodle that blocked the view between his spread thighs. He looked at Harry with a crooked smile.

'His quite a card,' laughed Harry, trying to think of something appropriate to say. 'He's a lucky devil!' He gave way to a daring comment. 'I bet he was rewarded for posing!'

She giggled. 'Oh, that was taken after the reward!' She handed him another picture.

Harry nearly gasped when he saw it. Max, naked and smiling like a Cheshire cat, was holding a gorgeous naked woman in his arms. Her breasts were quite prominent and her smile had dimples like Eleanor's.

'That's Max with my sister Sally,' she giggled. 'It was taken in the courtyard of my parents' house. My mother found it and said it was disgusting!'

'I can imagine!' he said, laughing. 'Gosh, she looks terrific, like you.'

'Sally's a lovely person,' she said coyly. 'Though she's my sister she's my best friend.'

'Well, you're obviously very close,' he smiled, still drinking in the picture. Then he looked up into Eleanor's eyes and detected a naughty glint. His hand burned with the impulse to touch her leg. He dropped his eyes and took in the white porcelain texture of her thigh. The delicate swell of the cheeks of her bottom were quite clear below the tightly drawn edge of the towel.

'Here's another picture,' she giggled.

He reluctantly drew his irises from her thighs to her eyes. He still held the other pictures in his left hand. He smiled into her eyes, almost paralysed with desire for her. Her intense smile and dimples seemed to tease the life out of him.

'Would you like to see one of me and Sally together?' her musical voice flowed gently.

'Why, that ...' He cleared his throat which had become clogged and constricted. He smiled helplessly and almost whispered. 'I'd love to.'

She handed the next picture down to him, like a goddess offering a worshipper some crumbs. He looked at the picture. Eleanor and Sally lay sunbathing on green grass together, the one as tempting as the other in the unpretentious, natural presentation of their perfect naked bodies. They smiled innocently at the camera, like two girls next door. The nubile breasts, Sally's larger and fuller, were pert, and each reclining figure presented a clear black triangle of pubic hair between soft sleek thighs. It took Harry's breath away.

'Gosh, Eleanor,' he said, stupefied with wonder, 'I wouldn't know which one to choose. Which one to make love to, if I had the choice.'

'Why not have both?' she dimpled her natural, innocent smile at him.

He returned the picture to her hand, still quite paralysed by her presence and generous act of showing the pictures. He was confused about the parameters she was allowing. Would she accept his hand on her thigh? Would she accept an embrace and melt into his arms if he stood up and reached out for her? Would she interpret it as an uninvited pass and complain to her husband? He was aware of the sweat on his brow and the uncontrollable beating of his heart.

'I'll just fix this,' he said, swallowing hard and side-stepping the issue. He reached out and pushed the socket back into place. He plugged in the television which flickered and presented a brilliant, clear picture.

'You're so clever, Harry,' she smiled, looking at the picture. It was a holiday programme and a dark-haired girl with bewitching green eyes smiled back at them. She was on water-skis and her hair trailed in the wind, water furrowing behind her. She waved.

Harry stood up, seeing the Abbey through the window, its stonework shining wetly in the faint squalls of drizzle that swept by. He picked up his little toolbox. Eleanor was still enticingly close to him, her smiling eyes on a level with his mouth. He smiled shyly down at her. 'Eleanor,' he said hesitantly, 'I...I hope I wasn't over familiar last night.' He gave an awkward little laugh. 'You know, when we said goodnight.'

Her eyes widened as she pushed her hair back behind her ears. Then her cheeks dimpled. 'Of *course* not, Harry,' she said sincerely. 'I think couples should be honest with each other, don't you?' She swept her fringe back in a quick flick of her hand. 'Max certainly didn't mind.' She frowned prettily. 'If people can't trust each other, they shouldn't be married! After all, sex is the most natural thing in the world, do you know what I mean?'

She put down the photo-wallet and switched on the kettle in the hospitality tray. It began to surge immediately. 'Would you like some coffee with me?' She smiled invitingly. 'You know, we have too many hang-ups about sex nowadays. Max and I have an open relationship. We don't hide anything from each other and we know we can be frank with each other.' She sat down on the little chair next to the tray and poured out two cups of coffee. The towel seemed to ruck up and expose the slightest hint of her pubic hair. Harry kept his eyes averted with an effort of will and sat down on the edge of the bed awkwardly. She handed him a cup with a sincere smile. 'Do you know what I mean, Harry? Max says a good relationship should be able to overcome the occasional slip or fling.' Her little laugh tinkled. 'I don't mean slip, of course, because in our relationship there can't be slips. We're open with each other about everything we do, or did.'

Harry nodded. 'That sounds like a difficult balance to achieve. You're an incredible couple.'

She shook her head. 'Max doesn't keep me on a tight string, like most men do, and there are times when he's been away and been frustrated, when I told him on the phone to find a dolly bird, for heaven's sake.'

'You didn't mind?' he smiled incredulously.

'Of course not, Harry.' Her cheeks dimpled with sincerity. 'He was going on about being lonely. I said, for goodness sake, Max, find yourself a dolly bird!' She sipped her coffee, her little finger outstretched daintily.

He smiled. 'That was incredibly generous of you. You're such a generous girl.' He summed up his courage. 'I think you're super, Eleanor.'

She tilted her head to one side, dimpling at him. 'I think you and Anne are both super,' she said. 'You're such a lovely, kind couple. You're both ideal for Speedway.'

Her words struck a discordant note. Why did she have to keep drawing in Anne? And the reference to Speedway, in the present sensuous context, jarred. He tried to bring her back to the magic of her open aura.

'I mean,' he smiled, 'you have such a lovely aura, with your crystals and open relationship. Does that mean you don't mind reaching out? To new relationships?'

She shook her head and her laughter tinkled sweetly. 'Of course not, Harry. That's the whole point. It's the essence, do you know what I mean, of our new age. We're moving into a new era of discovery, of togetherness, and that means reaching

112

out to one another. Especially as we move into the new millennium.'

'That's sounds fascinating, Eleanor,' he smiled. Her blue eyes held his and prevented them from straying down to her bare legs. But he was subliminally aware of her entire body, an awareness that was beginning to register in his groin.

Then she glanced out of the window, at the Abbey. 'It's a new age that's broken with the past age, Harry. The past lies in ruins, like that old Abbey. It stood for a new religious age that began with the beginning of our millennium.' She smiled. 'Do you know what I mean? But that's broken down, now, with the old church. Now we're exploring a new world. One which we're making as comfortable as possible with science and commerce. Speedway can give us all the material rewards we need. But it also gives us new relationships. A new brotherhood and sistership.'

'Only in Speedway?'

'Oh no!' she shook her head, laughing. 'Speedway can improve the quality of our lives. But I'm talking of everybody, do you know what I mean? Everybody in the world. A world that's not controlled by any group. We're all reaching out to a new order with a new understanding of our purpose in life. And the exciting thing is the coincidences and chance encounters that happen to us when we release this new energy in our lives. Do you know what I mean, Harry?'

'Gosh, Eleanor, this sounds very deep.' It was thrilling listening to her. He was certainly aware of her energy. His whole body was tingling with it. 'Is that why you use crystals and silver coins? To direct this energy?'

She nodded. 'And to help release it into our lives.' She smiled at him. 'You know, meeting open people like you and Anne, when we were looking for temporary accommodation, was another of those coincidences. And then you gave me that little Buddha.' She smiled, looking at the little bronze figure she kept next to her bed. 'It all suggests a focusing of that energy. Don't you feel it, Harry?'

He nodded. 'I certainly do, Eleanor. I certainly do.'

'And who knows where it will lead?' Her biting blue eyes were hypnotic. When she dimpled her smile his soul melted.

When she folded her legs his heart twisted. He was both paralysed and painfully aware of her power over him. Her energy and her sexuality were bound together.

The whine of a car in the car park below brought him back to his present situation. He got up and looked out of the window. 'It's Anne,' he sighed. 'I'd better be getting back. She'll need help with the supplies.' He put down his cup of coffee, picked up his toolbox and smiled sincerely at her. 'Thank you for a lovely chat, Eleanor. This has been ...' He searched for the right words, failed, and resorted to a cliché. 'This has been a new awakening for me.'

She tilted her head and her cheeks dimpled again. 'That's what it's all about, Harry.'

CHAPTER 14

New Dawn

HARRY SHIVERED and hunched his shoulders as he moved among the cars squeezed into the cramped car park of his hotel. There was space for six cars if everyone parked thoughtfully, but one of them, a Range Rover, had been carelessly abandoned halfway up the sloping drive, making it impossible for the last car to squeeze in all the way. The little red Escort's taillight stuck out at an angle, about six inches into the pavement area. This was not unusual since many guests didn't mind squeezing behind other cars, and many were quite happy to park half on the pavement or in the cul-de-sac directly across the road.

But Mr Ramsden, a stocky gentleman with an air of self-importance, had been extremely unhappy about not being able to bring his car all the way in. It was the second night of the New Year break and he was hyperaware of the possibility of vandalism.

'Unfortunately the owner of the Range Rover has walked into town,' Harry had explained. 'Though I asked him to pull his car in properly before he left.' He shrugged his shoulders, smiling apologetically. 'I'm afraid not many guests take me seriously, or listen to what I ask. But if you leave the keys of your car with me, I'll pull it in as soon as he returns.'

'Over my dead body!' Mr Ramsden complained, pursing his lower lip. He had stood in the reception area and squared his shoulders at Harry, his hands in his pockets. 'My wife and I are tired and we're going to bed. But I want you to go out there now and examine my car. Take a careful look at the taillight! You'll see there's no damage on that car.' His eyes bored into Harry's. 'If there's as much as a scratch on that car tomorrow morning I'll sue you personally for everything you've got! Do I make myself clear?'

Harry swallowed. No-one had ever spoken to him so gruffly before.

'And another thing,' the man stuck out his paunch defiantly. 'You can cancel my booking for tomorrow. I'm highly dissatisfied with the parking arrangements.'

'Very well,' said Harry, smiling thinly.

Mr Ramsden nodded. 'I'm from Lincolnshire and I like to speak my mind. The slightest scratch on that car, and my solicitor will have you for breakfast!' He stuck his jaw out, challengingly.

'I shall personally stand guard over your car all night, Mr Ramsden,' Harry said, gritting his teeth. 'If that will make you happier.'

'I don't care what the fuck you do,' he said, his mouth bent downwards by the upwards pressure of his lower lip. He gave a disgruntled snort and pushed past Harry. 'Good night!' he growled and mounted the stairs.

That conversation had taken place at 10 p.m. It was 1 a.m. the next morning when Max and Eleanor walked into the car park where Harry lurked in silence, dressed in a cotton-lined waterproof jacket that failed to keep out the cold of the night air. Max and Eleanor were enveloped in hooded quilted jackets that gave them a look of Eskimos. They stopped in surprise when they sensed Harry.

'Good Lord!' exclaimed Max. 'I thought you were a ghost!'

'Harry? Why are you here?' Eleanor lilted in her musical voice, concern touching her eyes. Her little nose wrinkled in puzzlement. 'You'll catch you death!'

Harry warmed to her sympathy. 'I'm standing guard over this damn Escort!' he laughed, trying to make light of the issue. 'It's owner said he'd sue me if there was the slightest scratch. It would be just my luck that if I don't stand guard a local hooligan will kick it in!'

'What!' exclaimed Max. 'You're going to stand here in the cold *all night*?'

Harry nodded. Their breaths escaped above them in little puffs of visible cloud. 'I didn't like Mr Ramsden's attitude. I reckon he's the type of person who'll creep down in the night and scratch his own car, so he can sue me. So I'm going to stick it out, just in case.'

'Good God, Harry! You can't be serious!' Max exploded. 'He's not worth it. What if it rains, or snows?'

'I'll sit in my car.' Harry flicked his head towards his garage. The door was tilted up as was the back door of his estate car. 'I'll put the garage light on in a moment and sit in the back. I've got a book to read and a flask of coffee.'

'Jesus!' Max shook his head.

'That's right,' smiled Harry. 'The book's about Jesus. About the historicity of Jesus and whether the miracles really happened.'

Max gave a double take. 'It'll be a miracle if you don't get ill.' He moved forward as though to lunge a kick at the Escort. 'This is what I'd like to do to the idiot's car!'

Harry cringed. A movement of the curtain in the window of Mr Ramsden's bedroom upstairs caught his eye. 'I think he's watching us,' he whispered. 'We'd better talk quietly.'

'Fuck *him*!' shouted Max, shaking his fist at the window. 'He must be paranoid. It's only a bloody Escort, not a Bentley!'

Harry's heart galloped. He wished Max would go inside. He and Eleanor were obviously returning from a pub and had been drinking. 'It's okay, Max. I don't want any trouble. He probably comes from a high risk area. Lincolnshire must be full of vandals and car thieves.'

Max addressed the window. 'He needs a kick up the proverbial!'

Harry smiled nervously. 'Never mind, I'll survive.'

While they were talking another couple sauntered in, arm in arm and laughing. It was the owners of the Range Rover that had caused the parking problem in the first place. They nodded casually as they passed them and entered the hotel, letting the door slam behind them.

'Whose serving breakfast in the morning, Harry?' Eleanor asked in her small voice. Normally Harry served the breakfasts while Anne cooked.

'I'll have to manage,' Harry smiled.

'After being up all night?' She shook her head. 'You'll *flip*, Harry! I'll help Anne with the breakfasts. You go to bed as soon as it's light, see?' She smiled sweetly. Harry could see her dimples, even in the half light.

'That's sweet of you, Eleanor, but I'll manage, really. I can't expect you to do that.'

She shook her head. 'No, I'll not let someone take advantage of you like this. You go to bed in the morning and I'll do your shift. I've worked in restaurants before.'

Max looked anxiously at his wife. 'Are you sure, snookums?'

She nodded and looked at Harry. 'That man has conned you out of your energy aura, Harry.' She wrinkled her nose, scowling. 'Most people go through their lives in a constant hunt for someone else's energy. You're the one left feeling weaker and hurt. It's not right.' Her cheeks dimpled in another sympathetic smile.

'Eleanor, you really mustn't...'

'Say no more, Harry! I'll report to Anne for duty in the morning!'

Max grinned at Harry in the dark. 'It's no good arguing with snookums, Harry! When she has an idea in her head, that's it!'

'She's too kind,' he smiled at her.

Max turned to go inside, but first pulled a face at the curtain upstairs which dropped quickly back in place. Harry breathed a sigh of relief when he saw the front door close behind Max and Eleanor. He walked up the driveway to the gate and studied the tail of the Escort, shivering. The reflected orange street light looked bleached in the baked red enamel of the car's paintwork. He felt he wanted to kick it himself. 'One day I'll dance on your grave, Ramsden!' he hissed. He read the registration letters on the number plate: BFS. 'I guess that stands for Bloody Fucking Shit!' he whispered to himself. But he smiled, mollified by Eleanor's sympathy and offer to stand in for his breakfast duty. That was a bonus he hardly expected and it warmed his heart. She had spoken of energy auras. If anything, he thought, he had felt the warm flow of her energy flood into him. He hugged the thought of her to himself. God, he thought, she really *cared*, and tears picked his eyes. He looked at the Escort. 'Thank you, you Bloody Fucking Shit!'

Then he turned and looked across the valley, seeing the floodlit Abbey with its bell tower and rows of tiered arches in the crumbling gallery arcade, like an impressive monument to a collapsed faith. More than that, thought Harry, it was a monument to the Christian tradition that began with Jesus, and it reminded him of the book he had started to read—a book that reduced the miracles that began the Christian era to fables invented to give impetus to the message of an ordinary man who believed himself to be fulfilling the prophetic role of a messiah. Harry's breath spiralled in white vapour as he regarded the Abbey through the crisp air. He sighed and returned to the garage where he switched on a strip light that flickered and flooded the garage with a cold illumination. He sat down on the lip of the open boot and the suspension creaked under his weight. He opened the book and read some more. He read of Jesus's alleged injunctions to his disciples to maintain secrecy about the miracles and the Kingdom of God. These injunctions, according to the writer, were inauthentic and added by later editors because they were the best way to explain the awkward fact that the Jews had unaccountably failed to accept his message that the end of the world and the beginning of the Kingdom of God was near. Jesus's message that the divine Kingdom was about to be consummated in the immediate future was obviously wrong, according to the writer, since no such Kingdom had materialised. The Galilean's admonishments to turn the other cheek, love thy neighbour, welcome sinners and render unto Caesar, did not so much indicate a love of peace or a sentimental affection for humanity, or a respect for the imperial government, as a desire to deal quickly with what he considered to be matters that were subordinate and secondary to the main issue, thereby enabling his disciples to concentrate wholly on the dawning and imminent realisation of the Kingdom of God. 'Seek ye first the kingdom of God'—in the end that was all that really mattered. His mission to the Jews in Galilee, in so far as it was rejected, was a complete failure—a failure that was converted, after his death, to a message of universal hope and salvation by the church that followed. Harry read with rising horror of the author's suggestion that even Jesus's resurrection was fluffed over, even invented, by a later tradition in the interests of that hope.

Harry looked up, across the roof of the Escort with its beads of condensation. The uppermost part of the roof had turned a frosty white, for the temperature had fallen to below zero. The air was crisp and silent, his breath a steady exhalation of white vapour. Surely, he thought, the New Testament said somewhere that if the resurrection didn't take place, our faith was in vain? The threads of his faith had already begun to disentangle some years before, with the bouts of deep depression that came in the wake of the debts incurred by Anne's secret spending on intangible goods. If only there were a higher reality to which he could reach out, to invest his life with purpose and direction. He shook his head, looking at the Ford Escort. 'To what end are we turning the other cheek and loving those who despise us?' he said aloud. 'We lick the boots of others and suck up to them merely because in some way we're beholden to them.' He was sick of people he had worked with in the academic world with their inflated importance. He was sick of the posturing of pride amongst his guests, of their foibles and the fuss they made of trivialities. 'It's a fucking pampered world,' he said angrily to the Escort. 'What we need is a good war to smash our smug society to pieces.'

He read on, but drooped with weariness. The cold seeped into his bones and he got up and turned off the garage light. He walked up and down the pavement, to keep his circulation going. The air was dead silent and the crunch of his footsteps on the frost icicles were palpable in his ears. He turned back into the car park towards the garage, and his heart missed a beat. Someone stood quietly next to the garage—a slight figure wrapped in a heavy coat. The face was small and white that peeped out at him.

'*Haloo*,' came the familiar musical voice.

It was as though she had materialised out of nothing and a sense of unreality, of disbelief, pervaded him.

'Eleanor!' he exclaimed softly. 'Is it really you?' He was aware of her smile, sensing her keen blue eyes and dimpled cheeks rather than seeing them.

'I've brought you a mug of coffee,' she said sweetly. 'I woke up and thought of you still out here.'

Then he saw she was holding a mug that looked large in her small hand—an earthenware mug shaped on a potter's wheel.

He took the cup from her. It was warm to the touch and he cradled it in his hands. 'Eleanor, this is so sweet of you,' he said. Her presence in that cold half light was like a dream. 'It's so cold. You must get back to bed. But this...' He smiled, resisting an impulse to step closer and kiss her. 'This is so incredibly nice of you.' He lifted the mug and the coffee was strong and sweet. 'What is the time?' He squinted at his watch, not able to see it in the dark.

'It's just gone four,' she said, shivering. 'God, it's so *quiet*— and cold—out here.' She looked at the floodlit Abbey which loomed close in the crisp air. 'God, the Abbey looks ethereal and ... huge, almost spooky, do you know what I mean?'

'Yes. I know.' He sat down gingerly on the lip of the boot. 'I've been reading a book that makes nonsense of it all. It says Jesus's mission was a failure—and that there was no resurrection.' He gave a hollow laugh. 'And they built that great edifice! It's like a powerhouse of prayer fallen into ruin.'

'That's not so far from the truth, Harry,' she said, taking a seat next to him in the dark. He felt her shiver. 'I said before, you know, that it stands for a bygone age—the same age that's still crumbling around us.' Her teeth began to chatter. 'God, it's cold. I don't know how you can bear to sit out here all night, Harry. And it's so quiet. Nothing's going to happen to this silly car.'

'I know, but I'm determined to see it through. But you must go back in, love.'

He nearly bit off his tongue. The term of endearment had slipped out so naturally.

'I'll go in a moment,' she said with a shiver. 'I'll just have a sip of your coffee.' She lifted up her hands and took back his mug of coffee and sipped it. She handed it back to him.

He smiled at her, receiving the mug once again, feeling the touch of her fingers. Her act of drinking from the same mug was like a communion. 'This is so sweet of you, Eleanor. It's made the night worthwhile.' He felt a surge of love for her, seeing her smile coyly at him with her head tilted in that disarming way of hers. 'I even feel less angry towards this silly old fool.' He almost touched the Escort lovingly.

'That man committed a crime, Harry,' she said quietly, staring directly into his eyes. 'He's stolen your energy field by controlling you, taking over your mind. And he *has* controlled you. The fact of you sitting out here all night in the cold proves that. He did that because he's short of energy. He hasn't learnt to take his energy from ...' She swept her hand across their field of vision, across the floodlit Abbey and the open sky. 'From the universe. The universe can supply all our needs if we can only open up to it. That man is really *pathetic*! He has a closed mind, do you know what I mean, Harry? There are so many people like that exploiting others, sapping others like parasites.'

'You really believe we can receive energy from the universe?' He smiled at her childlike sincerity.

She nodded. 'We're sustained by it. It's made of pure energy—everything comes from that energy, including the plants we eat. But so many people are disconnected from the larger force of the ... of the cosmos, do you know what I mean?' She gave him a half smile, her eyes still connected to his. 'That pathetic man feels weak and insecure because of a shortage, so he stole from you to increase his personal energy.'

Harry nodded. 'It's like the African belief in a common good—a limited good. If a man's very wealthy it means he's taken too much of the limited good that fills the universe.'

'Oh no,' she shook her head, concern touching her eyes. 'There's nothing limited about it. We only steal from others because we haven't been open to the unlimited energy of the universe. When we steal from others we damage our own personal growth in fulfilling our purpose in life.'

'You spoke about that before, Eleanor. It sounds fascinating. About coincidences happening that promote our personal growth.'

'Yes, Harry.' She gave him a full smile. 'Life becomes a pattern of coincidences when you surrender to this energy, do you know what I mean?'

He nodded. He felt thrilled by her continued presence, her willingness to talk to him in the cold pre-dawn of a January morning. The moment felt almost holy.

'It's leading somewhere, you see,' she went on. 'The energy stream is asking you to go with the flow of a new creativity,

Harry. We're a family of humanity. We're more aware of one another than ever before. There's a new reaching out, a new understanding, for one another. Don't you feel it, Harry?' She touched his arm and he felt the hair of his arm rise under his coat, like goose pimples. 'Ever since I met you I felt there was a destiny that binds us, do you know what I mean?'

He nodded and was almost speechless. 'Yes, Eleanor,' he said softly, 'Yes, I do.' He gave a little shiver, shaking himself out of the trance she'd put him into. 'I think you've made me aware of that energy. I was hardly aware of it before.'

She smiled understandingly. 'Our perception of the energy begins with an increased awareness of beauty.'

'Beauty?' he asked. He wanted to say that the beauty he had become so sensitive to was her own.

'Yes.' She looked across at the Abbey. 'That Abbey *is* beautiful, isn't it? You can see that, can't you?'

'I think it's exquisite, Eleanor.' It was the word he would have used to describe her own beauty.

'Well, there you are, you see.' Once again her smiling eyes engaged his. 'The ability to see beauty is like a barometer telling you how close you are to seeing, or being aware, of the universe's energy.' She looked across at the Abbey. 'I bet that Abbey is built on the intersection point of ley lines. Ley lines carry that energy and focus it, you know. The old canons who built the Abbey probably felt that power by seeing the beauty of the place where they built it. In building the Abbey there they were responding to the energy field of this place.'

Harry grinned. 'The curator of the Abbey told me that during an archaeological dig some electric cables were uncovered. An American tourist saw them and asked if *they* were ley lines!'

He expected her to laugh but she shook her head seriously. 'No, Harry, ley lines are invisible channels of energy. You can't see them. But I'm sure they're there.'

'No, I meant...' he smiled, wanting to hug her again. She was so naive but somehow that enhanced her beauty, for him. It was like an innocence. 'So how do I know when my energy reserves are topped up?'

'When your awareness of beauty changes to a feeling of love.' She smiled, shivering, and Harry heard her teeth click together.

Her reply amused him. His feeling of love for her had been flowing towards her uncontrollably for some time now. It had come almost simultaneously with his perception of her beauty. Everyone must love her, he thought. But her shiver reminded him of the cold.

'Eleanor, it's been so lovely talking to you, but you must go in now.' He stood up and took her hand. She rose and his stomach lurched with vertigo as he kissed her cheek, gently. It took all his self-will to stop his arms going round her. 'You must get back into your nice warm bed now, with Max.'

She gave a little giggle. 'Oh, I'd rather let sleeping dogs lie! I'll make some more coffee and get ready for my breakfast duty. Can I bring you some more coffee?'

'No, Eleanor. You've been out here long enough. I really appreciate it.'

He watched while the front door of the hotel closed behind her. Only then was he aware of his heightened sense of elation, his whole body aglow with the stimulation of her presence and her conversation. He saw the pale glow of light towards the east, brightening the horizon, and saw that a mist was softening the outline of the Abbey. Everything was serene, yet in the distance were the faint sounds of a thrush. The peace was ethereal.

He breathed in the crisp cold air and his soul rejoiced.

CHAPTER 15

Bubble Bath

IT WAS AFTER TEN in the morning when Harry stretched himself awake, secure in the knowledge that Eleanor had helped Anne serve breakfast and that Rosemary had come in to do the cleaning.

When he entered the kitchen he felt hung-over after the night outside and his nasal passages felt congested. He found Anne halfway through a cup of coffee. She poured a cup for him.

'How did Eleanor manage with the breakfasts?' he asked, a little apprehensively.

She shrugged. 'Okay, I suppose. It's a simple enough job, getting the orders and taking the stuff to the tables. But she's a long time coming back, she talks so much to the guests. And then when she's here, doing the toast and getting the tea and coffee, she natters on and on about makeup and health foods.' She laughed. 'God, she must have told all the guests about Speedway and its products. One woman complained of arthritis coming down the stairs and Eleanor nattered on about something called Milk Thistle and energy auras! I think the woman thought she must be balmy.'

Harry smiled. 'And what about that Ramsden fool? What was his attitude when he checked out?'

'Just as obnoxious as he was last night. I let him know you stood guard over his stupid car all night and that the night was dead quiet anyway. He just shrugged and said it wasn't his fault, it was the Range Rover's fault. And then he said: "I like to speak my mind and I won't be recommending your hotel to anyone, lass!" He had the nerve to call me "lass" as well as Eleanor in the dining room. Eleanor says she told him he needed some Slippery Elm Food to improve his aura!'

'She told him *that*?' Harry grinned.

Anne shook her head. 'And you should have heard the advice she gave Rosemary! You know how Rosemary keeps complaining about her husband? How boring he is because he just sits watching TV all the time?'

Harry nodded, sipping his coffee.

'Well!' Anne snorted. 'She practically told poor Rosemary it was *her* fault, and that she needed to improve her sexual aura.'

Harry's eyes widened. 'Her *sexual* aura?'

Anne nodded, wiping her untidy fringe out of her eyes. 'She said how important it was to experiment with different positions and make life more fun for Donald—that's Rosemary's husband.' She smiled above her cup. 'And Rosemary actually admitted they only used the missionary position.'

'As do we,' said Harry quietly.

Anne shook her head with a laugh. 'I don't know, really! She told her that variety was the spice of life and she should expect Donald to be boring if she didn't experiment with positions. She nattered on, a lot of nonsense about being flexible with each other, to adapt to each other's energy aura, that you've got to give and take and strike a sexual balance so that your mutual auras or energy levels don't compete.' She shook her head. 'Oh yes, she said there mustn't be dominance or the one will be stealing the other's energy field! So the bottom line was that poor Rosemary had sapped the life out of Donald and that's why he sits dispirited in front of the TV all the time! Harry, have you ever heard such a lot of tripe! She stood next to the toaster and spouted all this nonsense in that ridiculous little girl voice of hers. Poor Rosemary stood there, looking dumpy and perplexed! God, what a bimbo! She'll be giving Rosemary a copy of the *Kama Sutra* next!' She laughed, shaking her head.

Harry smiled indulgently, then looked thoughtful. 'Well, I know that ...' He cleared his throat, feeling awkward. After being so touched by her gift of coffee in the frozen small hours of the morning he felt compelled to speak up for Eleanor. 'I know she seems inane, the way she speaks about Speedway products and auras. But, you know, I think there is more to her. She does have a certain energy, you know. An energy field, if you like. I think she does have a sort of innocent beauty. When you sense that, you sense her aura.'

'You've gone crazy!' Anne slapped down her mug on the table, staring at him in hostile disbelief.

'No, no,' he laughed awkwardly. 'It's part of her innocence—and her charm.'

'You mean, like Marilyn Monroe, or Pamela Anderson, with their simpering smiles?' She pulled a face, retracting her chin back into a series of double chins. 'Gosh, Boy, can't you tell the difference between plastic sex appeal and true beauty of soul? Who would you rather go to bed with, a Baywatch Bimbo or me?'

He thought, a Baywatch Bimbo *anytime*. But he said meekly, 'You, of course.'

'There you are, then!' she said triumphantly, nodding and pursing her lips.

'Although,' Harry said, not yet prepared to relinquish his defence of Eleanor, 'she's not as plastic as she looks, you know. I heard her talk about that aura stuff recently and I thought she argued quite intelligently.'

Anne snorted. 'Then you've fallen under her spell!'

He steeled himself. 'That's not so far from the truth, Anne. You might say I've sensed her particular aura. You have to give her credit for her sincerity and inner conviction. If you give her a chance you'll sense it, too. There's an intensity about her eyes, you know, almost like...' He hesitated. 'Like a supernatural force. She's definitely tapped into something.'

'Oh, give me a break!' Anne rolled her eyes at the ceiling. 'Now she's supernatural! If anything, she's an alien entity. I've always thought there was something weird about those creepy blue eyes, and she with her pitch black hair.' Anne leant over the table, her squat torso sagging heavily on her stubby elbows. She sneered, looking at Harry through her matted fringe. 'So when are you two going to zoom off to the planet Zeta together? And is it with Max's blessing? Or is he the booby prize you're going to leave for me?' She made nodding movements of her head, looking disgruntled.

Harry gave a weak smile. 'Don't be silly, Anne.' He drained his mug of coffee. 'Anyway, you *like* Max. You laughed a lot at his jokes the other night. And he clearly fancies you.'

'So where's this leading, Boy?' She narrowed her eyes at him. 'That we do a swap?'

He stood up wearily. 'Well, if we can't have a serious discussion, I might as well get on with the dining room.'

'There's no need,' she said sulkily. 'Eleanor's already set it up.'

He walked into the dining room with disbelief. Not only was the dining room in immaculate condition, but the paper serviettes were folded tastefully in a different way, like spread-out fans. A vase with a spray of Hawthorn with bright red berries on the main buffet table drew his eyes.

'Where do the Hawthorn berries come from?' he asked Anne when he re-entered the kitchen.

She pursed her lip. 'Eleanor's idea of decoration. It's a bit twee, isn't it? She went out this morning in her boots looking like a fashion plate to collect those.' She shook her head. 'She's got lots of time to waste.'

Harry thought it was a lovely touch, and that it was incredibly sweet of her. But he kept his opinion to himself.

Later Anne went out in the car to get the usual supplies for the evening meal. She said it was easier to control her budget if she shopped on a daily basis. Harry's head felt quite stuffed up as he sat close to the fan heater that hummed impotently in the cold private lounge. But he pricked up his ears when he heard the throbbing drone of Eleanor's Golf in the car park. He wanted to go out and thank her for helping and rose to do so when there was a gentle knock at his door. The pleasure of seeing her swept over him like a hot flush when he opened the door. She stood there, smiling, looking immaculate in her fur coat and black leather boots.

'Eleanor! You did such a lovely job of the dining room,' he gushed, the prick of tears underlying his sincerity. 'And thank you for serving for me. You were so thoughtful.'

'That's all right, Harry,' she said sweetly. 'I wanted to see if you were all right, after last night.'

'All the better for seeing you, Eleanor!' he laughed, thinking that he sounded like the big bad wolf. He certainly felt like eating her up. 'A bit stuffy in the head, but that will pass. At least that Ramsden chap's out of my life—for good!'

She looked concerned. 'You should have a good hot bath, Harry. With some relaxing bath salts and essential oils.' She gave a little laugh. 'You need to get the perfume oil right deep down into your lungs, by pushing out your stomach.' She bent her knees, pretending to stick out her stomach which was non-existent. 'Get as much of the aroma into your lungs as you can.'

He laughed. 'We only have a shower in our private bathroom.'

'Use the hotel bath!' she said. 'There's no-one in at the moment.' Her eyes crinkled. 'Tell you what! I'm going to have a bath myself, and when I'm finished I'll prepare the bath again for you. I'll get it nice and hot and leave my oil burner lit for you. It will be a good opportunity to regenerate your energy level. You can feel at one with the universe when you lie back in the hot water.' She giggled. 'It makes me feel sexy, but that's great, do you know what I mean? Your libido rises with your energy level. You'll feel really turned on and alive.'

'We could have a bath together then!' he joked, turning red with his own sense of bravado.

Her eyes twinkled as she tilted her head. 'That would be naughty!' she laughed. 'No, but seriously, Harry, it will do you good, do you know what I mean? I'll call down the stairs when I'm finished. I'll clean up after myself and prepare the bath fresh for you. Would you like that?'

He nodded. 'It sounds great, Eleanor.'

He walked up and down the little lounge, hearing Eleanor run the water in the bathroom above him. He couldn't believe this was happening. He felt quite breathless with subdued excitement and the accelerated circulation of his blood cleared his head and his sinuses. It was as though her energy was suffusing into his own, increasing his own aura. He felt mesmerised by her beauty, by her attention and her concern. Her sexual aura was so palpable that it was almost as good as having sex with her, he thought. It was enough simply to bask in it. 'Oh Eleanor, oh Eleanor!' he whispered, aloud, glancing out of the window at the cold sharp image of the Abbey, the morning mist burnt away by the cold sunlight. 'You're such a divine little creature. God, I love you.' Then he blushed at his words. Did he really mean that, he wondered. 'Okay, I don't love you,' he whispered, 'I just adore you, that's all.'

Then he heard the musical call he was waiting for: 'Haloo!'

He bound up the stairs with his towel, just in time to see her lithe naked figure flit up the landing and disappear into her room.

'Oh!' he exclaimed, startled, the smile frozen on his face. The question flashed through his stunned mind: why hadn't she worn a gown or at least wrapped herself in a towel? The sight thrilled him afresh, like a new intimacy between them. He had had only enough time to see the back of her, a flash of white nudity as she streaked ahead of him. It was as though she had wanted him to catch a glimpse of her. He opened the door to the bathroom, excited by the thought that he was alone with her in the building. He deliberately left the door unlocked. If only she would come back...

The steam filled the bathroom like a sauna and the sweet smell of jasmine was heavy in the air. He undressed and folded his clothes carefully on a chair and stepped into the hot water that frothed with bubbles. He sank in slowly, feeling the water lap over him and cover him. He settled his head back and stared into the steam. The room was infused with her delicious presence. The water felt oily and slippery, sensuous on his skin, the bubbles tickling him as they drifted over him, caressing him. The warmth of the water seeped into him and he felt deeply relaxed. Then he remembered her remarks about feeling refreshed and sexy, and that reminded him of her earlier comment about masturbating. God, he thought, she actually admitted to masturbating—and that made him think she had prepared this sensuous bath for him for that purpose. It was a delicious realisation, but he didn't want to diffuse the magic of the moment with an orgasm, or to think of her in crude physical terms. No, it was enough to feel spiritually turned on to her, and he closed his eyes, drinking in her aura. Her image, her jet black hair, the fringe combed neatly down to her dark eyebrows, the crystal blue eyes and sharp pixie features in her oval face, swam before him. 'Eleanor,' he sighed.

'What the *fuck* is this?' demanded Anne, standing in the open door, looking like a Buddha conjured up by the steam.

He gave a guilty start, opening his eyes. 'Oh, hello Anne,' he said, smiling weakly. 'Erm, Eleanor thought this would do me good.'

Her eyes were unrelenting. '*Eleanor*! Is she under those bubbles with you?'

He held his smile. 'Don't be ridiculous, Anne. This is to clear my head. I'm all stuffed up.' He stopped himself from saying 'fucked up.'

She looked round the steamy bathroom with hostility, seeing the little burner shaped like an owl whose dark bright eyes glared back at her. Then she transferred her wounded eyes to him. She withdrew without any further words, closing the door behind her.

Harry closed his eyes and tried to recapture the magic of the lapsed moment, but guilt gnawed at his stomach. He gave up and pulled himself out of the water, dried himself and dressed. He extinguished the burner and dutifully cleaned the bathroom after him. He went back down, carrying the towel and the little owl.

He found Anne in the private lounge mulling over a cup of coffee. She said casually, attempting a brightness that failed to conceal an underlying morose mood: 'You've been having fun with Eleanor, then?'

'Not really,' he laughed, equally casually. 'She came home and suggested she run a bath for me. She had one first, then ran one for me. I do feel better, actually.'

She shot him a sideways glance. 'Are you sure she didn't leave the same water for you.'

Oddly enough, that had never occurred to him. The thought of it possibly being the same water was delicious. 'Of course it wasn't the same water,' he said ruminatively. Then looked squarely at her and said firmly: 'Don't be ridiculous, Anne.'

She shrugged and looked out of the window at the Abbey. 'Well, the next thing you'll be bathing together.' She sipped her coffee, still looking out of the window. 'You'll tell me the truth, if you're ever unfaithful to me, won't you, Boy?'

He began to feel impatient with her mood. 'Would you accept that? I mean, if I had an affair—would you accept that, and like me to be honest?'

She nodded, still surveying the Abbey.

He decided to call her bluff. 'All right then, Anne, I'll tell you the truth,' he said calmly and quietly, sitting down near her, still holding the little owl. 'Eleanor and I made love. I admit it.'

She turned her wounded eyes on him, darkly. 'What?' she whispered. 'What do you mean?'

He looked at her squarely, smiling thinly. 'I mean we had sexual intercourse.'

She stared at him in silence. 'When?'

'In the bath, about half an hour ago.'

She continued to regard him and the silence built up between them.

He challenged her eyes. 'I always find the best way to get a woman out of my system is to screw her. I've been feeling totally obsessed by her and when I heard her in the bath I went up and found the door open. She smiled and made no objection when I took my clothes off, so I got in with her.'

She held his eyes for a moment longer, scrutinising his expression, then turned back to the window, staring unseeingly at the Abbey. 'I see,' she said quietly. Her chin slumped onto her fist as she rested her elbow on her stout knee.

He looked at the back of her head for a moment, taking in the lifeless blonde hair with the ragged split-ends draped around her shoulders. The silence stretched between them. Then he spoke softly, concernedly. 'My God, Anne, you didn't really believe me, did you?'

She shrugged. 'You tell me.'

'Then I'm telling you nothing happened. She only ran me a bath. The first version was the truth.'

'I didn't think you could lie so easily.'

He got up and placed his hand on her lacklustre hair which felt greasy to the touch. 'I'm sorry, Anne, I didn't mean to hurt you. But you seemed so ready to believe I was straying. You don't have much faith in me, do you?'

She turned from the window and impulsively buried her face into his waist. 'I'm sorry, Boy,' she said in a small voice. When she looked up at him her cheeks were tearstained.

'God, Anne, I'm sorry. I was only teasing ...' He patted her head, as one would a grovelling puppy. 'Come on, I'll get us a drink.'

He poured out two sweet sherries and handed her one. He sat down and smiled at her podgy face. 'Anyway, you know, Eleanor and Max are extremely close. Haven't you noticed how he's always touching her, stroking her hair and pawing her?'

She shook her head. 'That's only for your benefit, Boy, can't you see that? To show how great he is. I never noticed her touching *him.*'

'Really?' Her reply was like a new revelation to him. He sipped his sherry and felt it's warmth slip down his sternum. 'But what I mean is, they're clearly devoted to each other. You remember what she told you—or Rosemary, rather—about a well-balanced relationship? They've obviously got it right.'

She snorted. 'You could have fooled me. They depend on a lot of artificial aids. I don't know how you can be fooled so easily by those two. There's a suitcase under their bed full of disgusting sex stuff.'

He was horrified. 'You mean, you *looked*?'

She nodded. 'Why not? When Rosemary's not in I have to clean their room.' She frowned. 'Boy, you'd be shocked by the stuff. There's playing cards of naked people having sex together. And games. I don't like the friendship you're building up with those two. It's...' She sipped her sherry and sighed. 'It's just not right. It's not natural.'

He stared at her. 'How do you mean, not natural?'

She pursed her lip. 'I told you, you should see those cards, and sex magazines, too. They're full of unbelievably explicit sex positions. There's close-up pictures of a woman's...' She hesitated. 'A woman's—you know, and with two male things in it at the same time. And then there's a sort of snakes and ladders game, with forfeit cards.' She shook her head sadly, gazing at the carpet in front of her. 'Each card has Max's handwriting on it, with instructions.'

'What kind of instructions?'

'Well, one was: "Explore your partner's bottom." You see, the game is meant for more than two people.'

He drained his sherry, swallowing it in one gulp. 'Maybe it's just a way to ...' He grinned mischievously. 'A way to share one another's auras. You know, make love, not war, that sort of thing.' Secretly, he thought, Max must have a voracious appetite.

Her sad eyes focused on him. 'If you believe that, Boy, you must be unbelievably stupid.'

What she told him didn't perturb him. If anything, it was further evidence that Eleanor wasn't Max's exclusive property, that they were both open to other relationships—one which put Eleanor into a sort of reach, for him. But what did horrify him was Anne's easy acceptance of her own spying.

'You shouldn't really have looked, Anne,' he said, trying not to sound self-righteous. 'What's in that suitcase is their own business, you know—unless they wanted to show you and share it.'

She pursed her lips, nodding disgruntedly at the Abbey. She remained silent.

'Anyway,' he stood up, picking up the little owl oil-burner with its glaring, knowing eyes. 'I must return this to Eleanor. I'll just pop up a minute, shall I?'

She flicked her eyes briefly at him, then stared back at the Abby. 'Go on,' she said, wearily, 'Go to your girlfriend.'

CHAPTER 16

New Horizons

HARRY WATCHED the blizzard through the open door of the aeroplane.

The snowflakes were sweeping horizontally in the night. He felt snug and warm in the lit interior of the plane. People shuffled into their seats, stowing their heavy winter anoraks and coats into the luggage cubicles above them. The heavy door slid securely into place and before long the small aircraft belonging to Air Malta was shuddering and screaming as it lunged into the sky.

The plane banked steeply and in spite of the snow the lights of Newcastle sprawled endlessly below. Anne, not used to flying, gripped her seat and pointed to the moving specks of light that were cars nudging their way through the amorphous maze of lights. Before long the lights fell away and the roar of the engines dulled to a low and continuous surge. Harry yawned and blew into his nose which he pinched shut between thumb and forefinger, and the surge was suddenly louder and closer.

'The break will do you good, you know,' he smiled, bending over to Anne whose flaxen hair spread out against the seat well below the level of the headrest. 'And if we do manage to attend one or two of the Speedway meetings, the positive input won't come amiss.'

She closed her eyes, relaxing to the dull vibration of the plane. 'Are you sure that's what you're going for, Boy?' She gave a half smile, the corners of her mouth tilting downwards rather than up. 'Not just to see Eleanor?'

'Now you're being silly,' he said, annoyed by her uncanny ability to see through him. 'But of course it will be nice to see them again. They always make me feel better about myself— they're such positive people.'

'Always riding on a wave?' she said, her eyes still shut. 'They just don't let you see the troughs, Boy.'

Harry dug into his top pocket and read again the little note that had come in the post the morning before. It began with a quotation: 'Success is the progressive realisation of a worthwhile dream or goal,' followed by the words: 'You can do it! We believe in you!' And it was signed: 'Max.'

Harry wished it was signed by Eleanor, but he took it to reflect Eleanor's thoughts as well. Max and Eleanor had moved out of the hotel the previous month, in January, and in a desperate attempt to see Eleanor again he had organised a Speedway meeting in his hotel. He had visited many of the local business people in Jedburgh, handing out invitations to hear about 'an interesting business idea'—a meeting which Max, as his upline, was more than happy to address. His spirits had been dampened by the unenthusiastic response. He had tried to invite a colleague, a woman who owned the rival Guest House the other side of the valley.

'This is a marvellous business concept,' he had said, feeling awkward. 'I'm involved with a group of dynamic business people who are looking to expand in our area. It may be just the thing for you.'

In the silence that had followed he could feel her bristling.

'Harry,' she had said, curtly, 'Is this Speedway?'

Damn, he had thought. She wasn't supposed to find out until the meeting. 'Why yes!' he had tried to sound bright. 'Yes, it is!'

'Well then you can forget about it! They're American and they're only here to rake people off! Really, Harry! I wouldn't have thought you were the sort of person to fall for it. Off all people, with your university background, you should have seen through it. No thank you!' And she had slammed down the phone. She had been friendly and used to send him her overflow guests. Now she never rang.

'Harry, this is the quickest way to lose all your friends!' another hotel owner had told him. 'That's their *modus operandi*—to exploit all your friends first. Be careful, Harry.' And she had put the phone down, too.

In the end the only person who turned up was Norma, the middle-aged widow who had just begun to do bed and breakfast up the road from Harry. She was a born-again Christian and was always friendly to Harry. He had sat there, with her in his hotel lounge with tea and biscuits, while Max focused all his sales techniques at her, squeaking the network of circles on the board, treading every now and again on the loose floor board that creaked embarrassingly. Harry cringed with each creak, sensing the rising hostility of his companion.

'Is *this* the sort of thing *I* would be expected to do?' Norma had asked, defensively. 'Serving tea and biscuits on the pretext of a social function, and then having a business plan rammed down your throat? If my husband were alive, he would have protected me from this.'

Harry had always liked Norma and felt awful. 'No, no,' he said quickly, 'It's only to benefit you in the end. You could double—treble—your income within ...'

'By conning people!' she had cut him short. 'I'm sorry, Harry, that's not my scene at all! I couldn't use my friends in this way.'

The next day he had phoned Norma to apologise. 'Harry,' she had said on the phone, 'Couldn't you see what a vicious person that Max is? Those eyes of his! Dark and beady, watching me like a hawk. Beware of him, Harry. He's using you!'

Harry had relayed her response to Max. 'She said she felt used, Max, and that you're exploiting other peoples' friends.'

Max had been furious. *'Exploiting*! For God's sake! I gave up my whole day to address that meeting, and it's not my fault she was the only one that turned up! Couldn't the bitch see that it was for her own good? What's wrong with her? Doesn't she *want* to make more money?'

'Well,' Harry had said defensively, 'I'm just giving you the feedback so you know the type of responses I'm getting.'

And then that encouraging little note had arrived in the post. 'I believe in you!—Max.'

The truth was, Harry missed Eleanor's presence awfully. Since they moved out life was like a vacuum and the only light on the horizon appeared to be via Speedway. At least the Speedway convention in Malta promised another glimpse of her, if not an actual sharing, once again, of her magical aura.

He gazed ahead of him. He was near the front of the aeroplane and the relaxed and friendly disposition of the flight crew permitted the door to the cockpit being left wide open. He watched with fascination the dense cluster of winking lights and instrumentation, predominantly luminous green dials and switches that covered every square inch of the otherwise black instrument panel—a sort of technical fairyland beneath the deep black windscreen. The Captain leant forward, caught his eye, and beaconed to him.

Harry smiled, surprised. He rose from his seat and went forward, stooping in the little doorway. No-one seemed to be flying the plane. 'Whose in control?' Harry smiled down at the Captain and the co-pilot who were both reclining in their seats. The co-pilot was drinking some coffee.

The Captain laughed. 'We don't fly the plane ourselves. We only take it up and bring it down.'

'Good heavens! So who flies it?'

'James!' smiled the co-pilot, lifting his eyes.

'James?'

'Sure,' the Captain smiled up at him. 'The Autopilot. We call it James.'

James did a good job. It was a smooth flight and it wasn't long before Harry, leaning over the sleeping form of Anne, could see the lights of Sicily crowding the dark coastline below.

The warmth of Malta embraced them as they descended the steps from the plane. No snow, no ice, no blizzard, and yet it had been just four hours from the clutching cold of Newcastle. The air fondled them with notions of lazy tropical nights.

It was three in the morning and the bus rattled through deserted streets, skimming potholes and hammering coil springs into the holes too wide to skim. Anne's head slumped onto Harry's shoulder and rocked with the movement of the bus. There was a dilapidated air about the pot-marked streets and flat-roofed biblical houses. They were pleased, at length, to collapse into their beds in the small chalet-apartment which was part of a complex owned by the Golden Bay Hotel.

In the morning they walked out onto their little terrace overlooking Golden Bay. The light was blinding. When Harry managed at length to squeeze his eyelids apart, the scene was dazzling, not only in sunshine but in colour. The sea was a deep azure blue, stretching across the curved bay, encompassed by crumbling golden cliffs. Dominating the nearest cliff, perched almost on the edge, was a tower—one of many towers built by the Knights of St John to guard against the Turks. Homer's phrase, 'the wine-dark sea,' came to Harry's mind. It wasn't exactly the colour of wine, he thought, but somehow the phrase captured the essence of the incredible depth of colour of the water.

'Do you suppose it's warm enough to swim?' asked Anne. She blinked at the golden sands and the iridescent water below her. She wore a pair of shorts and a T-shirt that emphasised her squat figure. Her legs had run to fat and had become chunky, her breasts sagging fluidly under the T-shirt.

'We can try,' he said, looking at the beach which was deserted. A bulldozer worked noisily in the distance, pushing seaweed debris out of the way and smoothing the sand. 'I was hoping to visit Valletta, actually. Chuck Halliday's giving an address tonight. You ought to hear him.'

'Why's that, Boy?' she glanced up at him, her eyes narrowed against the sunlight.

'He speaks with such quiet conviction.'

'Will Max and Eleanor be there?'

He shrugged. 'Possibly.' Then he said with more conviction. 'I guess so.'

'But that's on the other side of the island, isn't it? Couldn't we at least explore around here, first, and have a swim?'

'Sure we can.' He smiled down at her. 'It will only take an hour or so in the bus to Valletta, and Halliday's address is in the evening. We'll take our costumes and go down to the beach, shall we?'

They had vouchers for use in the Golden Bay Hotel's dining room for breakfasts and evening meals. It meant joining a long queue with elderly people, but Anne was a good eater and enjoyed the arrangement of being able to eat as much as she liked. It simply meant taking up a clean plate and rejoining the queue again.

'God, I'm stuffed!' laughed Anne after breakfast as they picked their way amongst the bits of broken glass and beer tins on the beach. It was a stretch of sand that the bulldozer hadn't yet reached.

They inched their way into the limpid water which crisped their skin with its coldness. Anne hunched over, her knees together, planted in the water, bracing herself against the cold. Harry took a deep breath and ran in, splashing, steeling himself against the cold. Then they were both in, floundering and laughing, and for a moment the years had dropped away and they were in the first flush of their marriage again. Anne swam to him and folded her thickening body around him, light and buoyant in the water. For a moment her blue eyes were the same bewitching eyes that belonged to the nymph that had hooked him years ago in the anteroom of her stepmother's fundamentalist church.

'Did you know,' he had said, munching a cheese sandwich, for the want of something to say to the pretty little thing that she was, 'that the moon's made of cheese?'

'It's not!' she refuted, smiling defiantly.

'It is!'

'Is not!'

The water seemed to wash away the years, and when they ran back onto the beach their bodies were alive and refreshed.

'God, I'm famished, Boy! Are you?'

He nodded. 'I guess, but we've only just had breakfast.'

She nodded. 'I know, but the water's given my appetite an edge. I could murder a fish with some chips!'

They had seen a fast-food restaurant near the hotel. They dried themselves and walked, hand in hand like honeymooners, following a sandy path through windswept shrubs that leant up the slope towards the crumbling honey-hewed cliffs overlooking Gnejna Bay.

'Do you remember those delicious savaloys we had with chips in East Dulwich, Boy?' She smacked her lips with memory. 'Maybe they've got some of those here.'

'I'm sure they'll have something you'll enjoy,' he laughed, then stopped dead in his tracks. His hand tightened on hers.

'What?' she whispered.

He pointed with his free hand, too spellbound to speak.

'Oh, God,' she said, drawing back, but his hand held hers firmly.

Just in front of them, crossing their path in a lazy, flowing movement, was an adder, about two feet in length. It had reddish diamond shapes all along its back. There was a strong wind blowing so it must have been unaware of them. And yet it must have known they were there, so close, Harry thought. It had no sense of fear—just a sense of its own sleek beauty. It slid silently and unhurriedly into a hole beneath a rock.

'Jesus,' he said in a hushed voice. 'I didn't think we'd actually see it.'

'What, a snake?' Anne asked, her nose wrinkled in distaste.

He shook his head. 'The viper that bit St Paul.'

'Don't be stupid,' she frowned with a laugh. 'That was two thousand years ago.'

'Yes,' he smiled, still keeping his eye on the rock where it had disappeared. 'And on the other side of the island, in St Paul's Bay. The Apostle shook it off into the fire, remember? And he was unharmed.'

'That's because he was holy. I didn't like the look of that critter.' She tugged his hand. 'Come away, Boy.'

He shook his head. 'No, you don't understand. It was so beautiful. No one could be hurt by something so beautiful. I feel so privileged, seeing it. And it was as though it knew I was seeing it and didn't mind a bit.' He felt a sense of awe, his skin crisped with goosepimples. He gave a little self-conscious laugh. 'It's like a bond with the Apostle, don't you see? With the energy of the island.'

'You're crazy!' she said with a touch of irritation. 'Come away, Boy. I hate snakes.'

They continued their way, mounting an endless series of steps that took them past a derelict hotel that was gradually disintegrating due to the crumbling cliffs upon which it had been built.

'God,' said Harry, 'I wonder if this is the way the Golden Bay Hotel will go one day! These cliffs are receding and breaking off into the sea at an incredible pace!'

Anne looked sad. 'That was somebody's dream, once.'

Harry shook his head, bemused. 'They should have had a better geologist's report first.' Sadly, he thought, that applied to marriages, too. He turned and looked at her, seeing the wind whip up her fringe. Her expression was podgy as she regarded the panoramic vista with the Golden Bay hotel, marooned like an ocean liner on seemingly sturdy cliffs—cliffs made up of the same friable chalky stuff that had given way under the fragmenting ruins of the derelict hotel. 'The coastline looks like the edge of a crumbling piece of cheesecake,' she said.

'Talking of dreams,' Harry said, brightening, 'maybe we should get a move on if we want to have your savaloy and chips and still make it for the Speedway dream-night talk. It's the second in the series of the Dream Weekend in Valletta.' But he sensed her reluctance since she lagged behind him. 'Don't you want to go, Anne?'

She shook her head, picking her way along the path that wound round the cliff edge. 'I'd rather we had dinner and went for another walk. We could follow the cliffs to the Popeye Village.'

He laughed. 'We'd never make it there and back before nightfall. Why not leave that for another day—tomorrow, maybe?'

'Would we have to miss the buffet supper then?'

He smiled. 'Yes, but there's plenty of restaurants in Valletta we can eat at before the function. They even have a MacDonalds. You could have one of their top of the line mixed grills.'

She brightened visibly, smiling up at him and tightening her grasp on his hand. 'That would be nice, Boy.'

The bus was a treat, Harry thought. It was at least sixty years old—a vintage Bedford that rumbled along the narrow roads at surprising speed. They sat sideways just across from the driver who propelled the bus with one hand in a cool and casual manner, using a swivel knob on the steering wheel. The narrow windscreen divided into two gave the front-end the feel of an aeroplane cockpit. It was like a fairground ride, Harry thought, gripping the seat with one hand and a handrail with the other, or anything he could find that was fastened. As they drew into Valletta the narrow streets, the rows of houses with ornate wrought-iron balconies, the golden stone porches, unfurled like a film in fast-forward. At the end of the run their stomachs felt quite tossed and shaken and it was a while before Anne, laughing, pronounced herself ready for the MacDonald's treat.

'Are you hungry, then?' Harry asked.

'Yeh! Yeh! Yeh!' she laughed, her smile mounted above the wreathes of double chins.

'You're easy to please,' Harry laughed. 'You're not one of those pretentious wives who are only impressed with *cordon bleu* stuff like caviar and salmon sauce with fettucini in a sophisticated setting. You could have had that in an upstairs restaurant in Mosta overlooking the Mosta Dome.'

She shook her head. 'No, Boy, give me a good nosh of solid fried stuff anytime. I can't stand some of the fussy eaters we get at the hotel with their posh accents.'

They found the Valletta MacDonald's easily enough. A large clown figure in yellow and red with oversized boots sat on a bench outside. A lot of smartly dressed people with American accents sat inside, but they managed to find a corner table where Anne was soon ensconced with a heaped plate of grilled and fried meats with cartons stuffed full of thin-cut French fries. A huge double sized carton of Coke accompanied the order. Harry watched her with sad amusement, wondering at her capacity to compress so much into so short a stature.

'Your metabolism is controlled by James,' he laughed.

'Whose James?' she queried with a full mouth.

'The autopilot. You only sit down and stand up afterwards. James does the rest!'

She wrinkled her nose at him in a manner that was meant to be coquettish. 'You're just jealous, that's all, Boy. If you worked as hard as me you'd have a decent appetite too.'

There was a general clamour and chattering as a smartly dressed couple walked in. The man wore a suit and his wife a lined suit outfit that had a pleated jacket with tailored collar. Her short-cut hair was swept back to form a tight helmet. Most of the occupants of the room stood up, clapping and offered their seats. The couple looked at everyone, eyes beaming.

'Who the fuck are they?' said Anne, looking up, her mouth still full and chewing, her lower lip pursed.

Harry shook his head. 'VIP's of some sort, obviously.'

CHAPTER 17

Dreams are Made of This

IT WASN'T DIFFICULT to find the Phoenix Hotel since
Valletta has very few hotels, the ancient city having been
squashed onto a very small peninsula. Harry and Anne found
themselves already in the main thoroughfare, Republic Street or
Trig ir-Repubblika, which was full of shops, running through the
heart of the city down to Fort St Elmo on the tip of the peninsula.
They had a glimpse of brilliant blue at the end of many of the
streets as they walked along the main street, so they knew they
were surrounded by sea on nearly all sides. They were flanked
by handsome balconied facades that stretched above the street-
level shops, and could hardly miss the Phoenix Hotel which
stood out as one of the most elegant buildings with its wide
portal and tiers of enclosed green balconies that stretched above
them, rows upon rows.

The foyer of the hotel was awash with flowers and polished
people in immaculate suits and flowing dresses. Anne was
nowhere near as self-possessed as she was in the MacDonald's
and kept flicking out a hand towards his, seeking a reassuring
contact. She glanced about nervously, rapidly, but suddenly
smiled, revealing her skew teeth when she recognised the one
face she knew.

'Haloo!' sang out Eleanor, tripping up to them in a flared
maroon dress with diamond patterns around the tight waist. She
took Anne's free hand and tugged both of them towards a group
of people who were chattering with bright, fervent eyes and
animated hand gestures. Harry grinned helplessly, barely able to
take his eyes off Eleanor's trim figure and sparkling eyes. She
looked effervescent and enchanting as she flounced around, from
group to group, flashing smiles in her elegant dress and trim
leather boots, introducing them to more faces with beaming eyes
and wide engaging smiles.

'This is Meg, from Florida!' Eleanor gushed, uniting their hands with the thin lanky hand of a tall woman who flashed a toothy but immaculate smile.

'Hi!' whined Meg, her sharp American accent slicing through the hubbub of noise like a knife. 'I'm kinda confused. Are you English too?' When Harry nodded she went on: 'I'm still getting used to the differences. You all put milk in your tea and we put ice in it. You put lemon in it to make it sour and we put sugar in it to make it sweet.' She laughed, making them all laugh. 'And what about your pounds?' she gushed on. 'And they tell me they're different from the pounds of Malta! You wanna tell me it's real money like dollars? And then I find I weigh only eight stone and I think hey! that's great! But then they tell me that's kinda high, just as heavy as 112 lbs! You wanna tell me that's not kinda crazy!'

Harry laughed. 'We're not in the mainstream of cultural development like you!'

She made wide eyes at him: 'Hey! You talk kinda cute! Gee, with an accent like that you could kiss a girl in the main street in Miami and get away with it!'

'Not with me around!' grinned Anne, averting her eyes and biting her lower lip. She still held on to Harry's hand, like an item of luggage.

'Oh Anne!' gushed Eleanor, noticing her. 'You look *super!*'

Harry glanced down at Anne, taking in her powder-blue tent dress which ignored the existence of a waist. Anne flicked her eyes briefly at her, then at Meg, with a twisted smile. Her right knee waggled to an inaudible rhythm.

'Harry! Anne!' yelled a man's voice, and they swung round to see Max striding towards them importantly in a dark suit with a red diamond-patterned waistcoat similar to the seamed waist of Eleanor's dress. 'All the way from Scotland, eh!' He grinned, reaching out and grasping their hands. 'That's the ticket! That's the ticket!' Then he dropped his voice marginally with a twisted leer at Harry. 'Listen! Do you know why Scotsmen wear kilts? It's because they like oats, you see!' When Harry gave him a puzzled look he guffawed. 'It's so he can have his oats without wasting any time, get it!' He guffawed again, stimulating a sympathetic raucous guffaw from Anne and an increased tempo of her waggling knee.

'You're a card, Max, you really are!' Anne conceded, in spite of her open criticism of him behind his back.

Max grinned, then placed a grip on Harry's shoulder, drawing him slightly apart from the womenfolk. 'Look here, old bean, what are your plans for tomorrow?'

Harry shrugged. 'Nothing much. Swimming or sight-seeing. I thought we might get together.' He was hoping to see more of Eleanor and his next remark played right into his hands.

'Well, I was wondering if the two of you would look after Eleanor?' He smiled, seeing Harry's eyes register surprise. 'You see, tomorrow's Speedway's day off and me and some of the boys here have organised a flight to Sicily for the day—and probably for the night.' He winked. 'There's a night-club in Catania and we've got some fluff lined up.' He gave a little laugh. 'If you and Anne can see your way to spend time with Eleanor—you know, museums, palaces, stuff like that?'

Harry couldn't believe his luck! The thought flashed through him: it's true about coincidences, reaching out and shaping your destiny when you reach out to a goal! He smiled open-heartedly at Max: 'Max, that would be a pleasure! In fact, I have a hire car that's included in our holiday package. I could pick her up!'

'Good man!' he slapped his shoulder. 'You make the arrangements with Eleanor.' He drew Harry back towards the girls and kissed Eleanor on the cheek: 'Hi, silly moo! It's all fixed up with Harry and Anne.' She grinned up at him and he winked. 'Got to take care of the boss now! The force be with you!' He lifted a hand and disappeared into the crowd.

Eleanor smiled coyly at them. 'That would be Chuck Halliday. They're becoming quite thick together.' She touched Anne on her arm. 'Thank you Anne. So you'll put up with me tomorrow? I was looking forward to seeing you again. You really are looking super, you know. Would you like to sit with me in the meeting? We better go and find a good place.' Eleanor tugged Anne towards the lecture room and Harry followed, walking on air.

They sat near the front, much as Harry had done in the Edinburgh meeting, but this time he was handicapped by the presence of Anne between him and Eleanor. Anne was nodding sagely, listening to Eleanor's chattering, her arms folded together and interlocked across her spongy breasts. Every now and then she gave a mirthless, twisted smile, as she took in another morsel of information that Eleanor was scattering liberally. Harry listened to the music of Eleanor's voice rather than her words, not being able to hear clearly in the hubbub of conversational noise. He looked past Anne's splayed square knees, her feet planted firmly on the floor, seeing the delicate shape of Eleanor's boot, suspended above the other because her legs were crossed. He could see Eleanor's small, delicate fingers protruding from the long sleeves of her velvet dress, resting on her lap, and he longed to enclose them in his own hand. 'Do you know what I mean, Anne?' he heard her say earnestly. He nodded automatically, smiling, leaning forward and hoping to catch her eye. He always knew what she meant and he always agreed with her. God, he thought, she's such a delicious, beautiful little creature. And tomorrow he could bask in her presence all day long. Perhaps she could even stay overnight...

His thoughts were interrupted by the rustle of people rising from their seats. He rose, too, and saw that everyone was clapping, and he clapped, too. He saw the back of the familiar bald head of Chuck Halliday, the fringe of hair on either side of his head uniting above the nape of his neck in a V-formation. His domed head was a bit like the back of the Abbot's head, he thought, the displaced wanderer in Jedburgh, but tidier and opulent in the way it glinted in the electric lights of the auditorium.

'What's with him?' Anne sneered with a sidelong glance at Harry.

'Sshhh!' whispered Eleanor. 'It's Chuck Halliday. He's a double diamond!'

'That's a multimillionaire!' whispered Harry, smiling.

Anne nodded, pursing her lips as though sensing a bad smell under her nose.

The clapping died down and everyone settled in their seats. Chuck begun in his usual unassuming way, saying he was not there to speak tonight but to introduce Ken and Fran Dolby who were Diamonds from Florida. They weren't brand new

Diamonds, he explained, having been established now, and still growing, for the last two years. Then he asked everyone if they all had pen and paper and whether they had ever travelled in an aeroplane by first-class. He assured everyone that he always travelled first-class and that it was 'the only way' to travel. Everyone cheered. Then he gave a blow-by-blow account of what it was like to travel first-class. 'Imagine being called to the front of the queue. Imagine being shown into a separate boarding lounge, not crowded like the main tourist section. Imagine being shown to the upstairs deck and given drinks right away. Imagine ...'

Everyone listened in hushed silence, and Harry wondered how many present could actually afford to travel first class and whether they ever did. You could hear a pin drop, the attention was so rapt. He glanced at Anne and saw that her eyes were rolled up under her half-shut eyelids. Only the whites were showing.

Anne's eyes sprang open when the cheering crowd rose to their feet. Everyone remained on their feet when Ken and Fran Dolby, the Diamonds, strode in. The clapping broke out afresh and whistling filled the auditorium. Anne was still blinking, looking resentful for having been so abruptly woken up.

'So what are Diamonds?' she queried, looking at Harry sourly.

'Millionaires,' he said.

She rolled her eyes towards the ceiling. She watched the couple mount the dais and her eyes registered shock. She turned towards Harry. 'God, it's that smarmy woman who walked into MacDonald's! The one everyone sucked up to!'

'Sshh!' said Eleanor, smiling at her. 'One day you might be a Diamond, Anne!'

Anne sat down with everyone else, squaring her body again with her arms folded tightly, glaring at the woman in her sleek designer suit. Ken, her husband, stood up and spoke first, one hand playing with some coins in his pocket, the other grasping the microphone.

'Once, when I was an astronaut,' he began. Everyone chuckled, and he raised his eyebrows at them. He was a lean man, his suit perfectly tailored to fit his tall, lean figure. Red fluffy hair sprouted out of the sides of his otherwise hairless head, black-rimmed glasses emphasising his round eyes. 'Oh, you don't believe me?' he smiled. 'Well, it was a good try. None of you know me from Adam!'

The tittering died down and he explained that he was, in fact, a road-digger. At least, he said, he *had* been, before he was introduced to Speedway. But no sooner had the plan been shown to him, he wanted to quit. Then he enthused up again and before long, he said, his wife Fran wanted to quit. Thank God, he said, neither of them wanted to quit on the same day!

Everyone laughed.

'But look where we are now!' he said. He couldn't stop Fran from buying crystals. Their whole house was crammed full of crystals and everywhere she went she bought crystals.

This time Harry did manage to catch Eleanor's eye. She bent forward, smiling open-mouthed in surprise and pleasure. Here was another crystal collector! But it turned out that Fran was into ornaments—glass creatures ranging from owls to ponies. Fran beamed from her seat on the dais, basking in the limelight and the focused eyes of everyone present.

Then Ken gave the microphone to his wife and Fran got up, tugging self-consciously at the hem of her lined jacket. Everyone cheered and she beamed. Harry had to give her credit for being a good speaker. The cut and sweep of her talk was electrifying. No wonder she was so successful, he thought. 'If you can merchandise just one thing,' she said, 'you can become a Diamond.' She looked at everyone and beamed. 'We are in the business of dreams,' she said. 'We are dream merchants.' She smiled around her, seeing their upturned, worshipful faces. 'How many of you are here for your first dream weekend, or dream night? Oh yes, I can see your wide eyes. And you're saying "Oh my God, who are these people?" Well, let me tell you, you're going to get some great things! We were brand new like you at one time.'

Harry could sense the way she felt the mounting *rapport* with her audience, the way she geared up her talk into a gushing flow. She stepped up the pace of her delivery. 'You're thinking, we look pretty spiffy! But if you'd seen us some years ago, you wouldn't want to include us on your prospect list. We just knew we were so broke, so desperate with no decent car, no decent house with nothing going for us. So when we were shown the plan, we said for goodness sake, what have we to lose? Let's try it for a year—just *one* year! If it works, great! I never believed for one moment we would be Diamonds!' She shook her head and smiled engagingly, running her fingers over her smooth swept-back hair. 'You've got to have a dream that'll make you get out of your living room each night and show the plan!' She switched onto dreams. 'Be serious about what you dream for, because that's what you're going to get!'

Harry glanced across Anne, seeing Eleanor's neatly folded hands. God, he thought, with a spasm of pain, I want you, Eleanor. *You're* my dream! God, I want you more than anything else in the world! He took a deep breath, trying to get a hold of himself. How could he ever have Eleanor who was married to Max, and himself to Anne? He glanced at Anne and saw again that she was fighting sleep, her eyelids half shut and flickering, her expression set with her lower lip pursed.

'I placed a picture of a baby on my refrigerator. Ken stuck a picture of a 40 foot yacht on the refrigerator. Those dreams soon materialised! The baby came only too quickly. The yacht took a little longer!'

Harry wondered whether Anne would tolerate photographs of Eleanor stuck on the refrigerator. He recalled that Max had a picture of her next to the bed when they were at the hotel—a picture of her in the nude. He'd like one like that, too, showing her two pert, resilient breasts. Perhaps he could place it in a secret place, the inside door of his wardrobe, or on the inside lid of his shaving kit?

'You wanna be goal oriented!' Meg urged in her strident American voice, her eyes connecting with the eager upturned eyes of the audience. 'Begin with just this much hope!' She held up her hand, as though holding something the size of a mustard seed between two fingers. 'Learn to be brave! Learn to be persistent! In five years we put together an Emeraldship! But then we reached danger-point. We got too comfortable at Emerald level. Get on a roll! Don't stop to admire the view, or you'll slide back. Keep climbing! We were Emeralds for ten years, and got bored with being known as the biggest Emeralds in the area, with our motorhome, five-bedroomed house and annual holidays to Disney World. So we said: why not *live* in Florida? Why not have one of those palatial houses where all those millionaires live, one that we never thought we could afford? So we put together a Diamondship! You see, you don't have to be a perfect person to do this! There are no barriers in this business. We decided we *had* to make that run! You see, all it takes is a *decision!*' She engaged the eyes that were already glued to hers. 'Wouldn't you like that option Chuck spoke of— to travel first class?' They all cheered and she smiled sympathetically. 'Yes, *you* can have that option down the road. Like us, you'll need to stop your spending and put it on the line! Then all of a sudden you're around a whole lot of new people, mountain-top people, positive people, terrific people.'

She had to pause for the cheering to stop. She smiled. 'It's worth it!' she gushed. 'I have to pinch myself to believe I am where I am now.' She continued to elucidate her present lifestyle. A split-level home, one section for the kids, one for themselves. A swimming pool. ('Wouldn't you just love to have your own swimming pool?') The trouble was, she said, she had to be careful what she said to Ken. If she as much as hinted she wanted a four-wheel drive Jeep, he would up and get it for her. 'Now I have the gold-trimmed Jeep as well as the Cadillac Eldorado. And both the kids each have two cars of their own!' She shook her head. 'Money isn't the goal, it's the *by-product* of your new lifestyle. It's the tool you need to get the things you need to go with this lifestyle. You know, when I go to buy a dress I don't look at the price tag. I buy it because I *like* it.' She opened her arms to the crowd. *'You* can do it too. You can walk across the stage, like we did, with your name in lights as a new Diamond! It's a worthwhile dream! Visualise it! If you can merchandise *one* product, you can go Diamond! Crystallise your dreams! It's the magic, the key, that will get you into a home like mine.' She caught the eyes of some of the women that gazed up at her. 'Be a Diamond-woman!'

She waited for the clapping to subside. Harry saw Eleanor's perfect little hands clapping, too. Anne's arms were still firmly folded. She was pulling a face, trying to raise her eyelids. Her irises alternated rapidly with the whites of her eye.

'I don't know what it is you want out of this business,' Fran gushed on, 'but I can tell you, you *can* have it! You are truly some of the warmest people you can get! I saw that when I went into the MacDonald's today.' She laughed. 'You know, being American, we kinda like American food, so we found a MacDonald's—and *there* you all were too!' Many of the people present clapped. She nodded in acknowledgement. 'Yes, when we went in we saw you there, and you were so warm and gave up your seats!' She smiled, radiating confidence. 'And we believe in you! And all it takes is one thing! That's getting plugged into your line of sponsorship! You can stop believing in yourselves, but *we* won't stop believing in *you!*'

Something she said really engaged Harry's attention—getting plugged into his line of sponsorship. Did that mean Max and Eleanor, or the persons he sponsored in return? Either way, it meant he had a right to be plugged into Eleanor! God, he thought, that image conjured up a delight of fantasy. He leaned forward, trying to catch her eye. Anne had given up the fight and her head lolled backwards, spreading her chins, her eyes closed. It opened the view to Eleanor who glanced at him, dimpling as her blue eyes flashed a smile. God, he thought, thrilling, I want to be plugged into you, all right.

'Be proud of your line of sponsorship!' Fran was saying. 'That's the magic ingredient. Don't ever stop sponsoring.' She smiled patronisingly at her audience. 'You know, there are so many of you here who are going to rise up this year. Yes, it may be *you.*' She looked straight at Harry and made him freeze with fright. He smiled sheepishly. 'Do whatever it takes, I believe in you! Look at yourself in the mirror every morning and believe you can do it! It's so important to be plugged into your line of sponsorship! You need to be around the dream all the time!'

Harry's whole body was a rash of goosepimples. Fran's engaging eyes seemed to be telling him to be around Eleanor all the time! One way or the other, he felt charged with energy.

Fran sat down and the whole auditorium rose to its feet. Harry got up with everyone else, adding his applause. He looked to his right and saw that Anne was missing. Eleanor looked radiant, standing, applauding, smiling at the dais. He looked down and saw the upturned, red-blotched and bloated face of his wife, her mouth lolling open in sleep.

That night, jolting back through the dark in the bus, Anne inflated herself into one of her pontificating moods. 'It's like they're prostituting themselves!' she complained. 'They're ...' She shook her head in disbelief, her hair duller than usual in the dim yellow light that illuminated the interior of the nearly empty bus. 'They're debasing themselves...' She searched for a more apt word. 'Yes, prostrating themselves before money. My mother would say bowing down before Mammon, and she's right! They have no soul! That woman! All she could do was brag, brag, brag about her split-level house, her swimming pool and I don't know how many cars! She ought to be ashamed of herself! God, I've never seen anyone so ... so shallow!'

Harry sighed, looking down at her, seeing the floppy outline of her breasts jiggling like jelly as the bus rattled and jolted. He was surprised that she had heard anything of the talk. 'Anne, you're missing the point! She was saying *you* could be just like her...'

'Over my dead body, the stuck-up cow!'

'No, no! She was saying you can have anything and everything she has, too, if you follow your dreams—whatever your dreams. You weren't listening...'

'I'm quite content with the way I am, thank you very much!'

He laughed. 'Didn't you hear what her husband said afterwards? He said when people say that, he tells them the only contented creature he knows is a cow!'

'So I'm a cow!' she snorted. 'God, Harry, they actually applaud and stand up, and give up their seats, when a rich person comes in! I was taught you do that to old people! Can you imagine what Christ would have said to them!'

'Anne!' He felt exasperated. 'You keep missing the point. They do that to encourage you to become rich and successful! Don't you see? Those people are more than happy to stand up because they're conditioning themselves willingly, saying it's great because this is what it will be like when *they're* rich! They're accepting that woman as a role-model for themselves, that's all.'

'Well, I don't want to be like them—like that strutting cow—thank you very much!' She locked her arms across her chest, flattening her breasts and glowering through the dark windscreen. 'I can't see myself going where they're going, crowing about how fantastic I am. Haven't you heard, Boy? Self-praise is no praise.'

Harry slumped back into his seat, surrendering the argument. 'Anyway,' he sighed, brightening and smiling to himself. 'We'll have Eleanor's company tomorrow. She's coming on the bus and I'll meet her at the bus stop by the hotel.'

'Oh, *great!*' said Anne, turning her head and glowering into the night. Her sour reflection in the dark window glowered back at her.

CHAPTER 18

Feeling Cosmic

THE MORNING was crisp with a fresh breeze when Harry reached the little enclosed bus stop adjacent to the Golden Bay Hotel. Some elderly folk had already gathered, expectantly watching the road that ran down from the rocky hillside for the first signs of the ancient yellow bus that would take them to Valletta for a day's shopping. They held capacious shopping bags, two or three clutching a paperback novel which they could read while sitting in a park, or on the rampart walls, soaking up the winter sunshine. Harry joined the little throng and watched the empty road with more eager anticipation than his elderly companions—an anticipation that accelerated his heartbeat.

'Oh, what a lovely day for it!' exclaimed a stout woman whom Harry had already mentally dubbed Miss Roley Poley, a woman of considerable circumference in her mid-fifties.

Harry followed her eyes. A row of people on horseback, some on ponies, were lurching across the road and picking their way amongst the loose stones. They were making their way towards the cliffs.

'They do this every morning,' explained Miss Roley Poley, smiling at Harry.

He returned her smile. He saw she had a young face enveloped in folds of fat.

'I'd love to go but I'm afraid the poor pony would collapse under my weight!'

He laughed politely. 'It *is* a lovely day for it,' he agreed, thinking how apt her words were. Then he saw the little bus round a corner in the bend of the road, its ancient radiator aimed straight for them. Excitement gnawed at the pit of his stomach. The elderly folk stirred, some standing up from seats, and gathered in a tighter group, laughing and chattering.

Miss Roley Poley regarded them with distaste. 'I'm supposed to be playing Bingo today,' she grimaced. 'I'm over fifty so I qualified for the Golden Years Holiday. What a bore! I thought I'd go to Valletta to escape! Are you going sightseeing?'

He shook his head, smiling. 'I'm waiting for a friend.'

Her face fell. 'Oh, pity. I thought I'd have someone to talk to that wasn't over ninety!'

He laughed, warming to her sense of humour. 'Oh, you'll find lots of red-blooded Maltese men in Valletta who'll pinch your bottom!'

Her stomach shook with humour. 'In my dreams! I have acres to pinch, my dear. But when you've got too much of a good thing nobody wants to know.'

They both laughed as they watched the bus swing round in a U-turn. It drew to a stop next to them, it's motor reverberating and rattling as people began to step out. When Eleanor appeared in the doorway Harry caught his breath. Her slim shapely figure was stunning, her legs revealed all the way up to her short and tight hot-pants out of which her pert little bottom peeped, protruding tantalisingly and, Harry thought involuntarily, just *asking* to be pinched.

'Eleanor!' he gasped. 'You look good enough to eat!'

She smiled coyly at him under the disapproving glare of the elderly folk, Miss Roley Poley included, who began to file past her into the bus.

He took the little bag she was carrying from her and they began to walk towards the apartment in which, he presumed, Anne was still fast asleep. 'Did Max get off all right, then?'

She nodded with a twinkle in her eye. 'He and his buddies left at the break of day.'

'You'll miss him,' he ventured.

'I don't mind,' she smiled, displaying her dimples. 'I think they've got some dolly birds lined up. Max needs time off for fun. He works so hard. Not just for Speedway. He's one of Fenetre's top sales executives, you know. I worry about him sometimes. He really needs to blow off steam. He was up late last night arranging the next leadership seminar with Chuck Halliday.'

'You mean,' Harry began, his steps faltering. 'You know about ...?' He began again. 'You don't mind him having a fling?'

Her crystal laugh tingled down his spine. 'Of course not! I *told* him to find a dolly bird! He can recharge his energy that way. For Max it works like a tonic, do you know what I mean?' She flashed a look of amusement at him out of the corner of her eyes.

'Good grief, you're certainly a remarkable girl, Eleanor,' he said, taking her arm as they negotiated the steep stone steps down to the level of his apartment. The flesh of her upper arm was soft yet resilient and a pulse skittered through him, leaving him with a sense of breathless exhilaration. But the steps were too narrow to walk abreast and he hung back, savouring her sleek thighs and pert bottom all the way down to the door of the apartment.

When they opened the door they found Anne was already dressed in a bulky track-suit and spreading raspberry jam onto some toast. The benefit of an apartment was that it had a self-catering facility, whereas the vouchers provided the flexibility to eat in the hotel. Harry was taken aback by Eleanor's effusive pleasure at seeing Anne, hugging her and planting a kiss on her ruddy cheek. He wished he'd been given the benefit of the same treatment, but then he may have responded all too effusively.

They decided to spend the day visiting the catacombs in Rabat and a prehistoric temple on the coast. If time permitted, they would take a boat trip into the famous Blue Lagoon caves. After a light breakfast Harry collected the keys of his hired car from the hotel reception and they found the car, a natty white Zen built in India, in the main hotel car-park.

The driving was exhilarating. Harry had felt ominous about the driving since so many had warned him that it was hair-raising. At least they drove on the left-hand side of the road, as in Britain. The Guide Book said the locals tended to drive on either side of the road, depending which was the shady side.

'I'm getting the hang of it now,' said Harry, though Eleanor (sitting in the back) was deep in conversation with Anne about a new Speedway nutrition supplement called Nutra-Mins which had the virtue of bringing together a proper balance of vitamins and minerals. ('Do you know what I mean, Anne?' her voice lilted. 'The nutrients you lose by chopping your food are so easily topped up.') Harry smiled, cresting a hill and speeding up towards a traffic circle below. 'All you do is drive like mad, like everyone else, as long as you can see a clear path ahead. It's aiming rather than driving!' He slowed down as he approached the traffic circle until he could see a gap in the flow of the traffic with a clear path through to the turnoff to Mdina, then put his foot down. The little car shot forward, slued round the tight circle and shot out towards the south.

'God, Harry,' objected Anne, clutching her seat and turning towards him. 'You're breaking the rules!'

'No, no,' he laughed, enjoying himself immensely. 'The only rule is not to hit anyone.' He slowed down behind a car sporting L-plates. It slowed as they approached a blind rise with a double barrier line. Just then another car flashed past Harry, overtaking him and drawing parallel with the learner-driver. A second car in hot pursuit flashed past, overtaking the learner-driver as well as the car overtaking it at the same time.

'Shit!' Harry laughed. 'Did you see that! I *told* you there were no rules!'

Eleanor stopped her nattering momentarily. Then she continued: 'The high temperatures used in canning foods can actually destroy vitamins, Anne, do you know what I mean?'

'God, that's a magnificent view of Mdina!' shouted Harry. 'It's like a medieval castle on a mountain!' The car whined upwards towards the ancient city with its honey-hewed walls and rows of arched windows. The spectacular dome and Gothic turrets of St Paul's Cathedral dominated the scene.

Eleanor broke off her chattering for a moment. 'That *is* a magnificent sight, Harry. It will be an energy centre, do you know what I mean?'

The road curved upwards, around Mdina and into the centre of Rabat where they parked the car. In spite of the earlier promise of a nice day it began to drizzle and they were pleased to shelter in the Catacombs of St Paul which once served as a Christian cemetery. It was a honeycomb of tombs, carved coffin holes, receptacles for corpses, a few with slabs on top to cover the now absent bodies. The place was crammed with tourists and they clambered up into a small opening that revealed empty tombs carved in rock. Pressed together and aware of Eleanor's shapely resilient legs, Harry felt it safe to touch her, as if by accident, repeatedly on the soft flesh of her arm, once dropping his arm and sliding his hand down against her naked thigh, like an affectionate contact. She didn't seem to mind, smiled sweetly though never acknowledged or returned the contact or pressure.

'Why aren't there any bodies?' she asked with a little shiver that Harry felt through the gentle contact of his hand on her small waist.

'Well,' Anne pontificated with an air of an expert. 'After so many years there wouldn't be anything left.' Her words echoed through the caverns. 'In any case,' she added self-importantly, 'it's a Christian burial place. It's a happy place.'

'A happy place?' Eleanor wrinkled her nose. 'I don't feel any vibrations here. There's no energy.'

'That's just it, isn't it?' Anne gave a knowing laugh. 'The bodies aren't here anymore. The tombs are empty, like the first empty tomb in Jerusalem. '

Harry looked at the love tables—stone slabs where the living relatives partook of the Eucharist in the presence of their loved ones. The links with Christ were everywhere. 'So you're saying that the dead have been raised and are alive with Christ?'

'Well ...,' Anne tugged her lower lip, shrugging.

'I don't like it here,' said Eleanor, allowing Harry to draw her closer. 'It's claustrophobic. There are no vibrations.'

Harry nodded. 'Let's go back up to the light then,' he said, encircling her compact waist with his right hand and drawing her towards the steps that led upwards. It took all his self-control not to squeeze her. The contact charged him with a flood of energy, his stomach somersaulting giddily with vertigo as she mounted the steps and he felt the sinuous movement of her hips.

The drizzle had stopped when they reached the outside air and they continued on their way to the Neolithic Hagar Qim Temple on the southern coastline of the island. They stopped, in the first instance, for lunch at the Hagar Qim restaurant, taking a seat that overlooked the sea. The sun was out again and the water sparkled, the small uninhabited island of Filfla a focus of attention across the mirror-bright water. Harry ordered black clam shells in an overgrowth of salads while Anne was keen to experience *lapuki*, a fish peculiar to Malta. Eleanor only wanted some cheese with salads, saying that she had an ulcer and didn't really eat meat. The *lapuki* was smothered in fried chips, much to Anne's delight, and she dug in with relish.

'What's it like?' queried Harry, seeing the dark chunky flesh of the fish.

'Try some!' said Anne, chewing, and passing a piece over to him on her knife.

Harry chewed, thoughtfully. 'It's meaty and quite tough, isn't it?' He laughed. 'A fish for the hungry, not the gourmet. It doesn't have the delicate white, layered texture of Carp or Cod. It takes some chewing.'

'It's okay,' returned Anne, chewing contentedly. 'I'm hungry, anyway.'

A short and swarthy Maltese waitress brought them a bottle of white wine, an unlabelled green bottle of a hand-crafted, irregular appearance that looked promising. But it was vinegarish, and the hunt for the tiny olive-sized shellfish was hardly rewarding for a healthy appetite. Harry ordered a slab of pizza and Anne said, 'Make that two, Boy! And with more chips!'

'You're a healthy eater, Anne,' smiled Eleanor, picking at her meagre salad with her fork. She looked down and wrinkled her nose. 'There's snails on this.'

'Did you order snails?' Harry queried and she shook her head, her eyes smiling. He looked closer at her plate and saw live snails trailing through the freshly washed lettuce. 'Oh, God, Eleanor, you can't eat that! I'll order something else.''

She shook her head. 'I've had enough, Harry. I really don't eat that much. I prefer to take nutritional supplements. Speedway has ...'

'Have you got snails on your lettuce, Anne,' Harry interrupted, watching Anne unconcernedly crunch her way through some salads and the last of the *lapuki*.

'What doesn't kill, fattens,' she said, smiling with her mouth full and wiping her plate with a chunk of bread. 'I'm ready for that pizza now.'

Eleanor stood up. 'I'm really not hungry. I think I'll walk over to the temple. You'll find me there.'

'Sure, Eleanor,' said Anne, munching through the first bite of an enormous slab of pepperoni pizza and swilling it down with a swallow of Coke. 'See you later.'

When Eleanor left Anne leaned over and swept the contents of her plate into her own.

'What about the snails?' said Harry, horrified.

She shrugged. 'I told you—what doesn't kill, fattens. It's a saying of my mother's. I don't like to see food wasted. Eleanor eats like a bird!' She pursed her lips, still chewing. 'Anyway, what's the point of paying good money for Speedway nutritional supplements when there's plenty to eat.' She snorted. 'Some people!'

Harry worked through a portion of his anchovy pizza and pushed it aside. 'I think I'll go and check on Eleanor.'

'Running after your girlfriend again, Boy?' she smiled crookedly at him.

'Don't be silly, Anne.'

'Aren't you going to eat the rest of your pizza, then?'

'Help yourself,' he smiled wearily, standing up and pushing back his seat.

Harry strolled across the car park in the bright sunlight to the site of the prehistoric temple. When he entered the enclosure he saw that massive slabs had been placed horizontally to form doorways or portals in the generally rectangular structure of vertical stones. He entered between two enormous vertical stones, wondering about the mystery that drove man to placate his concept of God—for clearly there were altars, heavy horizontal slabs, no doubt for blood sacrifices. The deep azure blue of the sea sparkled through openings and between the heavy sentinels of Hagar Qim. Then he stopped in his tracks, seeing the slight figure of Eleanor lost in thought, seated on one of the altar stones. She looked exquisite with her black bobs and trim figure, her thin T-shirt barely concealing the sharp mounds of her breasts. Yet, somehow, she looked vulnerable, like a child-woman. She seemed to be gazing short-sightedly through a window opening carved in one of the heavy vertical slabs. He walked softly up to her and sat down beside her, following her gaze. The small tabletop island of Filfla was framed in the opening, the sea shimmering and reflecting in a sheet of water that lay on the ground. Without hesitation and quite spontaneously he picked up her hand.

'What are you thinking, Eleanor?'

She spoke without turning towards him or looking at him. 'Harry, this place is so beautiful,' she said in a hushed voice. 'The vibrations are so strong. It's a powerful energy centre.'

He studied her fragile, sharp profile, his own voice low so as not to break the mood. 'It's older than the pyramids. I suppose it's evidence of the physical and spiritual strength of a prehistoric people.' Her hand was limp in his and he brought his other hand over and covered it so that her hand was enveloped gently in both of his. He followed her eyes again, resting on the distant uninhabited island. 'I suppose the place makes one ask the timeless questions—about the meaning of existence.'

She nodded almost imperceptibly. 'Yes,' she whispered. 'It's a sacred place, Harry. There's an energy field here that makes me feel stronger, do you know what I mean? It's a place where you can receive energy from a higher source.'

'The source of the universe you spoke about that night at the hotel?'

'Yes,' she smiled, nodding, her fingers twitching just perceptibly in his. 'You can tap into it here. I was feeling weak and claustrophobic in the catacombs, but here the vibrations are making me feel strong again. It's sort of like—' Her cheeks dimpled, her eyes still straight ahead. 'Like feeling cosmic, do you know what I mean?'

'I think so,' he nodded. 'You mean because you're responding to it's beauty.'

She nodded. 'The sea, and that island, has a bright aura.' Then for the first time she turned her eyes towards him. Her deep blue eyes were penetrating. 'Harry, I have an energy compatibility with this place, do you know what I mean? Can you feel it?'

He pressed her hand slightly. 'Yes,' he smiled. 'Oh yes.'

She turned her eyes back to the island. 'My energy is more focused. I can feel how my energy is increasing, and my aura. I feel open. You have to open, to connect, to ... to use your sense of beauty and ... and fill up.' She turned and smiled at him again.

'And then you feel love, don't you?' he asked softly. 'When you're filled up?'

Her smile broadened, her eyes deep in his. 'You can feel it too, can't you? I can see that you do—in your eyes. You're transmitting love-energy back—to this place.'

He wanted to say, I'm transmitting it back to you, but didn't dare. He wanted to draw her closer and touch those enchanting eyes of hers with his lips. Instead, he said, 'It's a kind of ... of euphoric connection with...'

'With everything,' she completed the sentence. 'So it makes you feel stronger.'

He looked down at her hand which he still held. Somehow he felt her vulnerability and his exploitation of her trust in him. He ran his free hand gently over her hand, seeing how perfect and fragile it was, how the thin blue veins stood out on it. 'But you don't eat enough, Eleanor. Look at these veins in your hand. You want to build up your physical strength more.'

She smiled coyly. 'You'll be telling me I'm a scarecrow next.'

He looked up and connected with her eyes again. His voice trembled. 'You're beautiful, Eleanor. I think you're beautiful.'

Her cheeks dimpled and she made no attempt to draw away her hand. 'Like Anne. She's beautiful, too, Harry. I think you're both beautiful people.'

It broke the spell. He let go her hand and turned in time to see Anne striding towards them. She strode purposefully, like a man, swinging her arms. Her track suit, bulging and bulky, made her stomach look larger than normal, the material of the legs bulging out and drawn in at the ankles. Once again, Harry thought, she looked like a Michelin man. Her mouth looked small, like a rabbit's, dwarfed by her plump cheeks.

'You two look like you're waiting for a bus!' Anne gave a raucous laugh.

Eleanor stood up and took Anne's hand. 'This is a magical place, Anne. Come with me and I'll show you some of the energy spots I've found.'

Harry watched them as they walked through a monolithic archway, hand in hand. He thought with irony, Eleanor was more demonstrative towards Anne than towards him. He recalled her limp hand in his. Only once was there a slight response, or had he just imagined it?

He remained seated and looked back towards Filfla, trying to recapture the magic aura he'd felt with her. Was Filfla a sacred island, he wondered? He knew that both Malta and Gozo had been sacred islands in prehistoric times. Pilgrimages were made to the megalithic temples to commune with a goddess, probably the Great Earth Mother, symbol of fertility. But instead of strength he succumbed to a sense of frustration. He stared across the sparkling sea to Filfla, yearning for an escape, a release from his frustration. A great yearning grew in his soul. The people being sacrificed on the altar upon which he was sitting would have seen the same view, he thought. It would have been their last and final view. Was it a window of hope, an opening to a new life? He yearned for escape, to Filfla or some distant island where he could live with Eleanor, far away from Anne or Max or pathetic guests or posturing academics. But a residue of depression settled in his stomach like indigestion. Somehow he doubted Eleanor would ever respond to him, let alone want to live with him.

In the end, he thought, every person was an island.

CHAPTER 19

Pooled Resources

THE DINING ROOM of the Golden Bay Hotel operated on a self-service basis. Perhaps because it was the winter season which allowed reduced rates for long stays at the hotel, the dining room was crammed with retired people escaping the cold of Britain. Harry and Anne—and Eleanor, as their guest— had to join a long queue for the evening soup and choice of main courses—excellent in quantity but not, Harry apologised to Eleanor, in quality. It was too bad that she was a near-vegetarian and didn't fancy the snails of the salad—an item the hotel fare shared with that of the Hagar Qim restaurant. When they settled around their table there was much by way of entertainment, if watching fellow diners was to one's liking. As was the case with Miss Roley-Poley, Harry gave other guests their special names and elicited some smiles and dimples from Eleanor when he pointed them out.

'That's Mr Wobbly-man,' he said, topping up everyone's glass of wine and seeing a man who wobbled to his table, two overloaded plates in each hand, beaming in anticipation of the meal and navigating carefully as he swayed amongst the tables. His skittle-shaped body gave him the wobble. His white hair was all he had in common with his wife, a scarecrow with a loud cackle. They beamed together at a table occupied by Miss Hair.

'Do you see Miss Hair?' Harry asked, sipping his wine and eliciting another indulgent smile from Eleanor. Miss Hair's crowning glory was her abundance of auburn hair, either falling in sumptuous waves down her ample shoulders, or tied back in a bundle behind her. Her freckled face was amiable and inviting and much admired by the Head Chef who spent long moments bent over her upturned visage in animated conversation, his tall hat bobbing. She was a handsome woman, younger than the rest, and walked with erect pride to replenish her plate, starched pointed breasts well in advance of her but unfortunately dwarfed by the ample stomach that stuck out further.

'Then there's Uncle Jess,' Harry said, nodding towards a moustached military gentleman whom they could hear expounding a point with telling authority: *'It's as simple as that!'* Uncle Jess banged his table, turning all heads towards him. *'And that's just the point!'* They never did catch the point, but Harry was to find out that he made it every evening.

'And look,' Harry smiled, 'There's the Odd Family!' Eleanor drank some more wine and giggled as her attention was directed towards the stocky side-burned father with his towering, lanky wife with short-cropped blonde hair who was always accompanied by a small energetic son whose face was a carbon copy of his mother's; close by was their mini-skirted teenage daughter, disproportionately large with huge thighs that rolled over each other as she walked.

'Oh, and there's Miss Pimms, my favourite person!' exclaimed Harry, seeing an elegant and slim grey-haired woman, immaculate and delicate in a long skirt. Her double-chinned husband loomed over her. 'Something from the bar?' his voice gravelled, and 'Pimms, please!' came her pert reply, her blue eyes sparkling.

'You're being ridiculous, Harry, giving people names!' Anne scolded, draining her glass of wine. 'They can't help the way they look. I wonder what you call me behind my back?'

Michelin woman, he thought without hesitation, smiling innocently.

'And what would you call *me*, Harry?' Eleanor asked, smiling sweetly over the brim of her glass.

'I'll have to think about that,' he grinned and topped up everyone's wine. A much better name than Snookums, he thought scornfully. Names flashed through his mind. *Super-girl, Fairy Queen, Miss Sweetness, Miss Exquisitely Delicious, Sexipants, Miss Titillating Tantalus, La Belle Dame Sans Merci.* 'Miss Crystal Blue Eyes,' he said lamely, taking a running gulp at his wine so that he all but finished it off at once.

'Mrs Blue Eyes,' corrected Anne, snorting into her wine. 'She's married, or haven't you noticed, Boy?' She pushed out

her chair with a rasping noise. 'I'm going for a refill. Can I get you anything, Eleanor?'

'I'll come too,' Eleanor smiled up at her, putting down her glass and rising from her seat. 'I'll just get a little jelly.'

Harry watched them as they weaved amongst the tables, Anne still bulky and squat in her track-suit, Eleanor with a sarong which, wrapped round her waist, decorously concealed her sleek legs and hotpants. Whereas Anne strode with heavy masculine strides, swinging her arms, her buttocks bunching and quivering, Eleanor walked like a model on a catwalk, her slim shoulders, waist and bottom swaying and undulating sensually, a sinuous and flowing movement which recalled to mind the gliding adder that had so enchanted him the day before.

He was still basking in the elation of the day's events since they had left the Hagar Qim temple. They had made their way further down the coast to the Blue Grotto caves where they joined a small boat with other sightseers, lurching and bobbing on the open sea. The lurching motion had given him the excuse to place a steadying hand on Eleanor's smooth thigh and she had made no objection. When they entered the magic world of the sea cave that mirrored the brilliant phosphorescent colours of underwater flora, the awe and rapture evoked by the incandescent and sublime beauty seemed a natural inspiration for his hand to slip down affectionately to the soft silken flesh of her calves. Again, she made no objection as he stroked them, her attention absorbed by the way her own hand turned the same colour of the iridescent water when submerged.

Then, after another hectic and exhilarating drive back to the hotel complex, they all tested the limpid water of the heated indoor pool. There was no-one else about and Anne had returned to the changing room, leaving Eleanor and Harry alone while they still sat and chatted on the edge of the pool. Eleanor had returned to a previous topic, expressing the need for sexual experimentation and novelty if a healthy relationship were to be maintained. The topic seemed to invite a natural pressure of his hand on her thigh. She wore a skimpy chocolate-brown bikini and the delicate texture of her skin was exquisite.

'You've got beautiful legs, Eleanor,' he had smiled daringly, running the palm of his hand gently up and down her thigh. His throat was quite dry with excitement.

She had ignored his remark, pursuing her argument in her musical voice. 'The point is, though, an older couple's relationship can be revitalised by the introduction of a younger person or persons, in a mutual sharing of auras. Do you know what I mean, Harry?'

He nodded, still stroking her thigh, feeling more turned onto her than ever. She was making no objection to his contact. 'But what you said about different positions in lovemaking. I'm afraid Anne and I have never ventured from the missionary position.' He was becoming bolder in what he dared say, congratulating himself that their relationship that day had progressed by leaps and bounds.

'Oh, but you *must* experiment, Harry!' she told him. 'You owe it to Anne, do you know what I mean? Otherwise your relationship will become boring and stultifying. Max and I realised that very quickly.' She giggled. 'We do it standing up and from behind.' She stood up, much to Harry's disappointment. 'You should read the *Kama Sutra!*' she said, picking up her towel.

'I don't think it's possible, doing it standing up,' he said, standing up. He took her hand and drew her gently to the wall. 'Do you think we would fit together, if we did it?'

She smiled coyly, her back against the wall. He pressed himself against her, lightly, his heart palpitating at the delicate touch of the whole length of her small lithe body against his. 'Do you think it would work?' he laughed, his mouth dry, his eyes on the doorway where Anne might at any moment appear.

'I don't see why not, Harry. You're a little tall, I suppose. Try it with Anne next time.'

'She's even shorter than you,' he giggled. He bent his knees and held her compact hips, pressing her against him, to see how well their bodies correlated. But the embarrassment and fear of Anne seeing him overcame his lust and he drew away, laughing awkwardly. 'Well, I'll have to follow your advice with Anne then, won't I?'

She had smiled sweetly at him, just as Anne strode out, still towelling her hair. 'Aren't you two going to get dressed!' she said. 'Hurry, or we won't get a good place in the supper queue.'

His mind came back to the present, seeing the two girls weave their way back towards him, each with a plate. He smiled up at Eleanor as she approached, aware of the bouncy resilience of her young breasts under the thin T-shirt. 'I thought I'd go back for another swim,' he grinned. 'That heated water was delicious.'

'Good idea!' Anne agreed in her raucous voice. 'You go down if you like, Boy. I'll join you later.'

He stood up, the room tilting a little under the influence of the heady wine he had imbibed. He smiled and left them, making his way a little unsteadily to his apartment where he changed back into his still wet costume. When he reached the heated pool in the now dimly-lit enclosure he was pleased to find no-one else there. He felt the warm and wet embrace of the water as he slipped into it, his body still numb from the wine. He slipped off his costume and crunched it up, wrapping it in his towel that lay by the side. He grinned to himself, hoping Eleanor would be the first to come down. His desire for her reached out hard and firm from between his legs, but his heart sank when Anne's stumpy body waddled in, bulging under her wet red one-piece costume.

'Where's Eleanor?' he asked.

'Still changing,' she said as she lowered her rotund body into the water. 'God, it's like warm blood,' she laughed, wading towards him. She came up to him, her cheeks more flushed than usual on account of the wine. She came into contact with his erection. 'God, Boy, you've got nothing on!'

'Why don't you slip out of this too?' he said encouragingly, pushing the straps of her costume off her shoulders. If they were both naked, he thought, Eleanor might follow their example. The thought was delicious and maintained his erection.

'God, you've got a *muckle een*, Boy!' she said, feeling his erection with her hand. 'Someone might come!'

'No they won't,' he said. 'They're all be playing Bingo, or going to the old-time dancing.'

'But Eleanor ...'

'If you hurry we can have a quick one before she comes,' he leered. 'It's delicious, under the water. Eleanor keeps telling us to try new ways, anyway.' He pushed down her costume further, making her squidgy breasts flow out.

'God, you *are* naughty tonight, Boy,' she giggled, stepping clumsily out of the costume underwater. 'I thought you were going off me!'

In spite of her rotundity she was buoyant in the water and Harry lifted her easily, manipulating her towards the side of the pool in the deeper end. She hung onto the side with her outstretched arms, grinning down at his bopping head. He splayed her thick thighs and sank into her effortlessly, his erection planted deep inside her generous and sumptuously wet interior.

'God, Boy,' she sighed, 'I really thought you were going off me!' Her grin twisted at him. He thrust into her a few times, hanging onto the side of the pool against her, one eye watching out for Eleanor. The anticipation of seeing her kept him firm and hard in Anne.

'Come on, Boy, Eleanor will come any moment,' Anne panted. 'We'd better stop.'

But Eleanor had already entered the enclosure. 'Halloo?' her musical voice called out. Harry looked up and his heart beat wildly. She looked irresistible in her almost non-existent bikini, the bellybutton in her flat stomach like another dimple.

'It's okay,' he whispered to Anne. 'Just stay underwater. She won't mind.' Then he called out to Eleanor: 'Won't you join us, Eleanor?'

He saw her come up to the side and glance at Anne's wet abandoned costume next to his towel. She smiled mischievously down at them, her cheeks dimpling, her head tilted to one side. 'Is that an invitation?' she said softly.

'Sure is,' Harry grinned up at her. He was still rooted into Anne and crazy with desire for Eleanor.

He watched her, breathlessly, as she tucked her arms back and neatly untied her bikini top. He tried his best to make out her small supple breasts as she bent down and stepped out of her bikini bottom. Then she slipped into the shallow end, surging into the water towards them. He broke loose instinctively from

Anne and swam towards her, touching her bare bottom as he swam past her. Anne followed him and for a while it was a game, chasing Eleanor as she swam, giggling, across the pool and back again. Both he and Anne caught up with her in the shallow end where she stood, waiting for them, allowing Harry to stop and settle in front of her. She smiled sweetly at both of them and her body was like a magnet to Harry. His arms slid round her lithe body instinctively, drawing her sinuous naked figure against his. The sensation was too delicious to control and his hands slipped down to her buttocks, squeezing their firm resilience, then, with a life of its own, one hand slid between her buttocks. The surprise was exquisite when his finger slipped effortlessly and deep into her moist velvet crevice which opened so unexpectedly to his touch.

He heard her mouth open with a glutinous snap followed by the sharp intake of her breath. He felt her body go limp against his in a swoon, her soft moan like music in his ears. He bent his head down to her upturned face and sank his lips onto hers. Her mouth opened under the slightest pressure, her thin delicate lips sliding sinuously, wetly against his. It transported him into a heavenly dimension and he became dimly aware of Anne's presence still there and the need to placate her. He reached out with his left hand, slid it down her spongy buttocks, managing to hook his finger into her damp interior. He held both women in a mutual embrace, one a token embrace, the other real and unspeakably intoxicating. His tongue and his finger were exploring her and he felt her lithe body quivering, one of her hands on Anne's arm which she pummelled frantically.

His desire for Eleanor became urgent and he moved his hand around to the front of her, feeling the soft pubic hair between her thighs, then sliding his finger back into her. The angle of his arm was awkward and he bent his knees, trying desperately to gain entry with his firm erection. He fumbled again and again, suddenly hot with frustration, confused as to why he couldn't sink in and desperate to feel the soft embrace of her femininity, to consummate his urgent love for her.

It ended when Anne broke away. 'I'm cold,' she said gruffly, and pulled herself out of the pool. Eleanor moved away, following her direction. Harry caught up with her again while she was in the act of lifting herself backwards out of the water, so that she still faced him. He was drunk with desire for her and still gave a half-hearted attempt to slide in his penis.

'No, I don't like it that way,' she said simply, pulling herself out of the water.

His disappointment was immense but his heart was still racing with hope. 'Shall we continue this in the apartment?' he asked hoarsely.

'Okay,' she said softly, giving him a half-smile.

They wrapped their towels around themselves in silence and followed Anne who had already gone on ahead to the apartment.

They entered the front door of the apartment and he found Anne in their bedroom about to get dressed. He went up to her and kissed her. 'Can I bring Eleanor in here so we can finish what we began, please Anne?' he begged.

She sighed. 'If you must—I suppose.'

He raced back down the little passage and took Eleanor's hand. 'Come,' he said simply. She took his hand and followed him willingly into the bedroom. He switched off the light as he went in and darkness covered them. He drew her next to Anne and they stood together in a huddle next to the bed. He put his arm round both women, once again, and felt for Eleanor's lips. Once again her mouth opened readily under the pressure of his own, and he was aware of light fingers gently around his swollen penis.

Anne broke away, wordlessly, and rushed out of the room, the light flooding in from the passage. Her sudden departure stunned them both.

'Oh dear, she couldn't take it, Harry,' came Eleanor's small voice. She went to the door and Harry followed her, exasperated. His heart thumped high in his chest.

There was no sign of Anne, but then they heard the car outside start and drive away quickly. They were still both naked as they opened the front door, just in time to see the glow of the red lights of the small Zen rushing away and up the length of road that led to Mosta and beyond.

They both came back in, Eleanor looking anxious. She picked up a towel and wrapped it around her. 'Will she be all right, Harry? Do you think we should get help for someone to go after her?'

He shook his head. 'She'll cool off, Eleanor. She'll be back.' He looked at her, wondering what to do, still wanting her desperately. He was so desperately unhappy with Anne. He would make a clean breast of it to Eleanor. Then she would understand. He wanted to exclude Anne, not hang on to her.

'Look, Eleanor,' he said, coming up to her and touching her arm. 'The truth is ...' He took a deep breath. 'The truth is I don't love Anne anymore. It's been on the cards for some time now. I ...' He hadn't formulated the thought that was often in his mind, and now he made a decision. 'I'm going to get a divorce, anyway.'

Eleanor looked horrified. 'A divorce?'

'Yes,' he said. It was as though a weight had lifted from his shoulders and he smiled. 'So you see, there's nothing to stop me...' He tried to slip the towel off her. 'Can we please make love, Eleanor? I ...I love you, and I want you terribly.'

She drew back, pulling the towel back tightly. She spoke firmly, reprimanding him. 'No, Harry. I wouldn't do anything behind Anne's back. I'd never have come between you if I knew you two were breaking up. I was prepared to share with you both, to let our auras mingle, to ... to revitalise one another.' She shook her head when he tried to approach her again. 'No, Harry.'

He stood there in the glare of the electric light, naked and humiliated. He watched her pick up her clothes and dress quickly. He found his towel and wrapped it round himself, feeling empty. Everything that a moment ago seemed so nearly in his grasp had slipped away, forever. He sat down on a sofa and watched her. She sat down on the opposite side of the room, as far away from him as she could.

'I hope Anne comes back soon,' she said with concern. She still wore her hot-pants and her bare, tempting legs mocked him with their sexual magnetism.

He sighed. 'I'd better get dressed,' he said disconsolately, and went into the bedroom.

When he came back he made them both a cup of coffee from the hospitality tray and they waited in silence.

It wasn't long before they heard the whine of the Zen as it pulled back into the parking space next to the apartment. Anne came in, ruddy-cheeked, her face under a dark cloud, still wearing the gown that she had hastily drawn on before racing for the car. She slumped into a chair, not looking at either of them. She glowered at the carpet in front of her.

Eleanor went to her and crouched on the carpet by her feet. She put her hands on her knees. Her voice was soft and contrite. 'Oh, Anne, I'm so sorry. I didn't mean to upset you.'

Anne flashed an angry glance at her, averting her eyes back to the carpet. She pursed her lips and nodded at the carpet, meditatively. She snorted.

'Anne,' Eleanor went on in a pleading voice. 'When you left, Harry still wanted to make love to me. I told him no—that I wouldn't do that behind your back.'

Anne pushed her bottom lip up still further, nodding gloomily at the carpet. 'Oh, that's *great!* That's just bloody *great!*'

'Anne?' Eleanor's small musical voice still pleaded. 'Will you forgive me, Anne?'

Anne nodded contemptuously at the carpet.

'So can we still be friends, Anne? Can I still come and visit, when we're back in Scotland?'

Once again Anne nodded contemptuously at the carpet, her eyes still averted from Eleanor and from Harry.

Harry felt sick, deep down in his stomach. He went into the bedroom and closed the door behind him. He lay on the bed and wept.

CHAPTER 20

Where No Birds Sing

'**B**OY?' Anne opened the door to the bedroom and came in. The lights were off and she crept nearer to the bed where he lay. 'I'm just going to see Eleanor off on the bus to Valletta. She's decided to go back tonight.'

He was silent. It had been more or less decided that a bed would be made up for her in their apartment and that she would return the next day. It was as though he'd lost Eleanor for good. 'Anne?' he said softly.

'Yes?'

He took a deep breath. 'Do me a favour. Please tell Eleanor that I don't love her. Tell her I know now it was just infatuation and that I got carried away. Apologise to her for me.'

She was silent for a moment. 'I'll tell her,' she said, her voice softening.

He heard them leave and the front door shut. He walked over to the dressing table and switched on the light, seeing his haggard expression in the mirror. He remembered the Speedway woman's exhortation to look at his expression in the mirror and tell himself he could have anything he wanted. The memory mocked him and the face that stared back at him mocked him. 'I hate you, you bloody fuck!' he spat. A wave of emotion hit him again and once again he collapsed, anguished, wanting Eleanor desperately. He couldn't shake the picture of her deep blue eyes from his mind. Everything about her moved him. Her jet black hair and the neat bobs, the fringe above those dreamy eyes, her perfect lithe body which he felt again against his own. She seemed to open so readily to him, and yet she was like the petals of a rose that closed as soon as he reached out to it. She seemed to promise but never delivered. But the voice of her eyes had penetrated deep into his soul, into the raw nerves of his being. She was just like Keats's *Belle sans merci*, he thought, with her wild eyes and the soft petals of a mouth that 'made sweet moan' when his finger slipped into her. He wanted to shut her wild eyes with his kisses, but her response was always conditional—always conditional that Anne was part of the union! Without Anne there could be no consummation! She always seemed to be drawing in Anne when he reached out for her. So Anne was the key! Dammit, he thought, surely she didn't harbour a lesbian attraction for Anne!

His mind went over and over the excruciatingly delicious moments in the pool. So near and yet so far! He felt her firm naked body against him again, heard that magical gasp as she swooned against him, and those kisses that transported him! He closed his eyes and closed his hand around his erect penis and pumped it, trying to pump his lust for Eleanor out of his system. He needed desperately to be free of her, to find a release from his obsession for her. He pumped and yearned for her, until his orgasm came in a hot flush, globs of white semen oozing over and through his fingers, making them sticky and glutinous. He opened his eyes, depressed, empty and drained. He collapsed into a bundle on the floor and began to weep again, shaking. 'Eleanor, Eleanor, oh shit, Eleanor, I love you...'

His throat felt strained and painful from the tight constriction of his desolation. He picked up his towel that still lay nearby and wiped away the traces of his semen. Then he got into his pyjamas and climbed into bed, pulling himself into a foetal position. He tried to clear his mind and find oblivion in sleep.

Sleep wouldn't come because he couldn't stop his mind working, resurrecting images of Eleanor. He remembered sitting on the prehistoric stone altar staring with her through the stone window at Filfla, holding her delicate hand in his. He had seemed so near to her then, talking about energy flows. Could he ever find another woman who evoked feelings as strongly as Eleanor? But there was Anne, too. There was always Anne, down at mouth, frumpy, ruddy faced, totally lacking in glamour. Anne, who had no aura, he thought bitterly.

He heard the door open and Anne walked in. He closed his eyes and pretended to be asleep.

'Eleanor was concerned about you, Boy,' she said, kicking off her shoes and climbing into bed in all her naked glory. Oh

God, he thought, squeezing his eyes shut, it's Michelin woman herself. He felt the bed sag as she settled in. 'She wondered why you didn't come with us to see her off on the bus,' she grunted.

He opened his eyes, staring at the opposite wall. Did Eleanor really care? 'Did you tell her I didn't really love her?' he asked. 'Did you explain?' The only hope, he thought, of hanging onto Eleanor was to make her think he didn't love her. Then she might accept him as a package deal—with Anne. A non-emotional involvement.

Anne gave a sympathetic laugh. The tone of her voice softened, like a mother reassuring a child. 'I told her, Boy. And she said *of course* she knew you didn't love her! She's not that stupid, after all. She said you were just sexually overcharged. She said I was to reassure you she understood.' She shook her head and gave a hollow laugh. 'Do you know what she said then? She said I should find you a dolly-bird, and ...' She snorted. 'This takes the cake, Boy! She said could I please help her out with Max? Can you credit that? She wants me to let Max have his way with me! So *she* can have a break!' The bed shook with her silent laughter. 'Give me a break, is all I can say!'

Harry still regarded the opposite wall. 'Couldn't you, Anne? It would help if you could.'

'Let Max screw me! Harry, I *couldn't*! I *couldn't*! I think he's course and common!' She sniffed, near to tears.

'He's very good with women, Anne. He told me so himself. You'll have the time of your life. You should try him.'

'Is that so you can screw Eleanor?'

He nodded.

'But I thought you said you didn't love her?' she whined.

'No—but ...' He sighed. 'Never mind. Let's just forget it.' He closed his eyes.

The silence lengthened between them.

'Harry?' she said, a note of despair in her voice.

He remained silent.

'Don't close up on me, Boy.'

'I don't want to talk about it.'

'Harry!' she pleaded, close to tears.

He squeezed his eyes shut. He hated himself for what he was doing to her, but he couldn't go on living a lie. He only felt pity for her.

He felt her get out of bed. She came round to his side of the bed and knelt down on the floor, next to him. She stuck her hand under the sheet and placed it on his knee. He opened his eyes, seeing her beseeching eyes on him, seeking out his own eyes. Then she moved her hand up his thigh, enclosing his testicles and his penis with her kneading fingers.

'I don't want it now, Anne,' he said, gritting his teeth.

But she ignored him, her beseeching eyes still on him, her little rabbit mouth hanging open, pitifully, in her podgy face. Her hand encircled his penis and began to milk it, as one would milk the teat of a cow. In spite of himself Harry felt the warmth of his erection returning, betraying him.

'I don't want it, Anne.'

But he didn't pull away, trapped by the returning desire. He channelled it into a renewed lust for Eleanor, thinking of her mystical blue eyes and trim naked body, hearing again the sweet moan which he crushed with his lips.

He tore out of bed and buried his face into Anne's ample, soft sagging breasts. He scooped them up into his hand and stuffed the flaccid nipples into his mouth, one at a time, sucking for all he was worth. She encircled his head with her stubby arms and crooned, resting her head on his. 'I've *found* you again, my boy! I've found you! Oh yes! Oh yes! Just suck me all you want!'

He sucked fervently, like a glutton swallowing milk. Then he pushed her back and splayed her thick thighs, burying his erection in her to the hilt, thrusting urgently and desperately. 'That's right, my boy,' he heard her cooing, panting with him. 'Take me. I'm here for you—just for you!'

He closed his eyes, thinking of Eleanor. He heard Eleanor's sweet moan and felt his dormant orgasm stir unwillingly, hesitantly. He focused his mind on her sleek legs and the way her trim buttocks peeped out of the hotpants and his orgasm rose higher, fluttering. He imagined her naked thighs splayed out for him, opening like a petal for him, and his orgasm shot into Anne, shuddering, draining him, emptying him.

Anne sighed. 'Oh yes, Boy. Oh yes. You can't tell me you don't love me.'

Afterwards he lay panting on the bed, closing his mind to Anne. But she was sitting up in bed and talking—talking at him rather than to him, smoking a cigarette and filling the room with smoke. 'You must appreciate, Boy, that I have feelings, too, hey?' She tried to soften her voice and sound reasonable. 'Can you imagine how I felt when Eleanor told me you still wanted to screw her after I ran out? You must admit that *that* was a bit thick, hey Boy?' She cooed, ruffling his hair. 'He-e-ey?' she drew out the word, as though talking to a baby. 'And when you were feeling her in the pool. She was kneading my arm like she was out of her mind! How do you think that made me feel? I had no idea what was happening down there, you see—whether you were inside her or not. All I knew was that your finger in me had stopped moving. I wouldn't have minded quite so much if you hadn't forgotten about me. How do you think I felt, he-e-ey?' She continued to play with his hair.

He remained silent, trying not to hear.

'Harry, why don't you talk to me?'

He sighed. 'You wouldn't understand, Anne. You couldn't. The problem is with me, anyway.'

'Try me, Boy.' She stroked his hair.

He took a deep breath. 'Well, the horrible truth is that I can't get Eleanor out of my system. I think about her all the time. She's bewitched me. I only wish I could get her out of my system, so I don't have to think about her.' He gritted his teeth and took the plunge. 'I just want her so badly.'

Her fingers continued to twirl his hair. She spoke simperingly, as though to a baby. 'Now that wasn't so bad was it, he-e-ey, my boy? Maybe I can help you to get her out of your system. What do you think it would take?'

He opened his eyes, staring at the wall again. He never thought she'd be so reasonable. 'I don't know. Maybe if we all slept together.'

'I don't think I could stand having you have sex with her, Boy. But I'm willing to try being in bed with both of you, if you made love to me and not her. Do you know what I mean?' She sniggered. 'Oh, God, now I'm beginning to sound like her!'

He laughed, in spite of himself. 'You're so reasonable, Anne. I just wish I could get over this.'

She bent over and kissed his cheek. 'I'll do whatever it takes to keep you, Boy. But just don't put your *muckle een* into her. And don't ask me to sleep with Max.'

The next morning they walked hand in hand round the back of the hotel, climbing until they reached the edge of the cliffs. Then they turned and walked along the rocky path, following the cliffs northward, in the direction of Gozo. It was a clear morning with a blue sky and an azure sea over which the sunlight sparkled. The champagne air was fresh and invigorating and only a slight breeze kissed their foreheads. Landwards a row of horses carrying the early riders picked their way amongst the stones of a different path.

In spite of the exhilarating morning, Harry couldn't shake the previous night's depression. Anne strolled with a rolling gait beside him, her hand clamped on his like a gaoler. He stopped and looked seawards towards the North African coastline which was beyond the horizon.

'Something's strange,' he said, listening.

'What is?'

'It's so quiet. It's too quiet. You'd think you'd hear bird's singing, on a morning like this. I don't even hear seagulls.'

Just then the air was punctuated by a gunshot.

'What was that?' she asked, looking round.

'A car backfiring, I guess.' He searched the landscape. 'I can see a couple of old bangers. Look, there's an old Morris Minor stuck up on that ridge. And further on there's an ancient Landrover.'

'Why are the cars so old here?' she squinted, looking at them.

'For one thing, there's not much rain. So there's not much rust.' He shrugged. 'I don't suppose there's much use for fast modern cars on a small island.'

They walked on and they saw a number of small enclosures crudely built with small stones. 'They look like miniature fortresses,' Harry said. They entered one and saw the remains of sandwiches and an empty beer tin. Then he noticed a number of spent cartridges on the sandy floor. 'Someone's been shooting here.'

Then they continued their way along the cliffs. Another car backfired in the distance. Harry stopped, his heart too heavy to continue. 'I don't know if I can go on, Anne.,' he said softly.

'Why not? Does your leg hurt, Boy?' She looked up at him with concern.

He shook his head with a sad smile. 'That business with Eleanor yesterday. I'm afraid it's all brought it home to me. It's not fair on you, I know, but I just can't go on.' He felt her hand tighten on his.

'But I thought we thrashed that out, Boy? I understand your infatuation for her. I'm trying to, anyway. I'll help as far as I can.' She looked across the sea and bit her lip. Another car backfired.

'I appreciate that, Anne. Yet it only makes me feel worse. I'm living a lie, you see. In a sense we'd be using Eleanor to whip up something in me that's already died.'

'So what are you saying, Boy?'

He took a deep breath, also looking out to sea. In the distance a small fishing boat bobbed on the sea. 'I'm saying I'm not in-love with you anymore.'

She was silent. She drew her hand away from his and slowly trudged along the path, alone. She came abreast with another small fortress and leant on the stone wall, wearily. He pitied her, seeing her fat masculine legs that bulged from her shorts. He came up to her and touched her cheek, brushing away a strand of lifeless hair. 'I still ... love you, I suppose. But I'm not *in*-love, if you know what I mean.'

She still said nothing and the silence built up between them. There was another explosion, much closer this time. Then they heard a sparrow, or a tiny bird, frantically fluttering. They turned and saw, quite close, a small bird bopping and twittering desperately in a tiny hand-wrought wire cage perched on a mound of small stones. Harry lifted his eyes and saw a pair of beady eyes in a leathery wind-beaten face peering at him from inside another of those small stone fortresses. He hadn't noticed the man before, or the caged bird.

'They're hunting birds,' he said, surprised. 'Those weren't cars backfiring. They were rifles.'

Anne pursed her lip. 'Poor little creatures. No wonder the birds don't sing in Malta.'

As they continued their walk, no longer holding hands, they spied many stone fortresses or 'hides,' almost every one surmounted by a sunburnt face with a cap peering at them. Invariably there was a crude wire cage nearby with a tiny bird trapped.

When Harry stopped to lean against a rock he felt Anne's hand slide back into his.

'Harry,' she said resolutely, 'I'm not going to give up. I'm not going to let you go. I'll even tolerate Eleanor, for your sake, until you get over her. What more can you ask?'

Another gunshot punctuated the silence that followed. A nearby cage fluttered.

He looked at her, desperately sorry for her. He had to swallow to ease his throat. 'I'd be using you as a decoy to attract Eleanor. She'll only share her aura, as she calls it, with both of us.' He smiled thinly. 'She probably even fancies you.'

She surveyed the sea, but flashed a sidelong glance at him. 'I don't mind being your decoy, Boy. Just don't think you can get rid of me.'

'But why would you want to stay with me, when I treat you like a decoy?'

Her lips pursed into a smile. 'Because I love you.'

They watched a pleasure cruiser come into view from the south, heading towards Gozo. It edged smoothly forward across the rippled water, leaving a wake behind it that looked like a thin line drawn with a ruler through the water. There was something captivating in its purposeful movement and they watched it in silence until it disappeared behind the cliffs to the north.

Then they turned and began to amble back along the cliffs, hand in hand, as before. Anne broke the silence. 'It wasn't all your fault, anyway, Boy.'

'About what?' He looked down at her dumpy figure.

'About what happened in the pool and afterwards. While we were waiting for the bus Eleanor blamed it on the fact that she was missing Max.'

Harry's eyes widened. 'But he was only away for a day—and she seemed pleased about his...' He shook his head. 'She was happy for him to find a dolly bird!' He gave a laugh. 'And she told *you* to find me a dolly bird, to give her a break from him! I think she's mixed up!'

She snorted. 'I'm glad you've noticed, Boy. She also said what happened was because we were touching her so much all day and it had turned her on. She's crazy. I never touched her! Did you, before the pool thing?'

Harry shook his head, confused. 'She's crazy!' he said defensively.

They went by another stone fortress in which they saw a man skulking.

'It's terrible,' Anne hissed. 'The way they lie in wait for poor unsuspecting little birds. They're like spiders and the caged birds are like bait. I suppose it satisfies their hunting instinct.' She snorted. 'Men can be so cruel.'

'Yes, I know,' he said, with a stab of guilt.

CHAPTER 21

Staying Centred

IT WAS ALMOST mid-February and a few days after Harry and Anne had returned from Malta. The sky was dull and overcast, the air wintry and biting as Harry ambled slowly along a narrow lane that led across the sloping hillside that overlooked Jedburgh. An occasional snowflake drifted above the hedgerows, the chilling wind seeming to pass through him, too lazy to blow round him. In a gap of the hedgerow a blackbird with ruffled feathers lolloped soundlessly.

He recalled his last walk alone in Malta, on the hillside where no birds sang, overlooking the sea on the last gusty day. He had seemed to make no progress in his hopeless marriage to Anne. He had allowed himself all too easily to slip back into a parody or pretence of love, through pity or guilt, he wasn't sure. He had stood there, looking out across a seamless sea, handcuffed by his pity for one woman and his infatuation for another. It seemed to him that if he discarded the one he would lose the other. Then, as now, he was like Keats's knight palely loitering on a cold hillside, so unlike the Knights of St John who were men of faith and action.

At the crest of the hill he paused. He gazed across the glen. The walled paddock of the cemetery jigsawed into the slanting slope of fields. It was bordered by trees like scattered cabbages which straggled down to the Jed. He sighed, recalling his neighbour who had committed suicide and who lay there, enfolded in the green cold earth. He tried to identify his tombstone, but it was just another speck in the stubble of grey stones sewn thick together in the little paddock.

His eyes drifted further down and northwards, seeing the broken Abbey brood over the rubble of conservation dwellings and mottled shops. The flat slab of the Tourist Information Centre jutted out like a sore thumb, uncompromisingly modern and prosaic. Below it the green park land, reclaimed from the old redbrick rayon mills and smokestacks, tumbled down to the squat leisure centre. The shoulder of the hill obscured his view of his hotel.

He wondered how those prosaic buildings got planning permission in a conservation area. Then he wondered about his neighbour. Had he, like himself, loitered palely amongst these hills? Had he allowed his aura, his energy field, to dissipate, unconnected from the life force that Eleanor proclaimed with her energetic eyes? It seemed just the other day that his neighbour was mending his fence. He saw again his lined face that never smiled, his furrowed brow, his enquiring eyes, blue piercing between ears like radar dishes. Every time he needed him—a broken window, a shelf that needed to be lopped off—he was there. 'Did ye get planning permission for this fence?' his neighbour had asked. He wondered if he had got planning permission to put a staple through his brain.

Sometimes the thought of suicide was like an anaesthetic. It was like a promise of peace postponed. He wondered what were his neighbour's thoughts when he locked his joiner's shop and held the staple-gun to his head. He was a man, he thought, of immense courage.

Harry's spirits surged when he neared the hotel and saw the bright yellow Golf angled in the sloping hotel car-park. She was back! His pace quickened and by the time he strolled through the gateway there was a spring in his step. He found her ensconced in the back kitchen with Anne, drinking coffee. She looked chic and elegant, like a modern princess, in the dim and drab interior lit by the artificial lighting. Her black bobbed hair, her long black dress and patent black ankle boots were in contrast to Anne's greasy hair, dowdy tent dress and smock stained and smudged from cooking oil.

It was as if nothing had happened in Malta. Eleanor smiled engagingly at Harry and chatted animatedly about her continuing search for a modelling job. She had just been in touch with an agency. 'I told them on the phone that I look much younger than thirty, if youth means that much to them!'

So she was thirty! That barely made him ten years her senior, Harry thought. He had always put her age around twenty-five. 'You barely look twenty-five,' he smiled at her. 'You have such a youthful aura, Eleanor.'

She smiled coyly. Anne flicked out a cigarette and a match flared, drawing their attention. She was only five years older than Eleanor but, Harry thought sadly, looked old enough to be her mother.

'How is Max?' asked Anne, spewing out a stream of blue smoke.

'He's away on a refresher sales training course for Fenetre in France,' she said, crinkling her eyes. 'That's the parent company and they want to increase motivational awareness in all their senior executives—not that Max needs motivation.' She shook her head and sadness touched her eyes. 'He phoned last night and he sounded lonely. I said for *goodness* sake, Max, find yourself a dolly-bird! France is full of dolly-birds, isn't it?' Her cheeks dimpled but her eyes remained sad. 'He works so hard, you know. It's hardly fair, going away like this just after Malta. But he works so hard, running about the country to promote his Speedway business, and repping for Fenetre at the same time. You know, it's beginning to eat into our capital. I told him, don't go into the capital set aside for the house.'

'You haven't found a house yet, then?'

She shook her head. 'We've got a good contract on the cottage we're renting. It's a super little farm cottage the other side of Ancrum. You must come and see it some time. It has the cutest staircase that twists up to the attic bedrooms. It's only twenty minutes from here.'

'That would be great, Eleanor,' Harry smiled. 'Perhaps Anne and I can drive around sometime this week?' He glanced at Anne who nodded absently, her eyebrows raised in casual affirmation.

'Sure,' said Anne distractedly. 'I'll have to run into town for some supplies,' she added. 'Perhaps you can give me a lift in your car, Eleanor?'

'Oh, there's no hurry!' Harry said quickly, his heart sinking at the prospect of Eleanor going so soon. She was the brightest star in his otherwise gloomy heaven. 'I can run you in, if you don't want to drive. You could stay for supper, couldn't you, Eleanor?'

Eleanor's cheeks dimpled. 'I'll take a rain cheque on that, Harry, thank you. I thought I'd drive down to the Abbey and have a look around. It's funny, when we were staying here and seeing it every day, we never went. With Max away it will give me something to do. I'm sure it's an energy centre, you know, and I need a top-up.'

'What a lovely idea,' smiled Harry. 'I could go with you!' His heart gave a twist of excitement. 'Anne could come with us as far as the Abbey. What do you say, Anne?' He looked at her, almost pleadingly.

She pursed her lips, then caved in. She smiled weakly at him. 'Sure, Boy.'

They squeezed the car into the cramped car-park outside the visitor's centre of the Abbey and Anne marched off, swinging her arms up the hill with her capacious shopping bag. Harry and Eleanor entered the Abbey grounds through the visitor's centre, Harry paying the entrance fee for both of them. The bell tower over the crossing area loomed solidly above them, the arched vault of the southern transept gaping darkly at them between thick broken walls. They stood there in the crisp cold air, Eleanor smothered in a fur coat with its sumptuous collar hugging her delicate chin.

'It's super, isn't it, Harry?' she said with awe. 'There's such a weight of power here. It's almost frightening.'

'It's more overwhelming when you get close,' said Harry, remembering the feeling he had before of being drawn into its power, and he shivered, also recalling Thomas's crazy notion of being sucked into the past. He gave a short laugh. 'You remember that simple fellow, Thomas Cranston, that day outside the hotel? He spoke of the curative effect of herbs in the Abbey cloister, remember?' He paused, but went on when he saw her cheeks dimpling. 'Well, he seemed to think the Abbey could suck you into the past—through a sort of time-gate.'

Her smile broadened. 'He was responding to the energy vibrations here, Harry. The people who built this Abbey in the first place were responding to a new spiritual energy that was being released. Perhaps we need to go back and relive the millennium that followed it. It would help us to understand our own time.' She shook her head, creasing her brow. 'No, we need to go forward from the old controls. We don't want to imprison our minds in the old way of thinking, when the church controlled men's thoughts.'

'I always saw this place as a powerhouse for prayer,' Harry said. 'It's an Augustinian Abbey. It was open to the people, not a closed community.'

'That's good,' she nodded. 'It's the original energy field we want to get back to—the one that existed before the church, like the one we felt at that temple in Malta.'

He smiled. 'You're a deep thinker, Eleanor.'

Her deep blue eyes flicked across his face, flashing a quick smile. 'Shall we go nearer?'

He dared to take her arm through the padded fur as they made their way up the steep steps. On their left was a wide rectangle enclosed by a yew hedge. A circular herb garden was set within, a small evergreen Juniper tree at the centre.

'This is lovely,' said Eleanor, pausing.

'It's the cloister garden,' said Harry, chuckling. 'It's the one poor old Thomas thinks he tends in the twelfth century. Actually, it's a replica of the old medieval garden with the same plants the old brethren used for their herbal remedies. Thomas told me that the yew hedging can bear heavy weights of snow. It's a symbol of protection and immortality.' He pointed to the juniper in the middle. 'The juniper is evergreen and at the centre, representing the Tree of Life. The branches were used for sprinkling holy water in the Abbey.' He gave an awkward laugh. 'Some of those herbs are for curing lust. I suppose I need some of that after the way I carried on in the pool in Malta.' His face turned red, taken by surprise at his own remark.

But she shook her head and smiled indulgently at him. 'No, Harry. What happened in the pool was quite natural—at first. We were all responding spontaneously to one another's vibrations. It went wrong when ...' She gave him a quick sidelong glance. She went on, almost inaudibly: 'When it stopped being spontaneous.'

She walked ahead of him, looking at the plants, preventing him from replying. 'You know,' she said, 'the old brethren weren't so far from the truth in seeking healing energy from plants. They probably learnt to project their energy towards the plants to make them more effective for cures. We do the same with people when we focus on a person's beauty. When the energy goes into them, it helps them to grow stronger. Then they give back this strength to us. Isn't that the idea of a tree of life?'

He moved closer to her, thrilled by the implications of what she had just said. It was what Anne reported her saying, in Malta. She hadn't excluded him at all—provided his intentions were spontaneous and included Anne. He wondered how his very conscious love for her could be channelled into spontaneous actions—or at least actions that *appeared* spontaneous and acceptable. He'd have to play his cards right, he thought, looking at her small delicate hand that peeped so temptingly from her fur. He longed to take it in his and walk hand in hand into the Abbey.

She turned and walked closer to the Abbey. She stopped at a sign that read 'Chapter House.'

'What was this place?' she asked, staring into the rectangular area surrounded only by the foundations of a wall. Some stone blocks lined the old foundations, except where the floor area was excavated to reveal rows of stone-lined spaces, like coffins.

Harry stood close, brushing against her coat, his hand nearly touching hers, reading the smaller writing on the signboard. 'It's the meeting room of the community. This is where the canons were allowed to talk in their daily gatherings. Where sins were confessed—or accused.'

She wrinkled her nose. 'I don't like it. I wonder how much they really helped one another? I think it's awful to accuse anybody of...of sins. I think they were stealing one another's energies, exploiting their auras.'

Harry laughed. 'It was part of their organisation. Their rules.'

She shook her head. 'What you're saying is...' She puckered up her little face. 'You're saying that they were institutionalising love. Controlling it with rules. You can't do that with love, Harry. Love is a spontaneous flow of energy.'

'Quite,' he agreed, sensing a sudden gush of love for her. Her porcelain face, so white and fragile and framed by her black fringe and bobs, was so striking, so vulnerable. When she heard his sigh she looked up at him with concern. 'Are you all right, Harry?' she asked with a tender inflection of her musical voice.

'I'm all right, Eleanor,' he said, then decided to risk some confidence, to draw her sympathy. 'It's just that I've felt rather depressed, so low in energy, I suppose, since Malta and that pool incident. I'm afraid I took our friendship too far, Eleanor. I'm sorry. I meant to apologise to you.'

She smiled sweetly at him, her eyes still touched with concern. 'I didn't mind, Harry. I told you, it only went wrong because you began to exclude Anne. Love—the energy of love—is not meant to exclude.' She looked at the stone seats against the crumbling foundations of the Chapter House. 'Like these canons or monks, whatever they were. Fancy *accusing* one another! They were excluding their brethren from love by doing that. Love doesn't exclude.'

'I realise that now,' he said contritely. 'Anne and I are both making an attempt to recover our relationship. I have you to thank for that.'

Her eyes brightened. 'That's good Harry!' She lay her hand lightly on his arm. It thrilled him. She had never made an attempt to touch him before. 'Try to see the silver lining in every situation or event, Harry. Only by doing that can we evolve in our personal development. If we're positive and sharing we can move to a higher level. You need to stay centred in your situation and open yourself to the free energy that's all around you. Try to see the beauty in everything.' Her blue eyes thrilled him when they smiled, penetrating so deeply into his. 'I really enjoy helping people to evolve to a higher vibration, to fulfil themselves in their personal destiny, do you know what I mean? If you're positive and open, I can help you and Anne, Harry. I'm a natural healer, you know. I have healing properties in my aura. It depletes me, but I can be recharged, too, when I help. Do you know what I mean, Harry?'

'It's so kind of you to help, Eleanor. You're so generous.' He felt the tears prick his eyes. Her own eyes seemed so earnest and it touched him. He resisted the temptation to bend down and kiss her.

'Not at all, Harry. Love is the way we keep our vibrations up. You must rise out of your depression, see? I realise that what happened in the pool went wrong for you and I want to mend it. But first you must mend your relationship with Anne.'

'Yes, I know,' he said softly, her eyes still holding his.

'Our biggest danger is to take too much control of one another, Harry. Especially in a marriage. We must be careful not to manipulate our partner and steal their energy. I'm only trying to help you and Anne, do you know what I mean? To build up your personal energy fields. You have to learn to draw your energy from the whole cosmos, not to sap each other. Then you can share that energy and strengthen each other. When we radiate it we can all share it.'

He felt a stab of injustice in what she was saying, as though he alone was to blame for not sharing. 'But what about Anne?' he asked, frowning. 'It seemed that she was unwilling to share—in what was happening to us in Malta.'

She shook her head and smiled sweetly. 'You were taking too much control, Harry. I told you before—most people go through their lives in a constant hunt for someone else's energy, like that awful Mr Ramsden. They were like these people here.' She pointed around the area of the Chapter House. 'I hate to think of the canons accusing one another here. Is that really what they did? It means they were sapping energy from one another!'

Harry laughed, seeing her stern expression like a petulant child. 'And when they sapped their victims' energy out, they must have buried them here too! You can see their graves over there!' He pointed to the exposed coffin-shaped graves. Each was lined with a row of upended stone slabs.

'Oh, Harry, that's horrible!' She shrank back.

'No, no,' he smiled. 'I was only teasing. Those were the graves of the senior Abbots. I think it was a special privilege to be buried here, Eleanor. You can see the photographs of their skeletons in the visitors' centre.'

'I still don't like it,' she said, wrinkling her little nose. 'I don't feel any energy vibrations in this part. Like those catacombs in Malta.' She looked up at Harry with concern. 'Be careful not to sap Anne's energy, Harry. She needs love—lots of it, and she needs energy. You can give it to her—we can both give it to her. Don't let your marriage turn into a power struggle. The loser always pays the price. Don't suck the vital energy out of the people you love. Don't take a manipulative posture. Do you remember Chuck Halliday's talk on posture? We must transcend our natural urge to control others.' She shook her head, smiling. 'Stay centred in love, Harry. Remember who you are. We all need to maintain a positive posture, not only towards ourselves but to others. That way we can learn to live at a higher vibration.'

Her energetic exhortation took him by surprise. 'You certainly are a deep thinker, Eleanor.' He smiled at her. 'Is that how we maintain our personal fulfilment? You spoke of fulfilling our destiny. Do we do that by feeling cosmic, as you said in Malta? Becoming cosmically aware? Can we do that in a place like this?'

She looked down at the exposed graves. 'Not here. Maybe inside the Abbey. When we first came I felt stronger. There was definitely an energy field.' She placed her hands in her coat pockets and walked further along the path, towards the truncated transept. 'How do we enter?' she asked, looking up at the vaulted arch of the transept under the bell tower.

'This way,' he said softly, taking her arm. He led her to the left through a small processional portal. They found themselves at the inner end of the long nave with its rows of giant arches embracing two tiers of openings. The upper storeys and the tall galleries above the aisle vaults gave an impression of tremendous power, in terms of height and distance.

'Oh Harry,' she whispered, standing close and placing a hand on his arm, 'this is *magnificent*.'

'Yes,' he said, thrilled by her closeness and by her touch. He could tell that she was deeply moved for she didn't say 'super.' He felt the natural impulse to slip his arm around her, but inhibited the action, clenching his fist instead to control himself.

They walked in silence under the massive structure of the bell tower into the eastern limb of the Abbey with the broken structures of the presbytery. They turned and looked back, under the tower towards the far end of the nave, facing west. Two lofty arches within the bell tower embraced the openings into the aisles and they could see into the galleries above the aisles. It was like the inside of an enormous ocean-going vessel, like an ark, and the sense of power was immense. Without forethought Harry took Eleanor's hand and drew her forward, sitting down on a wide slab of rock that might have been where the high altar once stood. They looked past the canon's stalls, their eyes drawn by the series of arches and giant cylindrical columns to the intricate rose window high up in the gable at the far end of the nave.

'You know,' Harry spoke softly, 'this reminds me of a moment when I was a child. At school they used to hand out small bottles of milk for us to drink. I was draining the last of my bottle, upending it to the open sky, when suddenly I was hit by a strange awareness. It was such a strange moment. I began to wonder who I was, and what I was. Why did I exist at all? It was like a sudden epiphany of consciousness.'

He felt the pressure of her hand on his. 'I know what you mean,' came her voice, sounding mellower and softer than before.

He sat there, holding her hand, staring at the fine fretwork of the rose window. He felt he was soaking up the beauty of the place and he gave way to a sudden flood of buoyancy, a surge of elation. The rose window seemed to glow, exhibiting more presence, like the antediluvian temple in Malta. He felt a rush of love for the girl beside him, a love that made him feel protective and gentle. Without turning his eyes away from the rose window, he sensed her aura, as though she was dressed in a flowing white robe. He sensed that she was somehow taller, her dark hair on a par with his own. Her hand in his felt larger, firmer, and trembled with a shared energy. It was as though they had both been lit from within. It was more, far greater, than a sexual energy, he realised. It was a spiritual force, and he felt a spasm of love for her that brought the realisation that he would be willing to go to the ends of the earth for her, to die for her, if necessary. She was like a spiritual mentor. Their hands clasped together like a bond of unity, allowing a mutual flow of energy. He felt strong and powerful, his chest swelling with elation.

He thought he would burst with happiness. He was subliminally aware of a low vibration, of the soft hum of voices in harmony that seemed to emanate from the canon's choir at the base of the tower.

The elation began to overflow and he couldn't stop himself.

'I love you,' he whispered.

'I love you too,' came her mellow voice, sounding strange yet familiar.

The surprise made him turn and look at her.

There was no-one there.

He looked back and saw Eleanor a long way off, examining the stonework of a pillar near the end of the nave. Some wispy snowflakes were filtering down. One touched his nose and began to melt. He was confused and a surge of dizziness hit him. Then he had a blinding headache, like a hangover.

He shook his head and stood up. Another dizzy spell hit him and he had to steady himself on the stone slab. The ground tilted and sloped beneath him, then slowly began to right itself.

He walked unsteadily down the nave, towards Eleanor. He felt totally confused. One moment she was beside him, close and magnified, holding his hand, and said she loved him! The next moment she was far away, small and vulnerable in her fur coat, casually examining a carving on a pillar. It didn't add up.

'Eleanor,' he said, coming up to her. 'When did you leave? I thought you were next to me.'

She turned and smiled. 'Oh, there you are, Harry. You seemed to be in a trance, sitting there. I could see you were connected, so I left you alone. I didn't want to disrupt your flow of energy.' She looked concerned. 'What's the matter? You seem to have lost your aura.'

'But you were sitting next to me. You said ...'

She smiled indulgently and shook her head. 'No. As soon as you sat down you began to speak to yourself. You had a faraway look in your eyes and your lips were moving, but there were no words. It's like you were speaking to someone else.'

'I was telling you about that moment when I was drinking milk at school, you know ...'

Her crystal laugh tinkled. 'You were completely silent, Harry. Except for when your lips began to move.' Her smile broadened. 'You had a mystical experience, didn't you? You felt the cosmic energy of this place. I *told* you it was an energy centre, Harry.'

'And you didn't say anything to me?'

She shook her head. 'I came over here. I didn't want to disturb you, do you know what I mean?'

CHAPTER 22

Spontaneous Combustion

'**A**RE YOU ALL RIGHT now, Harry?' Eleanor asked as she unlocked the door of her Golf. The odd snowflake scurried across the top of the car.

'I'm fine, Eleanor,' he said, smiling and pulling the collar of his coat up around his neck. 'I think I must have had some sort of dream, that's all. It just seemed so real.' He laughed awkwardly. 'In the dream you were still sitting next to me, on that altar stone—whatever it is.' He didn't dare say what she had told him in the dream.

'I think that's significant, Harry.' Her crystal eyes smiled. 'I think I better run you back to the hotel. It looks like snow, doesn't it?'

He climbed in next to her. 'I suppose the Abbey's been a sort of escape for me, occasionally,' he said, fastening his seat-belt. 'I mean, the hotel gets so boring that I stand in the window, sometimes, dreaming about the past. About what it would be like to go back to the twelfth century.'

'It's not such a bad thing to dream, Harry,' she said, slipping her key in place. Instead of starting the car she sat back and smiled at him. 'All kind of dreams are good. Not just dreams when you're asleep, but dreaming while you're awake. It's an important way of getting in touch with your energy flow. That's why Speedway urges you to dream—to visualise goals.'

'Like the Dream Weekend in Valletta?' he smiled languidly. 'That's a way of conditioning yourself, I suppose. The types I have are more like wish fulfilment.'

'But those are good, too, Harry. Our dreams and daydreams guide us. It's a way of making your energy flow, do you know what I mean? They help to encourage the coincidences and chance happenings that will lead us forward in life. They can even be prophetic.'

'You mean, like an intuitive process?'

'Yes,' she screwed up her nose prettily. 'If you mean a spontaneous process. But by daydreaming you make it a conscious process, too, don't you? In a way, one that you're controlling.' She shook her head, thoughtfully. 'No, I tell a lie. Too much control is dangerous, Harry. Energy flows spontaneously when you're centred, and you felt that just now, I think. Also like the time in the pool in Malta.' Her voice softened and she smiled coyly. 'That was a wonderful moment, Harry, as I said, because we were all opening to an energy flow together, for a time. But it came too strong for you, and Anne too, didn't it? You were trying to assert your control over the flow, and you stepped out of it and then it became a manipulation, do you know what I mean? The energy, when it flows spontaneously, will lead you naturally in the direction you need to follow. But you tried to use too much control and that got in the way of the natural flow, and Anne felt it first. She got scared and ran off. I can't blame her. As I said, your control was excluding her.' She touched his elbow lightly, smiling. 'Do you know what I mean, Harry?'

'So I must try to ... what did you say? Reconnect with the spontaneous flow of energy that comes from outside ourselves? Like I did in the Abbey?'

She nodded. 'Yes, by staying in a state of love—of giving. And by staying alert, too, to every coincidence or opportunity that life presents to promote that love. A love that binds us together, that doesn't divide us into selfish islands, that doesn't make us just sap energy from one another.'

'Opportunities?' He smiled, struck by an idea. 'Do you know what day it is tomorrow?'

'It's the 14th of February, isn't it? Oh yes, I *see*!' Her smile widened.

'St Valentine's Day!' He nodded, pleased by her reaction. 'It's like one of those coincidences you were talking about! Do you think it's an opportunity for us all—for Anne and I—to reconnect with the universal energy?' Reconnecting with Anne was the only basis whereby he could reconnect with Eleanor, he thought. He hoped this was sounding spontaneous.

'You need to do something spontaneous, Harry,' she smiled, as if answering his thoughts. 'Have you bought Anne a Valentine's day gift?'

He shook his head, looking at his watch. 'I haven't, I'm afraid, and the shops are closed by now.' He beamed at her. 'Look, Eleanor, why don't you come round tomorrow, and we could all go out together for a St Valentine's dinner? You could choose something appropriate for Anne on your way over here from Ancrum. I'll reimburse you.'

She smiled hesitantly. 'I'd love to, Harry. Especially with Max away, it's very lonely in the cottage. But would Anne like that?'

He nodded, holding his smile. 'I spoke to her. She said she was willing to go along with ...' He searched for the right phrase. 'With the energy flow, if it happened again. We've talked about it. I think we'd both love you to be with us, to help us reconnect.'

She smiled generously. 'You two are both such lovely friends. Of course I'll come, if you think it will help. What do you want me to buy for Anne? Wouldn't it be better if you chose something tomorrow?'

He shook his head. 'The problem is that it's Anne that runs into town for the supplies. She says it's easier for her to budget that way. If I went in she'd be suspicious. The gift wouldn't seem spontaneous, if you know what I mean.'

'Of course, Harry,' she nodded, her eyes intense with sincerity. 'We'll make it a wonderful evening for Anne.'

It was a sort of conspiracy that brought them closer together. Harry was delighted. 'It will be wonderful for all of us,' he grinned.

The next day the snowflakes were filtering down more thickly and Harry was anxious that the weather would stop Eleanor coming around that evening. Her cottage was at least two miles off the main trunk road, on a narrow farm road that wound steeply up a hillside. If it snowed heavily she could easily be blocked in—or out. After lunch Anne drove into town for her daily shopping for supplies—'to get her messages', she said, using the local jargon—and Harry glanced restlessly through the front windows of the hotel, straining his ears for the throaty throb of Eleanor's car. He had received a Valentine's card in the post that morning. Although it was anonymous, he knew, of course, that it was from Anne and he thanked her. She had acknowledged his hug with a twisted grin, not saying anything about there being no card for her. If only the card had been from Eleanor, he thought, and he hatched an innocent plan whereby he could legitimately hug her. He would pretend he thought the card was from her, not Anne, and give her a spontaneous hug when she arrived! But he could only carry out the plan if she arrived before Anne returned. He ensured that all the storage heaters were switched on. Intuitively, he wanted the place to be warm.

It was about four in the afternoon when he caught the yellow flash of her car and heard the throb of the little diesel engine. He took a deep breath and opened the door.

'Halloo!' she sang in her musical voice, wrapped in her fur coat with some parcels in her arms.

'Eleanor!' he enthused, his heart in his mouth. He closed the door behind her. 'Eleanor, that was *so sweet* of you!' he went on, opening her coat and slipping his hands around her small torso, holding her close. Her small firm body felt resilient and delicious under the coat. 'Thank you so much, Eleanor!' He kissed her on the cheek and hugged her again, getting as much mileage out of the pretence as possible.

'Harry!' she giggled. 'What do you mean?'

'The Valentine's card!' he said, smiling into her eyes so close to his own, his hands still locked round the small of her back. He felt her soft breasts against his chest. She never wore a bra.

'Don't be silly, Harry,' she giggled, smiling sweetly at him. 'That was Anne. I didn't send you a card.'

'Oh, well,' he grinned. 'It was a nice cuddle, anyway.' He dared to hold her a little longer, for she made no attempt to pull away. After what felt like half a minute of bliss but was only three seconds he drew his arms away, reluctantly.

'Look!' she said, still smiling broadly. 'Look what I brought for Anne. Would this make a suitable present from you?' She placed a little trinket, wrapped in silk paper, into his hand.

198

Harry unwrapped it. It was a delicate silver chain from which was suspended a piece of thin silver metal shaped into a tiny heart, hollow in the middle except for the thin metal words 'I love you.'

'Eleanor,' he enthused, 'this is just perfect! You have such good taste!'

'Well, as long as she thinks it's from you,' she smiled, pleased by his reaction.

When Anne came home clutching shopping bags under each arm she found them drinking coffee in the small private lounge.

'Now then, Anne!' said Harry, getting up and raking up all the enthusiasm he could muster. He fastened the little chain round her neck. 'Here's a little St Valentine's gift for you. I bet you thought I'd forgotten! And guess what? Eleanor and I are taking you out to dinner tonight!'

She was overwhelmed. Perhaps because she never expected a love-token from Harry she easily accepted the notion of Eleanor making a third at the dinner. 'Boy, this is so lovely of you!' she said with her twisted grin, flicking a glance at Eleanor to include her in her pleasure.

That evening Harry suggested they eat at the only Italian restaurant in Jedburgh, knowing that Eleanor was partial to pasta and ate very little meat. Anne was only too happy to agree since it was such a novelty for Harry to take her out to dinner.

'You don't take me out often, Boy!' she said, settling down at a corner table and eagerly examining the menu. 'Are we going to order some wine too?'

'Of course!' said Harry, remembering how the flow of wine at the Golden Bay hotel in Malta had helped to precipitate the spontaneous flow of energy in the pool. He ordered a bottle of expensive *Chianti* red wine which was served in a bottle wrapped in wicker work.

'Boy! This is not like you!' laughed Anne, surprised by her husband's extravagance.

'Nothing too good for two such lovely ladies,' he smiled, seeing the approving glint in Eleanor's smile.

The proprietor of the restaurant, a well-endowed rotund woman with a round face wreathed in smiles, was delighted to see them chatting and enjoying themselves, and placed a generous serving of *Tortelloni con spinacci e ricotta* in front of Eleanor, who looked shocked at the amount of food. 'No rabbit food for me!' said Anne with her plump rabbit-smile which welcomed the arrival of her *Spaghetti di Polpetti*. Harry plumbed for *Spaghetti Arciuche* and found the anchovies rather over-salty, which in due course required a second bottle of *Chianti*.

'Gosh, Boy,' proclaimed Anne with shining eyes, her mouth full of spaghetti and half a meatball, 'You're really pushing the boat out tonight!' She laughed, recalling some of Harry's adventurous eating in Malta which included octopus salad and the national dish of rabbit stew. 'Give me a pizza or bangers and mash anytime,' she said, chomping through another mouthful of meatball.

They walked back through the falling snow, arm-in-arm, Anne in the middle, laughing and chattering, careful not to slip on the snow where it had been compressed into mushy ice by the preceding footsteps. Harry longed to be in the middle instead of Anne, to link his arm with Eleanor's, but was being careful to play his cards right. Everything had to look spontaneous and wasn't to exclude Anne on any account.

'I really think you'd better stay over the night, Eleanor,' Harry said. 'I don't like to think of you being stuck in the snow, and we have plenty of empty bedrooms. There are no guests this time of year.'

'Thank you, Harry,' smiled Eleanor. 'Would that be all right, Anne?'

'Sure! Sure!' she proclaimed fervently. 'Be our guest! Just don't do anything we wouldn't do!' Her raucous laugh was dulled by the falling snow as they reached the sloping entrance into the hotel's car-park. 'Whoops!' she shouted, losing her footing, sliding forward, but Harry had his hand hooked under her arm, steadying her as they reached the door.

They drank some coffee with mint chocolates, and Harry felt they were sobering up all too quickly. 'What about some Cherry-Brandy, or some Drambui?' he suggested, getting up from the settee he was sharing with Anne. 'And why don't you sit here with us, Eleanor, nearer the fire?'

'Oh, no, I couldn't, Harry,' Eleanor said sweetly, 'Not after all that pasta and garlic. Really, I'm stuffed!'

'Stuffed!' laughed Anne, 'You hardly touched it! If I hadn't finished it for you, most of it would have landed in the bin! You eat like a bird, Eleanor!'

Eleanor smiled indulgently. 'I have to think of my weight, Anne. I've applied for a modelling job. As it is, my stomach feels enormous. It's not good for my energy field, do you know what I mean?'

'Well, come and sit with us anyway, Eleanor,' urged Harry, trying not to appear manipulative. 'We'd like to share your aura, wouldn't we, Anne?'

'No,' Eleanor smiled ruminatively at them. 'I'm going to get my beauty sleep, if you don't mind. I don't normally have so much wine and I feel quite heady. I'm going to go to bed so you two lovebirds can be alone together.' She stood up, picking up her coat which lay over the back of her chair. 'It's room 2, isn't it? The one with the proper bath? I'll have a nice soak and go to sleep.' She came nearer and bent over Anne, planting a kiss on her flushed cheek.

Harry stared in disbelief at the door that closed behind her as she made her way to the guest bedroom upstairs. His spirits reached rock-bottom, depression settling in his stomach. He wondered what had gone wrong.

Anne placed a stubby arm round him. 'This is very nice of you, Boy!' she said, her small mouth smiling rabbit-like in her plump face. She looked down and fingered the little heart round her neck. 'I can't tell you how chuffed I am about this, and the dinner. Gosh, Harry, you're not often so generous! It was like old times tonight!' She bent over and kissed his cheek wetly. Her stubby fingers worked at his fly. Her voice dropped into a simpering tone. 'Have you got a *muckle een* for me tonight, Boy?'

He sighed. 'I've got a thrashing headache, actually, Anne.' He got up and walked to the window. The floodlit Abbey was almost obscured by the now thickly-falling snow. A few streetlights along the A68 cast dull fuzzy yellow pools of light and a snowplough made its way silently southwards, towards the Carter Bar and the English border.

Anne got up and staggered, nearly falling. She giggled. 'I'll be in a better condition in the morning, Boy. You won't escape me then!'

He listened to the creak of the back stairs as she went up to their little coffin-shaped bedroom. He heard the water gurgling into Eleanor's bath upstairs, and wondered briefly if she would regard an offer to scrub her back a spontaneous impulse. His heart fluttered painfully at the thought, then steadied as his mood relapsed into despondency. It was easier to procrastinate his desire for Eleanor. He consoled himself that she was still present, only just upstairs, and with the thought that the morning might bring a fresh flow of spontaneous opportunity. For the moment he felt drained, his dry brain dizzied by the effects of the dry wine.

In the morning he woke up early. He remembered Eleanor asleep and alone in her bed, probably naked, and restlessness gnawed at his belly. Anne's occasional snore or grunt was magnified by the uncanny silence. He took a deep breath and pulled himself out of bed, slowly so as not to wake Anne. He padded carefully on his bare feet to the window, grimacing every time he stepped on a floorboard that creaked, and drew the curtain aside, peeping out.

It was magical, like a Christmas-card tableau. The snow lay everywhere, on the sloping roofs, the weighted bows of trees, the tops of hedges and fences and on the street, glowing in the dull yellow pools of light from the streetlights. Occasionally a car crept by, soundlessly, as it followed deep ruts in the fresh textured substance. Snowflakes were still filtering down, adding to the thick white blanket that smothered and cushioned the scene.

He closed the curtain, his heart palpitating from a thought he couldn't shake off. It was only a half-formed idea, but he discarded his pyjamas, shivering, and drew on his gown, tying it at the waist so that he was naked except for the gown. He made his way gingerly down the stairs, keeping to the sides to diminish the creaking. The strip light in the kitchen flickered and bathed the room in brightness and he made himself a cup of coffee, sat down at the table and thought.

Things just didn't happen spontaneously, he told himself, unless you gave them a push. A car didn't start spontaneously unless you turned the starter, he thought, swallowing the hot sweet coffee. He ran a scenario through his mind. What if he took Eleanor a cup of coffee? He looked at the electric kitchen clock. The second hand moved round silently, unbelievably slowly. It was only just after six. A bit early to take her coffee, he thought. But what if he just went up and peeped in? Maybe she was awake. 'I've just come to see how you are,' he heard the words silently in his brain. He shook his head. She was hardly going to invite him into her bed. Besides, it was no good if Anne wasn't involved. Somehow he *had* to involve Anne. But he couldn't see himself waking up Anne and towing her to Eleanor's room. What if she rejected the advance?

He took a deep breath. This was madness, he told himself—planning an act of spontaneity in cold blood. He breathed more deeply, steadying his galloping heart. He stood up, swallowing. If he just went to her room, and then considered his position. He was already half way up the stairs when he got a hold of himself and paused. But he could see the door of her room and it was open!

A dim light radiated out through the open door. He tiptoed up, slowly, until he could peer in, casually, and caught his breath. A bedside light was burning next to the low king-size bed. She was sleeping like a child, spread-eagled, the bedclothes half thrown off her. Her jet-black hair stood out sharply against the white pillow, her eyelashes closed peacefully, one of her small breasts uncovered, peeping out petulantly with a taut pink nipple. He released his breath and breathed slowly, soundlessly. She was like a princess, so pure, innocent and desirable.

He slipped off his gown and crawled in next to her, gently kissing her eyelashes. His heart beat wildly.

Her eyelashes fluttered once, twice. Her eyes stared at him blankly, nonplussed.

He smiled at her, his heart in his mouth. 'Hi,' he whispered. 'Just dropped in. Saw you here and couldn't resist you.'

She looked bewildered and he panicked. 'Shall I fetch Anne? We could both give you a cuddle, if you like.'

She squinted at him, confused, but she nodded. 'Okay,' she said, unsmiling.

He bent over her and kissed her, taken aback by her stale, garlic-laden breath. But her lips were unspeakably sweet and he lingered, tasting them, savouring them, and he felt them twist deliciously under his. He drew away and smiled into her puzzled blue eyes.

'I'll be back with Anne,' he said breathlessly, and dashed off, naked, unthinkingly. He dashed up the back stairs and shook Anne whose eyes snapped open, confused.

'Come, Anne,' he urged, pulling her hand. He spoke quickly, excitedly. 'Come. Eleanor says we can give her a cuddle. Remember we discussed this and you said you would? Would you come now? Please?'

'I don't know, Boy,' she said, wide-eyed. 'I don't know if I can ...'

'It will be all right,' he assured her. 'I won't make love to her. I promise. I'll only make love to you.' All he could think of was to get back into bed next to Eleanor, naked, with her delicious, sinuous body, and reconnect with those lips that tasted like wine and made him so alive. To gaze into her biting blue eyes, kiss them and kiss her breasts, slide over her and ... 'Come, Anne, please. I'll do anything if you'll come. She doesn't want ... I don't want to exclude you. This will revitalise our love.'

She allowed herself to be dragged down the stairs, her naked stumpy legs following him dutifully. They found Eleanor waiting for them, wide awake now, but looking bemused. Anne gave her a twisted smile as Harry drew her into the bed, on the other side of Eleanor. He crawled in next to her again, sliding his leg over her naked body, feeling the smooth silk-texture of her warm skin, covering her mouth with his again, taking in the delicious soft lips and the foul garlic breath together, like a package deal. He felt her pelvis under his thigh twitch and begin to buckle rhythmically, mechanically, up and down against his thigh. Then he looked up, seeing Eleanor's still perplexed eyes and Anne's wide helpless stare at the same time. He smiled reassuringly at Anne. 'It's all right. I'm just going to lie on top of her for a moment. Nothing will happen.' He slid over on top of Eleanor, taking his weight on his elbows, heady with the smooth taut feel of her body under him. He splayed his thighs around her, nudging his erect desire against the soft wiry texture of her pubic hairs, kissing her again and feeling her mouth open to him. He kissed her for as long as he dared, savouring the soft silk of her lips, the stale garlic of her breath, for as long as he dared. Then he slid off her, lying between the women on his back, groping Anne's spongy breast to placate her, the other hand enveloping one of Eleanor's nubile breasts. It was a delicious handful and when he squeezed gently he heard her sharp intake of breath.

He pushed both his hands downwards, until each hand rested on the fuzzy hair between each of the women's thighs. He twirled the hairs in his fingers, feeling the smooth softness of Eleanor's thighs, the lumpiness of Anne's, and worked his fingers down into their clefts. Both women parted their thighs obediently for him, his fingers sinking easily and unexpectedly into them.

At this point Harry was only aware of Eleanor, drunk with desire for her. He heard her moan as his fingers sank deeper into her surprisingly sodden cleft. The deeper he explored the more intense her moans became. He sensed her back arching and her slim pelvis buckled under his hand, her head thrown to one side, away from him. He was spurred on by her rising, shrill cries of ecstasy. They grew higher and higher in pitch and he moved in more fingers, massaging energetically, deeply, frantically. She began to yell with all the power of her lungs, long sustained screams that rose and trilled, hitting the high notes with the piercing intensity of an opera singer. Harry was enormously excited, barely believing this was happening, never in his life having ever heard a woman scream in such fervent ecstasy. She held her high notes for an unbelievably long time, trilling in a high soprano voice in an ear-splitting frenzy. His fingers pistoned frantically.

Then, abruptly, her screams stopped. She turned her head and looked at him with wounded eyes. Her slender arm reached down, her small hand finding his penis. Her agile fingers found the sensitive spot she knew was there and began to whip around in a strange, circular and rapid motion. Harry guessed it was a technique that must have worked well for Max, but which did

205

nothing for him. He stopped her hand gently and smiled. Then he mounted Anne. She splayed her thighs obediently and he entered her, plunging and thrusting while he kept his eyes on Eleanor, longing for her, not Anne.

Eleanor's eyes caught his and glanced away, as though embarrassed.

At that moment Harry forced his orgasm. He spasmed quickly with rapid jets into Anne, and while he was still throbbing he lunged forward and bent Eleanor's head towards him, kissing her passionately, crushing her head between his hands.

Then it was all over. Apart from Eleanor's violent screaming, neither she nor Anne had spoken a single word during the encounter. Both women lay there now, still in silence, waiting for Harry to speak.

He lifted himself onto his elbows, and knew that the world, for him, would never be the same again. From outside the dull sounds of the normal world filtered in, hushed by the snow—people commuting to work, going on as before. He lifted himself onto his elbows with a sense of strange unreality.

Somehow the experience had gone horribly wrong. Anne had already left the room and as he got out of bed, Eleanor got up and looked for her clothes. He took her into his arms just once more, awkwardly, and kissed her.

'Thank you, Eleanor,' he said with a self-conscious smile. 'You're so very generous, and sweet. You're the most generous person I know.'

She gave him a half-smile, disentangling herself from his arms. 'I've got to go early,' she said. 'I've got a modelling interview. I won't wait for breakfast.'

'But the snow?' he objected.

'I'll manage,' she said, almost curtly.

He felt he was dismissed and left. He found Anne back in their bed, waiting for him. She wrapped her arms around him and kissed him. She looked at him with hurt, urgent eyes. 'I can kiss, too, Boy,' she said fervently. 'I can kiss too!' Then she planted her damp mouth on his, kissing passionately, as though wanting to draw the life out of him. She drew apart, breathlessly, and her eyes were wet with tears. He noticed that the little silver heart still dangled round her neck.

'I can kiss too, Boy!'

CHAPTER 23

Addiction

WINTER PERSISTED and spring came reluctantly with the appearance of some stunted crocuses in the front garden of the hotel, followed by straggly daffodils soon blasted by a late frost. The hotel filled again with elderly people seeking short breaks at cut-rate prices, where the evening meal was more or less thrown in free for the sake of the bed and breakfast money. It was what Harry called the 'Scarborough syndrome,' typical of seaside resorts where the rash of guest houses and bed and breakfast establishments competed fiercely for the dwindling supply of short-breakers. Guests began to expect free dinners and shopped around until they found the lowest tariff. They were impressed by quantity rather than quality in dinners. They preferred lashings of mashed potato and sliced-beef piled high with three steaming servings of vegetables to such fare as *salmon paupette* or *duckling a la orange*, which was preferred by the more sophisticated clientele of the summer season. But the cheap spring tariffs also attracted the hordes of overweight Americans who expected quality and spacious *en suite* rooms with all mod-cons for a nominal cost.

'They're aggressive consumers,' Harry said disgruntledly. 'They demand brown toast placed hot before them, hash browns, poached eggs not too runny and not too hard, a generous supply of freshly-baked muffins, pancakes and honey. Their demands are aggressive and their smiles reluctant!'

'I thought Americans had the reputation of being friendly,' complained Anne.

'Well,' Harry explained, 'to them we're part of a service industry. They don't see us as a husband and wife team, doing what we can for their comfort. We're supplying a commodity and they're paying for it.'

'But they don't want to pay for it. That's the point. They want everything for nothing!'

Harry nodded. 'That's what Angus, the curator of the Abbey, told me. He said when they go through the Abbey shop they tick things off a list, or make a note of their spending in a notebook. They query all the prices.' He laughed. 'One grumpy American guy brushed his suit accidentally against one of the pillars of the Abbey. He was angry and demanded that British Heritage pay for the dry-cleaning.'

'Typical!' Anne pursed her lips. 'Yesterday a fat American who had booked Room 1 refused it, saying it was too small. He said he came to us because we were so highly rated. He asked me to hold the room for him while he looked around to see if he could find a bigger room at another hotel. Bloody cheek! Fortunately the TIC sent a German couple half an hour later who loved it!'

'If only all our guests were like the Germans,' Harry sighed. 'I've never come across such good breeding and friendliness before. To think we were actually at war with them! They're not like the Dutch, stiff and formal, or the French who inspect everything and want to beat your price down. Give me the Germans any day!'

It was about 10 a.m and Harry had just finished cleaning the dining room. Anne had just brought down a bundle of washing from the bedrooms and they had stopped for a coffee break. They felt physically exhausted, trying to save money by not employing a cleaner. The winter had depleted their available cash and Harry was averse to having Rosemary back who was slow, inefficient, and constantly talked to ghosts she believed populated the hotel.

Harry recalled something Rosemary had said when she cleaned the rooms the previous season. 'When Rosemary was here last year she said a German woman went on and on to her about something. She said she didn't know if she was German or Dutch, but that it sounded like German. She sounded angry and wouldn't shut up. Rosemary said she tried to tell her she didn't speak her language. It was in one of the attic bedrooms.'

'You mean, a ghost spoke to her? The German woman was a ghost?' She wrinkled her nose in disdain.

Harry nodded, draining his cup. 'Yeah. She said she thought the lady was angry because of the way the guests were treating us.'

'Oh!' Anne gave a raucous laugh. 'Then she *must* have been German. That was nice of her, to stand up for us.'

'Yes,' he smiled wearily. 'I told her to thank the lady for her concern.'

She shook her head. 'God, this place is full of weirdoes. And that includes that crazy screeching woman with her energy auras! I do hope you're over her now, Boy! Really, I don't think I can take any more of her ranting.'

'You mean Eleanor?'

She nodded with pursed lips. 'She and Max have been a very bad influence on you, Boy.' She shook her head. 'Honestly, that session in the bedroom was the limit! And the carry-on she made! There's no need to carry on like that.'

He looked hurt. 'But she must have enjoyed it, to scream like that. You never moan or scream.'

She shook her head, snorting. 'It's not necessary, Boy. I don't know what her game is. And I don't want her to come crawling around here anymore, do you hear? Enough is enough.' She looked at him squarely. 'Do you hear that, Boy? I'm putting my foot down now. I went along with it and let you try it. But enough is enough.'

He felt desolate. 'You mean, you won't tolerate Eleanor any more? Even if it means saving our marriage?'

She put her cup down and faced him, squatting on her seat, legs apart. Her manner was bossy but friendly. 'Look, Boy, how would you feel if I dragged you into bed with Max?'

He stared at her, but for once she out-stared him and he looked away. 'That would be different,' he said sulkily.

'Oh yes? How?'

'Well,' he hesitated, thinking. 'Women are more tolerant about that sort of thing, aren't they?' His argument sounded lame, even to his own ears. 'Eleanor is so gentle and generous. Max is more forthright and ... and bumptious.'

'You don't fancy Max screwing you, then? Or Max watching you screwing me? Come on, Boy, be honest.'

'Oh, this is ridiculous, Anne!' He stood up and stared out of the window.

'No,' she went on remorselessly. 'I want you to face this, Harry. For my sake. Tell me that you don't see my point.'

He continued to stare at the bell tower of the Abbey. He couldn't deny that she was right, as far as her argument went. He knew that he had overstepped the mark and he felt trapped. His infatuation or love for Eleanor, whatever it was, was in no way diminished. He craved for her but remembered the wounded look in her eyes, in spite of her ear-splitting orgasm. He craved for her, and it had been weeks since the encounter that snowy morning—and she hadn't returned or made any attempt to contact them. And now Anne was closing the door permanently. Eleanor had been the only light at the end of the drab tunnel of his mundane, unglamorous life. Each day he listened eagerly for the sound of her car. Each day he was disappointed. He spoke disconsolately, still staring out at the Abbey. 'I told you, Anne. I'm not in love with you anymore. I explained that to you in Malta. Eleanor was a desperate attempt to ...' He swallowed. His throat had become clogged and constricted, and he cleared it noisily. 'I love Eleanor.'

'No you don't, Boy!' she said tenderly, coming up to him. 'I know you better than that.' She placed her arms around him, standing against his back. 'You even gave me this.' She drew one hand back and fingered the little silver St Valentine's heart which she wore constantly.

'What?' he said, turning round and disengaging himself from her, seeing the heart. 'Oh, that.'

'Yes, *that*! Tell me you didn't mean it, Boy!' She smiled confidently with her rabbit-like mouth, dwarfed by the fleshy cheeks and her double chins.

He shrugged, depressed, no longer able to sustain any pretence. 'Eleanor bought that for me.'

'Eleanor?' She paled, staring at him. She touched the chain with the tip of her fingers.

He saw the reaction and tried to soften the blow. 'Oh, I asked her to choose something for you. I'd left it too late, you see...'

She clenched the chain in her hand and ripped it off her neck, breaking it. She stalked out of the room, her head bent down.

'Anne...?' He followed her, concerned. He followed her out of the back door. He saw her walk across to the fence and fling the trinket over the bank, into the Jed river.

She turned and walked back past him, her eyes as black as thunder.

It was one of those coincidences again, he thought, later that day when he was tidying up the upstairs bedroom Eleanor and Max had once occupied. He heard the throaty purr of her car and he rushed to the window. There it was, jolting to a stop in front of the brittle brown branches of a conifer that had been killed by the severity of the winter. He rushed down the stairs and found Anne stomping towards the private section. She glanced darkly at him. 'Get rid of her, Boy!' She slammed the door and he heard her bolt it shut behind her.

Harry opened the front door to Eleanor. She looked chic and debonair in her fur coat, a small black beret tilted at a rakish angle on her immaculate black hair. She held a little package but didn't smile, though her cheeks dimpled slightly.

'Harry,' she said, her sharp blue eyes edged with sadness. 'I came to see Anne, actually. I brought these for her.' She gave him the parcel.

'You look gorgeous as usual, Eleanor,' Harry said brightly, trying to recover his former composure as if nothing had happened. He couldn't bring himself to tell her Anne had barricaded herself inside and didn't want to see her. 'Anne's washing her hair at the moment, I'm afraid. Shall we sit in the front lounge? I'll get the fire going.'

'No, really, Harry, I don't want to stay. I just wanted to apologise to Anne.'

'Apologise to Anne?' He felt cold fingers clutch his heart. He looked into the packet she brought and saw that it was a box of chocolates. There was also a little handbag lined with pink silk inside. 'This is all very generous of you, Eleanor.' His heart was heavy and he could see her mood was one of intransigence.

'The man Anne works with phoned and told me off, Harry,' she said. 'I felt I should say something to her.'

Harry was confused. 'Works with? She only works with me. What man? What did he say, for heaven's sake?'

'He told me to stop wearing revealing clothes in front of you.' She gave him a thin smile. 'I can only think he was referring to the way I dressed in Malta.'

Harry felt outraged. 'But who the hell was he? And what gives him the right to phone you!'

Eleanor shrugged. 'Never mind. The thing is, Anne got someone to speak to me on her behalf. She could have approached me herself. I'd feel better if I apologised, anyway, and said something about that other time.'

'You mean, about what happened in the bedroom?' he asked softly and contritely. 'I meant to apologise to you about that, Eleanor.'

She nodded, still standing in the hallway. 'It wasn't right, Harry.' Her clear blue eyes held his. 'What happened in the pool in Malta—yes, I could tell Max about that. That was quite spontaneous and he would understand. But I couldn't tell him about the bedroom. I can't tell him about that.' Her eyes, wounded again, looked accusingly at him. 'I know what he would say. He would say I was being used.'

'But I *wasn't* using you, Eleanor,' he insisted urgently. 'You must know that.' If anybody was being used, he thought, it was Anne. His throat constricted and his words slipped out, breaking as they did. 'Can't you see that I'm in love with you, Eleanor?' He felt the pressure of tears just held back.

She shook her head briskly. 'You don't love me, Harry. You're going through an addiction phase. You've hooked into my energy field and that's blocking your flow of energy from the outside. Obviously we have some kind of connection, but it's not a connection with your real source.'

'Won't you come in and sit down, Eleanor? Then we can talk about this.'

She shook her head with determination. 'No, Harry, there's no point. You first need to break your addiction to ...' She took a deep breath. 'Your addiction to *me*. You only think you're in-love because of the high you get from my own energy. And you're depleting me, Harry. My aura suffers every time I get near you. You've become addicted to my energy as a substitute for what you're really looking for. Your addiction's cutting you off from your true source and in the end your energy will run out. I can't keep replenishing it for both of us, you see? I'm sorry to say this, Harry, but I think we better not see each other again.'

His heart sank and he didn't know what to say. When he found his voice his argument sounded ridiculous. 'But you're my upline,' he said pathetically.

But she didn't laugh. She didn't even smile. She spoke seriously. 'I'll arrange for another line of sponsorship for you, Harry.'

He looked at her, seeing her delicate porcelain skin and brilliant eyes that surveyed him sadly and mercilessly.

'Goodbye, Harry,' she said. She gave him a half smile and walked out briskly. He heard her car start and watched it reverse back into the road. He felt stunned and helpless. He moved closer to the window and her eyes met his briefly as she drove away. He heard the throaty sound of the engine fade away and he still stood there, numb with shock and disappointment.

He heard the inside door open and was aware of Anne's stocky figure next to him.

'So what did she want?' Anne demanded.

He spoke distractedly. 'She came to apologise. I told her to get the hell out of our lives.'

'*Good* for you, Boy!' she said, putting her hand on his arm and shaking it approvingly. 'Good for you! I'm proud of you!'

CHAPTER 24

Cold Turkey

THAT NIGHT Harry's sleep was restless. His mind kept returning to Eleanor's curt and brisk manner, so untypical of her sweet and loving nature. He knew it must have gone against her grain to speak to him that way. He kept blaming himself for his stupidity in trying to precipitate a spontaneous episode in their relationship through a manifestly crude and clumsy sexual exploitation of her childlike friendship. She didn't have to tell him he had once again stepped out of a creative and loving energy flow and resorted to the manipulation of control.

Not that he believed all Eleanor's picaresque philosophy about energy flows and personal auras! It was something he was willing to accept as unique to her world, like the Speedway business plan with its range of health, beauty and utility products. It was all part of her world which he was happy to imbibe as part of her aura. But she had told him, in effect, that she was cutting herself off from him. In doing so she was cutting him off from her thinking and way of life. Without her, her energy auras and crystals became a mere phantasmagorical superstition. And he couldn't care a fig for Speedway. He bit his lip, lying in the dark and listening to the spasmodic grunts of Anne's sleep.

He forced his mind into a blank, closing his eyes and focusing on darkness, and eventually his mind abandoned its ceaseless replay of Eleanor's orgiastic screams and her cold rebuttal. His consciousness resurfaced in a weird dream scenario in which he was involved in the reburial of his grandparents. He dreamt he was in an area where rows and rows of coffins and bodies wrapped in shrouds were placed on trellises. A benign and industrious man had arranged a new cemetery or vault in his private grounds, and Harry was afforded the opportunity of carrying the shrouded corpses down to their new burial place. A dispute arose as to whether all his other relations should be allowed into the new sanctum. But Harry was in favour of restricting the reburial to his grandparents since he didn't recognise any of the other names in the records. There were piles of old documents beside each group of bodies. He saw others carrying corpses down, a string of people, and he stood back to allow them to pass. He asked one to help him with his grandfather's body since he was reluctant to start handling the corpses.

The next morning Harry worked through his breakfast shift, beaming at the guests and laughing effusively at their jokes to conceal his heavy heart. It was a brilliant spring morning with champagne air and a fleckless blue sky. Outside the dining-room window a red robin bounced from branch to branch, attracting the attention of the early diners who laughed every time they saw it.

'It's like being in a tree-house,' a plump and jolly young woman said. 'And the view of the Abbey through the treetops is magical! You're so lucky to be living in a place like this!'

'Yes,' smiled Harry. 'One forgets the beauty of the place. One takes it for granted, I suppose.'

After the morning's cleaning Anne said she would be in town for 'her massages' or daily supplies and would be a while. As soon as she was out Harry went to the phone and dialled Eleanor's number, but put the phone down before it finished ringing, He made himself a cup of coffee and sat in the window-seat, watching a large pigeon settle on the still bare branch of a sycamore tree that grew on the river bank. Because of the hotel's elevated position above the river bank he was ideally placed for observing bird-life in the close upper branches of the trees. But his mind was on Eleanor and the unfair advantage he had taken of her childlike trust. He missed her friendship desperately. He missed her musical chatter, however inane Anne thought it was—a chatter that flowed like a stream and was difficult to interrupt. At best, he thought, one could deflect it by a nudging comment. It was difficult to get a word in edgewise when she talked, but he was always happy to nod and throw in the occasional prompt, like 'Quite!' or 'Absolutely!' It gave him pleasure to listen to her as one would enjoy the twittering of a canary. But his lust for her had got the better of him and he had crushed that fragile friendship with his clumsy act! He was desperate to hear her voice again, and desperate to apologise to her. As he stared distractedly out of the window a second pigeon joined the first, then flew away with its companion in a whirr of wings.

Harry put down his coffee, deciding he couldn't make things any worse by phoning her. He wrote down a few words he might say, to prompt him if his mind went blank. His heart fluttered as he dialled again and listened to the ringing tone, rehearsing his words from the paper in his hand. The ringing went on and on, followed by a click and the sound of her musical voice on an answering phone. He replaced the receiver, drawing a deep breath of frustration rather than of relief. In half an hour he tried again, if only to listen once more to the sweet dulcet tones of her recorded voice. His imagination began to work overtime. What if she had a screening facility on her phone so that she knew it was his number and refused to answer? He knew Max wouldn't be home in the morning and that was all the more reason for him to try to phone her then. He consoled himself with the thought that she was most likely out and that perhaps she would return his call. So he phoned once more, listened to her musical inflections on the tape, and left a brief message to say he had called.

He tried to take his mind off her by picking up a book. It was something he had taken out of the library on energy auras, to prime himself with her way of thinking. It was a self-help book in which the author maintained that the power of imagination could bring him whatever he wanted. She cited the fact that as a teenager she wanted to go out with someone who looked like David Bowie—and lo and behold, a Bowie look-alike stranger asked her out. That sounded very much the sort of thing Eleanor had said! Developing an intuitive mind was part of one's personal evolution, or something like that, and thinking positively could precipitate the fortuitous happenings that led one on to success and fulfilment. His thoughts flew apart when the phone rang.

He leapt up, his heart in his mouth, with the certainty it was Eleanor. But it was a man's voice, polite and friendly with a hint of a Welsh accent.

'Mr Morgan?' he said, his heart sinking as he recognised the voice of the bank manager.

Mr Morgan drew his attention to the beautiful morning. Wasn't it time we had a nice day, he asked, and wasn't spring a long time coming this year? Harry breathed in deeply, wondering where this was leading. 'I wonder,' went on Mr Morgan, 'if you could find the time to pop in for a minute? There seems to be some difficulty with your account we need to clear up.'

Harry went in right away, sensing something ominous was about to be revealed. He needed to know the worst and get it out of the way as soon as possible.

He was ushered in right away. Mr Morgan's eyes were soft, as before, but touched with sadness. His Hitler moustache looked out of place on his lean, sympathetic face.

'Not to put too fine a point on it, Harry,' lilted Mr Morgan, 'I'm surprised that, after our previous discussion, you haven't taken more care with your account.'

A stab of panic went through him. 'What do you mean?'

Mr Morgan shook his head, examining a balance sheet in front of him. 'You've overshot your overdraft facility by a thousand pounds. I thought we should talk about this before it went any further.' His watery eyes transferred their gaze to Harry. 'You're into your spring season now, aren't you? Your cashflow needs to improve a lot to cover your daily Switch drawings.'

Harry swallowed. There had been enough in the bank to cover expenses. 'Switch drawings?' he asked, confused.

Mr Morgan nodded. 'You've been purchasing on a daily basis.' He squinted at the balance sheet. 'Mainly from the supermarket, it seems.'

Harry shook his head. 'We've been using cash for all our purchases. Every day I give my wife the cash she needs for the daily shopping. She said she found it easier to budget that way. Apart from my own withdrawals of cash and the mortgage payments, no demands should have been made on the business account. The account should be well within the overdraft limit.'

The manager shook his head and handed over the copy of the balance sheet. 'Haven't you been keeping an eye on the balance? We send monthly statements.'

'No, I ...' Harry frowned. Anne always got up ahead of him in the morning and was the first to collect the post. He looked at the statement in his hands and the truth dawned on him. Anne had been using the Switch facility on his banker's card instead of using the cash he gave her. She knew how to sign his signature, of course. So what was she doing with the cash? 'I guess my wife has been using my bank card,' he said weakly. 'I better do the shopping myself in future.'

Mr Morgan cleared his throat. 'You have to get this under control, Harry,' he said quietly but firmly. 'I'll allow the present debt provided the overdraft is repaid in two months. After that I shall have no choice but to foreclose, I'm afraid.'

When he left the bank Harry blinked in the bright light that bathed the High Street. It was full of busy shoppers and happy laughter from high-school children who were out for the lunch hour. He was about to turn back towards the hotel when he caught sight of Anne's dumpy figure down the road, turning into the Pheasant, one of the High-street pubs. Anger rose in him and he followed her, wanting to confront her with a copy of the bank statement which the bank manager had given him. He entered the double doors of the Pheasant and, through the crowd that had gathered for lunch, saw her at a side table tucking into what looked like a heaped plate of chips and meat pie. A large glass of Coke stood by her side, some full shopping bags dumped by the side of the table. She seemed to be studying a slip of paper and from time to time, as he watched, she underlined or ticked something with a pencil.

He began to walk forward when he recognised the man he thought of as the Abbot. The man was grasping a half-pint of beer and took a seat at Anne's table. Harry froze, seeing him take up the piece of paper and nod. He watched, fascinated. The Abbot leant his pallid tonsured head forward and engaged Anne in earnest conversation. He looked unshaven and more dissipated than ever. Then he drained his glass and they both stood up, as if to leave.

Harry dashed back outside and waited there, to see what her reaction would be when she saw him. He waited for five minutes without a sign of her or her companion. He went back inside, glanced round the room which was dominated by the large bar with barstools. He squeezed his way through the crowd to see if she was in the dining room at the back. There was no sign of her. He went out of the back door into the small street that ran past the turreted stone house in which Mary Queen of Scots once stayed on a quick visit to Bothwell.

The street was deserted and he walked back to the hotel disconsolately, catching the twang of American accents as he walked past the group of tourists coming out of Mary Queen of Scots House. Once in the hotel he went straight to Anne's little desk and tried the drawer. It was locked as usual. He fetched the screwdriver as he did before and unscrewed the back, dipping his hand into the drawer from the back. All his hand found was a few cancelled lottery scratch cards and, to his surprise, what looked like an outdated betting slip.

He re-screwed the back of the writing desk and left it as before. The front doorbell shrilled and he found a group of elderly Americans looking for bed and breakfast. He showed them the rooms he had available and they inspected them minutely, turning back the sheets and looking into the toilets of each room. 'I wanna room with a tub?' a scrawny sun-dried woman whined.

Harry said the only room with a tub was already let that night.

They queried the tariff and Harry told them £21 for Bed and Breakfast.

'Is that per person or for the room?' an oversized man with a paunch queried.

'Per person,' Harry said, sensing his hackles rising and wondering, as he always did, where they had spent the previous night.

The portly man shook his head. 'That's beyond our budget.'

Harry sighed. He wished they would leave. But then an idea rippled through his weary brain. It was an experiment he always wanted to perform. 'I tell you what,' he said with a smirk, 'since you're all such discerning people and because it will be a great honour to have you stay in our establishment, I'll be happy to offer you a special tariff. Say, £5?'

The scrawny woman glared at him. 'Is that per person or for the room?' she whined.

He gave a double take. 'Oh, per room, of course.'

They all looked at one-another and glared back at him. 'Well, I dunno,' said the plump man. 'We'll have to discuss it.'

'By all means.' Harry mustered an engaging smile. 'And you can have the room with the tub. I've just remembered the booking on it was cancelled earlier.'

The scrawny woman considered the offer. 'So that's twenny for *all* of us?'

'That's right,' Harry conceded, and added as an afterthought. '*And* you can have a further fifty-percent discount if you don't use the *en-suite* facilities.'

'Where do we go then, when we gotta go?' demanded a lady with a bulbous bottom, hitherto silent.

'You're welcome to use the facilities in our private section. I won't be here tonight, but my wife will be happy to share them with you. You just need to ask. Ring the cowbell by the private door.'

The scrawny woman looked up at her husband. 'What d'ya think, Henry?'

Henry pursed his lips. 'Sound reasonable to me,' he said gruffly. Then he eyed Harry suspiciously. 'Just one more thing. Where do we park?'

Here it comes, thought Harry. 'In the car-park,' he said wearily.

'Where's the car-park?'

Harry walked over to the window on the landing and looked down. Their car was abandoned at an angle in the middle of the car-park, preventing the entry of any further cars.

'You're *in* the car-park,' said Harry, wondering if he should offer to bulldoze the retaining walls of the bank so they could pull onto the garden and flower beds. Normally he would ask them if they would mind pulling forward out of consideration of any other guests wishing to park their cars. 'That's fine,' he said. 'You've parked *beautifully*. If only our drivers here were as courteous and as considerate as you are.'

'Yeah, well,' conceded the paunchy man, appeased, 'we get along.'

Harry left them to settle in while he went to his own bedroom and packed a suitcase. He picked up his passport,

221

resolved to put into effect a plan he had entertained many times. He pulled on his coat and was about to leave when he stopped, seeing an old 10-lb weight with a handle, like a small suitcase, which had belonged to his grandfather. Harry used it as a doorstop, but its real purpose was a weight for the antique scales his grandfather once used in his grocery shop. On impulse he bent down and lifted it, putting it into his suitcase which became substantially heavier. He took out a heavy length of string from one of the kitchen drawers and stuffed it into his pocket.

It was a glorious afternoon, the avenue of trees along which he drove a haze of light green through which the sunlight filtered. The shadows from the tree trunks slanting in rows across the road reminded him of the nave of the Abbey, and he recalled that day when he thought Eleanor told him she loved him. It was an abiding memory, with the elation and effusive high it had provoked. But the memory mocked him now on this, his last desperate bid for freedom.

The car ran smoothly in spite of its age, and in spite of being a Lada with its rusted wings—a car which everyone mocked as a cheap substitute for a real car. He had picked it up for a mere £200 and it more than served its purpose, for he and Anne rarely had occasion to drive. Its main handicap was the incredibly hard steering, but Anne managed it well with her stocky muscular arms. He was thankful that that day she had walked into town and left it in the garage. He even felt happy, succumbing to a sense of release because he had made a decision.

The road stretched ahead, across the green dales of the countryside, like freedom. He even felt a desire to sing. The road swung southwards and the sunlight glared in the windscreen, refracted by grease marks. He dipped his hand into the side pocket of the door for a rag. It came out, lifting and spilling scraps of paper onto the floor. He wiped the window and replaced the rag without losing speed. He dipped his hand down and picked up some of the papers. He squinted at them. There were more scratch cards and two old betting slips.

CHAPTER 25

Absconded

EXTRACT from the front page of *The Scottish Courier:*

RIDDLE OF RUNAWAY HOTELIER
Jedburgh wife sobs:
'Please come home'
A heartbroken wife last night spoke of the anguish caused by the mysterious disappearance of her husband, the owner of the Abbeyview Hotel in Jedburgh.

London-born Anne Denton, who runs the hotel with her husband, begged: "Harry, I love you very much. I'm very worried about you.

"Please get in touch—just come back to me."

For Mrs Denton, the past 24 hours since her husband's car was found abandoned at a seaside beauty spot have been a nightmare.

The couple shared an idyllic relationship. They are both prominent figures in Jedburgh and are well-respected by the community.

But last night it emerged that the hotel business they shared may have been the main reason behind Mr Denton's disappearance.

Mrs Denton, 36, reports that a dispute arose with some American guests staying at the hotel about the tariff quoted by Mr Denton and that demanded by Mrs Denton the following morning. She also reports that the guests made unreasonable demands to use her own private facilities in the belief that Mr Denton had said that in so doing they qualified for a hefty discount. One of the rooms was also double-booked by Mr Denton prior to his disappearance, resulting in a heated argument between Mrs Denton and guests who arrived later in the evening.

Mrs Denton concludes that the strain of running the hotel may have led to her husband's nervous breakdown with his subsequent disappearance.

Her 39-year-old husband, who was born in Dulwich, is a graduate of the University of Wales, has a PhD in literary stylistics, and was for a time a professor of English at the University of London before a career change into the hotel business.

He had recently been anguished over recurring disputes with guests concerning the limited parking facilities at the hotel. On one occasion during January, Mrs Denton reports, he stood guard in near freezing conditions to ensure the safety of a car belonging to a guest who threatened legal action if any damage were to occur to the vehicle.

Recently he took a week off to spend time talking over his difficulties with his wife during a short break in Malta.

Mr Denton is thought to have left the hotel in his maroon Lada, registration number B808 CHD, at 3pm on Tuesday.

The vehicle was found five hours later by police in the parking area adjacent to the beach at Bamburgh, about 50 miles away on the Berwickshire coast.

Yesterday, Mr Denton's wife appealed for her husband to come back and discuss his work dilemma.

She said: "Whatever problems you are thinking about we will sort them out together. Nothing is insurmountable.

"This is so out of character for Harry and that's why it is so shocking. He's been depressed for two or three weeks; before that he was coping with the pressures of work.

"We discussed this as much as we could but he found it quite difficult to talk about. He's never done anything like this before. It is completely out of the blue."

Detective Chief Inspector David Blair of Roxburghshire police appealed for anyone who saw Mr Denton's car or a man answering his description—6ft, dark brown hair, blue eyes, wearing dark navy trousers and a grey sport's jacket—to contact officers on 01835-862189, extension 36663.

"He may have booked into a hotel or guest house under a different name," said DCI Blair. "We are concerned for his welfare because he has never left his home before without letting his wife know."

*

'I just don't *understand* it!' wailed Anne, frumpishly spreading her knees as she leant forward to put down the cup of tea. 'And he's left me to cope with all these demanding guests on my own.' She shook her head, pursing her lips. 'I've had to call in Rosemary to help and she's so nervous she spilt coffee all over one of the Americans. Now I have to pay for the stupid man's dry-cleaning!' She pulled out a cigarette and a match flared. She drew heavily on the cigarette. 'I don't know what I did to be treated like this.' She shook her head. 'Ever since I was a child things went wrong for me. Not even my own mother wanted me.' She flicked her eyes briefly to gauge the reaction of her audience, at the same time flicking ash into an ashtray. 'I was adopted, you know.' She hung her head, dolefully surveying the pattern on the carpet. 'One day I came across my adoption certificate. I saw that my original name was Martha. What got to me, though, was that the name change had only cost half a crown! The paper had 2/6 stamped on it. Can you believe it? That's all I'm worth. Half a crown!'

'I'm sorry, Anne,' Eleanor said softly.

'Poor dear,' soothed Max, shaking his head. 'I'm sure he'll be back, you know. He probably just needed to blow off steam.'

'Well, we came around as soon as we saw that newspaper report, Anne,' Eleanor said with concern. 'Did you know he left a message on our answering machine?'

Anne eyed her suspiciously. 'What did he say?'

'Oh, just that he'd phoned. Do you suppose he was trying to reach out to us? I don't like to think that we weren't there for him.' She gave Anne a half-smile.

Anne flicked her eyes back to the carpet. 'I don't know what was in his mind. In the morning he was laughing and joking with the guests. Then I went into town to do my messages. When I came back there were these awful Americans wanting to use my toilet and no sign of Harry.' She shook her head again, tears gathering in her eyes. She drew deeply on her cigarette. 'I don't

225

know what got into him. The Americans wouldn't pay me more than £5 for a room! It was *unreal*!' She crushed her cigarette in the ashtray and picked up a copy of the newspaper report. 'What must people think when they read this! And they put this awful picture of me in, holding a photograph of Harry. And also this picture of the car on the back of the police recovery truck!' She shook her head, looking at the picture of herself in which her eyes and chin were almost enveloped by the surrounding folds of flesh. 'But at least people can see how much I miss him and want him back!' She wiped her eyes with a damp handkerchief before crushing it into a side pocket of her smock. She pursed her lips and nodded disconsolately at the carpet. 'And now Harry's bank manager wants to see *me*! He said he saw the newspaper report and may be able to throw some light.'

'Is there anything we can do, Anne?' asked Eleanor, tilting her head sympathetically.

'Sure, Anne,' Max nodded. 'You've only to ask.'

Anne bit her lip, still surveying the carpet. Her arms were folded tightly in front of her. 'Well, the fact is, I can do with some financial help.' She flicked her eyes up at Max and gave him a twisted grin. 'The truth is, I've been a bit of a naughty girl.'

Max's eyes widened. 'In what way?'

Anne continued to bite her lip, still grinning twistedly at the carpet. She rocked her head to and fro. 'Harry has been very stingy with money, you know. Recently I've got into a bit of debt. I met someone in the Pheasant who gave me a tip. He said it was a sure thing.'

'You mean, a bet on the giggies!' laughed Max. 'You're kidding me! What was the sure thing?'

Her smile twisted up at him. 'Fairy King.'

'*Fairy King*!' he guffawed. 'That's a donkey, Anne! *I* could have given you a better tip than that! You should have gone for Deep Water! That's Aldan Black's unbeaten colt that won the Grand Criterium at Langchamp yesterday. He's a 4-1 favourite for Saturday's Dewhurst Stakes. Look here, Anne, how much are you short?'

'About £2000,' she smiled, looking flushed. Hope gleamed in her eyes.

'Mm, *that* much?' he said, grasping his chin. He surveyed her with his Panda eyes. 'I tell you what, Anne. £450 both ways on Deep Water should get you out of your hole nicely. Can you lay your hands on that much?'

'Max,' Eleanor frowned, placing her hand on his elbow. 'I don't think this is the help Anne wants.' She looked at Anne, her voice soft with concern. 'I wish we could help you, Anne, but our own capital's needed for our house purchase. As it is, we've made too many inroads into it already, haven't we, Max?' She looked back at Max and flashed a worried smile at Anne. 'Max likes a flutter himself but they don't always pay off. Do you know what I mean, Anne? A horse can never be a sure thing.'

'Snookums,' Max objected, smiling. 'Deep Water is a sure thing if anything is!' He narrowed his eyes at Anne in a knowing smile. 'In fact, if you can lay your hands on just a couple of hundred I'll put it on Deep Water for you. I'm not exactly a stranger at the betting shop, you know.' He winked. 'I'm surprised we haven't bumped into each other there. Who do you generally deal with? That huge Amazonian blonde? I bet she could manhandle three men at once! I can see why they've employed her. Cor, I wouldn't like to argue with *her*! Then again...' He winked. 'Cheer up, Anne! Things are never as bleak as they seem. Have you heard what the elephant said to the naked man?'

She shook her head, still biting her lip.

'He said, "Cute, but can it pick up peanuts?"' He squeezed his eyes shut and shook with silent laughter. 'You have to think *big*, girl! Don't go around trying to pick up peanuts when you can have gold nuggets! Fortune favours the brave, as they say. What do you say, Anne? Can you at least manage a hundred?'

'No, Max, *no*!' Eleanor stood up. 'I think we better leave now, Anne.' Her eyes softened. 'You know, the best thing is to go and see the bank manager and see how he can help. You'll be surprised how helpful bank managers are.'

'Not in my experience, they're not!' said Max, standing up. 'They don't like risks. They're addicted to caution. Have you ever come across a wealthy bank manager?'

Anne sighed. 'I don't think Harry's bank manager likes me. Or the staff at the bank. I can tell by the way they look at me when Harry gives me a cheque to cash. They take the cheque to the back and get into a huddle. Then they phone Harry to make sure it's all right. It's awful. It makes me feel like a criminal.' She brought out her crushed handkerchief again and wiped her eyes. 'Why me, is what I want to know. Why *me*?'

CHAPTER 26

At Sea

HARRY LAY ON HIS BUNK with a glazed mind, cocooned from reality by ample administrations of Bacardi and Coke. He stared through the porthole at the huge moon drifting purposefully from cloud to cloud, lighting the dark sea with a luminescent glow. He smiled. He had given them the slip, all right. He felt pleased by his strategy. After abandoning the car in the deserted car park by the beach, he took the first bus that came along. It took him to Newcastle from where he caught another bus to the docks—just in time to use his credit card to buy a return ticket to Amsterdam on the *King of Scandinavia*.

It would attract less suspicion if he bought a return ticket, he thought. Not that he intended to use the return half. He closed his eyes, willing himself to succumb to the energy vibrations of the ship as it surged through the placid sea. But he couldn't erase the residue of uneasiness in the pit of his stomach. He couldn't altogether detach his mind from the plan which, in due course, he intended to execute.

'Let's have some fun! Let's have some fun!' a megaphone bellowed nearby, making Harry's eyes snap open. *'Horse racing will begin in the Columbus Lounge at 10 pm ship's time!'* Harry made his way down and watched others betting on the cut-out horses hobbling to the throw of dice. Thereafter he watched the frantic cabaret presented by the portly cruise manager who belted out *Hello Dolly*, smiling exuberantly while Harry tried to avoid eye contact to prevent himself being drawn into the act. He allowed the entertainment to work on him like a drug, massaging his mind from the reality that loomed ahead. The ageing blonde Danish cruise manageress in sprightly tights shot into the arena with an effusive smile, belting out a love song. If anything, Harry thought, avoiding her beaming eyes, she had nice legs.

He returned to his cabin where he doused his mind with further liberal helpings of duty-free alcohol. He kept up the administrations until he felt himself well insulated from reality. Then he pulled on his jacket and picked up the 10lb weight which he had placed near the bunk in readiness, tying it securely to his left wrist with the sturdy length of string. It wasn't much, he realised, but at least it would help to propel him downwards into the glassy sea.

He tucked his hand with the weight awkwardly under his jacket and picked up a half-bottle of whisky. His legs felt heavy and he made his way with a shuffling gait to the deck above and to the stern of the ship, feeling the gentle pitch and lurch of the deck through the soles of his feet. He stood by the railings and gazed at the frothing wake that stretched to the horizon.

Beyond the horizon was Anne, whom thankfully he would never see again. Sadness clutched his heart since Eleanor was there too, beyond that darkly shimmering stretch of water—and he would never see *her* again, either. He brought the whisky bottle down, awkwardly, to his left hand so he could unscrew it without revealing the weight. He lifted the bottle to his lips and pulled deeply, feeling the burning chute of coarseness down his sternum. The moonlight illuminated the wake into a turbulent iridescence. Fear clutched his heart at the thought of sinking into that turbulence, and he took another pull at the bottle. There was plenty of time, he told himself. He had the rest of his life for the right moment—as long as it came before morning.

He thought with irony, as he watched the iridescent foam, that everything in his life had brought him to this point. It was something Eleanor had said about personal evolution. It made nonsense of all his experience, his childhood struggles from learning to walk and learning to read to his university degrees and appointments, not to mention the anguish of his marriage. Death came to everyone eventually, anyway, so what was the point? You were doing yourself a favour by pre-empting it, escaping the forlorn and lonely days of old age, he told himself. Yet nothing happened by chance, Eleanor had said. Did that apply only if you were 'centred' and engaged in the energy flow of your life? What about the millions of suicides who successfully terminated their pointless lives before him? No-one ever stopped *them*, no coincidences, no voice from God, ever intervened. In death you were ultimately alone—not like birth where a midwife or a doctor and possibly other caring persons helped to ease the trauma. He thought of dogs or cats who sensed death and willed it, going out alone into the countryside to die. You knew when your time was up, he thought as a cloud obscured the moon and the sea darkened.

Was life that hopeless, he wondered, that he had to take this initiative to end it? Certainly his life with Anne wasn't *that* intolerable. He had seen her that morning with the Abbot. Clearly she had some sort of liaison with that seedy, displaced person. Not that he cared. There was no twinge of jealousy, though obviously she had forged some kind of relationship that was draining their income. He felt he just couldn't be bothered to dig out the truth and confront her again. It would require a major effort to break out of his spiralling complacency, to start again afresh. It was just the last straw, the final nail in the coffin, that was all. More depressing was the thought of Eleanor's friendship withdrawn. He hadn't realised how dependent his spirits had become on her, how much he was buoying himself up by the vibrations of her spiritual and sexual energy. He brought up the bottle again, feeling a further plunge of heat into his numbing body. He told himself that it wasn't lust alone that had kept him going. He saw her sharp blue eyes again before him, the dimples of her cheeks, and felt the radiance of her sweetness. But she would be forever married to someone else—someone who knew how to love her and to care for her. His only hope of sharing her world, in the end, was via Anne for whom a closer union with another woman was understandably repugnant. He had stepped so low as to force them both—Anne and Eleanor—into an unacceptable union. Yet, he thought bitterly, all the avenues, the openings that Eleanor seemed to be holding before him, were illusions, like mirages. He wanted so desperately to consummate his love for her, on any terms, but she closed the door whenever he reached out. He swore at himself and took another swig.

'For God's sake,' he said aloud, 'she's a married woman, you fool! What did you expect?'

But why had he felt the need to be drawn into her world in the first place? Was his life at the hotel so drab, an inescapable prison of daily smiling and scraping to petty demands? Most of his guests were uncomplaining and behaved themselves, after all. They were even self-effacing, preferring to stir their coffee with a soup spoon or the handle of a knife if he had forgotten to provide teaspoons! Once he'd overlooked the butter and when clearing found that everyone had spread their marmalade or jam directly onto the toast. They only needed to *ask!* And if they *did* ask, they apologised for bothering him. At the end of the day, he had to agree, courtesy and politeness *was* the rule, not the exception. Why, then, had he found the mundanity of the hotel, the grumpiness of guests, so much of a burden? He thought warmly of the two elderly sisters, both in their eighties, who came to stay repeatedly because they so much enjoyed chatting to him. He had to hide in his private lounge and peep through the door first to see if the coast was clear, to make sure he wasn't going to be waylaid by either of their beaming faces, testing his knowledge of English literature. They had both been headmistresses and were proud of the magnitude of their own reading.

'You're no *ordinary* innkeeper, you know!' he recalled the shrill voice of Avril, the older sister who was also the taller and leaner of the two. 'I told Judith you'd read William de Morgan! You see, you didn't let me down! Now what was the name of his most famous character?'

'Joseph Vance?' smiled Harry.

'You *see!*' shrieked Avril, turning to her sister. 'What did I tell you, Judith!'

'Yes, yes,' Judith smiled coyly at Harry, tugging her sister's elbow. 'I'm sure Dr Denton has plenty of work to get on with now, Avril.'

'But there's one more point to clear up!' beamed Avril, swaying as she bounced from one foot to the other. 'Which Victorian novelist did De Morgan emulate?'

'That would be Dickens, Avril,' smiled Harry, his arms sagging under the weight of the loaded tray he was carrying. 'Which of course is why he failed to become as famous, don't you think? For the turn of the century he was just *too* Dickensian.'

Harry smiled, remembering how they would hobble off to the Tourist Information Centre and engage everyone there in tales of how wonderful he was. Denise, the team leader at the TIC, sighed every time she saw them shuffle through the glass doors. She reported to Harry that his two dear old ladies were taking up an inordinate amount of their time singing his praises. So when the two sisters arrived on a repeat visit, Harry was quick to tell them that Denise at the TIC couldn't wait to see them again.

'Och *no!*' Denise would moan, when Harry informed her that they were back.

During the last visit Avril had turned ninety and Harry filled her bedroom with flowers. They were exhausting with all their literary questions, but he loved them, all the same.

They were as endearing, he thought, as the retired brother and sister who sought a twin-bedded room every time they passed through Jedburgh en route to their farm cottage near Inverness. They belonged to the salvation army and Gordon, the brother, invariably looked spruced up in his uniform while beaming his toothy smile. Wendy, his sandy-haired sister, always arrived in a dingy kilt that displayed her knock-knees and wrinkled stockings to advantage. Harry smiled, recalling how on each visit Wendy gave him a blow-by-blow account of how the local planning officer in Invernesshire gave official recognition to their ancient cottage as a dwelling house.

'He stood against the wall in the middle of the room. "Now I'm not saying the room's less than six feet high. And I'm not saying the ceiling slopes too steeply. And I'm not saying the floor isn't level. But I am saying I can stand up straight here, like. And that's good enough for me!" Then he ticked it off on his paper!' She beamed her misty blue eyes and angled her square jaw at Harry, whose arms felt weak with the weight of the tray he was holding. Gordon nodded, beaming toothily. Harry had to make his escape quickly or she'd trot the whole story out once more. After that she would explain how they furnished the cottage with upended tomato boxes and scraps of carpet donated by all their friends.

Then there was the overweight Mr Falconer who wore a hearing aid, breathed stentoriously and had a voice like a foghorn. Harry recalled how Mr Falconer tended to step nearer and nearer when he spoke, bellowing in friendliness and exuding bad breath. 'Do you know,' he bellowed in his nasal, sepulchral voice, stepping forward and attracting the attention of the whole dining room. 'Do you know who I saw on the cruise round the Outer Hebrides? It was Vincent Price! He was being interviewed! I tell you, it was Vincent Price!' Harry nodded amiably as he backed against the radiator, nearly overcome by the benevolent fumes and in danger of dropping the crockery on the tray he held.

There was a host of delightful people, he remembered. There was the lady doctor and her daughter he found dancing to the piped Scottish music in the dining room early one morning. And there was a nurse who radiated peace and calm, who came back with her aunt because the place felt like home. She even wrote and recommended the hotel in the Nursing Journal.

There were too many to recall, he realised. Most of them were delightful and slipped into oblivion as soon as they left. It was only the eccentric and the rude guests he remembered clearly, like Mr Ramsden. Why couldn't they all be sweet and charming, like Mrs Pimms?

He smiled, recalling Mrs Pimms as he took another swig from his bottle. She wasn't one of his guests. She was the sweet elderly lady in the Golden Oldies holiday group at the Golden Bay Hotel in Malta. For some reason she resurfaced in his mind now. She was always dressed so immaculately and he loved the bright and clipped way she responded to her husband's offer of a drink: *'Pimms, please*!' One morning she was sitting in the foyer with her Golden Oldies Group, waiting for the airport bus amidst a debris of luggage. He saw her there and turned his head for a last look. Her eyes met his and stopped his heart, crinkling and flashing a smile that reduced everyone else to dust. In that instant he had even forgotten about Eleanor! He shook his head, bemused. Even an old lady had the power to excite him. How come Anne had lost that ability altogether? But the old lady had a radiance, he realised, capable even of eclipsing Eleanor's! If only he could meet someone who had a radiance like that! Someone who wasn't twice his age or married to someone else.

All the best women in the world were always married to someone else, he thought bitterly.

No, he thought, looking distractedly at the bubbling wake of the ship. In spite of the flashes of happiness, life was a general drama of boredom. It was like the myth of Sisyphus, he thought bitterly. Everyday he wrestled pointlessly with his burden, pushing it up to the crest of the hill. Then it rolled down and he had to start over again. Day after day, season after season, always getting older and deeper into debt. The bubbling water would give him the peace he sought, in an abiding and continuing absence of consciousness. As the ship rose and fell gently beneath him, he imagined himself sinking into the turbulence, as in a whirlpool of oblivion. He would be unaware of the cry of gulls, the deep sea swell, the profit and loss of life. There would be peace, peace ...

He leaned forward over the rail, watching the white water boil against the steep side of the vessel. He watched it, hypnotically. A drop here would go straight down, he thought, avoiding the frightening turbulence of the propellers. He dropped the almost empty half-bottle of whisky and watched it plunge down, ricocheting once against the steel sides of the ship and sinking noiselessly into the white wake. He didn't want to hurt himself going down, he thought. He needed to find a position with a clearer drop into the ocean, with less danger of hitting the sides. He didn't fancy being sucked into the propellers, either. All he wanted was to sink quickly, safely into the depths where he could breathe the dark current under the sea and sink smoothly into oblivion.

He pulled himself up and began to shuffle a little further away from the stern and the boiling froth from the propellers. He was watching the sides, studying the water that slipped darkly past the ship with fascination, when he sensed some other people nearby.

He froze. He would have to wait for then to move away. He tucked the weight which he held in his left hand further under his jacket, pretending to watch the moonlight which shone in a rippling silver band across the sea.

The dark shapes of two women shuffled closer, the taller with white hair that gleamed in the moonlight.

'*Can* it be?' the smaller one said in a hushed voice. 'Is this Dr Denton I see before me!'

'Let wonders seem familiar!' shrieked the taller of the two. 'And in the *middle* of the North Sea!'

They shuffled closer, peering closely at Harry.

He didn't know whether to be amazed, pleased, or annoyed. 'Judith and Avril?' he blinked, wondering if he had already jumped overboard and that this was a near-death experience.

'It *is*!' shrieked Avril, delighted and hobbling from one foot to another. 'It's a miracle! It's our Dr Denton! It's our Innkeeper, I declare!' She lay her skeletal hand on her sister's shoulder. 'You see, Judith, I *told* you he's no ordinary innkeeper!'

'This is quite a coincidence,' smiled Harry, feeling detached. He wished they'd go away and at the same time gave way to a wave of relief. After all, he told himself, there was plenty of time.

'Shouldn't you be looking after your guests, Dr Denton!' chided Avril, shaking a crooked finger at him. 'Putting flowers in their rooms!' She gave a scintillating laugh.

'I'm sure Dr Denton deserves a break, Avril,' put in Judith with her coy smile. 'I always said, he works too hard, you know.' She smiled up at Harry, though she addressed her sister.

'Now then, young man!' shrilled Avril, hopping more quickly from foot to foot in her excitement. 'I've got a question for you! What was the name of Charles Kingsley's book on natural theology? In it, he says nature is no less sacred than the Bible, and that the naturalist acknowledges the finger-mark of God and wonders—and worships! *There*! See if you can answer *that* one!' Her eyes sparkled in the moonlight as she watched him.

Harry gave a half smile. 'I suppose that would have to be *Glaucus*, his work on marine biology.'

'You *see*! You *see!*' Avril shrieked at her sister. 'I *told* you he's no ordinary innkeeper!'

Judith smiled apologetically at Harry. 'Avril's been catching up with her reading on Kingsley. She's made me reread the *Water-Babies*.'

'Physical and spiritual evolution!' announced Avril, nodding energetically as she continued to hop from foot to foot. 'The one's a parable for the philosophy of the other. You know, when Tom drowns he evolves into a higher spiritual being! In marine life he saw that God was perfecting nature. Just as we continue the evolution towards the Kingdom of God. Even the polypses under the sea here are part of that greater plan. Do you agree with that, Dr Denton?'

'Avril is a deep thinker,' smiled Judith. 'I hope we're not keeping you? You look tired.'

'No, no, I'm fine,' Harry lied. His left arm was beginning to ache, concealing the weight tied to his wrist. It was a familiar sensation. Usually he was holding a tray when they waylaid him with their questions. 'It's a beautiful night, isn't it?'

Avril nodded frantically, her shining eyes fixed on him. 'The true schoolroom, according to Kingsley, is the ocean, the prairie and the forest! He sees the universal in the particular! The infinite in the most worthless of sea-vermin! Every act of life is a step in the right direction, to the infinite good. His contemplation of the idea of God's perfection gave him an intuitive light, not derived from any book! He said it was something he felt in his brain! What do you think of that! Don't you just feel things in your brain, Dr Denton, when you just *know* you're going in the right direction?'

He sighed. The weight in his hand was tedious and he longed to stretch out his arm and let it hang down. 'Yes,' he said. 'I've heard something like that before. You sense a development to a higher level of vibration. A friend of mine ...'

'There!' shrieked Avril to her sister, hopping madly from side to side. 'Just look at the power of his mind! I've never heard it put that way before! A higher level of vibration! I *told* you he was no ordinary innkeeper!'

Judith smiled. 'I think Dr Denton's tired, now, Avril.' She put her hand on Avril's arm and tried to steer her away. 'It's late now, and we were just getting some air.' She gave Harry another apologetic smile. 'Avril gets a little excited, you know. But she's very sharp for ninety, isn't she?'

'You certainly are,' he smiled sincerely at Avril whose eyes beamed back at him. 'I've never seen anyone so vibrant. I don't know where you get the energy from, Avril.'

'Listen to his silver tongue!' Avril proclaimed. 'Are you taking the return crossing tomorrow night? Will we see you then? I've got some questions on Wilkie Collins I want to put to you!'

'I might spend a few days in Amsterdam,' he replied. 'I'm afraid I won't see you again.'

'Oh, but you *will*! We'll see you in the summer! We want the same room with the view of the Abbey, do you hear!' Avril's voice was high with excitement. 'We want to see that nice lady at the Information centre and tell her all about you!'

'That would be lovely,' he smiled sadly. 'You two are my favourite guests.'

'Listen to him!' proclaimed Avril. 'I bet he knows that Dickens and Wilkie Collins wrote a play together! Do you know the name ...?'

'Avril,' protested Judith, a little more firmly. 'It's time we were in bed now. You don't want to get over excited, you know.' She smiled coyly and apologetically at Harry. 'She gets a bit overexcited.'

'Yes, yes, bed!' Avril began to bounce from foot to foot again. 'Did you know that Wilkie Collins wrote a story about a bed? A terribly strange bed ...'

'Come, Avril,' Judith said, steering her away firmly, She looked back and smiled at Harry. 'She's very sharp for ninety, but she needs her beauty sleep. We'll look for you at breakfast. We'll be in the Seven Seas Restaurant.'

'I'll see you there,' Harry said lamely. He relaxed his arm as he watched them shuffle away, Avril still bobbing from side to side. 'I *told* you...,' he heard her saying as they disappeared behind a bulkhead.

He turned to face the railings again and sighed. He watched the water slip by, bubbles catching the moonlight as they frothed and broke against the moving side of the ship. The moon was as large as ever as it drifted in a purposeful line from cloud to cloud. The deck vibrated and shifted almost imperceptibly beneath his feet. The night was calm and peaceful. The effects of the alcohol had largely worn off and he felt too sober to kill himself. And something Avril had said about the most worthless of sea-vermin being important had brought tears to his eyes.

There would be no harm in procrastinating the act until the return crossing, he thought. There was plenty of time. He could even treat himself to some window-shopping in Amsterdam. Who knows, he might even see a girl that looked like Eleanor!

How strange, he thought as he fumbled his way back to his cabin, that he should bump into his two old ladies on the ferry. It was like one of those strange coincidences that Eleanor talked about. He was looking forward to his bunk. He could lie down and let the gentle movement of the ship rock him into oblivion. He might even dream of Eleanor.

CHAPTER 27

Amsterdam Inferno

HARRY FELT as though he'd already joined the ranks of the damned. He watched his compatriots trudge from the dark hole into the porno cinema to fill the faded tiers. The live show was about to commence and no one spoke. The uneasy silence punctuated by the occasional cough made him think of the sanctity of a church. The difference here was that each person was anonymous and isolated by his own loneliness, shrouded by the half light that concealed his identity.

This was hardly the environment that would promote his personal evolution, Harry thought ironically, but then he had abandoned all hope for a future in whatever form. Before his selfish act had destroyed his friendship with her, Eleanor had spoken of the power of thought and the need to be alert to the mysterious intuitive way in which one's life evolved. She had spoken of the way people came into one's life at just the right time to give one the right answers at the point of need. But here he was isolated from his companions. Nobody wanted to be recognised by anyone else. Everyone shrank back into themselves, alert only to the expectation of lust.

The music shattered the silence on cue, tearing, piercing the tympanums of dead ears. Harry felt himself instantly at one with his voiceless companions, gawking at the rhythmic posturing of a floppy-breasted dancer who took them by storm. She ran amuck among them, climbing and clambering over their dormant bodies, extorting polite laughter as she prodded bloated middle-aged bellies and ground her velvet, pointed nipples into deadpan faces. Harry sank back into his seat, hoping to avoid audience participation.

In the next act the music settled into a monotonous jangle. A leering ethnic actor surveyed the dead sea of staring faces with impudent superiority, churning his nonchalant manhood in the upturned portal of the leading lady who lay flattened, on her back, face turned away from the gaping eyes.

Harry wondered what kind of fascination had brought him here. Eleanor had blamed him, saying what he had done was a manipulation for her energy. But at least his manipulation was motivated by a form of love so anguished for consummation that it had resorted to a desperate contrivance. But what he was witnessing here was not even a manipulation for energy. It was mere soulless exploitation for money. He sank into his seat, watching the loveless mechanical act. His own sense of revulsion, he thought bitterly, was merely an emotional justification for being there. 'You're a bloody hypocrite,' he accused himself, forcing himself to watch, yet feeling sickened and empty. There was no fulfilment here. The actor grinned and winked at his audience, thrusting mechanically into the lady who remained flattened and motionless on the stage floor. The wonder was that he maintained an erection, Harry thought. And the woman, whose face was turned away like Eleanor's ... At least, he recalled, Eleanor had responded by twitching and screaming like a banshee. And she wasn't doing it for Max, either. That, at least, proved something, whatever it was.

Someone had said Amsterdam was a city made for wanderers. Its concentric streets, like its concentric canals, brought him back, time and again, to the inner core of decay. His path wound and twisted, bustled by the crowds flowing across the bicycle-lined bridges, past near-naked women in windows, flesh oozing from every cup, and then into a glass-covered boat, moving under bridges and glimpsing famous towers. He winced as he saw a young woman knocked over and arrested for shoplifting just in front of him in the crowded main street. It was the day after the resurrection, he thought, the hordes flowing on the pavements. He was caught up with the flow and moved on, along leafy avenues where yellow trams snaked and barrel organs yelled. Sightless black windows in rust-coloured walls watched his progress, funnelled by wrought-iron railings over bridges with chained bikes decaying, wheelless.

Then he was back again, like a moth's fluttering return, to the neon lights reflected in zigzag patterns in the opaque water, rainbow-iridescent and sluggish with oil slicks. One sign read:

'EROTIC VIDEO—CABINS'—spiced with the shimmering outline of a naked lady in fishnet stockings; another read 'PORNO supermarket—Demonstration Video.' He was bustled again by the thronging hoards along Oude Zijds Achterburgwal and back again by Oude Zijds Voorburgwal with its rows of signs—*kamer te huur*—and into Warmoesstraat, with more signs—*kamer te huur*—then back again, circling the great Ouderkerk that loomed majestic from the tortured twisting cobbled passages, red-lit, glaring, illuminating the bare legs and bulging boobs, the blue-luminous panties and black bras of winking widow girls—each pinpointed by a red glow and a sign that read *kamer te huur*.

The passages narrowed and the milling throng squeezed through. A young fresh faced blonde whom Harry guessed was somebody's loving daughter leant out and smiled at him. She spoke in dulcet tones: 'You want to come in now? Have a nice fuck?' He returned her smile and flowed back again, along the Oude Zijds Achterburgwal where the canal slid sluggishly and cars crawled and growled, nudging the dormant perambulators under the signs that read: *kamer te huur*. Then he moved over the narrow bulging-bridge and a flash of light picked out a girl in black lingerie in a window above him. He saw her start, turn and fling shut the curtains, erupt from the door with her thin black-stockinged legs sprinting over the red glare of wet cobbles. She was a wildcat that clutched a startled fur-coated woman, shouting: *'You took picture! You took picture! Give me the film!'* Her voice tore into the red-lit night, rebuffed by the nasal transatlantic whine: *'Na! na! She was only photographing the canal!'*

Harry froze, seeing the wildcat strike and the furred lady sprawl horizontally. *'You bitch! You took picture!'* screamed the wildcat, wrestled away by the lady's husband. But she screamed and clawed: *'Give me the film! Give me the film!'*

Harry melted away from the melee, frightened, his heart a spasm of pain and pleasure, and flowed again around the cobbled apron of the Oudekerk that tolled and peeled—*kamer te huur*—a musical jangle insistent, persistent, striking the hour like a gong of doom.

His time was running out, he realised. Soon he would be back on the dark sea, waiting for the right moment to hurl himself into black oblivion. He had one chance left to throw himself at life. He circled again and sought out the fresh faced blonde. She had the look of a girl next door, he thought.

He humped and strained in a darkened room, buckling over her prostrate female flesh, fighting for release while he felt desire fade, inexorably leaving a vacuum filled with frustration and fear.

His frustration beat against his ribs. His fear of death began to pound in his temple. The Ouderkerk tolled the hour for more spirits to stir the sterile water that slid red in the night.

'What is your name?' he asked.

'Angel!' she smiled.

'Do many find it difficult ...?'

'*Ach*! So *many*!' She shrugged her slim pretty shoulders. 'But *why*? They are all so nervous!' She shook her golden locks. 'I know not why!'

Then they're not yet dead, he thought bitterly.

His feet flowed into the night and the bells tolled as the Ouderkerk chuckled a jangle of musical peels. A little girlchild, thin and ugly in bedraggled jeans, pulled his arm on the humped Ouderkerk bridge. *'Don't you want to fuck with me? Only twenty-five guilders!'* Her words shocked his arm away, but she clung still: *'For one hour! I give you blow job!'* Her angular face, her starved eyes pleaded with his. He broke loose through Damstraat and Damsrak, past signs sprouting—*kamer te huur*—away from the damned, his soul an agony of twisting pain.

'This is fucking hell,' he thought, and the remembrance of the words that followed went through his throbbing brain: Nor are we out of it.

He followed the concentric canals while the yellow trams rumbled and sparked. Somewhere a barrel-organ ground out its wild agony. He saw a skater, wired for sound, streak in the bicycle lane, past the food slot machines and the Rijksmuseum where a bagpipe pierced the night in a thin squeal. Two youths loomed, unkempt, unshaven, and asked him: 'You speak English?'

'Nein!' he shook his head and melted away.

When he returned to his hotel and collected his key, he saw a red-haired girl at the receptionist's desk. 'My name's Bell,' she said brightly. 'You know, as in Ding-Dong!'

He liked her. There was something robust and healthy about her. He hoped he might get a chance to speak to her, but then he saw she had a companion—a pimply-faced youth with a haunted look. He sighed. All the best girls were spoken for, he thought.

She and her companion were in the room next door to his. He heard then making love. It must have taken all of half a minute. There was the sound of energetic thumping, a sudden rattling of the bed's headboard against the wooden partition. It put him in mind of rabbits copulating, it was so rapid and quick. He lay awake for hours in the stretched silence that followed, thinking of Eleanor and her high screams of ecstasy, her face turned away from his.

The next day Harry sat in Vondel Park, shell-shocked by the altered course of his life. There was no point in delaying the inevitable, he thought, and he resolved to release himself from the burden of consciousness when he took the overnight ferry the next day. He watched the dawn suffuse the Arcadian setting in green auras of chestnut trees and spread around the steaming water. He stared at the little figurine in the middle of the fountain, a statuesque nymph of stone, spray-painted, her legs mauve, her torso green and little breasts a gaudy pink running down her olive stomach.

Around him, like a machine starting, the joggers panted and strained, neck muscles pulled taut. He watched them circling, following the infinitely twisting paths that interlaced and interlocked the lake, seeing the fountain spurt, off and on, off and on. Dogs, great and small, walked their owners, pursuing the concentric paths that wound and twisted.

His disconsolate eyes lifted up to a sculpture that stood above him, big and bulbous, stout-bellied and large-breasted, head uplifted to the steeple that inspired Anne Frank with hope through twenty-five weary months. Its body of forged metal appeared to crumble and sag—black fragmented iron, charred remains that made him think of a soul burnt-out with neglect. It filled him with a sense of poignant loneliness. Her soul, like her body, appeared purposeless, hollow and aerated, sagging unwanted, her eyes forgotten holes turned up appealingly to the spire that stood silent and erect, aloof from her world.

Harry took one last journey that day, visiting Anne Frank's house. She would have been an old woman now, he thought sadly. He saw that the Nazi's found her in 1944—so near the end of the war. His heart went out to her again and again, seeing her diary so neat and meticulous: 'I still believe that people are really good at heart.' What he'd like to know was who betrayed her—who made that mysterious phone-call to the Nazis? He hoped sincerely that the cruel informer had lived long enough to see the girl he or she betrayed become famous.

He had little to eat that night and felt weary from all the walking he'd done. He was weary of life and was almost impatient for the ferry. He looked forward to the release it would bring with a new and firmer resolution. He made his mind go blank and sank almost immediately into sleep.

He dreamt he and Anne were walking around a strange city. It was a foreign city, since the sun was too bright and the air too warm for Scotland or England. They were chatting happily and holding hands. Then they met a girl, a brunette who was tall and slender and they fell into conversation easily. The girl's natural, easygoing and unpretentious girlish charm pervaded the scene without being obtrusive. They spoke cheerfully and the girl laughed freely, as though she'd always known them. In a moment they were all chatting like old friends, not realising so soon the impact of her presence. Harry became gradually aware that the girl by his side was no longer Anne but Eleanor. It made no difference that it was Eleanor, not Anne, who was laughing. He was aware that she was much shorter than the newcomer who stood in front of him and now drew all his attention. This girl, whoever she was, radiated a natural energy and a natural enthusiasm for life. Her eyes were bright and lively, her smile wide and generous.

Eleanor was saying that her sister and brother-in-law were coming to stay with them the following week and the girl replied with a laugh, going to the heart of the matter at once: 'Oh dear, doesn't that *always* happen? Just when you thought you've got some time to yourself!'

Harry smiled broadly, amazed. He thought, how did she *know*!

He was spellbound as he watched and talked, seeing how naturally and effortlessly she carried herself as they walked together. But there was an awareness of a cloud, of some time that must elapse, some upheaval that must take place, before he would see her again.

'Will we see you again?' he asked innocently as she turned gracefully to leave.

'Who can say?' she laughed, making the sun rise in his heart.

'Where do you live?' It was a natural thing to ask but he had to know.

'Here, I'll show you,' she said, her eyes twinkling. 'This is how you can find me!'

It was a game. She wrote all sorts of clues on a piece of paper in an incredibly short space of time. When she handed the paper to him he couldn't believe how much she'd written. Her handwriting was neat but spidery towards the end of the page. It would lead him, as far as he could tell, to a certain tree.

'But how will we know where to go from the tree?' he laughed. It was like a treasure hunt, and he noticed his use of 'we,' as though he pretended the game was to include Eleanor.

'Oh, *this* is where I am,' she said with another burst of good humour, handing him a silver bowl. On the inside of the bowl were arrows—like a compass.

It was intriguing. But he still felt uneasy about not being able to find her. He turned over the piece of paper she had given him and there it was! She had written her address down, as clear as day: 31 Elgin Street, Durban.

He looked up, amazed—but she was gone. Eleanor was gone, too. He looked around and saw a toilet. He needed the loo, he thought, and went in. The urinal had piles of wood next to it, as well as an axe. He urinated and felt incredibly excited at the same time.

He awoke, still half in the dream, feeling the need to urinate. He staggered up and made his way down the passage to the toilet. When he returned to his room the excitement of the dream was still with him. He kept rerunning it through his brain, as if it were a video-recording.

He was aware that Eleanor, like Anne, had diminished to dust the minute the strange brunette walked into the scene. She had come over so naturally and so easily that he hadn't even realised the impact she was having on him. He knew now that in that moment he had fallen in love! And yet it was only a dream! She was like a goddess that stepped into time, appearing like an ordinary happy-go-lucky girl, rather tall, a brunette with bright eyes and a ready laugh—and with an uncanny ability to catch his drift. He had been smitten by this incredible creature—and it had only taken a moment! But, he thought, bemused though excited, it was only in a dream.

Then he remembered that she had written down her address, though she hadn't given her name. She was like a girl next door, though never in his life had he known a girl next door like her. He still remembered the address she gave. He took out his pen and wrote it down: 31 Elgin Street, Durban.

That's ridiculous, he told himself. It was only a dream, and he'd never ever been to Durban, though he knew it was a place somewhere in Africa. He'd never even been to Africa. He knew that it couldn't really be true, that the girl couldn't really exist, let alone live at that address. It was only a dream. But he hugged himself, still in a cocoon of excitement. If he could feel that way about another girl—a girl who wasn't Eleanor—and a girl in a dream!—then there was a chance he could feel that way about a real girl in the real world!

It was like a new discovery. God, he thought, it was as though she was real, and that she *wanted* him to find her!

He got back into bed, pulling the bedclothes tightly around himself, squeezing his eyes in excitement. The dull siren of a police car wow-wowed in the distance. If she existed, he thought, he would find her.

The next day, when the cleaner came in to clean the room which Harry had vacated, she was surprised to find a 10-lb weight under the bed.

CHAPTER 28

Thistle Cottage

THE TREES formed a spidery network of bare branches along the narrow country lane. Snow powdered the tar, decorating the hedgerows and the fine filaments of branches. He would miss this country, Harry thought, as his Lada jolted to a stop next to the small farm cottage that lay alongside the road, low and long like an abandoned railway carriage. Smoke twisted lazily from the chimney.

'Halloo,' smiled Eleanor as she opened the door. 'Come and sit by the fire, Harry. Max will get you a drink.'

Max gave him a half-smile. 'Got some Scotch somewhere.' He rose from the settee and shook Harry's hand. 'Back from the dead, eh? The whole town thought you'd skedaddled or kicked the bucket. I told them you were just blowing off steam.'

Harry laughed awkwardly. 'I'm afraid I gave a lot of people a lot of trouble, including the police. The truth is, things just got on top of me. I needed to sort things out, you know. I came to a decision.'

Harry sat in silence while Max poured them both a drink. He tried to catch Eleanor's eye as she put the final touches to the dinner table. She looked soft and elegant in a flowing blue dress that accentuated the blue of her eyes. Her jet-black hair was tied back, but she looked drawn. She kept her eyes on the table. The small black stove on the hearth radiated warmth, the lapping flames visible through the glass in the metal doors. It all felt incredibly cosy and the plush carpets in the depressed area in front of the hearth surprised him. It was like a love-nest, he thought, and made him think of languorous love-ins, or relaxing sex-games, Max exploring a dolly-bird's taut little bottom while Eleanor watched, smiling.

'Rumour has it that you sold the hotel?' said Max, offering him a glass of Scotch. 'And that Anne's no longer with you?'

'Thank you, Max.' Harry accepted the drink, cradling it in his hands. 'Yes, the new owners are moving in next week. I was lucky to sell so quickly, really. And Anne's with her mother in Streatham. Our divorce is in its final throes, you might say.'

'She was worried about you,' Max stated. 'Worried to death.'

Harry swivelled his glass in his hands. He was aware of a certain tension in the air and felt certain Eleanor had told Max about his bedroom exploitation. 'Perhaps. But the marriage had run out of steam, you might say. I made my decision to go ahead with the divorce while I was in Amsterdam. As I said, I needed time to think.'

'How did Anne take it?' Max sipped his Scotch and placed the glass near him on the carpet. He trained his eyes on Harry.

Harry gave another awkward laugh. 'Not very well. She took a running kick at me and called me a bastard. I suppose that's what I am, but I couldn't go on any longer. We were just living a lie.' He didn't want to go into all the sordid details of Anne's mounting debts and addiction to gambling. He felt he deserved the guilt for giving up. 'There just wasn't any love left on my side, I'm afraid. She'll get half of whatever's left of the hotel money, after the mortgage is repaid.'

'You could have spiced up your sex life.' He winked and gave a smile that failed to include his eyes. 'I suggested the wheelbarrow position to Eleanor last week. That's when you grab the woman by the legs and she holds herself up by her hands. You know what she said?'

Eleanor gave a sidelong glance at Max. 'Don't believe everything he says, Harry.'

Max grunted. 'Oh, she agreed, but only when I promised not to push her past her mother's house!' His eyes pinched shut, his belly quivering in a half-hearted attempt at silent laughter. 'She's not very bright, is Snookums.'

Eleanor walked quickly into the small kitchen where Harry heard her busying herself with the meal she was preparing.

'Look at these, Harry.' Max leant over and picked up a calendar. 'It's the *Sun's* girlie calendar for this year. Which one do you prefer? I fancy Miss July best with everything spilling out of her T-shirt.'

Harry smiled and perused the pictures. He stopped at a petite dark-haired girl with radiant blue eyes and small supple breasts. 'She's rather nice.'

Eleanor came back in and set a serving dish on the table. Max called her over. 'What do you think, Snookums? Which girl looks the nicest?'

Eleanor came over politely and flicked through the calendar. She stopped at a picture of a lean girl in a transparent gossamer gown. It was in soft focus, suggestive of autumnal mist. 'Miss October,' she said, without a smile. As she turned back to the table her foot caught Max's glass on the carpet, spilling the Scotch.

'You *stupid* cow!' shouted Max angrily. 'Why can't you open your fucking eyes!' He picked up the empty glass and returned it to the sideboard. He lifted the bottle. 'Damn Scotch is nearly finished, too!'

'Well, I'm sorry,' said Eleanor meekly. 'Dinner is ready.'

Harry felt awkward and wished he'd brought a bottle of Scotch with him as a peace offering. He noticed that Max hadn't refilled his glass.

Supper consisted of leek soup and a curry made from a diced vegetarian substance called Quorn that looked and tasted like chicken. Conversation was desultory, though Max tried to lighten the mood with a question: 'Have you ever thought why condoms are called French letters, Harry?' he asked with a little smirk.

'I've no idea, Max,' Harry smiled politely.

'Well, it's obvious, isn't it?' He scraped the last of his soup with his spoon. 'If they were called Welsh letters, they'd have leeks in them.'

Harry grinned broadly and Eleanor gave Harry a half smile. 'Max is a laugh a minute, Harry. Especially when we have guests.'

'Well,' retorted Max, putting down his spoon and helping himself to the curry. 'I'll tell you this, Harry. We eat a lot better when we have guests. Snookums takes a little more...' He shook his head and grunted. 'She took a lot more trouble with you coming tonight, Harry. Perhaps you'd better come round more often. Things might become a little more edible around here.'

Harry was touched and flicked a smile at Eleanor. 'I think this is a superb supper. Since I've been on my own I've been making do with fish and chips or the occasional take-away from the chinky.' The silence that followed was broken only by the sounds of forks clinking on plates. Harry tried to change the subject. 'What are your plans? Have you found a suitable house yet.'

'We're moving out at the end of the month. I've found a flat that's much more reasonable and takes less heating. This place is just burning up capital.'

Eleanor stopped chewing with her mouth full. She looked at Max with wide eyes. 'You didn't tell me we were moving at the end of this month. I just paid next month's rent today into the landlord's account, as we usually do.'

Max dropped his fork and paled visibly. His Panda eyes drilled into Eleanor. 'What?' His voice was ominously quiet.

'Well, you should have told me, Max.' She smiled and Harry saw she had gone very pale. 'I'll just ask for a refund. It's not the end ...'

'You *stupid bloody bitch*!' roared Max, standing up in vexation. 'You know *damn well* we'll never get that money back!'

Harry self-consciously broke a piece of Quorn into fine pieces with his fork, not trying to look conspicuous as all hell broke loose around him.

'Max, Mr Shem is a reasonable man. All we have to do is tell him ...'

'Shem is a bloody shyster!' He banged his hand on the table. 'You *stupid* bloody cow! You can't get *anything* bloody right! I fucking told you we were moving *out*. You even started to pack your damn crystals! Most of the time you're in some bloody dream! It's time you woke up and got your feet on the ground.'

Max slumped back onto his chair and snorted. 'Sorry, Harry,' he said half apologetically. 'It's just that she *knew* we were moving.'

Harry smiled tactfully. 'I'm sure there won't be a problem about a refund, Max. You just have to explain a payment was made in error. If I were the landlord I wouldn't hesitate...'

'Oh, if *you* were the landlord!' he snorted. 'Not all landlords are gentlemen like you, Harry. And you don't have to deal with a simpleton of a wife, either.'

'Max, that's not *fair*,' Eleanor protested, lifting her eyes from her plate, her tears just held back. 'I was only trying to be efficient.' She stood up and began to remove the empty dishes. She went out with a sense of subdued sadness. Harry's heart went out to her. He longed to go after her and put his arms around her.

'Bloody cow,' Max said gruffly in an undertone. 'She just won't grow up, you know, Harry, with her crystals and Buddhas and silly talk about vibrations. I went along with it for a time because, well...' He shrugged. 'I guess it all seemed sort of cute, at first. But she's just the same in everything she does. Like a child. You know, she hasn't signed anyone up for Speedway in over two months!'

Harry felt he had to say something in Eleanor's defence. He spoke diffidently. 'These are difficult times, Max. You must admit she's very sincere.'

'Sincerity's *one* thing, Harry!' Max leaned forward confidentially. 'But imagine Eleanor, aged 30, still trying to get a position as a model! And if she does manage an interview, she talks about crystals and energy auras. No wonder people think she's bonkers! And I'll tell you something else.' Max's penetrating eyes burned in their scorched sockets.

'What's that, Max?'

Max dropped his voice. 'She's been having a close relationship with the single mother who lives next door here. A pretty enough creature that I invited to share—you know—a bit of slap and tickle. She wouldn't play ball, if you catch my drift. But she and Eleanor took to each other right away. Whenever I come home Sandy—that's her name—is either here, or Eleanor's *there.* '

Harry shook his head. confused. 'She's probably quite lonely during the day. I'm sure it's quite innocent, Max.'

Max pursed his lips. 'Well, I don't know. Eleanor claims she's a healer, you know, and has long sessions with Sandy. Laying on of hands, that type of rubbish.'

'I never saw her as evangelical ...'

'No, of course not,' Max dismissed the suggestion contemptuously. 'It has to do with auras. You know the sort of mumbo-jumbo she speaks.'

Harry was nonplussed. His emotions were a cauldron of confusion. He had never entertained the notion of Eleanor and Max not having a perfect and enviable relationship. Harry was surprised by his own question. 'Max,' he began, his heart in his mouth. 'Surely you two ... surely you still make love? With each other, I mean?'

He grunted. 'Not in a month of Sundays!'

Harry saw that Max was in his own private hell—something he never thought possible. He had always envied Max and now his heart went out to him, as it did to Eleanor a moment before.

'Max,' Harry said, and cleared his throat. He steeled himself, feeling he had to say this, for friendship's sake. 'Don't get me wrong, Max. But I've heard Eleanor—um—in the throes of ecstasy when you made love to her in the hotel.'

Max's eyes widened and bored into Harry. They registered genuine shock.

'Don't get me wrong, Max. I didn't mind. In fact, I was delighted to know how happy you two were together—and how compatible.' He smiled apologetically. 'Surely that's evidence of how much she appreciates you?'

Max eyed Harry for some time, almost suspiciously. Then he pursed his lips and spoke sneeringly. 'Harry, it could be *anybody*! That's just the point. She'll carry on like that with *anybody*!'

It was a double blow. Harry felt he was as much a victim as Max was. Yet he felt painfully concerned for Eleanor. Maybe it was just that she was so wrapped up in her own energy field, he thought. Or was it because she was so totally plugged in to a higher source of energy? But the sad and drawn girl he loved so much hardly looked as though she were receiving a higher inflow of strength that evening.

Max flicked out a cigarette and struck a match. 'What about you, Harry? What are your plans now?'

'I'm just waiting for the new owners to take over. Then I'm off to London. I have a temporary job at a language academy in Crystal Palace. Teaching English to foreign students. With any luck it could become a permanent job.' His mouth crinkled in a half smile. 'I've also applied for a professorship at a university in South Africa. It's a bit of a long shot, but this particular university is one of the newer ones. They may be desperate enough to consider me, though my previous professorship in London may stand me in good stead.'

'Why do you say desperate?' Max frowned, drawing on his cigarette.

'Well, I've been out of touch with the academic scene. And the university is in an unstable political area, in the north. They've been looking for someone for some time. There's even an extra regional allowance, similar to the London allowance.' He smiled. 'In this case the staff call it danger pay, I believe.'

'From the sublime to the ridiculous!' Max smiled. 'Or is it the other way round? At least you're out in the front line, out there. Not like a cosy hotel proprietor. You'll be engaged with brains, not bodies.'

Harry smiled non-committedly. 'That's one way of looking at it.' He shrugged. 'Anyway, beggars can't be choosers. And I have to do something with my life. What's left of it.'

Max's eyes took on a knowing gleam. 'Talking about bodies. You'll be in London for a time, right?'

Harry nodded.

'Well, do yourself a favour, old man.' He winked and tapped some ash into an empty plate. 'While you're there, visit a nice little number called Geena who gives a wonderful massage.' He lowered his voice. 'She has the nicest pair of tits in London.' He took out his wallet and thumbed through some cards. 'Here you are. Stick that in your back pocket—and give her my love!' He handed the card to him just as Eleanor came in with the coffee.

They moved to the comfortable seats near the fire. Max rattled the stove and threw more coal onto the fire. Then he excused himself, saying he needed to look over a list of prospects he wanted to call on the next day. He settled back at the table with some sheets of paper.

Eleanor brought her cup of coffee with her and sat down on the plush carpet near Harry's feet. She cradled her cup in both hands. She sipped her coffee and looked up at him over her cup.

Harry was aware again of the blue of her eyes and her long lashes.

'Harry,' she said quietly, unsmiling. 'I want to apologise to you.'

'Whatever for, Eleanor?' He was surprised. If anything, he felt the need to apologise to *her*.

'I know I've been a very silly girl, and I probably led you on, without meaning to, or realising it.'

'How do you mean, Eleanor?' But he knew exactly what she meant.

She gave a little half smile. Her voice was soft and contrite. 'The way I dressed in front of you and perhaps some of the things I said. It's in my nature to be very friendly. I should have realised I was overstepping the lines of friendship. I took advantage of you, didn't I, when you were in a very vulnerable condition?'

'You did no such thing, Eleanor ...' He wanted to say by all means continue to take advantage of me! He glanced quickly at Max who seemed to be absorbed in his work. 'I loved every minute of your ... ' He smiled down at her, tears in his eyes. 'Your friendship has meant everything to me. You opened up a whole new world to me.' He knew his voice was trembling with sincerity.

'I know.' She smiled quickly. 'But I wanted to say I understand now what I was doing—what I did. And I'm sorry, Harry. It won't happen again.'

The lump in his throat prevented him from replying. He also didn't know how to say it. He wanted to say *please* make it happen again—she was the most wonderful thing that had ever happened to him. He was trying to think how to put it when she spoke again.

'I heard you tell Max that you might be going out to Africa, Harry.'

'You heard everything he said?' He raised his eyebrows in surprise.

She smiled. 'It's not a very large cottage, Harry. But I'm glad you're going to follow your star. You may even find someone who's just right for you.'

He felt a wave of sadness, as though she were slipping forever further out of his world, or he from hers. 'When I was in Amsterdam I had a dream of someone like you. Someone I might meet and love.' He lowered his voice. 'I'd like to think it was you.'

She shook her head, smiling. 'You don't want to find someone like me, Harry. But you remember what I told you about dreams? Sometimes they're events that cast their shadows before them. Reach out to your dreams, Harry. Find the girl who's on the same wavelength as you. Someone who's plugged in to the energy source of the universe. Do you know what I mean, Harry? Someone who doesn't drain your own energy. Don't make the mistake of falling in love too easily, with someone who merely provides a closed circuit of energy. You want a partnership, not an exploitation. Do you know what I mean, Harry?'

He knew exactly what she meant. What he didn't understand was why it couldn't be her.

CHAPTER 29

Agape

HARRY sat on the stone where the high altar had been. It was within the presbytery area of the Abbey, where he had once sat with Eleanor. He focused his eyes on the rose window at the top of the west front, as he did before. It was like looking down the length of a disembowelled ship: the enclosed space was empty, yet contained by the series of arches supported by the colonnade of pillars.

He had come to say a final farewell to the Abbey and, he hoped, be energised with the energy he had felt the last time he sat there.

He was aware of none of the reverberatory power he had felt before, and the rose window with its spoke-like tracery of honey-hewed stone remained in focus, no aura of light glowing through the intricacy of its pattern.

He thought of the black-robed Augustinian canons sitting in rows in the canon's choir, or moving slowly, heads bowed under cowls, absorbed in one of their daily eight Offices, or set services. Perhaps it was Vespers, at the close of day, and he tried to hear the resonance of their Gregorian chant. He half closed his eyes, trying to slip back in time.

The Abbey was a spiritual island in a changing world of lawlessness, a world of petty warfare where wolves roamed and chieftains plundered one another. But the Abbey was an island of peace. 'In this place I will give peace.' The words registered in his brain. Were they words he had read in the visitors centre? 'Everywhere peace, everywhere serenity, and a freedom from the tumult of the world.' Yes, he thought, that's what the world needed. A sanctuary withdrawn from the world, yet a place that was a beacon of peace for nations crying out for peace. 'In this place I will give you peace.'

A place where one could be recharged, finding peace with one's fellow man and peace in one's own heart.

It was like a new insight. That's what the Abbeys were for, he realised. Not centres for suppressing the masses with rules and laws, or for manipulating the many by a few. They were arks of peace in a stormy world flooded with wars and power struggles. The sea and the waves roaring. They may have been broken down in the storm, shipwrecked in the modern world of accelerated change, but the seeds of peace they bore were still there, waiting to germinate and take root in a new millennium of peace.

The rose window was alight, glowing from the horizontal light of the setting sun. He thought he could hear the harmony of the chanting now. It was easier, now, to visualise the black canons, their hooded black cloaks over white surplices and black cassocks which they wore at all times, even in bed. They had taken the three oaths of poverty, chastity and obedience. No brash materialism here, no flaunting of pride. The air reverberated with the peals of bells, reminding men that from dawn to dusk prayers were said for them here, a place withdrawn from the world yet in the world—for the Augustinians, unlike the Cistercians, worked amongst the people and served the people.

He closed his eyes and tried to feel again the presence of Eleanor, or whoever it was, besides him. He felt the companionship and was aglow with love. He needed her, to walk together in a new world order of peace and love.

But when he opened his eyes and turned, there was no one besides him.

CHAPTER 30

Hands-on Experience

'**H**E TOUCHED ME!'

'Where?' The Director of Studies raised his eyebrows.

'On my arm,' said the outraged, pimply-faced EFL teacher.

'On the underside or the outside of your arm?'

'Oh, on the outside.'

'Through your clothing, or... on the flesh?'

'Well, I was wearing a jumper.'

'Oh,' interposed another mousy EFL teacher. 'And he chinned Karen!'

Karen was the Assistant Director of Studies. She had short dark hair and striking jade green eyes. She pouted just perceptibly and nodded in affirmation.

'He... he *what*?'

'He took me by the chin and said "Bootiful!"' Karen grimaced a little self-consciously.

'And,' interposed another—a frail skeletal woman called Helen, whose parents had apparently laboured under the illusion that their cherished offspring would be tall and striking, like the original of Troy. 'And ... yesterday, when we were walking to the Ladies' College, he put his hand on ... on my shoulder.' The last phrase was almost inaudible.

The Director of Studies shook his head. 'We must... must keep an eye on Oscar. Keep me informed. We don't want trouble—especially not at the beginning of the season.'

'Who exactly is Oscar?' asked Harry.

The Director of Studies turned his ruddy, boyish face towards the new speaker. 'He's one of the Spanish students. The oldest of the students we have.'

'The middle-aged man? He usually wears a blazer.'

'That's the one.' Keith Chalmers, the Director of Studies, smiled. 'We call him the Toucher.' He turned towards his staff. 'Now, any other matters?'

They were crammed around the long table, some munching stale sandwiches, some scribbling notes or figures on the attendance registers.

Harry surveyed the scene with an air of sadness. His appointment was only for two months, but at least it was something to keep him going while he adjusted to his new life as a single man in London. His dingy ground-floor flat a block away was a lonely retreat after running a small hotel in Scotland, but at least it was an escape from the harassment of demanding guests and the loveless life he had led with Anne.

He enjoyed the company of the students, and he especially enjoyed teaching in a multicultural classroom. It was a welcome escape from his loneliness. He was confronted daily with fourteen students, a mixture from Bangladesh, Indonesia, Japan, Oman, Quater, Greece, Germany, Holland and Switzerland. 'You name it, I've got them,' he joked when asked what nationalities were in his class.

The charm of the third-world students was irresistible, and he particularly liked the enthusiastic friendliness of the Bangladesh students. 'Now this exercise is being a horse of another colour,' laughed one of them, flashing an array of white teeth. 'It is telling me that what I am learning is a bird in hand! It is better than two in the bushes!' They didn't like it if he went too quickly through the grammar exercises. Unfortunately this meant that the European students were often bored. Though younger they were clearly more advanced in their use of English and often completed their exercises while the others were still struggling through theirs. Harry nevertheless gave each student as much personalised or individualised attention as possible, going from student to student, bending over their work, hand on shoulder, giving encouragement and praise whenever possible. It was his careful attention to individuals that made him well-liked, especially by the third-world students. They were often shy and unsure of their ability, but Harry had the knack of drawing them out of themselves and making them feel confident.

He felt tired as he walked from student to student. The European students were not as bright, he thought, as they liked to think, and he found many errors in their constructions. But they were often reluctant to accept his explanations, or to believe him when he pointed out their mistakes. One Dutch girl produced a construction that read, 'Tomorrow I will have been eighteen.' She looked suspiciously at him when he corrected her. A Swiss girl and a girl from Germany vociferously supported her, quoting rules to explain why the sentence *had* to be correct.

'But, you see,' he explained gently, 'English is a very inconsistent language. The rules are helpful, but you can't always trust them.'

But they clearly didn't trust *him*. He had a gentle, hesitant manner, which failed to convince them. When he asked each student, in turn, to read a paragraph from an article, so he could hear their pronunciations, the Dutch girl refused flatly. 'I wish not to read, thank you,' she stated primly. He accepted the rebuff without rebuke, and the next student, from Bangladesh, phonetically mangled the paragraph with disarming eagerness.

The afternoon class was a Study Skills lesson, and he felt tired though flushed with success at the end of it. The young Arab students were keen and had participated energetically. But he felt all of his forty years when he climbed the interminable stairs to fetch his bag in the staff room at the top of the building. Karen Elgin, the pretty Assistant Director of Studies, was there and gave him a message: would he call in to see Keith, the Director of Studies, on his way down?

Keith Chalmers had stopped him on his way out before. Flashing his benevolent smile, he had conducted him into an empty classroom and elaborately closed the door. He had asked Harry to give details about what and how he had been teaching. Harry detected a little embarrassment, and at the end of the interview asked him: 'Is everything all right? What has the feedback been from the students?'

'Fair,' Keith had said. 'But you've lost a few, of course.'

Three of the slower students, including one of the young Spaniards, had in fact requested to be put into a lower level. Harry was teaching the Advanced group, and those three felt they would cope better at the Intermediate level. Apparently they had found it difficult to keep up and, largely because of this, Harry had given even more careful attention to each student, especially the slower ones.

Now Keith conducted Harry into an empty room again, this time with more furtive ceremony than before. It made Harry feel mildly anxious, but he hoped secretly that this time Keith wanted to compliment him and perhaps even ask him to stay on longer.

Harry couldn't help liking Keith and he warmed to him, seeing him now, looking more boyish than ever, with his large head and ruddy cheeks, cramping his large body on the little chair opposite him.

'Um,' Keith coughed, his embarrassed smile sliding into a painful grin. 'I've had a delegation from your class.'

'Oh?' Harry's heart missed a beat. He sensed disaster.

'It's the European students, really. They feel you're going too slowly.'

'But you said last time I was losing students, going too fast.'

'Perhaps you should have more solid language work. Something they can get their teeth into. Brainstorm them first thing in the morning.'

'Well, look at the work we went through this morning.' Harry dipped into his bag and brought out the prescribed textbook for Advanced students. 'We got through all these exercises here. In fact, there are only two units left. We'll finish the book within the next two days.'

Keith thought for a little, rubbing his chin with a large hand. When he spoke he looked more serious.

'When you prepare your lessons, I think you should include a lot more fun-type activities. Ask Karen to show you the book *Games in Language Acquisition*. Everyone uses it.'

'Oh, but we do a lot of relaxing work. I've been doing exactly as you said at the outset. Solid language work during the first part of the morning. Then open-ended activities. Believe me, the students have been very enthusiastic. We've had a lot of fun ...'

Harry was confused. He was going too slow. He was going too fast. He wasn't making them do enough solid language study. He ought to make them do more games to relax ...

'Well,' he said, 'I'll try my best, of course. But what do you think the real solution is?'

Keith looked through him, bemused. Then his eyes focused on Harry. 'I suppose, really, we'll have to separate the Third World students from the Europeans.'

'You mean, separate development, as in South Africa?' Harry couldn't help laughing, but Keith failed to see the joke.

'Yes, I suppose so.'

He smiled. 'Never mind, I'll try harder.'

'Yes,' said Keith. 'It's the Europeans, really, that we want to keep happy.' He looked serious. 'It's a pity they couldn't feel they could approach you directly.' He stood up. 'And when you go back to the class, don't say, "I believe you've all complained to Keith!"'

'Good Lord, no!' Harry laughed, but his heart was in his shoes.

'Thank you, Harry,' Keith smiled his disarming boyish smile. He was so sincere. He *had* to be right.

Harry walked out of the Academy with a total sense of unreality. No one had ever questioned his competence before. Perhaps it was the sense of dislocation, the intervening period running a hotel that distanced him from the real problems of teaching. Yet how strange it was, he thought: the students really seemed to enjoy his lessons—apart, perhaps, from the Dutch girl.

He put himself to sleep with a sleeping tablet and a double whisky that night. He slept fitfully and dreamt that Keith was plunging his erect penis into the Dutch girl, his face flushed with boyish energy.

'You not touch me!' screamed the girl.

'Don't be a silly girl!' Keith panted.

When he went to work Harry tried to be bright and breezy. He particularly paid attention to the Dutch girl, but she was friendly and interested, like all of the other students. Surely he had imagined her animosity. 'We need to go a little faster,' he said. 'Get through more language study first thing, and have more fun later.' He gave them a series of language exercises. 'You only need to get through the first three by teatime. But those who can—and want—to work faster, please go ahead. Finish them all if you can. Work in pairs, as usual.' And then he walked amongst them, giving more personalised attention to the Bangladesh students who got bogged down in the noun clauses. By tea time he felt he had satisfied all of his motley crew. They joked together and the Europeans asked a lot of serious questions. By the time the Spanish, German and Dutch students satisfied themselves that their work was perfect, the Third World contingent caught up too.

Harry enjoyed his tea. He felt he had regained confidence—in his students and in himself. The work was fun, after all, and he liked helping people. Keith finished his mug of tea and beaconed to Harry. 'Could we see you for a moment, please?'

Karen, the feathery curls of her black hair stirring softly as she moved, led him upstairs—to yet another empty room. Keith followed.

Keith closed the door with concentrated solemnity. Karen hovered solemnly in the background. Her girlish appearance, the way she tilted her head to one side, reminded him of Eleanor, though she was taller.

'I'm afraid,' said Keith, 'we've had more representations from your class.'

'Since *yesterday*?' Harry asked with disbelief.

'Apart from that,' Keith quickly added, 'there have been rumours. I'm afraid, under the circumstances, we have no choice but to let you go.' Keith's expression was pained again.

Harry was stunned, but managed to hang on to a show of friendly politeness. 'I never realised it was that bad.'

Silence. Harry couldn't understand *when* his students could have had the opportunity to see Keith again. It was closing time when he left Keith last night, and he had been with all of his students since the beginning of the morning.

'Of course, I understand,' resumed Harry, who felt the ball had been placed in his court. 'Of course, I shall finish off today, then. I might have suggested it yesterday, but thought you might have difficulty finding someone else at such short notice.'

Keith said quickly: 'No, no! It happens that at this time of year there's no trouble finding people.'

'Very well, then. I'm grateful, in any case, for the experience ...'

Keith was relieved. 'Thank you for taking it so well. For being so nice about this.'

'On the contrary, thank *you* for being so nice.'

'There have, of course, been many good things said about you, too ... I hate to think what a mess some of my old colleagues at the University of Lancaster would have made of the job. You've done a lot better than they would have.' Keith was growing magnanimous. 'Your gifts are obviously in a different direction ...'

'Of course. I'm used to academic degree students...'

'Quite,' Keith readily agreed.

'Yes,' put in Karen, softly. She had crept a little closer. Her bright green eyes were arresting yet sympathetic. 'Perhaps you should enrol for an EFL course. There's a good one at Pilgrims ...'

'I've heard they're very good. Quite.'

It was painful, teaching through the rest of the morning and afternoon. But Harry kept up appearances, saying nothing about the interview and of his impending demise. He mustered up a great deal of enthusiasm from somewhere, and the Bangladesh students kept the ball rolling with their spontaneous mirth and zest. He even gave them some homework to finish over the weekend, making it look as if things were as normal as usual.

But he knew he would never see the class again. On Monday they would be surprised—or would they, really?—to find a new EFL teacher: one fresh and undoubtedly younger, brimming over with brainstorming and the latest high-tech techniques from Pilgrims or some other language school with new theories about language acquisition. Someone with real punch. Someone with a hands-on attitude, undimmed by months of serving bacon and egg, from repeated apologies about a cramped car-park and the steep stairs to the small attic bedrooms.

His feet wound their way through the crowded shopping centre of Crystal Palace. When he looked up his eyes fell on Oscar, the Toucher. The man, middle-aged and thickset, was walking ahead of him, wearing his black blazer, his hand resting gently on the Dutch girl's shoulder.

At least, Harry thought, *he* had the right attitude. A hands-on attitude...

The thought stopped him in his tracks. It was part of his personalised approach, when attending to students, to lay a hand lightly on a student's shoulder. Might that explain ...? Was *he* a Toucher, too?

It was a damp evening and had been raining all day. The large wheel of a bus slued round the corner and spewed dirty water over his suit.

'Oh *shit*!' he swore.

CHAPTER 31

Eros

IT WAS A COLD, damp evening and the lights of cars glistened on the wet tarmac of the streets. Harry's footsteps became heavier and more reluctant as he traced his route back to his dismal ground-floor bedsitter.

If only there was someone he could talk to, he thought. His dismissal from the language academy was so sudden, so unexpected. He needed to thrash it out with someone. The thought of contacting Anne flashed through his mind. She would be only too willing to sympathise with him and listen to his tale of woe over a glass of whisky. And then it would all start over again. He sighed and dismissed the temptation from his mind. His thoughts went to Karen, the Assistant Director of Studies. He remembered her sympathetic look, her sad smile just touching the corners of her mouth. It was as though she wanted to say more, but held back. She looked so sweet and understanding— but she was part of the team that had dismissed him, he reminded himself. It was like a betrayal. Yet there was something uncannily familiar about her—a feeling of *déjà vu*. Was it because she reminded him of Eleanor? That was it, he told himself.

What would Eleanor say about this turn of events? They were hardly part of a positive personal development or evolution, he thought bitterly. He could phone her, but then more than likely Max would answer the phone. Then he recalled the card that Max had given him, about a girl called Geena. He sighed. This was definitely the night for visiting Geena. Comfort or female balm, in whatever form, would be welcome. He felt alone and abandoned in London. He stuck his hand into his top pocket. Yes, the card was still there.

What a fool he was, he thought, allowing himself to be drawn into the spell of Eleanor. He longed for Eleanor who seemed so incapable of real love and sympathy. He felt drained of hope and deeply depressed, much of his incentive for going on draining away.

He reached a bus stop and stepped onto the first 185 bus that came along. He still wore his splattered suit and his briefcase lay on the empty seat next to him. The bus jolted through the night, past the row of dismal shops that fronted Peckam Rye and through the concrete blaze of the Elephant and Castle. At Piccadilly Circus he got off the bus and took the tube to Knightsbridge. It was a route he knew well from his old university days in London.

In Central Knightsbridge he found the seedy building next to a Chinese take-away. It sported a neon light that flashed temptingly: 'Black Forest Massage Parlour.'

He hesitated a moment before entering. A young hard-faced woman with fuzzy blonde hair sat at a desk chewing gum. She looked up and slid a card towards him without smiling or ceasing to chew. 'Which one?' she said with total disinterest.

Harry looked at the menu. He could have a 'straight massage' or a massage with assisted shower. 'What's an assisted shower?' he asked, slumping in a chair. He felt nervous and a little breathless by his own audacity in coming into the place.

'It's a shower,' she said, unhelpfully. 'Assisted.'

'Well, I'll have the massage and assisted shower, then.' It might be intriguing, at any rate. 'Could I have Geena, please?'

'That'll be fourteen pounds,' she said, ignoring his question.

He handed her the money and followed her instructions to go down some steep stairs. He found himself in a gloomy underworld—a dimly-lit corridor lined on either side with doors. A young girl, plump, blonde and buxom, met him. 'Know where to go, luv?' she screeched. Harry was obviously lost and was already regretting the impulse that made him enter the place.

'Um ... no,' he stammered. 'Are you Geena?'

'Oh, this is your first time? Shame! Come this way.' And she waddled off, stopping before a door. She opened it and led him in.

'Take off your clothes and wait here, luv. Your lady will be with you in a minute.' And she disappeared into the gloom.

Harry found himself in a dingy cubicle, open at the top. A dilapidated loudspeaker in a corner mangled some music meant to be mellow and seductive. He undressed self-consciously, laying his briefcase and clothes neatly on a chair. He sat on the raised narrow bed which would have served equally well in an operating theatre or mortuary. There was a telephone on a low table and a faded notice stuck on the door with sellotape: 'Please phone for assistance.' Harry lifted the receiver, gingerly. A woman's voice said 'Hello.'

'I ... I'm waiting in..'

'Your lady will be with you shortly.' The voice was brisk. The phone clicked.

Harry sat there, feeling a little cold and more than foolish. Somewhere in the distance a young man's voice called out: *'Wow, what incredible tits!'* and a woman giggled. The music blurted discordantly. Ten minutes went by. This is ridiculous, he thought. His mind wandered and conjured up the image of Eleanor when she sat by his feet and apologised. He recalled her sad, contrite expression and felt a spasm of love for her. But his mind went back to the memory of her light firm body against his on that fateful night in the bedroom and his love straightened into lust. 'God, I have to get her out of my system,' he thought. He felt altogether burnt-out and rudderless.

He looked at his watch. Another ten minutes had gone by. 'This is ridiculous,' he said under his breath and picked up the phone again. The same brisk voice reassured him: 'Your lady will be with you in a moment, sir,' and clicked once again into silence.

At last the door opened.

She took his breath away—a dazzlingly beautiful creature dressed in a tight mini-leather skirt and a loose see-through fishnet blouse generously filled by liquid breasts. 'I've kept you waiting,' she smiled, tossing her raven-black hair to one side. Her cultured voice surprised Harry. She sounded incredibly like Eleanor—the same inflections of voice. She looked down at him with clear brown eyes. 'What is your preference? A dry, or wet, massage?

'Whatever you prefer,' Harry gulped, mesmerised by her beauty. 'Are you Geena?'

'I am,' she said archly, smiling and flicking her hair again by an easy movement of the head. 'Do I know you?'

'My friend Max says you have the...' He hesitated. 'He said you're the nicest girl in London.'

'That's nice. Which Max is that?'

'Max Merchant.'

'Never heard of him,' she replied casually.

'Oh, you should remember him. He likes to tell rude jokes!' He laughed awkwardly.

She shook her head and repeated her former question. 'What will it be, a dry, or wet massage?'

'Whatever you prefer,' he said.

'Very well, then,' she said, smiling condescendingly, 'a dry massage.'

Not altogether dry, since she first lubricated her hands with something squeezed from a tube. Then she ran her fingers lightly up his inner thighs. Her breasts filled the fishnet blouse even more tantalisingly as she leant forward. 'Of course,' she crooned, full of self-confidence, 'you can have more than a simple massage.'

'Oh?' he said casually, cupping his head in his linked hands.

She spoke musically as she ran her fingers delicately round his testicles. 'You can have a simple hand relief. Or a breast relief. Or more. It will cost a little extra, of course. Twenty pounds. Twenty-five, fifty, a hundred.' She smiled sweetly. 'As much as you like.'

This broke the spell somewhat since he had to grope in his wallet. 'I can manage twenty-seven pounds,' he said. He was quite hooked, but had no more money on him apart from what he would need for the return tube and bus.

'Well,' she crooned, businesslike, 'for that I'll give you a nice breast relief.'

He tried to relax and control his palpitating heart as he lay back. She began by running her hands along his chest and torso, casually jerking down her blouse and allowing her breasts to spill out from the top. They were like living entities, supple, milky, cheeky and pert with uplifted brown nipples.

'Am I allowed to touch?' he asked, hoarsely.

Without a word she smiled indulgently, cupping one breast and bringing the pert nipple to his lips. His lips swallowed it instinctively, sucking the hard core into his mouth, harder than he intended. She closed her eyes and he heard the sharp intake of her breath. He did the same to the other nipple, but more gently. Then she moved to the lower end of the bed and smoothly, generously enveloped his erect member between her breasts.

Harry gasped. The feeling was like electric silk, warm and bewitching. She smiled at him through her lashes. He took in her brown eyes and the beauty spot on her cheek, unconsciously, dazed by sensation. He lost all awareness of time.

But before long she became impatient. She smeared more of the lubricant on her hands and wrapped them around his member, increasing the firmness and intensity of the rhythm. When this failed to produce the result she was looking for, she bent over him, her breasts swinging forward, while she rubbed with her hands like an impatient washerwoman. Harry felt increasingly numb and the enchantment had evaporated.

'Um,' he said diffidently, 'I don't think that's going to work.'

'Oh, what a shame,' she said, smiling and looking up, 'Did you enjoy it anyway?' She began to fold the towel and cloth she had brought with her.

To his dismay Harry realised the session had ended. But there was still the assisted shower to look forward to.

She led him out of the cubicle to an area of sterile tiles and showers. She ran a shower and he got in, expecting her to follow. But she simply handed him a towel and disappeared. Standing under the tepid water, he felt an utter clot. This was it, then? He found his clothes and his briefcase on a stool, got dressed, and was soon rattling disconsolately on the Piccadilly Line.

By the time the bus neared the crest of Crystal Palace the clouds had dispersed. He cursed his own stupidity as he reached the top of the hill. Moonlight bathed the countless serrated ridges of terraced houses, like petrified teeth in a fossilised landscape. 'God,' he said, 'this is not the England I want to live in.'

When he opened the door of his flat he found a neatly-typed envelope that looked official. It bore the stamp of the South-

African Consulate General. His fingers trembled as he opened it. He read quickly, holding his breath, then sighed with relief.

At least, it was a new direction, he thought. The letter was a request to present himself for an interview at South Africa House in Trafalgar Square in order that he might be considered for the Chair of English at the University of Lebowa.

The letter was dated 3rd April 1986. Harry had mixed feelings about accepting a Chair at an apartheid university. But then, he was desperate to try anything.

CHAPTER 32

Into the Fire

THE BUS rattled speedily north along the Jan Smuts highway while the daylight shifted into red with darkening clouds. It was going to be another of those late thunderstorms, a fellow passenger told him—a thickset man with heavy jowls who had since slumped into sleep next to him. Civil Servant storms, the man had called them, to coincide with the commuters going home in Pretoria.

Harry watched the dry featureless plains of grass, or veldt, drift by. It was like an alien planet, he thought. He recalled the first sight of the landscape from the aeroplane as it banked over Johannesburg—sun-baked mine dumps, tin roofs and sparkling pools. One or two flat-topped mine dumps, yellow stained with grey and running black, still blemished the horizon. He had been jerked into this strange land overnight, as though translated into a different universe. It felt a long way from the London drizzle with its cold dawning of spring.

He had made two final calls before leaving. One was to Eleanor, during the morning when there was a good chance of Max being out. The musical lilt of her voice wished him well. 'I hope you have a *super* time, Harry,' she had said. 'Remember to keep your eyes and ears open, Harry, for the coincidences of life. If you're centred, nothing really happens by chance, do you know what I mean? Pay attention to the people you meet and listen to your dreams. Always follow your dreams, Harry.'

He wished her well, too. But concern touched him, even now in this strange place in another hemisphere. It seemed only too apparent to him, on the last occasion he had seen her, that her personal evolution was passing through a turbulent phase. Could she be right that serendipity was the whole principle of life, underlying natural and personal evolution? He tried to swallow the lump in his throat. He wished he could have taken her away, to begin a new life with him.

His second call had been to Karen Elgin, the Assistant Director of Studies at the language academy. It was merely routine, to request that his final salary be sent on to a bank in South Africa. Once in South Africa he would contact her again, he had said, with the name of the bank and account number. She expressed surprise, saying she had been born in South Africa.

'I never realised you were South African,' he had said.

'I was only born there,' she replied. 'I came out with my parents when I was ten. My parents are British. My father worked for a firm that made floor tiles—in Durban.'

'I once dreamt of Durban,' he laughed.

'Well, do be careful,' she said. 'It's a dangerous country now.'

'Thank you,' he replied, and added with a sudden sense of mischief: 'Watch out for the Toucher!'

She gave a burst of bubbly laughter. 'Oh, I'll soon put *him* in his place!'

'Well, I hope you have a good season. Give my best wishes to Keith.'

'Thank you, Harry,' she said softly. 'I'm sorry things didn't work out here.'

Harry had wished her well and replaced the receiver. He had detected a certain inflection about her softly mellow voice— something he couldn't quite put his finger on. It must have been a trace of a childhood accent, he supposed. He suspected she and Keith were an item, as the saying went. They certainly presented a united front when they dismissed him. Thinking back to the whole episode, now, increased his desolation and loneliness in the strange environment that streamed past his window.

He asked the black bus driver to drop him outside the railway station in Pretoria instead of taking him into the city centre. No point in wasting money on a taxi, he thought.

When the bus growled past the station it was already raining quite hard. He pushed past his sleeping companion and stumbled forward on the lurching floor. He gripped his suitcase, expecting the bus to stop.

But it didn't stop. He shouted to the bus driver who obtusely ignored him, driving on. 'I say, I wanted to get off here!' Harry shouted again. He thought the driver was deaf when the bus suddenly ground to a halt. The street was dark and the station was at least a block further back. Nevertheless, Harry alighted, stumbling out into the soaking rain.

The bus was swallowed by the chaos and he lurched his way under the covered pavement. It was a decaying Colonial-styled tin covering supported by pillars festooned at the top with ornate wrought-ironwork. Harry immediately had a sense of deep misgiving. It was a totally deserted area with no streetlights, and the rain soaked, machine-gunning the tarred street with relentless power. Water ran fast and deep in the gutters.

His heart lurched to his throat when he saw two figures approaching in the dark. He struggled back into the thick of the rain, away from the gloom of the pavement. But there was no one else in sight, and the two figures came running up to him, shouting. They were black youths in shabby clothes shining from the rain.

'Where you going, boss!' they demanded. Before he knew what was happening one had him in a throttling grip from behind. He lurched and fell, sprawling onto the wet tar. Yet he never let go his suitcase. He staggered up again and one of the men gripped the suitcase, pulling.

'What's in here, boss?' shouted the man, teeth white in the dim light.

'That's not for you!' Harry hung on for all he was worth. The case contained clothes and a bank draft, all he had left, apart from some travellers' cheques in his jacket pocket. He felt the other man's hand clawing his chest. The first man tried to wrench the suitcase away.

'Jesus Christ!' Harry screamed, putting all his might and soul into the scream.

His inside pocket ripped and the men ran off. But Harry still had hold of his suitcase. *'Jesus Christ!'* he shouted again at the receding figures. Then he was alone in the rain, soaking. He stumbled and lurched with the heavy suitcase, going as fast as his legs, weakened with shock, would carry him. He climbed up the steps of the railway station and entered the Victorian portal, dry at last in the vaulted entrance of the station. People seated on benches looked up at him, surprised and with disdain, as if he were a tramp.

I must look like a tramp, he thought. He put the suitcase down, gasping for breath. He looked at his hands. They were shaking. His left palm was bleeding from being scraped on the tar. It still felt numb.

He collapsed on top of the suitcase, panting. Curious eyes frowned and looked away. Then he got up, heavily, and staggered to the ticket office. 'I want a policeman,' he said to the sullen girl at the counter.

'Over there, by the cafe,' she sneered, tilting her head to indicate the direction.

He found a young policeman, barely nineteen, who shrugged at the information. 'The bus driver ... *ja,* he will have been in on it, all right. Can you describe him?'

'Not really,' Harry said. It was dark.

'*Ag,* in any case, we'll never catch them,' he said casually, in the flat vowels of the South African accent. 'They're like rats, these people.' He scribbled something on a blue form. 'I'll report it, anyhow.'

Harry humped his suitcase to the empty platform. The Pietersburg train was expected shortly from Johannesburg. He slumped in an empty bench, his heart still pounding from the ordeal. God, he thought, what a country. A lump grew in his throat. He wished with all his might that he was back in England.

He examined his torn pocket. The travellers' cheques and his passport were missing.

CHAPTER 33

Northbound

LIZ FELT DESOLATE as she boarded the train in Pretoria. She lifted a tatty briefcase into the doorway of the carriage, then humped a heavy shopping bag up the steps. She clumsily lifted both items of her luggage and made her way into an empty compartment. The shopping bag clinked as she let it slide to the floor. She sat down, wearily.

Her eyes followed the ragged line of roofs and chimneys as the train pulled out. Before long the tin roofs of cheap suburban bungalows fell away beneath her, and she saw the dark outline of the horizon. The train set out at an even pace across the elevated plains that flattened towards the distant hills of the Northern Transvaal. She sighed heavily.

The hills of the north held many memories. They cradled the memory of Koos, the rugged farmer she had met one evening in the Great North Hotel. Their love had flared up immediately, for they recognised in each other the same untamed spirit, the same daring love of adventure. He had been a sailor before he tried his hand at farming, supervising a tea plantation on the slopes of Magoebaskloof. She, in turn, had been a wild spirit, unable to settle to any permanent occupation. She had won a bursary and completed an Honours degree in Accounting, and instead of settling down to a progressive career and a steady income, had responded to an advertisement to join the small crew of a 12-metre ketch. She spent two years on the ketch—no radio, no engine—sailing the Caribbean and the seas of South and central America. Eventually the ketch struck a reef off the coast of Brazil and the crew was stranded, without money, in Rio de Janeiro. Liz's ageing father in Durban paid for her flight home, but she was restless at home. A lectureship at the University of Lebowa brought her to Pietersburg where she had met Koos.

When her university post wasn't renewed she got a position at a bank.

For a year, she and Koos had been blissfully happy. They lived together in a ramshackled farmhouse high on the slopes of a mountain. It could only be reached in the Landrover they owned—a second-hand vehicle they had sunk their last savings in. Koos was as rugged as the surroundings—a stalwart figure with a face swamped by a black beard. But it wasn't long before the disease that would indirectly claim his life manifested itself. He had muscular sclerosis, and the doctors didn't give him more than two years. Soon his vision deteriorated and he could no longer drive. They both began to drink too much, and one evening, after an argument, Koos drove off into the night. His failing eyesight by then had left him with little more than three-percent vision. She fretted all night and half expected the call from the police. They had found his mangled body in the twisted remains of the Landrover at the foot of a cliff.

The darkening veldt drifted by, the odd rectangular shape of unlit African houses seen darkly through the rain-streaked window. She thought again of her wasted years at sea and the lost year with Koos. She picked up the shopping bag and extracted one of the bottles of Scotch she had brought with her to fortify the overnight trip to Pietersburg. She sloshed a liberal measure into a plastic tumbler.

As she sipped the whisky she stared at her reflection in the window. Her tiredness was accentuated by the bags beneath her eyes. She'd allowed herself to go to seed, she realised. Her once healthy and lithe body had thickened, too—from too many evenings of sumptuous meals prepared for Koos followed by liberal supplies of lager stockpiled from the supermarket in Pietersburg.

The whisky produced a warm glow and before long she dozed off. She woke up when the door of her compartment shot back and a scruffy and harassed-looking stranger in a rain-soaked suit shuffled in with a heavy suitcase. He hesitated when he saw Liz.

'Sorry,' he said. 'Is ... is anyone sitting here.' He pointed to the seat opposite.

Liz peered short-sightedly at the empty seat. Her voice was gravelly. 'I don't see anyone. Can you?'

The man blinked. 'I hope you don't mind. The train's rather full ...'

'God!' she exclaimed, focusing her eyes on the intruder. 'What the hell's happened to you?' She took in the wet suit and torn jacket.

'Mugged,' he said, bitterly. 'A couple of thugs outside the station, in the rain.'

'You need a drink! Here!' She sloshed another liberal helping from her bottle. She handed the plastic cup to him and he drank it gratefully.

'Thanks,' he smiled. 'You're a brick!' He handed back the tumbler.

The train swayed gently. She sat back and looked at him. He seemed sad and worn out, slumped on the seat. His lean body might have been appealing had it not been for his slouching, hangdog appearance. But his harassed and lost look appealed to her mothering instinct. She liked to be needed. He wiped his forehead and she saw the blood on his hand.

'Here,' she said, reaching out with her handkerchief. 'Let me bind that for you.' But she was still cocooned by her whisky and felt detached from any real concern.

'It's nothing,' he said, wrapping his hand in his own handkerchief. Then he got up and removed his wet jacket. 'They took my travellers' cheques and passport,' he said bitterly.

'Traveller's cheques!' she said, glad at being able to help. 'Never mind. You can report them lost on Monday, at the bank. I work at the bank!'

'You do?' he said, sitting again and brightening a little.

'Yes. The Standard Bank in Pietersburg. Are you going to Pietersburg?'

'Yes.'

'Well then! Come in first thing in the morning and I'll give you a form. You'll get all your money back. What cheques were they?'

'American Express.'

'No problem. I can fix it.' She smiled reassuringly. 'Or are you with a different bank?'

'The cheques are from a bank in England. I'll need to open an account in Pietersburg, anyway.' He relaxed a little. 'Thanks,' he said. 'I'll come to your bank.'

'I'm Liz Evans, by the way.' She stretched out a limp hand.

'Harry,' he smiled. 'Harry Denton.'

'Welcome to Apartheid country, Harry,' she grinned. 'Have you just arrived?'

'Yes.'

'Nice welcome you've had.'

'Yes,' he agreed, unsmiling. In his mind he had shot those two thugs again and again.

'Why Pietersburg?' she shot the question at him.

'I have a post at the University of Lebowa. English Department.'

'I was with the Accounting Department there,' she said. 'They didn't renew my contract. So thank God for the bank.'

She took another swig from her tumbler. 'Sorry,' she said, her mind still unfocussed. 'Don't usually drink alone. Got another tumbler somewhere.' She groped in her bag, producing another bottle of Scotch and another tumbler. 'Here.'

'Thanks.' Harry wasn't in a mood to refuse. She seemed to be drinking rather a lot. 'You're surely not going to go into a second bottle,' he said, bemused.

She gazed at him, not taking the slightest notice. Then she put down her tumbler and produced a packet of cigarettes. 'Would you...?' She offered the packet to him.

'I don't smoke,' he shook his head.

'Please yourself.' A match flared and she gratefully inhaled.

'Have you lived for long in Pietersburg?' he asked.

'In a way.' She sighed. 'I was helping my boyfriend to farm. He died.'

'I'm sorry.' His voice softened. 'May I ask what happened.'

She told him about Koos. As she spoke, tears betrayed her hardened exterior. 'I loved him. All I ever wanted was to love— to look after somebody. I let him down. We argued and he died an awful death.'

'But you helped him,' he said.

'Did I?'

280

'He had to die. You gave him companionship in his last days.'

The tears pricked her eyes afresh. 'I hope so.' The knot in her throat stopped her saying anything further.

'His death was quick,' he said, answering her thoughts. 'He might have had a lingering death, from what you've told me.'

'I've had a hopeless life,' she blurted out. 'I'm such a drifter.'

'Why do you say that?' He felt the same could be said of himself.

'Well,' she said, draining her tumbler, 'I spent two years on a ketch, just drifting.'

'There must have been some good memories.'

'Yes,' she smiled, feeling better. 'Here!' she refilled his tumbler and then her own. 'Sorry, no ice or mixer.' She lifted the tumbler and pulled a face. 'That's better,' she said, then resumed her story. 'We—the skipper and I—had some narrow escapes. Like the huge ship at night.'

'Huge ship?' He was feeling mellow and as the train rocked gently his recent ordeal lost its sting. Liz was a welcome diversion and her whisky couldn't have been better timed.

'We were travelling in a shipping lane, in the middle of the Atlantic. It was absolutely dark and I was on watch duty. It's awful being on watch, alone.' She lit another cigarette and watched the smoke spiral upwards like incense. 'I kept awake by chewing—sucking toothpaste.' She laughed at the memory. 'We had no radio or lights, you see. The skipper—Ken—he was asleep below. I dozed off, anyway, and suddenly there was this ship, like a block of flats, blazing with lights and bearing down on us.'

'Good heavens!' He leant forward. What an amazing woman, he thought, in spite of her dowdy appearance.

'I screamed for Ken. Ran below, shook him awake. He ran up onto the deck, stark naked. He held a flare straight up in his hand, the sparks flying all over his naked body. He was a sight! There was some choice language from the ship as it ploughed past us.'

Harry smiled. 'Didn't you have a motor?'

'No!' It was good to talk and she enjoyed the recollection of her adventure. 'It meant we were often becalmed and had to sit for days waiting for a wind. We drank a lot of beer.'

'I can imagine,' he said, taking another sip and enjoying the warm glow as the liquid slid down.

'We were hot and bored, once, waiting for a wind. So Ken suggested we had a swim. I warned him about sharks. He said, "No problem. We'll put a shark watch out." He posted Bryan, the other member of the crew, near the stern. We had a great time swimming in the clear water.

'And?'

'When we climbed back on board, Bryan, as calm as you like, said, "You took a chance, swimming with that big chap about." Ken asked, "What big chap?" Bryan pointed to the shady side of the boat. There, apparently asleep in the shade of our sails, was the biggest shark I'd ever seen. Not so deep down, either. The water was so translucent, you could see him perfectly.'

'Why didn't your watch warn you?'

She shrugged. 'Don't know. He was drinking beer. Said he didn't want to disturb us—or the shark.'

Harry nodded. The train lurched and swayed and they poured another drink.

'We tried to catch it,' she laughed. 'We were bored out of our minds.'

'Catch the *shark*?'

'Yes!' She gazed into her tumbler, studying the golden liquid. Then she lifted the tumbler and swallowed the rest of the whisky quickly. The warmth spread rapidly and smoothly down her body. 'That's better,' she sighed. 'Yes,' she said, picking up her narrative. 'We opened a can of bully beef and fixed the opened can to a line. We dropped it in and the bully beef fell out. But the shark went after the tin, all the same. I suppose it was the bright reflection. It took the tin, and Ken pulled on the line. He pulled for all he was worth. "Are you mad?" Bryan shouted, and he cut the line. We could never have pulled it aboard.'

'I should say not!'

She smiled, enjoying her role as raconteur. 'We had a problem with the marine toilet. We couldn't figure out how to work it properly. It was too much bother, anyway.'

'Oh ...?'

'We just hung over the stern and ... did it ... straight into the sea.' She took another swig and coughed when it went down the wrong way. 'Pardon.'

He looked at her with eyes that seemed paradoxically sad and amused. He was a sympathetic listener, and that spurred her on.

'I suppose that's how poor Tibs went,' she said. 'Leaning over too far, I mean.'

'Tibs?'

'The ship's cat. He was very adventurous. A little black cat. Would chase all over the boat. I knew he'd fallen overboard—in the night, some time. He used to lean over, thrashing his paw at the flying fish. He must have missed and fallen over.'

'Couldn't he have clambered back on board?'

'No chance. When there was a breeze the boat would have moved too fast.' She lifted her tumbler again. 'Poor Tibs.'

'Poor thing.'

'Yes.' The knot was back in her throat. She loved cats. She loved everybody.

'Poor Ken—and Bryan.' her eyes were misty. 'They used to fight so much.'

'How so?'

'Over me. That's the trouble with men. They're always so jealous.' She took a drink and looked at him, swaying with the steady rhythm of the train. 'You've got such egos, you men.'

'I hope we're not all ...'

'Oh, but you *are*.' She took up her cigarettes and lit another. She sucked in some welcome smoke and coughed. When she spoke again her voice was husky with smoke. 'I was the only woman on board, of course ... obviously, we made love.'

He stared at her. '*Both* of them?'

'Naturally.' She broke into a coughing fit. Her voice became gravelly. 'We used to have orgies—the three of us. There was plenty of beer, and ... but it didn't work out really. Men are such jealous creatures. Always wanting to compete. They well nigh

283

threw each other overboard.' She poured another tumbler-full and drank liberally. She shook her head sadly at the memory. 'Poor dears.'

Harry looked at her in sad disbelief. 'But you don't often ...?'

'Oh no.' She blew out the smoke in her lungs, adding to the musty air in the compartment. 'Don't get me wrong. I'm a bit of a hedonist, but I'm a one-man woman. I believe in dedication. Like when I was living with Koos.' She looked thoughtfully into the distance. 'Kevin used to jump in through the window some nights, of course.'

'Kevin?'

'Oh, he was just a kid. A nice kid. Son of a local farmer nearby. He used to get lonely and needed to talk. It was silly of me to leave the bedroom light on, of course.'

'Couldn't you have told him to go away?'

'Oh, but he was a *nice* kid. I didn't mind, really.'

'Didn't Koos mind?'

'He often wasn't there—loading tea or something. Anyway, Kevin was just a kid.'

'I see.'

'It wasn't his fault.' She giggled. 'He used to get randy, you see.'

His eyes widened. 'Just how old was he?'

'Eighteen. Maybe younger.' She sipped her drink. Her eyes looked tired and distant. 'One night he couldn't make it. He said he felt guilty. He was betraying his girlfriend. Such nonsense.'

'Nonsense?' His sad eyes took on a look of horror. She surprised him, but she had also struck a raw nerve.

'Sex is so natural, isn't it? What's there to be ashamed about it?' She obliterated the remains of her cigarette on the windowsill. 'It's one area where I can be of help, isn't it?'

He looked at her. She seemed vulnerable in spite of her bravado, swaying gently to the steady rhythm of the train. She turned her head and gazed blankly out of the window, into the inscrutable darkness of the night. In spite of her ample breasts and blonde hair, she looked worn out, clutching the remnants of her drink in her left hand. Would she find her Mr Right, he wondered? Would she find the one person that could absorb her desire to give generously of herself? In a sudden collapse of caution he told her about Eleanor.

'I had an encounter with a married woman,' he blurted. 'She sort of threw herself at me, like your Kevin.'

'So?' she smiled at him sleepily, her head resting on the stiff pseudo leather cushions of the seat. 'You slept with her?'

'Well, not really.' He had that lost look again. 'In a way, it's why I left Britain. She had a strange hold on me. I was married too, at the time.' He took a swig of his whisky. 'I dragged my wife into her bed, one night, while her husband was away. But it wasn't an orgy, like you had. Both women were reluctant, really.'

'But you didn't screw the married woman?' She watched him through hooded eyes.

'No, not really.' He gave a twisted smile. 'I just masturbated her. She seemed to enjoy it, but I could see afterwards that I hurt both women terribly.'

She continued to study him through half-closed eyes. 'As I said, Harry. Sex is natural. I wouldn't have thought any less of you if you'd screwed her.'

He smiled. 'You're from a liberated background.'

'I'm *intelligent*, Harry,' she said, with sudden vehemence. 'God, I'm intelligent. I don't have to abide by stupid customs and conventions.'

He was silent and they listened to the rattling of the wheels on the rail for a minute. Then he continued: 'Anyway, it's a closed chapter of my life now.' He sighed. 'What's important is to keep alert for the right opportunities in life. To keep tuned to the energy vibrations.'

'Come again?' she squinted at him.

'That's what Eleanor—the woman I fell in love with—told me. She said you have to stay centred.' He smiled at her confused expression. 'You can increase your personal aura by plugging into the energy field of the universe.'

'Plugging in ...?' She smiled and drained her glass. 'Sure,' she said, feeling too sleepy now to concentrate. 'She sounds balmy, if you ask me.' Then she nestled her head back on the headrest and the steady motion of the train seduced her into sleep.

Harry looked at her. She was a forlorn figure in her soiled skirt, her ample breasts sagging in her blouse. He and she made quite a pair, he thought: he in his still wet and torn suit and she looking no less presentable. But at least he wouldn't be arriving in Pietersburg alone.

He sat back, turned his face to the window and succumbed to sleep himself. He dreamt that it was dawn. A wall drifted by, almost in arm's reach of him. He started when he saw a little black cat, running excitedly on the wall. It stopped, glanced at him with mischievous jade eyes, then gave a playful swipe at a fluttering butterfly. It lost its balance and dropped down the other side of the wall. 'Eleanor!' he heard himself calling. He opened his eyes but the wall had disappeared. The train was swaying gently, slowing down. Heavy goods vehicles, covered in tarpaulins, drifted past in the morning light. An untidy array of railway lines sprawled in different directions.

Soon he would be in Pietersburg.

CHAPTER 34

Colourful Relationships

HARRY checked into the Great North Hotel in Pietersburg, a pseudo-Tudor building that emanated the smell of stale beer, before accepting the temporary use of a room in a ramshackled house rented by Richard Emslie, a colleague from the Linguistics Department of the University.

Richard, or Dick, as he was called, was an Englishman of forty-eight. Harry thought him the most colourful (by dint of being colourless) character he'd ever met. Dick was stout or lean, depending on the state of his larder and bank balance, always ravenous and slightly balding. He had a dry sense of humour and a Cambridge degree, and had lost his virginity only two years before to a roly-poly Welsh nurse who used sex as part of her therapy to cure him from depression. (He was at the time in a nursing home in Pretoria as a result of a nervous breakdown—or, as Dick put it, 'in the nuthouse as a result of going nuts'). The therapy may or may not have worked—but it did awake in him a certain craving to repeat the therapy with a more permanent partner.

After a miserable courtship with a skinny divorcee who was as dry as a seed pod, he gave up, for she came to share the common view about Dick's eccentricity and kept his advances at arm's length. The fact is, Dick could never muster the courage to make an actual advance; instead, he would spend a great deal of money taking her to Mike's Kitchen, paid for by Dick's cheque book, and telling her how his Department Head (a gregarious Lesbian the size of a bus) should 'look Melanie in the face and tell her frankly that he wished to have sexual intercourse with her.' Of course, Melanie, conservative and sterile, in spite of her extant three children conceived by immaculate conception, was shocked and disgusted, so Dick never did get to sample her brand of feminine therapy.

Hitherto, Dick had spent his lecturer's salary buying unreadable and unspeakably dry books from Dillons of London. The same rows and rows of books still adorned his walls, unread, as best as Harry could determine. Nevertheless, a great deal of Dick's uncorked sexuality had—and continued to be—siphoned off through hours of listening to Bach, and repeated singings of the B-minor mass. While Harry stayed with him he was frequently entertained by the thronging and sombre tones of Dick's tenor voice. At these moments Dick's face assumed the look of bliss, and yet was oddly frog-like, his stoutish (at that time the larder stood in reasonable stock) middle-aged body swaying rhythmically from side to side. He was also a faithful member of the Methodist Choir, for the sake of the singing, though he would be the first to admit he was a confirmed agnostic. The choir, after all, was a legitimate outlet for his creative energy, or, in the absence of a female therapist, his sexuality.

Having been unsuccessful in gaining the therapeutic favours of Melanie, he turned his attention to a source of companionship that proved more amenable. He had two friends, young black men who belonged to the Bahai faith, who rejoiced under the names of Amos and Jonas and repeatedly promised to supply a female companion. They were about twenty and were still 'at school'—though they had moved into Dick's house which, being in Pietersburg, was in the heart of Terrablanch's Conservative Party (though these were the days before the Swastika was openly displayed). At any rate, Dick was pleased to have them stay in spite of, if not in defiance of, the Group Areas Act.

Harry didn't feel comfortable with the two young men, though he was certainly susceptible to Amos's wide smile and innocent white eyes. Unfortunately one day he confided to a colleague in the English Department, a prejudiced white South African steeped in the prevailing right-wing mentality, saying that, in his opinion, Amos and Jonas 'were a couple of ne'er-do-wells who were sponging off Dick'. (He did add, to give him his due, that one could hardly blame them, given their impoverished and repressed condition in South Africa.) The Boorish colleague (named Pieter van Niekerk) wrote a note to Dick, saying he agreed with Harry that 'those two pimps were sponging off him' and that he should 'throw out those two *kaffirs* and marry a good woman who can look after you.'

In the small hours of the mornings, on his occasional sojourns to the toilet, Harry would be aware of Jonas lurking in the shadows. He felt instinctively that their distrust for each other was mutual. One evening, when he returned late from a lecturing trip to dark Giyani (one of the University's northern outposts), Dick followed Harry into his room. He was clutching Van Niekerk's note and Harry detected that his friend's hand was shaking. A mild sense of alarm suffused him as he sat on the bed. He recalled that Dick, as he had put it himself, had been in the nuthouse.

'May I talk to you?'

'Of course,' replied Harry.

Dick handed him the note. He read it and realised he was in danger. Bloody Van Niekerk, he thought.

'Well?'

'I never said that!' Harry lied through his teeth.

Dick gave him a friendly biff on the arm. 'I *knew* you couldn't have!'

Well, what the hell, thought Harry. Amos and Jonas were Dick's pets. Touch them and you touched his soul. Dick was lonely and terribly reserved and in the two youths he had found a lasting companionship. Harry thought how you could tease him anyway you liked—but when it came to those two, you're at the very nerve centre of his being. The next day when he bumped into Van Niekerk in the corridor of the English Department, he told him how his note had placed him in mortal danger. Van Niekerk was profuse in his apologies and studiously avoided any further communications with Dick.

Through the kind offices of Amos and Jonas, Dick was eventually introduced to Emilie, a village maiden with a little English. This happy event had already predated Harry's introduction into Dick's house, but he was brought up to date with the state of Dick's love life over a late breakfast one day in the university canteen.

It was a characteristically hot day, the sun beating down out of a steel-grey sky. Depression clogged his heart as he gazed out of his office window across the open campus. He hardly thought of Eleanor now, or her theories of energy fields and vibrations. It was as though she were in another dimension. He thought bitterly of how he had tried to establish a future in that other world—the vibrant romantic world of Walter Scott, or even the picaresque world of Dickens; but all he had experienced there was a desolate loneliness. It now seemed that, in the wake of his divorce, he had fallen into the vacuum of Africa with its spreading deserts of loneliness. Yet here there were twilight figures in a crumbling world who proffered forms of friendship. How like twilight figures both he and Dick, and Liz too, were: it was no wonder they had fallen into a form of friendship. They shared a makeshift raft in a turbulence of change where hard and fast values and rules were no longer discernible.

The campus was void of students who were currently on strike. He had forgotten the reason, this time—whether it was poor food in the hostels or the refusal of the mathematics professor to pass sixty percent of his students in the last exam. The silence filled his ears and was almost audible, like a thin siren wailing in the background. It was like living in a vacuum. On occasions when he walked across the rough cobbled stones embedded in the crude paving slabs of the campus, he felt he was in an alien world.

The sudden roar of engines brought his mind back to the scene outside the window. A convoy of dull olive-skinned vehicles, bristling with guns, aerial wires and uniformed youths, trundled around the campus, circled twice, and receded across a half-made road in a swirl of dust. He waited for the noise to recede, and the silence, the vacuum, reasserted itself, a dead-weight in his ears. 'God, I hate this country,' he mumbled. There was a tap on his door.

Harry lifted his eyes to see Dick's weather-beaten face.

'Shall we sojourn for brekkie?'

'Yes,' replied Harry.

They made their way across the rough hot cobbles towards the canteen. It was more convenient to have breakfast ready-made than go to the bother of cooking it themselves, so they usually found a gap between morning lectures for a canteen visit. On this occasion the strike gave them ample free time.

Soon they were confronted by the usual rubber eggs on toast and tasteless sausages. Dick stirred the ingredients into a matrix of tomato sauce and chutney.

'So running a hotel was worse than this?' Dick stuffed half an egg into his mouth and his words slid out in muffled chunks. 'I mean...,' he chomped, 'the guests ... bed and breakfast.'

'Dreadful,' sighed Harry, then drew his brows together. 'Well, not really. There were some lovely people. A couple of old ladies who kept coming back and testing me with literary questions. And a married couple who became good friends.' His eyes took on a glazed look. 'She had jet black hair with crystal blue eyes. She was like a fairy queen. I suppose you could say I fell in love with her. But she's married, of course. I guess that's one of the reasons I came out here.'

'*Ag*, shame,' mumbled Dick. He still spoke with a good Cambridge accent, but had imbibed South African clichés. He poured coffee down his throat. His face was wizened, sun-baked and wrinkled, like an old man's.

'Anyway, you had something going with a nice South African girl. Melanie, I think you said ...'

'Stuff Melanie!' Dick crushed a sausage between his teeth. 'She's frigid.'

'Didn't you ...?'

'Fuck her? No.'

Harry nearly choked on his coffee, startled by Dick's bluntness. Dick had been forty-six when the Welsh nurse introduced him to the delights of sex. Ever since she left he was in a quasi-permanent state of frustration. For years he had been totally immersed in the dubious pleasures of Turkish and remote dialects of the Nguni language. His rows of books on esoteric dialects and grammatical functions bore evidence to this lost world.

'What happened, in the end?' Harry nudged sympathetically. Like it or not, he thought, he shared much of the older man's frustration and wondered if he was a beacon for what he would become.

'Nothing.' Dick shrugged his shoulders. 'She took me home, after dinner at Mike's Kitchen. But I had locked myself out of the house. She wouldn't put me up at her flat though I had nowhere to go. In the end she put me up on her couch and locked herself in her bedroom. I left in the morning. It was the last time I saw her. I wrote and told her I'd grown considerably poorer in the process of knowing her.'

'I'm sorry,' Harry commiserated. He felt that somehow the one hope for Dick was to find a responsible woman—someone who could control his bank account and keep him well fed.

'Doesn't matter,' he said, swallowing the last of his coffee. 'I love Emilie.'

'Emilie?' Harry looked up in surprise.

'I thought you knew. She's Amos's sister. Jonas and Amos are like two adopted sons to me.'

'Yes, I know,' Harry said quickly. 'But I didn't know about Emilie. You mean she's ...'

'Black? Naturally.' Dick was unconcerned about Emilie's colour. 'She's beautiful,' he added with a touch of youthful naiveté that made his wizened face look ridiculous.

'She can't be very old, if she's Amos's sister.'

Dick shrugged. 'Eighteen, I suppose.'

Harry's cup froze within centimetres of his lips. He put it down slowly. 'We have much in common. As I said, I found myself falling under the spell of one of my guests—a woman much younger than me.'

'Did you fuck her?' asked Dick nonchalantly, draining his cup.

'No, I ... Surely you didn't ...' Harry stumbled.

'Have sex with Emilie? Yes.'

Harry paused for a moment. The age difference, he realised, must be astronomical—considerably more than the ten years that intervened between his and Eleanor's ages. He said, politely: 'Emilie must be a village maiden.'

'She's highly intelligent.' It was like a factual statement.

'And you're forty-eight?'

'Love knows no limitations.'

Oh for a Cambridge education, thought Harry. You could use clichés like universal truths. He wondered if Dick was insulated from reality by his classical education. He had a fleeting vision of Dick's bleached body running to fat, heaving on top of Emilie's black youthful body spread out for him like a sacrifice.

Dick picked up his cup and refilled it at the coffee urn. He sat down again at the table.

'Was it any good?' ventured Harry.

Dick raised his eyebrows.

'Emilie, I mean.'

'Not really,' he confessed. 'It only happened once.'

'Oh?'

'It was before you moved in. Amos and Jonas brought her round to the house. They told her she should have sex with me.'

'Good Lord. You mean they sat in the lounge while you and Emilie ...?'

'No!' Dick grinned. 'They were discreet. They went for a walk.'

'And then?'

'Then I asked Emilie if she would like to make love to me.'

'Just like that!'

'Well,' he knitted his brows, recalling, 'She didn't appear to understand. So I said: "Will you have sex with me?" And she said: "You want sex? No problem!"'

'And you managed it ...?'

'Well,' Dick chuckled over his coffee. 'She asked me to redirect my penis.'

Harry's eyes widened. 'She put it like that?'

Dick gave way to a laugh that escaped like a belch. 'No. She said, "Put your penis here!" It hurt a bit.'

'It must have hurt *her*!' Harry said with a touch of horror.

Dick shrugged. 'She was very quiet. Not like Gwen.' Gwen was the Welsh nurse. 'Gwen used to scream like a banshee.'

'Like Eleanor,' said Harry.

'Eleanor?'

'Oh, the woman in my hotel, in Scotland,' Harry said wistfully. He frowned. 'But if Emilie's still visiting, or moving in, I'll be in the way, Dick.'

'No, you won't be. It only happened once, anyway.'

'That was the only time? She hasn't been back since?'

'Well...' Dick twirled his hand noncommittally. 'She's been around a couple of times, before you moved in. But it didn't come to sex again.'

'And you really love her?'

'Yes. She's super.' He touched his cup with the tips of his fingers, gazing wistfully at it with his head to one side. 'Her skin's like silk.'

My God, Harry thought. 'Are you sure she doesn't just come for money? Or food?' He hoped the question wouldn't offend him.

'I bought her some groceries last time,' he said thoughtfully. 'No. The trouble is, when I escort her back to the taxi rank, the taxi drivers think she's a prostitute and charge her double.' Dick didn't drive.

'You mean, because they saw you with her?'

'Yes.'

Harry looked at his friend. 'Jonas and Amos stay with you—with us—though, and you feed them?'

Dick raised his eyebrows. 'They're finishing school. They don't work.'

'So...,' Harry went on awkwardly. 'You don't think Emilie's been asked to sleep with you ... as a kind of payment for their board and lodging?'

But Dick didn't take any offence. 'No. She's a super girl. Super.'

Harry smiled, thinking how strange that Dick should use a word that Eleanor was so fond of using, and with as much feeling.

The main complaints that beset Dick's life were the complaints from the occupants of the neighbouring houses. When the landlord called to collect the rent he told Dick that the neighbours had objected to black people who obviously stayed the night. It was against the law—the Group Areas Act which stipulated that blacks and whites stay in their separate areas. Dick's black friends could visit but they shouldn't stay the night, the landlord had explained. So for a time Amos and Jonas moved out, back to the black township or location, as it was called, to keep a low profile before filtering back into the house.

When Harry came home from lectures one night he found that Dick was sleeping on only half a bed—the mattress.

'What happened to the base of your bed, Dick?'

'Oh, I leant it to Jonas. He hasn't got a bed.'

Dick was a Bahai, yet he was a better Christian than many Christians Harry knew—in practical terms, anyway. He was feeding the hungry and sheltering them—and when he couldn't continue to provide shelter, he gave them half his bed. 'Jonas lives in a shack,' he explained. 'He's got nothing else.'

'But surely, Dick, to give half your bed away ...'

'You'd do it for me,' Dick said matter-of-factly.

But Harry knew he wouldn't. You've got to draw the line somewhere, he told himself. Living in a third-world country, where the overwhelming majority (who happened to be black) had nothing, you had to draw the line or you'd be swamped. Harry recalled the story behind a statue of a hero on horseback in Cape Town—a story Van Niekerk in his Department had told him. There was a shipwreck and the man had tried to save a crowd of drowning people by swimming out to them on horseback. Everyone clutched at the horse until hero and horse, all together, were pulled under. That was why Dick never had any money, Harry thought. When he had anything, he was generous. He gave till he had nothing—and still gave. Then he had to borrow and sponge off others until his next paycheque came in. 'Mean Dick', people called him. But he wasn't mean at all. He just didn't know where—and when—to draw the line.

As a Senior Lecturer of some years standing, he ought to have had a substantial house in the suburbs—a house with a swimming pool, a double garage, and at least one Mercedes, like the rest of the whites in Pietersburg. But Dick had nothing. The house he lived in wasn't his and, apart from the rows of books on the dialects of Upper Volta and the Niger Delta, it was bare—no carpets, and only one table and two chairs. Occasionally he did receive a ten-pound note from his seventy-year old mother in Norwich. It helped, occasionally, to provide some mealie meal whereby Dick and his two black protégés eked out the remaining fortnight of a month. In this way a seventy-year old woman in England, unbeknown to her, was fighting apartheid—by putting in her two mites.

'Emilie might come this afternoon,' Dick announced.

'Oh, really?' Harry smiled.

'If I fuck Emilie, I'll be in good singing form tonight.'

But Emilie didn't come. Harry began to view her as a mythological figure in Dick's world of would-be reality.

CHAPTER 35

African Vibrations

BOB RIMMER, the new British Council officer in the region, invited Harry and Dick for Sunday lunch.

Bob rented a huge disintegrating house on a plot—a smallholding outside Pietersburg—which had a rondavel, a round house or hut with a straw roof. Bob very magnanimously invited Harry to stay in the rondavel, a blessing which enabled Harry some relief from the overcrowded condition of Dick's house where Amos and Jonas had crept back with the addition of a cousin. Bob preferred the anonymity of a country house away from the prying eyes of white neighbours, though his liking for young black women put him in a tenuous position in a country which, as Harry put it, was 'about to go nova.'

The house reflected the past glories of a decadent white society. It had a huge lounge and dining room, a bar, and a spacious patio overlooking an open vista of faraway mountains under a sky of steel blue during the day, and deep black at night with brilliant stars. It was after lunch and Harry, Dick and Bob were seated comfortably in the weakening afternoon light drinking beer. Bob, a slight figure in jeans and loose T-shirt, leant back in his wire chair. He looked foppish with his long curly hair, but peered benignly through the thick lenses of his glasses at the thronging array of 'young ladies', as he was pleased to call them—local black lasses swirling and twirling to synthetic recorded music that blared from a portable radio-cassette player.

They were dusty young maidens, stamping the earth with their bare feet, releasing the dust of the earth that swirled about their ankles, while the music throbbed, repeating the same phrase with monotonous regularity. Their voices trilled and wailed as they hurled remarks at one another with vociferous abandon. Nubile bare legs, clad in tight yellow shorts, beat out the untamed rhythm of Africa, while stouter bodies in bright dresses—mauve, red, pink—gyrated monotonously, arms raised and dropped, fingers clicking.

The tallest of the dancers was clad in a tight red skirt that stretched across wide thighs. Her course features were turned towards the sky, eyes closed, a deep, almost base voice bellowing musically. She was Sophie, Bob's young lady who worked (and lived) in the main house. She presided over the cooking though Bob in fact did his own cooking while she hovered over his shoulder, or leaned languidly against the stove, throwing in comments with raucous laughter. Harry could never actually perceive what she did for her money and her free board, for the house was always covered in dust and Bob was always shouting at her to do various jobs which she never did.

'Exactly!' said Bob, gesticulating with his raised arm. 'They'll all be murdered, at this rate. There's a tidal wave of hatred building up against them!'

'They're blind to it,' suggested Harry. 'They're comfortable in the lager.'

'Exactly!' returned Bob, running his hand through his long hair. 'Take the Boer who owns this house! It was raining last Monday, when he came here. Jacob and other labourers were sheltering in the garage. "Why aren't you kaffirs working!" he shouted. And then he fired the lot of them!'

'Incredible!' said Harry.

'Disgusting!' said Dick.

They all drank their Lion Lagers and shook their heads in disbelief.

'But those poor people!' continued Bob. 'In the rain, they had to move out. Women with children. They had to walk for miles, no doubt, to take refuge in some village.'

'Surely he must have relented?' put in Harry. 'The owner, I mean?'

Bob shook his head, his eyes magnified unnaturally behind his thick lenses. 'That damn Boer just roared off in his bakkie.'

'A Boer in a bakkie,' said Dick, swallowing another mouthful.

Raucous laughter interrupted the monotonous beats of the music and Sophie, the tall maiden, picked her way across the bricks of a wall that had collapsed the week before. (It had killed a small dachshund which Bob had buried nearby. The artificial flowers on the little mound of its grave could be seen next to the nearby cement dam.)

'Hey Dick!' bellowed Sophie. 'You dance with me!'

It was an order rather than a request.

The three men squinted against the light of the sun. Sophie in her red apparel stood planted, feet apart, before Dick. 'You come!' she ordered. She ruled the roost and was used to obedience—even from white men. She put out a dusky hand and pulled Dick from his chair. He rose, half reluctantly, half willingly, and allowed himself to be towed across the rubble of the wall. Her laughter cackled in deep staccato bursts.

Once in the dusty clearing, Sophie gyrated opposite Dick. He was dressed in the trousers of his smart grey suit and blue shirt, since he was to sing in the church choir shortly. He gyrated in response to her, picking up the African rhythms. The others stood back and began to clap rhythmically. Sophie repeatedly brushed her large thighs against Dick's trousers. Then, as the excitement of the dance overtook her, she repeatedly tugged her skirt forward, in a parody of an enormously concealed erection. Dick did the same, tugging the front of his trousers, imitating an erection. Then she backed her large gyrating posterior against his now obvious erection and he, quite oblivious of indwelling inhibitions, groped at her large breasts flattened beneath the tight blouse.

'*Look* at that!' gasped Bob in mock horror.

'Dick has to appear in the choir in an hour,' Harry said with genuine alarm. 'I have to take him.'

'Don't worry,' laughed Bob. 'Let's see where the evening takes us!'

Sophie and her friends had been dancing and drinking continuously throughout the afternoon. Harry wasn't sure he wanted to see where it would lead. The vibrations of Africa were too heady, too spontaneous and uncontrolled for his liking and he wondered what Eleanor would have made of them. If this was an energy centre, he thought, it was wild and untameable.

At length Dick broke away and returned to his seat, flushed.

'Had a good time, Dick?' Harry smiled uncertainly.

'Why, yes,' said Dick, resuming his drink. His suit trousers were covered in dust.

Sophie picked her way across the rubble again and sat heavily on his lap. 'Here!' she said. She slid a handful of silver into Dick's shirt pocket.

'What the bloody hell's that for?' he asked.

'It was money given by those who were interested to watch us. We were the best to dance.' Her voice was husky. Then she rolled back, veritably squashing Dick with her posterior, easing back against his chest. She squirmed her posterior against him, sensing his erection. She looked down at him with a superior smile. 'I think I will ween you,' she said. 'I think Emilie will lose you. I will ween you from her, Dick.'

'Yes,' said Dick, half suffocated. He was always polite to women. Harry wondered if his erection hadn't been completely crushed.

'I think,' said Harry, 'that it's time for us to leave, Dick. The choir, you know. If you're still interested, that is.'

From somewhere Dick resurrected a sense of responsibility. 'Yes,' he said.

When Sophie returned to the gyrating dancers Dick took the opportunity to retrieve his tie and jacket from the house. He and Harry got into Harry's battered Beetle and as they drove away Sophie ran forward, waving them off. Bob smiled benignly behind her.

At church Harry felt amused, seeing Dick march in, single-file, with the choir members, dressed in the formal green gown of the choir. Harry tried to catch his eye, but Dick kept both eyes aloof, his face stern in assumed sanctity. His resonant tenor voice filled the auditorium, his eyes fixed sternly on his music sheet.

It was dark when Harry returned to Bob's rondavel. The wind had got up and the trees above the rondavel moaned with restive energy. He was picking his way through the dark when Bob's slight figure came out of the darkness.

'Harry!' Bob whispered.

'Bob!' Harry was surprised to see his friend materialise so unexpectedly.

'Quick!' Bob said, stopping Harry's advance towards the main house. 'It's dangerous here. Let's go to the rondavel.'

Fear clutched at Harry's heart. What was the matter? He fumbled the latch key against the lock of the rondavel until it opened. The two men entered the sparsely furnished room, dominated by a small table with a typewriter in the centre of the round room. Only then did Harry see that Bob's arm was soaked in blood. A few crimson drops had already appeared on the floor.

'Bob! My God, you're hurt!'

'Harry, Sophie's gone berserk!'

'What!'

'After you left ...' Bob was breathless. Clearly he was suffering from shock. 'I went to lie down on the sofa. I was asleep. Suddenly she was there. On top of me, strangling me. "It's your life or mine!" she kept shouting.'

'Good Lord.'

'I got away. Then she started throwing things at me. Cups, saucers, glasses. My cookery books. Anything she could lay her hands on.'

'And your arm?'

'One of the glasses, I think. It caught me on the arm.'

'It's still bleeding!'

Harry found some plaster. Bob wiped his wound with a damp cloth and Harry stuck two pieces on it, in the shape of a cross. Harry motioned to one of the two upright wooden chairs.

'Sit down, Bob. Where is she now? What happened afterwards?'

They both sat down and looked at each other. Bob's eyes stared, bewildered, through his thick lenses.

'She was berserk,' Bob continued. His long strands of hair made a wild mess around his damp temples. 'I managed to get the door between us. I put all my weight against it. Gertrude and her boyfriend were there, too, tugging at Sophie, trying to stop her.' Gertrude was another of the young ladies employed by Bob. One of the dusky and dusty dancers a couple of hours ago. 'Anyway, she gave up, ran round the house, and burst through my bedroom window. Then she came at me again.'

'Good Lord!'

'Yes.' Bob's eyes stared. 'I escaped into the garden. I was still in my socks. And she chased me round the house a few times.'

Harry imagined the scene. Bob's practice was to jog round the house early every morning. Harry was used to having fleeting and sleepy glimpses of his friend flitting past the window. Datchy, the little dachshund that met its demise under the wall, used to be in pursuit, scampering on its tiny legs. The scene with Sophie, the mad woman, in pursuit, was a modification of the remembered images. Instead of the tackies, there would be the blue socks; instead of the long hair rhythmically quivering around his temples, there would be the wild locks flying in the wind: and then there were Bob's eyes, staring in terror as he ran.

'Good Lord,' said Harry.

'Nothing like this ever happened to me before,' said Bob. 'Not even in Aden. In Ethiopia, once, a girl slapped me on the cheek because I refused to sleep with her. But *this*!'

'Quite,' said Harry.

'She's berserk.'

'She's been drinking too much.'

'She's possessed.'

'She has a demon.'

'Damn right she has. She has a demon.'

'You didn't do anything to provoke her?'

'No! I just called her a sex maniac.'

'You did? When?'

'After you left. It was just banter. The way she was dancing with Dick, you know.'

'Then you went to sleep on the couch?'

'Then I went to sleep on the couch. Exactly!'

'She's a big woman. She could have killed you.'

'Exactly!'

'Where is she now?'

'God knows. She ran into the veldt. I looked in the dam.'

'She's not there?'

'She's not there.'

'She might come back.'

'She might come back,' Bob echoed. 'She has murder in her heart.'

They talked noncommittally and eventually Bob went back to the big house, barricading himself behind locked doors. Harry was left with a sense of unreality, suspended between exhaustion and apprehension. He didn't dare go to sleep but sat, fully dressed, in case the mad woman came back to renew her attack.

He sat on the hard upright chair waiting for the dawn. Why, why had he come to this desolate land? He thought of Eleanor, again, far away, in a world beyond the horizon, and her naive chatter about energy vibrations. He recalled his strange experience at the Abbey when he sat on the altar stone, as he thought, with Eleanor. It was the one moment in his life when he felt truly centred. But these people here, he thought, were hardly centred. They were twilight people, flotsam people, like himself, drifting, looking or not looking for some sort of meaning or purpose. They were circling and wheeling about a pivot that didn't exist. The centre cannot hold if the centre doesn't exist, he thought. 'We're all falling apart,' he said aloud, addressing his harassed image in the small mirror over the washstand. 'We're all flotsam, circling around the plug hole. Soon we'll all be sucked in ...' Sucked into what, he thought bitterly. Life was a void and nothing satisfied.

A knock on the door made him jump.

'Harry!' said a woman's husky voice. It was Sophie.

Now it's my turn, he thought, jumping to the door and keeping his weight against it. 'What do you want?' he said, steadying his heartbeat.

'I must speak with you,' she said.

He felt stupid standing there, not knowing what to do. But she sounded calm and in control. He took a deep breath and unlatched the door.

She came in, immaculately dressed as though she were going to church or a wedding. She wore a beret and carried a neat handbag.

'I am leaving Bob,' she said in a husky and controlled voice. 'You tell him I am having no more to do with him.' She pulled a ring from her finger. 'You give him this. You say I say goodbye!'

She was gone before he could take in what had happened. The whole thing was meaningless to him.

CHAPTER 36

Twilight Zone

LIZ was hardly the sort of woman Harry would date. But she had been pleased to see him when he came to the bank, and she had so efficiently restored the financial value of the travellers' cheques stolen from him at Pretoria station. She was friendly and in the vortex of loneliness Harry was experiencing he was happy to clutch at any companionship. When he left the bank he had accepted her suggestion to see the new movie at the Drive-in cinema.

At seven he parked his Beetle on the wide pavement under a Jacaranda tree in Magazyne Street. The evening was cool with a brisk breeze sweeping the branches above him. He walked up the steps of the old colonial-styled house. He walked along the wide veranda under a red tin roof and stopped at an open door. He could hear Liz's laughter and looked in.

She was seated on the carpet between two men, one slouched on a settee, the other reclining on the carpet and propped up on an elbow. They were all drinking from cups and turned to look at Harry.

'Harry!' Liz said, looking pleased. 'Come in and have a drink!'

Harry entered awkwardly. There was a stale aroma he couldn't quite place, but then he remembered that Liz smoked.

'Here!' she patted the carpet next to her. 'We don't stand on ceremony here. We're not in the bank now.'

He sat down on the floor, leaning his back against the bed uncomfortably. 'Hello,' he said uncertainly.

'Hi,' said the man on the settee. The other drained the contents of his cup.

Liz lit a cigarette and coughed. 'Harry's taking me to see *Gorillas in the Mist*.'

'That's a good flick,' said the first man. He had a wizened and pruinlike face.

The other, with a swollen red face, coughed politely. 'It's about Gorillas, you know.'

'*Ja,*' said the first. 'You know, there was a baboon on the wall at the back of my flet the other day. It had escaped from the zoo. A 'oke from the police came and shot him.'

'Hey,' said his companion, 'did they find his bicycle?'

They laughed with high-pitched giggles, the red-faced man's paunch shaking spasmodically.

'Hey, no,' said the lean man, 'you mustn't call them baboons, hey. The new word is plural gentleman, like in the Department of Plural Affairs!'

The fat man shook with laughter again. 'Ag no, man, you're *killing* me, man. So I can employ a plural gentleman to work in my garden!'

'And the Kaffirboom is now called a Plural Tree!'

The fat man's laughter turned into a coughing fit. 'Yislike, man...'

Liz smiled at Harry and responded to his lost look. She touched the fat man on his shoulder. 'You guys must bugger off now, hey?' She sat up straight and ran her hand through her blonde hair. She spoke with mock superiority. 'Can't you see I've got a hot date with a distinguished professor from the university?'

'Ja, ja, okay, Liz,' said the man, rising with effort. 'But thenks for the drink, hey.'

'Ja, likewise,' said the thin man. 'See you later, hey.'

'See you later, you vagabonds,' Liz smiled up at them through her curling cigarette smoke. 'Thanks for the visit.'

They left and Liz filled a teacup from a carton of red wine next to her. She handed the cup to Harry. 'I suppose you think I'm a bit of a tramp, having those two here?' She smiled with hooded eyes, drawing up one knee under a blue cotton skirt. She was barefoot and was enjoying relaxing.

Harry shook his head, not willing to admit his misgivings about her company. 'Not at all,' he said quietly.

'I met those two in the bar of the Great North. You meet some real characters there. I'll take you there.'

He laughed. 'I've tried to avoid it, actually.'

'The fact is, Harry,' she said, taking a sip from her own cup. 'I'm damn intelligent.' She wasn't smiling. 'I'm intelligent enough to appreciate the worth of any human being. I can relate to any human being at any level.'

'Like a chameleon?' he smiled.

'Like a chameleon, sure!' She lit another cigarette which made Harry look at his watch. 'Harry, do you really want to see this film about baboons?'

'Gorillas,' corrected Harry.

'Gorillas, then. I mean, we could be just as comfortable sitting here. There's plenty of wine.'

'Well, it's already started...'

'Just be honest, Harry. What would you rather do?'

'I'd rather sit here and get totally sloshed with you,' he heard himself saying. He laughed. 'No, of course ...'

'That's settled, then,' she said, taking his cup and topping it up. 'Are you sure you won't have a cigarette?'

'No, no,' he said meekly. He really regretted coming now and would have preferred to escape from her dingy little bedsitter. 'I was being ironic, actually...'

'It's true, though,' she said, not hearing his reply. 'I *am* a chameleon. One has to be, to survive. But that doesn't mean the chameleon isn't true to its own self.'

'Like Hamlet,' he laughed.

She drank from her cup and Harry drank from his. It was like a communion, he thought. The wine was surprisingly sweet and heady. His sense of desolation and loneliness seemed to retreat with every sip.

'To your own self be true,' she repeated, lifting her cup. 'Your chameleon self.' She laughed, shaking her head. 'Oh dear. You're out of wine, Harry. Help yourself.'

'Thanks.' He helped himself from the small plastic tap in the carton. The thin stream of wine tinkled into the cup.

'Oh God, I need to pis,' she said. 'Now I'm going to shock the hell out of you.' She got up unsteadily and walked towards the wash basin in the room. She laughed. 'I can't be bothered to walk down the veranda and into the house. I always just do it here!' She began to lift up her dress.

But Harry was already stunned by the effect of the wine. The novelty of Liz's honest bravado amused him. 'You do that sort of thing too!' he laughed. 'Well, I won't look.'

'Oh, look all you like. I don't care!'

He turned away but allowed his eyes to drift back to her. She was half seated and half leaning over the wash basin while a steady stream tinkled into it. She caught his eyes and smiled archly, but not before his eyes were drawn fleetingly to the black matted mound between soft thighs dimpled with cellulite. His eyes remained in focus long enough to notice how the mound was folded and neatly tucked into a delicate cleft.

He laughed self-consciously, feeling a tight spring inside him begin to uncoil. 'I usually keep the cold-water tap running, to make sure everything flushes away.'

She got off and her dress fell loosely about her knees. 'You see,' she said, 'we're both chameleons!'

'The other day,' he said, taking in a deep breath since the rhythm of his pulse had altered. 'I was caught with my pants down because my colour wouldn't change.'

She laughed, lighting up a new cigarette. 'Do tell!' She inhaled and coughed. 'Your pants down?'

'Yes,' he said. 'It was in the square opposite the supermarket and museum. I needed a loo, but the whites' loo was locked. It was urgent so I walked round the other side and found the blacks' side unlocked. It was a bit smelly but needs must ...'

She laughed liberally and he broke off, smiling. He went on: 'I pulled the door shut. It didn't have a lock. I was in midstream when a burly white Afrikaner yanked open the door. *"Hey,"* he shouted, *"this is for blecks! I'll report you!"* Have you ever had to stop the flow in full flow? I think it went all over my shoes ...'

She laughed volubly with pinched eyes. 'Harry, you're a scream!'

'The point is, though, I was feeling so bloody angry! I stood there with my penis hanging out, and I wanted to hit him!'

'You should have pissed on him!' Her breasts shook with laughter. 'Harry, you're the limit!' She smiled. 'You know, it's amazing how relaxed I am with you. It's easy to talk to you.'

'It's easy to talk to you,' he said.

'Then tell me what's really bugging you,' she said. 'How's your drink, Harry?'

'It's all right.' He drank some more and settled more comfortably against the bed. His whole body felt relaxed, including his eyes which abandoned the need to keep in focus. He looked at Liz and she swam lazily into focus. 'How do you mean, what's bugging me?'

'You're so damn withdrawn, Harry, like a little boy lost. Yet you're an important buff, running the Department of English. Are you like this at work, too?'

He smiled. 'Work insulates me from loneliness, Liz. This is a very lonely country, with its open spaces. Maybe I suffer from a form of agoraphobia—you know, fear of open spaces. The sky seems so high and open, the land so bleak and desolate. And the people are so... ' He hesitated. 'The culture is so foreign, I guess.' He sipped his wine. 'The whites and the blacks seem to be so trapped in their own cultures. They're so insular. I guess you—and my friends Dick and Bob—are the only people I feel relaxed with.'

She smiled sympathetically, stretching out her legs and placing one over the other. 'We're kindred spirits, Harry. What you're experiencing is the aftershock of a divorce. I've been there myself.' She reached out for his cup. He surrendered the cup to her which she refilled, handing it back to him. 'I know what it's like. You're looking for the Holy Grail. Someone—or something—to fill the vacuum that divorce creates. Do you know what you're looking for?'

He laughed. 'I had a dream once of a girl in South Africa. I wonder if that had something to do with my looking for a job here? In the dream she even wrote down her address. When I woke up I remembered it and wrote it down!'

'A dream!' She laughed, finishing another cupful. 'My God! What was the address?'

He shrugged. 'Somewhere in Durban. I can't remember now. It was only a dream. anyway.'

'But you wrote it down? I know Durban pretty well. My father lives there. I'll soon tell you if the address really exists. Where did you write it?'

'Liz, it was only a stupid dream!' He laughed. 'I don't have the piece of paper anymore, but I remember I did copy it into the back of my Bible.'

'Your Bible! So where's your Bible?'

'In the rondavel.'

'Let's go there, then.'

'Now?'

'Sure.' She looked at him languidly through her hooded eyes. 'I'd like to see your rondavel. Sounds nice. I've got another carton of wine and we'll stop on the way and pick up some Kentucky Fried Chicken. Make an evening of it.'

Harry thought the rondavel would be better than Liz's dingy room and at least it had a proper toilet. 'Fine,' he said, 'but I don't know ...' He chuckled. 'I don't know if I have more than fifty per cent vision left!'

'Oh,' she laughed. 'I've got at least fifty percent left. Together we'll find the way.'

Harry made his leaden legs push up his body. Liz collected her new carton and he navigated his numb body to the Beetle. 'God, Liz,' he said, starting the car. 'I'm not sure I'm safe to drive.'

'Just go slowly,' she said.

'I'll stay in second gear,' he said, and held the steering firmly in both hands. The little bonnet of the car drifted steadily and slowly along the left-hand side of the road. He concentrated on keeping it on the left and was pleased at how steady he could manoeuvre the car.

'God, it's like going to a funeral!' said Liz.

'Never mind,' he said, chuckling. 'At least it won't be our funeral.'

He stopped at the Kentucky Fried Chicken take-away and gave Liz a ten rand note. She came back with a box of chicken breasts and two packets of cigarettes. Then Harry manoeuvred the car slowly out of town, into the dark countryside. The stars were brilliant but occasionally eclipsed by dark shapes of clouds.

'There's going to be a storm,' said Liz. 'We need some rain.'

'Sure. But I can hardly see,' he said.

'It would help to turn on your headlights,' she laughed.

309

'Oh my God,' he said, switching them on. The black ribbon of the road sprang into brilliant focus. 'That's better.'

'You're really a card, Harry,' she laughed, then added soberly: 'This reminds me of driving with Koos. He was nearly blind, you know.'

'Oh yes,' he said, concentrating on the road. 'You told me about him.'

'He might still be alive if...' Her voice choked. 'Oh God, I loved him.'

'It wasn't your fault, Liz.'

'In a way it was.'

'In what way?' he asked sympathetically, daring to ease the car into third gear. It growled comfortably up a small hill and relaxed to a gentle purr as the road dipped downhill.

'What he really wanted was to experience another woman. To make a threesome.'

'What!'

'So we got into his bakkie and found a black woman. We took her home and gave her some money. But she got cold feet and ran off.'

'You went along with ...?' he said with disbelief, but also with a twinge of guilt.

'I loved him enough to comply with his whims.' Her voice broke again. She went on softly. 'Whatever it took to make him feel fulfilled.'

'And so?' It sounded all too familiar.

'And so he rushed off again in the bakkie. To find another woman. I didn't want to go again ...'

'Of course you didn't, Liz.' She would have felt like Anne did, that night in Jedburgh.

'And...,' she hesitated, 'And he never came back. He couldn't see, of course.'

Harry drove with a sense of unreality. Abandon hope, all ye that enter here, he thought, slowing down to take a left turn off the main road. The car lurched and rumbled on the corrugated dirt road that led to the plot.

'Well,' he said, comfortingly, 'he's at peace now, Liz. He's out of it.'

'Out of what?'

'Out of ... everything, consciousness, I suppose. No more awareness of his pain. You know, I can understand someone wanting death.'

'But Koos wasn't looking for death ...'

'He's at peace, anyhow,' he said, turning into the small winding track that led to the house and rondavel. The car bumped over the uneven surface. 'Being conscious—of our existence as well as our agonies and pleasures—is what makes us human, I think.' The car nudged into the dark next to a Bluegum tree that grew by the rondavel and spluttered to a stop. 'Here we are,' he said with relief. 'Still alive and still conscious!'

They got out. The leaves above them shook in a sudden chaos of frenzy, then settled into a restless stirring.

'The winds of change,' Harry said, looking up at the scudding clouds. A gap in the clouds revealed the brilliant points of the Southern Cross. 'Look,' he said, pointing. 'You can see the Southern Cross.'

She stood behind him, looking over his shoulder. 'I can see Halley's comet,' she said.

'Really?' He looked and could just make out a hazy patch with a wispy tail. 'It looks like a star that's been smudged. Is it really a comet?'

'Yes,' she said. 'The last time it came was in 1910, I think.'

As they watched the comet blurred and was enveloped by the creeping clouds. The leaves above them shook angrily again.

'Not bad for fifty-percent vision!' she laughed. 'We better go inside before the rain comes.'

Harry fumbled at the lock and opened the door. They went in and he put on the light.

'This is *nice*,' she said, taking in the round Spartan room with its single bed, table and two chairs. She put the wine carton on the little table and drew the two wooden chairs together. 'Come along, I'm starving.'

CHAPTER 37

Cesspool

THE RONDAVEL was like the still centre of a cyclone. There were distant thunderclaps and the single light bulb above them flickered. Then the heavens opened and a deluge of water washed the outside panes of the window. Harry got up and drew the curtains shut, closing out the night.

He had eaten and drunk more wine while Liz talked of her aspirations and dreams, and now he felt quite bloated. He took off his clothes and put on his dressing gown. 'That's much better,' he sighed, allowing his stomach to expand. 'Those trousers were getting tighter!'

She laughed. 'Come on, sit down and have another drink!' She helped herself to another glass.

He sat down. 'You were saying you loved living by the sea. You should go to Durban and work towards a managerial position in a bigger bank. You're wasted here, an intelligent person like you.'

She looked at him sadly. 'You don't know me, do you?'

'How to you mean?' He leaned back and stretched himself. The rain eased its intensity to a steady patter on the straw roof.

She sipped her drink and looked at him earnestly. She had kicked off her shoes again and folded one leg across the other, allowing the skirt to ride up her bare thighs. 'All I ever wanted, Harry, was someone to look after—and someone to look after me! I'm not a career person at all.'

'I thought you were well embarked on a banking career.'

'And get posted from bank to bank? Battling along on one's own really takes it out of a person.'

'I know,' he said with feeling.

'One of my happiest moments,' she said, 'was when Koos and I were on holiday on the East Coast, near the Transkei.' She lit a cigarette again. 'Harry, you wouldn't *believe* the beauty and

312

tranquillity of the place. We walked on the beach. There was a full moon. The sea was as warm as soup and there wasn't a breath of wind. We felt as though we'd stepped into a dream. Even before we met, Koos and I cherished a dream of a place like that—a cottage near the sea with the freedom to be undisturbed—to make a garden, to make love.'

He smiled. 'You're a romantic and an idealist, Liz. You should follow your dreams.'

'Yes.' Her eyes were damp. 'We had both spent long lonely hours in empty, haunted hotel rooms, boarding house rooms, hostel rooms, with no one to come home to or even to fight with.'

'Yes,' he said softly. 'I know the feeling.'

'We are—were—both ex-Rhodesian with a lost war and a lost country in common.' She drank again and smiled. 'Sorry about the self-pity.'

'We're all looking for paradise, I suppose,' he said kindly.

'I thought I had it for a while with Koos,' she said. 'He was the sparkle in the wine of my life!' She laughed, raised her glass and drained it.

'I hope you find your sparkle again, Liz.'

'And yours!' she said, refilling her glass. 'In the meantime I'll find it in here.' She lifted her glass.

His body felt more numb than ever. 'Maybe we've had enough,' he said.

'Oh, why bother. I know I shouldn't drink, of course. I belong to the A.A. I don't mean the Automobile Association, either!'

'You're an alcoholic?'

'No, I just drink because I like it.' She took another sip and laughed. 'Of *course* I am, Harry. I go to meetings. I should be at one tonight. You know, you meet the nicest people at A.A. meetings. They're the nicest people I know.' She meant it sincerely.

'I'm sorry, Liz. Here I am encouraging you ...'

'Never mind, you're doing me the world of good. You're good for my ego.'

'You'll find your dream, Liz. Maybe a transfer from the bank ...'

'Fuck the bank,' she said quietly and tearfully. 'Harry, I haven't told anyone yet, but ...' She took another swig and blinked. 'But the fact is, I've been given the push. Notice to leave, I mean. They know about my drinking problem.'

'Liz, I'm so sorry. Perhaps I can put in a word for you at the university. We need a secretary in the English Department. I'll talk to the Dean ...'

'Harry,' she said, reaching out and touching his knee, 'why are you so *nice*? You're so nice. Why?'

He smiled. 'Perhaps I share your pain of loneliness, or loss of identity. You know, in my own life, somewhere a light went out ...'

There was a sudden thunderclap. The light flickered and went dead.

They sat in stunned silence for a moment in the dark. Then Liz burst out laughing. 'Oh God, Harry ...' She laughed again, then drew close to him and put both her arms round him. 'You're a prophet! You just said ...' She laughed, then held him tight. 'Oh God, Harry, you're so *nice*. You're so good for me.'

He put his arm round her more out of politeness than desire. 'You're nice too,' he mumbled.

She kissed him and the smoke on her breath was potent. Still holding him in the dark, she said: 'I'm going to light a candle, if you've got one. Then we'll have some more wine and after that I'm going to make love to you.'

'Right,' he said, drawing away and stumbling in the dark. It was difficult to balance without the bearing of light. The electricity often went out in storms and the candle was always on top of the fridge. He found it and felt his way slowly back to the table, knocking his knee painfully on his chair. 'Here,' he said.

A match flared in Liz's hand and she lit the candle. A soft glow suffused the rondavel with dancing shadows.

'There,' she said, 'That's improved the atmosphere, hasn't it? This is really *nice*.' She had a clipped way of saying 'nice' which made it sound special.

Harry eased back onto his chair which Liz, in his absence, had drawn close to hers. She placed a warm hand comfortingly on his knee which made his stomach lurch dizzily with vertigo. It was as if he stood, for an instant, on the precipice of an abyss.

'Now tell me,' she said soothingly, 'what your girlfriend's address is. You said you wrote it in your Bible.'

Harry had forgotten the Bible. 'I was going to show it to you, wasn't I? I've got it right here.' He took a deep breath. He leaned over to a set of drawers just in reach and took out a Bible bound in black leather. He opened it at the flyleaf, but he could barely focus on the writing. '31 something ...' He handed it to Liz. 'Here you are.'

She laughed, looking at the page. 'Harry, I'm as blind as a bat, especially in this light. Leave it until the morning.' She took the Bible with one hand and it slipped to the floor. 'It'll be safe there.' She nudged it under the table with her bare foot. Then she took out a cigarette, leaned over and lit it in the candle. She put her hand back on Harry's knee but ran it a little higher up his thigh. 'You've got nice legs,' she crooned.

Harry was enjoying the closeness and the detached headlines the wine produced. The vertigo in his stomach, the stirring of his desire, seemed in a different realm.

He touched her knee and moved his hand gently up, feeling the soft contours of her inner thighs. 'You're so soft,' he said.

'That's *nice*,' she sighed, leaning against him. They were quiet, listening to the steady pattering of the rain. 'God, we need this water. It's so cosy in here, isn't it, Harry?'

'Um,' he said, agreeing, stroking her thigh gently with his thumb. His eyes were closed and the touch of her own fingers on his legs produced a falling sensation.

'Who owns the rondavel?' she asked.

'Bob,' he said. 'No, he rents it, I mean, from a farmer. Bob works for the British Council. He lives in the big house with a couple of black girls.'

'You're joking!' she said, waking up from her sleepy mood. 'They *sleep* in the same house?'

'Sure.' He laughed. 'At any rate Sophie, the tall raucous girl he sleeps with, has run off. She went berserk!'

'What!' she laughed. 'He actually screws her?'

'Why, yes. Bob says he has an exotic taste in women. It seems common with unmarried English expats. Dick, my other English friend and colleague, is trying his best to bed a young black girl. He thinks he's in love with one, but I suspect any

315

candidate will do. He lives with two black youths and one of them has promised him his sister.'

'God, Harry, you keep strange company!'

'Yes,' he laughed. 'But they're nice chaps.'

She pulled away and looked at him with narrowing eyes. 'God, Harry, do you screw black women, too?'

'No,' he laughed. 'Not to date. Bob tells me it's an acquired taste!'

'You haven't tasted, then ...?'

'No!' he laughed. 'I haven't infringed the Immorality Act.'

She lit up a cigarette and filled her glass again. 'Hell, Harry, me neither.' She drew a deep breath through her cigarette, then exhaled slowly. 'No, I don't mind what other people do. I just couldn't sleep with a black guy, that's all. It just gives me the willies.'

Harry chuckled. 'You mean you won't let him give you the willie.'

Her breasts shook with laughter and she broke off, coughing. 'Oh God, Harry. You're a real tonic ...'

Harry filled his glass from the little plastic tap. The intimate mood of the moment before had given way to a new bout of drinking camaraderie. 'I haven't told you yet about my peppermint?'

'Peppermint?'

'Well, one of my students came into my office the other day. He was very shy and awkward. He sat down uninvited and picked his nose.'

She began laughing again. 'Oh my God ...'

'It's a sign of respect, you see. Picking your nose ...'

'Oh Harry, shut up!' she giggled.

'Well, he said, after a moment, "Sir, I'm worried, I'm really worried."'

'"About what?" I said.'

'"Sir, I'm worried about my peppermint."'

'"Your peppermint?" I said.'

Liz's chest heaved again in silent laughter. 'Whatever did he mean?'

'He said, "Yes, sir, I'm really worried about it!" And then I realised he was saying performance. He was pronouncing it like *performence* and to my ears it sounded like peppermint!'

She howled with laughter. Harry enjoyed her company. She was such a good audience.

'But that's not the end of the story,' he went on.

'Oh God, tell me!'

'Well, the next day another Sotho student skulked into my office and sat down.'

'And picked his nose!' she prodded.

'And picked his nose,' he said. 'I waited, but he didn't speak. So I said impatiently: "I suppose you're also worried about your peppermint!" And he replied at once: "Yes, truly sir, I'm worried about it!"'

She howled again, shaking. 'Oh shit, Harry ...' When she recovered from her laughter, she said: 'You seem to have a lot of fun in your English Department.'

'Not really,' he said, sipping the wine again. 'Some of my colleagues are very negative. At least I try to keep the peace. Dirk Moolman, one of my colleagues, tells me my staff think I'm a bit of a hypochondriac. I usually get a migraine, especially before meetings. "I've got such a migraine," I say, so everyone feels sorry for me and won't disagree with my proposals.'

She laughed. 'Here we go again!'

'No, I do try my best. But it's impossible to solve the problems with a teacher-student ratio of one to a thousand. There's only six of us and six thousand students.'

'That's impossible!' she exclaimed. 'Ask for more staff!'

'Do you think I haven't! No, the authorities are really more concerned with window dressing, you see, than real education. It makes the country look good to the rest of the world.'

'Well, it won't wash!'

'No, it won't. Not while there's separate education for blacks. It's the main issue that Pieter van Niekerk keeps undercutting me on, negating my proposals to bring our teaching in line with the white universities.'

'*That* little shit!' exclaimed Liz.

'You know him?' Harry raised his eyebrows, surprised.

'Do I know him!' She blew out some smoke in contempt. 'He's got an account with the bank. He's the most quarrelsome little bastard I know, always arguing about his balance. Or bank charges.'

Harry laughed wholeheartedly. 'That's him, all right.'

'And he was in the Great North the other day. The little shit shouted: "Hey Liz, I bet I'm the only man in Pietersburg who hasn't screwed you!" What a bloody thing to say! I'll kill the bastard.'

'That was a terrible thing to say. Take no notice, Liz.' He patted her knee. 'Everyone knows what he's like. I've a good mind to write a memo to the Personnel Department recommending that his contract isn't renewed. No one likes him.'

She laughed. 'He's like the little man in church bewailing his misfortunes. He says, "Why me?" The minister says, "Yes, why him, Lord?" and the little man repeats, "Why me?" And a big hand comes crashing through the roof like in Monty Python, pointing at him, and saying, "Because you're a little shit, that's why!"'

A thunderclap stunned them into silence and the rain turned into a downpour.

'Christ,' Liz said. 'Sorry, Lord!'

They laughed hysterically, moving closer to each other. Liz refilled her glass but the flow of the wine had diminished to a thin trickle. The shadows shifted as her hand moved nearer the flame.

'We should save some for the morning,' she said. 'I need a drink first thing, you know. God, this rain is heavy.'

'Yes, it's quite a deluge.' He had to raise his voice against the noise.

They sat quietly listening to the rain, sipping the last of the wine. She ran her hand gently up his thigh, her fingers enveloping the hardness of his manhood.

'God, Harry,' she said with a lecherous chuckle. 'I think you're ready for bed. Time to test your peppermint!'

Harry felt quite removed from reality. It was like a dream. His heartbeat had accelerated, yet he felt detached and relaxed.

When her hand squeezed him it was like a pleasant sensation in another dimension, like someone else's pleasure.

'Come on,' she said, standing up. She stepped out of her skirt and pulled off her blouse in a practised movement. She bent her arms behind her back, unclasping a black bra. Her breasts flowed loosely on her chest, flattening. 'Time for bed, my man,' she said, taking his hand.

He undid the cord of his gown and let it fall to the floor. They lay on the single bed against each other, she on her back and he on his side. He placed his hand on one of her loose breasts, gathered it up in his hand and squeezed gently.

'That turns me on,' she sighed.

He slid one leg across her and continued to play with her breasts. Her body was warm and fulsome. Her breasts were fascinating because they were so liquid and he messaged them in a circular movement before pinching the fat nipples.

'Harry,' she crooned, 'this is *nice*.'

He carried on messaging, absent-mindedly, listening to the rain.

'Come on, Harry,' she said, gripping his arm softly. 'Come inside me.'

He slid over her, surprised by the fulsome feel of her body. Her legs opened and he slid into her. She sighed. Her eyes were closed and her mouth curved in an angelic smile.

'Fuck me, Harry,' she whispered.

Harry increased his rhythm, drawing his excitement to the point of explosion. But he became more detached and his desire ebbed. He panicked and felt his erection going. Suddenly he was numb, frustration and fear at once attacking his heartbeat.

'Liz, I ...I'm sorry,' he panted, collapsing at her side.

She ruffled his hair. 'You've had too much wine, my dear.' She surveyed him sleepily from under her puffy eyelids. 'Don't worry,' she crooned. 'We'll try again in the morning.' She smiled. 'It's the one thing I can do for you, Harry.' She closed her eyes and drifted off to sleep.

Harry lay there, uncomfortably balanced on the edge of the narrow bed. The rain subsided and Liz snored loudly, still fast asleep on her back. He got up and tapped a little more of the dregs of the wine into his glass, ensuring there was some left for

Liz. He placed the nearly empty carton and her glass under the bed. He sat in the chair, sipped the wine and looked at her languid body in the dying flickers of the candle. Her breasts had flowed back, nearly flat under her armpits. She snored gratingly and he felt utterly depressed.

'God, I hate this country,' he thought.

The rain pattered almost silently. He blew out the candle and squeezed his body into the narrow space next to Liz. The rain stopped and Liz snored. It was a long time before he dropped off to sleep, his head swirling like snow in one of those little glass paperweights.

He dreamt crazy dreams. On one occasion he was driving a bakkie with a long fishing rod strapped to the back. Two young women or girls sat primly at the back, holding on. He did a U-turn and swung too quickly. The bakkie careered round and crashed into a bank, crumpling the mudguard and telescoping the extendible fishing-rod right across the road. 'You'll have to report to the police now,' said one of the girls crossly. She had raven black hair.

When he awoke the sun was radiating the sunfilter curtains in an orange glow. He lifted his head but dropped it back on the pillow when the pain hit him. His head felt like it had been hit with a baseball bat. Liz was still snoring in plaintive grunts. As he listened he became conscious of something else—a putrefying and insidious smell. Somewhere there was a dripping noise.

He forced his head up, slowly. His neck was stiff and he turned his head with difficulty. It felt full of cotton-wool. He raised himself gradually, then swung his feet onto the floor. But instead of the expected cold touch of the hard cement, a squelching liquid sucked the soles of his feet. His feet came up with a reflex action. He looked at horror at the floor. A film of mud and putrid water covered the surface, the water refracting iridescent colours from the filtered sunlight.

'Shit!' he said, thinking that muddy water from outside must have flooded the rondavel. His bladder needed emptying and he realised he would have to wade through the mud. He forced his toes into the cold sticky ooze and tiptoed carefully towards the bathroom. When he looked in at the open door of the bathroom he gasped.

'Oh, God. Oh, bloody hell!' The ooze was coming out of the toilet bowl, gradually dripping, splotching onto the floor from whence it had spread throughout the rondavel. He remembered Bob saying something like this had happened before. The heavy rain had flooded the septic tank, forcing its contents backwards.

'Oh, shit!' he said aloud, raising his feet as far as his toes would allow him to. 'Oh shit. Now I'm really in the shit!'

When he minced back into the main room he found Liz sitting up, blinking. 'Where's the wine?' she asked.

'Under the bed—in the shit,' he replied.

She caught his look of horror and bent over. 'Uuugh!' she said. She found the carton and the glass next to it. She lifted the carton and it came up with a sucking sound. She manipulated the tap and squeezed some drops into the wet glass and drank gratefully.

'For goodness sake, Liz!'

She blinked at him, coming back to life. Then she burst out laughing. 'God, Harry, look at you! Naked and toe-deep in shit!' Tears were in her eyes. 'God, you're a sight for sore eyes!'

Harry wasn't amused. He spotted his Bible under the table, half submerged in the ooze. 'Oh damn!' he said, sloshing forward. 'Damn! The Bible's all wet!' He picked it up, dripping. There was nowhere to put it, to dry. He glanced around and swore. Then he put it on the table. His bladder was bursting.

'I need a bloody pee!' he said.

Her laughter burst out again. 'Just let it rip! What's it matter? You've got a wall-to-wall bog!'

CHAPTER 38

Merry-Go-Round

STAYING ON in Bob's rondavel was an uncomfortable affair. It was meticulously cleaned out, of course, by no less a personage than Bob's raucous Sophie who had stealthily crept back into Bob's house and into Bob's trust. She cleaned the floor with the help of a hosepipe after Harry had rescued his meagre belongings. The Bible was almost beyond redemption: though dried out, it was difficult to read through the brown and yellow stains. A precursory glance at the flyleaf showed that the address he had written there was still legible. The love-hate relationship between Bob and Sophie continued. Bob took it upon himself to teach her to drive so she could shop for groceries by herself. They often returned from a lesson, both in a furious mood.

'You *shout* at me! You shout all the time, Bob.'

Harry heard the commotion from the rondavel and peered through the window.

'You *stupid* girl!' Bob's raised voice echoed between the house and the rondavel. 'I'm *not* shouting! I'm just saying you can't slam your foot on the brake...'

The door slamming cut off their conversation.

Not being able to use the unflushable toilet made the rondavel particularly uncomfortable. The septic tank was over full and Bob recommended it should receive no further input. This meant creeping about at night to find a suitable tree. Squatting with his pants down and trying to maintain a certain elevation through levitation while emptying his bowels was not to Harry's taste, which was reasonably aesthetic.

So in the end, while he waited for one of the university's houses to become available, Harry moved back to Dick's house, grinning and bearing the company of Jonas and Amos who were once again firmly established. Dick was only too pleased to have Harry form part of his extended family since it comfortably augmented his already stretched income. Harry had a horror of the boarding house rooms that Liz haunted, and Dick had a ready sense of humour which he enjoyed. Furthermore, it was interesting to witness Dick's progress in fostering a secure relationship with a young woman, as he put it, 'of the black persuasion.'

Harry convinced himself that it was entirely through unjustified prejudice that he attributed Amos and Jonas's motives to the food they imbibed, or the shelter they enjoyed in Dick's capacious house. No, they surely acted from the highest and noblest motives in securing Emilie, and surely the food, the endless chickens, the *wors en pap* (sausages and porridge) they consumed daily had nothing to do with the deal. On two occasions Harry attempted to restock the refrigerator but the contents evaporated within twenty-four hours: it was like trying to fill a bath without the plug.

The hypothetical affair with Emilie lingered on but there was never a sexual reunion or any hint of a repeat of that first encounter. It wasn't necessary, Harry thought unkindly, from the point of view of Amos and Jonas, for the bulk of Dick's salary continued to be cajoled into the pockets of the two young gentlemen on the strength of an imminent future union—and, he presumed, a reasonable percentage was channelled to Emilie. At any rate, Emilie benefited materially though *in absentia* from Dick's account at Price and Pride or Woolworths, while chickens and *mealie-pap* flowed quite unhindered from Checkers into the digestive tracts of the young gentlemen.

Dick continued to build a substantial mansion in the clouds from the ectoplasm of dreams and hopes woven around Emilie to whom he referred as 'my darling.' But in the end he grew weary of waiting. Emilie only turned up when the young gentlemen were firmly implanted in the kitchen, or lounging in the sitting-room listening to Soweto pop on Dick's expensive Bang and Olufsen equipment. Her visits were brief and rare and she effectively warded off his advances.

Harry was dimly aware, one afternoon, of Dick's raised voice reprimanding her—on the last of her rare visits. Later there was a soft knock on Harry's bedroom door, and there she was with a tear in her eye. She wanted to say goodbye to him. It was the last time he saw her—and the last time Dick saw her. He was quite touched, her saying goodbye to him, with all his secret disapproval of the relationship engineered by Amos and Jonas. Perhaps she was simply a victim of those two gentlemen—and of Dick's need for therapy, of course. But to give Dick his due—in his naiveté he was perfectly sincere. He was childlike in his belief that a mature and fulfilling relationship was possible between persons so unequally yoked. That was what made him endearing, Harry realised. 'You're spearheading change in South Africa, Dick,' he told him. 'Especially in Pietersburg.'

Eventually the young gentlemen introduced a substitute woman into Dick's life. Harry strongly suspected she was Amos's girlfriend. At any rate, that was how she was initially regarded by Dick, having been first introduced to him during the Emilie days. Harry suspected that because Dick finally dismissed Emilie from his unrequited dream, Amos and Jonas cooked up the new scheme—in the interests of their continued enjoyment of Dick's larder and income. Since Dick seemed to adore those two vagabonds anyway, Harry's interpretation of the matter was no doubt most uncharitable—but there it was.

The new woman rejoiced under the name of Sivongila—a name to conjure with. Dick, having been told by the young men that she was in love with him, at once conjured up a new superstructure of castles in the air. At length he would marry 'his darling' and their mixed offspring would attend the convenient nursery just up the road (currently run by a prim Afrikaans lady for Afrikaans children, the *crème-de-la-crème* of Pietersburg's racial future). Harry saw the new candidate on just two occasions. The first time she was sitting in a car parked outside. She was wearing dark glasses through which, quizzically, she surveyed her new territory. The second time was when she arrived for the weekend.

Dick was all excitement. 'Sivongila's here,' he whispered as he came in on Friday evening. His face was bright with anticipation. Sounds of running water came from the bathroom. Harry retired early and rose the next morning to find Jonas and Amos in a huddle of giggles in the kitchen. Dick and his beloved had not yet appeared from the bedroom. Since Dick was generally an early riser, this was regarded as significant. But apparently he had put in a brief appearance to fetch the tea and had said something about 'pumping' all night. This word, 'pumping! pumping!' was frequently uttered by Amos and Jonas in their native Sotho that sounded like gobbledegook to Harry's ears. '*Jabber jabber jabber* pumping pumping!'—followed by roars of hysterical giggling.

Harry caught a glimpse of Sivongila later, in the passage, on her way from the bathroom. She was in a pink dressing gown, but what startled him was that she was no more than a child. Later Dick spoke of her 'delicious smooth skin,' and of the unimaginable softness of her breasts which he liked to cup while they slept. Dick was thereafter a man reborn and, it seemed, the 'pumping' activities were repeated with sufficient regularity for Sivongila to persuade Dick to invest in a double bed.

Once, when Dick was presiding over his teapot and teacups (being English, he made a ceremony of tea), Harry asked him the question he had always wanted to ask but had been afraid to: 'Tell me, Dick. When you and Sivongila make love... all that black and white flesh rubbing together, as it were ... does the black come off?' Dick replied with a good-humoured biff aimed at Harry's shoulder and giggled, as was his custom, with his tongue between his teeth.

This blissful condition continued for some time when Harry began to feel more acutely the loneliness of his condition. Dick's friendship was all very well, and frequently they got together with Bob and Liz for evenings that generally turned into late-night drinking sessions with consequent hangovers. But it was hardly a fulfilling existence. Liz had on more than one occasion offered to stay for the night and had even prepared herself for such an eventuality by bringing along a small bag of clothing. But Harry managed to maintain an arm's length friendship with her following the 'night of the bog', as he thought of it. He really hadn't felt well after that for weeks and he didn't feel he could rise to the complicated challenges of Liz's world of alcohol and vagrant drunks.

One evening he picked up his Bible and read the address on the flyleaf again: '31 Elgin Street, Durban.' He smiled whimsically, remembering how the dream in Amsterdam of a dark-haired girl with a bubbly laugh had stopped him from committing suicide. It was a very fanciful idea that the girl of his dreams actually lived at that address, yet he recalled how Eleanor had urged him to pay attention to his dreams. Durban was on the east coast and some four hundred miles away, and he wasn't going to be crazy enough to go all that distance on the flimsy basis of a dream! He didn't share Dick's ability to construct castles in the air, and he certainly didn't wish to live in such a fool's paradise. Nevertheless, it was easy enough to verify if such an address existed. The next day at the university library he inspected a street map of Durban. There was no sign of an Elgin Street. He felt foolish, but put a call through to the Durban Municipality from his office phone. Not surprisingly, he was told that no such street existed. But he couldn't help feeling a sense of disappointment as he replaced the receiver.

A diversion in his life was presented by the introduction of a new temporary lodger in Dick's capacious house. Harry had himself introduced Derek Mann to Dick since he was looking for a place to stay—and, indeed, Harry was hopeful of moving into a house to be provided by the university soon. The university owned a number of houses which Heads of Department could have for a nominal rent, and it was just a question of waiting for one to become available. Derek was a younger member of Harry's Department, just arrived—like himself—from England. Harry liked the younger man who in many ways reminded him of himself.

One Sunday morning Harry accompanied Dick and Derek to the Methodist Church, especially since Dick would be singing in the choir. The church was close enough for them to stroll over. Harry was amused by Derek's youthful innocence and listened politely to his notion of finding an opal mine in the Cape that belonged to a redheaded girl in England.

'You actually think the mine exists?' Harry smiled. 'Just because there's some mention of it in an old diary?'

'It's a long shot,' laughed Derek. 'It's no more than a dream, I suppose.'

'Dreams are important, Derek.' He smiled at the young man. He had fair hair that fell over his forehead and blue eyes that were still bright with hope. He didn't have the tired, wasted look that stared back at him from the mirror every morning. Harry wished he had the younger man's youth. He was clearly in love with a young girl who, he said, had given him his mission. He envied him his sense of purpose.

'How old is your friend, Derek?'

Derek blushed. 'She's still at school. Nineteen, I guess.'

Harry smiled at the man's embarrassment. 'Well, that's only ten years' difference,' he said. It was the same difference between himself and Eleanor. But Eleanor was out of reach. At least Derek was in-love with an identifiable person—a girl who wasn't yet tied to someone else. 'Follow your dream, Derek,' he said reassuringly. 'You only live once, you know.'

When they reached the church Dick went round the back to join the choir procession. Derek paused in front, watching the road.

'There's a woman who might be coming,' he explained, smiling. 'Someone I invited to hear Dick sing. She came to see me last week because she thought I could help with some translation work. Somehow I thought she might be a better match for Dick than Sivongila!'

'Someone who's not a village maiden?' laughed Harry. 'Dick certainly needs looking after.'

They stood, watching cars arrive. The avenue of Jacaranda trees were in full bloom and a veritable choir of mauve. Before long a white Mercedes emerged from the haze of mauve that fuzzed the tunnel of trees. The woman who stepped out was neatly dressed in a blue suit and blue suede shoes to match. She gave them a ready smile and Derek introduced her.

'This is Zola Skepper,' he said. 'Zola is the matron at the Cripplecare Home.'

'Pleased to meet you,' smiled Harry. He found himself drinking in her heart-shaped face, her immaculate blonde hair, her delicate nose and lips, and almond eyes that slanted upwards. It was a sweet and calm face that went well with her sweet smile.

They all sat together and watched Dick enter in the procession of green gowns. He stared short-sightedly at them, looking stern as was his custom when singing or waiting to sing. The prelude of silence filled the church and Dick cleared his throat. Then the choir burst into a resounding rendering of 'O Come All Ye Faithful,' and Dick's resonant voice filled the arched roof. The male voices fell silent and the gentle melody of the female chorus was underpinned by the base staccato of Dick's throat clearing. Then the full choir sallied forth again. When it was over Harry, Derek and Zola were enchanted by the lingering aural memory of Dick's powerful voice and by the authoritative way in which he cleared his throat between verses.

When they filed out of the church a lady wearing a bright smile to match her bright yellow hat pinned a little red-rimmed heart on Zola's blue jacket in token of mother's day. She gave a heart to Derek and to Harry, too, saying it was for their mothers. Harry accepted the heart graciously, not wishing to disrupt the atmosphere of sanctity by explaining that his mother had been promoted to higher service.

When Dick joined them outside the church Zola spoke in her slow, measured way. 'After that beautiful performance you deserve some lunch, Dick.' Her smile included the other two men. 'Would you all join me for lunch? We could drive to the Magoebaskloof Hotel.'

It was an invitation Dick couldn't resist. 'I'm all mouth!' he said. Derek demurred, saying he had arranged to phone his girlfriend in England that afternoon. But Harry was happy to accept. He felt relaxed in Zola's company. She seemed so poised and graceful with her easy smile, her freshly laundered hair falling in silky curls around her neck. In fact, he thought, she was quite stunning—in a quiet sort of way.

CHAPTER 39

Spiritual Healing

THE **DRIVE OUT** in the hot afternoon was rendered deliciously cool by the efficient air conditioning of the car. It was much cooler, too, in the crisp mountain air of Magoebaskloof, and it wasn't long before the car crunched the gravel outside the Magoebaskloof Hotel which was thronged in multi-coloured bougainvillaea. They chatted easily during lunch and Dick confided how he had made an awkward attempt to kiss his old girlfriend Melanie on the veranda of the same hotel.

'Our glasses got in the way,' he laughed. 'She told me it was a bit soon for that. Our relationship never progressed any further.'

'What a pity,' drawled Zola in her calm voice. 'You should have tried again.'

'Well, I ...' Dick cleared his throat as he did between hymn verses. 'I told her I thought it was time we consummated our relationship.' He popped a mushroom into his mouth and gave a little laugh. He cleared his throat again. 'My Head of Department told me I should tell her frankly I wanted to have ... ' His throat cleared again. '...to have sexual intercourse with her.'

Harry chuckled, glancing at Zola whose eyes took on a look of sad amusement. 'What did she do, Dick?' she drawled. 'Slap you in the face?'

He looked down with a laugh, tongue between his teeth. 'I think she said "Good grief!"'

'Dick,' Zola said kindly, 'I don't think your Head of Department gave you good advice. A woman likes a man to be more subtle, you know.'

'Yes, quite!' grinned Harry.

'I'll bear that in mind,' Dick laughed.

After lunch they sat out on the veranda at the back of the hotel and ordered drinks. There was a lovely view across the valley to the blue Mogoebaskloof lake snaking in the distance. At the foot of the garden and sliding down into the valley were scattered Azalea bushes, like rounded lumps of blancmange melting into the greenery. Some Jacaranda trees nearby cast dappled blue shadows on the lawn. From time to time a blue flower, like a butterfly, fluttered down to join the shadow.

Harry laughed, saying that his students believed that every time a Jacaranda flower fell on their heads it was a sign they would pass one subject in the exam.

'In that case,' Zola said, 'they should take a book and study under a Jacaranda tree.'

They chatted on and Dick fell asleep in his chair, his head awkwardly lolling to one side.

'Does he often do that?' Zola asked, amused.

'Well, yes,' said Harry. 'I think he takes antidepressants. It makes him sleepy, of course. He often drops off in Faculty meetings.' He grinned. 'Sometimes he snores and I have to nudge him. He's a very endearing chap, you know. One has to look after him.'

Zola was concerned. 'It sounds like narcolepsia, a sleep disorder. A brain-wave test might diagnose it.'

'Oh, he had shock treatment. I know that.'

'That's not good,' she said, worried. 'If he could only find his soul level.'

'Pardon?' Harry looked at her. 'What on earth's that?'

She laughed and went on calmly. 'It's exactly to do with the earth. He needs to feel the power of the earth holding him safe and secure, like a mother holds her child. We all need to find our soul level.'

Harry chuckled. 'I've heard of being centred in the energy vibrations of the universe. The beauty of this place could mean it's an energy centre. Is that what you mean?'

'Something like that,' she went on calmly, smiling. 'Haven't you heard of spiritual healing? We all have the right to be harmonious and fully-realised beings. Do you have a birthstone, Harry?'

He shook his head, drawing his eyebrows together.

She laughed and touched his hand. 'Now you'll think I'm preaching, but I'm not. It's just what I believe. I believe I can experience the mineral level of my being by finding a stone or crystal that corresponds to me. Look.' She held out her hand showing him her ring. 'Do you see this gem? It's my birthstone—a tourmaline opal.'

He was amazed. 'I had a friend in Scotland who believed in crystals!' He looked at the little stone that flashed pink and green colours.

'My birthstone is a tourmaline opal because my birthday is in October. It has healing properties.'

'So how does this help you become a fully realised human being?' he said, taking her hand and touching the little stone.

'You're laughing at me, Harry,' she said, but still smiling.

'I'm not,' he said, smiling with his eyes. 'Really, I'm not. I'm intrigued. I've heard about crystals and auras before. It's quite a coincidence.'

'Well, you mustn't force the stone's healing or spiritual harmony. I just touch it and sense its willingness to be with me.'

He was still holding her hand that lay limp in his. Her fingers were long and slender and he ran his own over them, feeling the stone. 'I feel very calm and holistic, feeling the stone. Does that mean it's working for me?'

'Holistic? You're laughing at me again, aren't you?' The corners of her mouth lifted gently. 'There are many different ways to well-being, Harry. We are all different, and this is only one way. Another is to experience the plant level of your being.' She smiled her slow smile, allowing her hand to rest in his. 'You know, your students aren't imagining the help they get from the Jacaranda flowers! I don't need to wait for one to fall on me. I can let my body lead me to a tree, but I can only pick a flower with the tree's consent. If I sense its willingness, the flower will impart a deep calming to my soul.'

Harry was looking into her hazel eyes and listening to the slow calm of her voice and felt himself pleasantly falling under her spell. Silky strands of her hair stirred in the almost imperceptible breeze while her eyes and her smile held his attention. He laughed self-consciously and placed her hand gently back on the arm of her chair. 'Sorry, I've commandeered your hand. But I think you have healing properties, even without the opal.'

Dick began to snore and Harry laughed. 'Look what a relaxing effect you've had on both of us!'

Their conversation was interrupted by the arrival of the drinks. Harry clinked some ice into his whisky and sipped it thoughtfully. 'My friend in Scotland told me that life was full of apparent coincidences that make us grow if we're tuned to the energy fields of nature—especially in beautiful places, like mountain peaks and forests.' He smiled. 'It seems quite a coincidence that you should talk about soul levels and healing properties—especially in a place like this.'

'Well, you may be right,' she said, gazing into the distance and sipping her lemonade. 'This is such a beautiful view, Harry.'

The afternoon crept on and they fell into silence watching the soft mist creep into the valley and up the hill towards them. A pigeon was cooing in the distance and Zola gazed into the valley, her thoughts lost in the mist.

She had been a widow for some years now and the desolation of her so-called freedom had really set in. Life without her ruthless and strict husband was at least a solitude of peace, free from his uncontrollable outbursts of temper and the occasional beatings she had to endure. And yet, there was the loneliness of her new life, her two daughters having been married and established with their own families. She might just as well have joined a nunnery as the Cripplecare Home which failed to provide any real companionship. She felt relaxed, sitting with Harry. She had only just met him, yet felt deeply comfortable with him.

'Penny for your thoughts,' said Harry.

'Oh, nothing,' she smiled. 'It's just so peaceful here. I come here from time to time, you know, to enjoy the deep peace. There were times when this hotel in its remote mountain setting was like a sanctuary or retreat for me.'

'You haven't always been happy?' Harry smiled.

'I'm happy now, sitting here with you two gentlemen.'

Dick snored and Harry laughed. 'One of us is a gentle dreamer.'

CHAPTER 40

Dangerous Liaisons

HARRY WAS IN HIS OFFICE, having just collected his post. There was an envelope from London. He opened it and a bank draft fell out. He was pleased. It was the final payment of his salary from the language academy. With the collapse of the South African rand it meant the exchange rate was very favourable. There was a compliment slip with the draft, signed by the Assistant Director of Studies with a short note scribbled at the bottom. He was squinting at her fine writing when Fridah Mminele entered softly, tapping gently on the door.

He slipped the draft with Karen's note into his top drawer and looked up, pleased to be interrupted by Fridah whom he especially liked. She was a young Xhosa woman recently appointed to a junior lectureship, having proved herself an exceptional student in the Honours course. She had full and soft arms with an ample bosom—built, Harry thought, for comfort rather than speed. He liked her because she was bright but also kind and gentle.

But he was alarmed to see tears in her eyes.

'Fridah, whatever is the matter?'

She sat down on one of the chairs in front of his desk.

'I'm ... I'm really troubled, professor. I need to tell you something, but ...'

To see the sadness of her soft brown eyes, normally bright with humour, made Harry more alarmed than ever.

'Tell me, Fridah.'

'You see, professor, you ...' She sniffed, then began again. 'You've been a kind teacher, so I thought I could tell you about something. It is about Lucas.'

'Lucas?' Lucas Mashike was the other junior lecturer, equally bright, appointed from the Honours course.

'Yes, Lucas. He has been approaching me in the hostel.' She dropped her eyes and her long lashes. 'He comes to my bedroom and tries to force himself on me.'

'Good heavens!' Harry blinked. 'Lucas is such a nice chap! I would never have believed it, Fridah.' He spoke softly. He recalled the time when, in effect, he had forced himself on Eleanor.

She shook her head, still watching the floor. 'Everyone says he is so nice. But he is really vicious. Last night I had to fight for my life. He is very strong.' She dabbed her eyes with a small white handkerchief.

Harry was speechless, surprised she should talk to him about this, and surprised that Lucas, his star student whom he himself had recommended for the post of junior lecturer, should behave in such an a-social way. But then Harry felt he had himself been guilty of a similar exploitation. He swallowed and found his voice. 'I'll have to report this to the Dean. But are you sure he did this?'

'Would I be lying to you, professor?' She looked up at him, her eyes red with crying.

'No, no,' he said, feeling awkward and sorry for her at the same time. 'Fridah, you must tell the ...' He was going to say she should tell the Dean, but realised as Head of the Department it was up to him to take some sort of action. And somehow, he felt implicated. He stood up. 'Fridah, please wait here.'

He went out into the corridor and knocked on Lucas's door. He opened it and Lucas looked up from his marking with a bright and shining face. 'Hi Harry.'

'Lucas, please come with me. We really need to resolve something.'

Lucas accompanied Harry to his office. Fridah looked up, alarmed, remaining seated.

'What is it, Harry?' Lucas said brightly, taking a seat next to Fridah. His round face shone with youth and enthusiasm. Fridah hung her head.

Harry sank back into his chair behind his desk. 'Lucas, this is very awkward, but I need to say this in front of you both, to give you both the chance to speak the truth.' He paused. Lucas looked puzzled and smiled. Fridah glanced up but dropped her

334

eyes again. Harry went on: 'Lucas, Fridah tells me you have followed her into her bedroom and... and asked her...'

'And asked her what, Harry?' he smiled, but his eyes were wide with surprise.

Harry cleared his throat. 'Well, to let you make love to her.'

'*What*!' Lucas sprang up as though hit by an electric shock. '*What*!'

Fridah stared at him, alarmed.

'*What*!' Lucas repeated, collapsing back into his chair. 'I don't *believe* it! I *never* did such a thing!'

'Haw! Haw!' Fridah shouted, looking daggers at him, half rising from her chair. 'Oh Lucas, oh Lucas! I knew you were bad! But I never thought you were this bad!' She spat out the word 'bad' and it sounded like 'bat.'

Lucas banged his fist on the table. 'You are *lying*, Fridah!'

'Oh Lucas, you are *bat*! You are *bat*!' She fell back into her seat.

Harry blinked, nonplussed. He spoke softly. 'I like you two so much, both of you. But one of you is lying.'

'It is *she*!' shouted Lucas.

'It is *him*!' She shook her head. 'You are so bat, Lucas. So bat!'

Lucas shrugged and looked wide-eyed at Harry. 'She's mad,' he said helplessly.

'*Oh, you are so bat*!' she screamed at Lucas. She looked at Harry beseechingly, tears running down her plump cheeks. 'He is *lying*, professor. He thinks he is God's answer to women. He comes to me and he forces himself on me. He says, "Fridah, I want you!" Then I have to fight to keep him off. Oh, professor, I *can't* go on like this!'

'She's mad!' Lucas protested.

Harry sighed. 'I appointed you both, you know, because you were the brightest and nicest of my students. And I'm fond of you both. You two are my friends. How can I take sides with one of you and against the other?'

'But she is *lying*, Harry,' protested Lucas.

'*Haw! Haw*!' shouted Fridah, shaking her head and glaring at Lucas.

Harry stood up and walked around the desk, close to both of them. He placed a hand on Fridah's shoulder. 'If it happens again, Fridah, you're to come straight to me. Then I will have no choice but to refer the matter to the Dean and the Disciplinary Committee.'

'But she's lying through her teeth, Harry!' Lucas continued to protest.

'You may leave now, Fridah,' Harry said softly. He turned to Lucas, still speaking gently. 'Just stay with me a moment, Lucas.'

Fridah looked darkly at Lucas as she got up. She gave Harry a half smile as she went out and closed the door behind her.

Harry sat on the corner of his desk and looked down at Lucas whose fresh ebony face had paled, looking ashen.

'She was lying, Harry,' Lucas said defensively. 'I don't know what's her game.'

Harry sighed. 'I must admit, she's a good-looking girl, Lucas.' He decided to throw caution to the winds. 'You know, there's a woman I know in Scotland—a beautiful young woman with black hair and the most incredible blue eyes you ever saw. I'd give anything in the world to sleep with her.' He smiled at Lucas whose eyes widened with surprise. 'I'm mincing my words, Lucas, aren't I? What I mean is, I've got a real passion for her. I've often felt, if I could just screw her once—a really *good* screw with a good orgasm—then maybe I'd get her out of my system.'

'Why are you telling me this, Harry?' Lucas's eyes were wide and white. 'I don't want to screw Fridah!'

'Then you must be crazy—or gay, Lucas. I certainly would, if I had a chance.'

'What?' he looked at Harry, his mouth open.

'I mean, you've got to admit, she's lovely. Soft and buxom. What healthy male wouldn't want her?'

'What are you saying, Harry?' He looked at Harry suspiciously.

'I'm saying that lust for a gorgeous woman is natural—almost inevitable, for just about any man. That's myself included.' He laughed awkwardly. 'Oh, I know that most men would deny it. Most respectable men. But I've a sneaking suspicion that every man is susceptible to lust. You look at a gorgeous girl and it's automatic. It only takes a second, but mentally, in that second, you've screwed her. By the time you've suppressed the thought it's too late—you've already committed adultery, in the Biblical sense. I suppose none of us qualify for the right to throw the stone. And I'm certainly not going to throw any at you, Lucas.'

He shook his head. 'Harry, I told you, she is *lying*!'

Harry ignored his outburst. 'The thing is, I won't make a pass at Fridah since I know I don't stand a chance! She's got her own agenda, and it doesn't include me.' He smiled whimsically. 'And I respect her too much to do it. I made a pass at that girl in Scotland, you know, ignoring the fact that she was married. She didn't like it. She had her own agenda, too.' He sighed and shook his head. 'No, I'm afraid sex is meaningless if the desire isn't mutual, don't you think? If it isn't mutual, then I'd just be using the woman. Like that randy pebble in Blake's poem, who warbles: "Love seeketh only Self to please." You'd be robbing her of her energy, let alone her dignity. You'd be manipulating ...'

'God, Harry, I *told* you, she was *lying*!' Lucas stood up and made for the door. 'She's *lying*! She's mad! She's just jealous that I'm brighter than her! She wants to break your trust in me! Who's manipulating? *She* is!' He walked out and closed the door behind him.

Harry sat on his desk, drained by the encounter. University degrees in literature hardly qualified one for leading a department, he thought bitterly. And he was the last person to unravel a sexual issue. He was himself far too susceptible. For too long lust, for him, had been a means of escape—though it hadn't worked in his encounter with Eleanor. All he managed to do was use her. 'And builds a Hell in Heaven's despite,' he said aloud, completing the quotation from Blake.

He thought of Zola and her sweet smile, remembering her talk of healing properties. In some ways she was like Eleanor and yet so different. There was a soft sadness about her—and, to top it all, she wasn't spoken for.

He wondered how she'd feel if he asked her out?

He picked up the phone and dialled the number of the Cripplecare Home.

'*Matroon hier*,' said Zola's calm voice, sounding like balm.

'Zola? This is Harry,' he said softly. 'Do you remember? Harry Denton.'

The phone crackled as though it had been dropped. Her voice came again after a pause. 'Oh, Harry? How nice of you to call.'

'Would it be presumptuous of me to ask you out, Zola?'

There was a moment of silence. 'Ag ye-e-es, Harry,' she said at length, drawing out her reply in her slow voice. She spoke English, but with the occasional Afrikaans word or inflection. 'Ag you know, I was just thinking ... you know, I really like you.'

'Really,' he smiled. 'I like you too, Zola.' He thought she sounded like a young girl on her first date and was charmed by the unexpected frankness of her compliment.

She repeated her words. 'Yes, I really like you.'

'Well, that's nice. Shall we say a movie? The Drive-In or the Plaza?'

'Whatever you like, Harry. I don't mind.'

'I'll pick you up tomorrow evening, then, at seven?'

'Yes, Harry. I'll be at my daughter's house at 37 Blesbok Avenue.'

Harry was surprised to hear that she had a daughter old enough to own a house. When he got out of the Beetle outside her daughter's house in Blesbok Avenue and walked up the drive his ears drank in the swinging melody of happy organ music. Castanets and light drums rattled rhythmically to an insistent beat. The door was open and he looked in. Zola was alone, seated at the organ, her slim torso swaying slightly as her hands deftly followed the keyboard with a life of their own. She was wearing a loose-fitting pale-orange dress that left the shoulders bare. She tossed her head as she played and her hair fell down lightly in front of one shoulder and behind her neck, leaving the other shoulder uncovered. He crept in, enchanted, and touched the uncovered shoulder with his lips.

She stiffened and the music stopped abruptly. She looked up and laughed. 'Oh, Harry, you startled me,' she said languidly.

Zola chose to see the current film showing at the Kinekor Drive In called *Dangerous Liaisons* with Uma Thurman. Harry felt honoured that such an elegant woman as Zola, with her long graceful legs and perfumed silky hair, and who drove a new Mercedes, should condescend to grace the cramped interior of his little Beetle. The car chugged dutifully to a sloping stop, nose in air, next to a speaker which he hooked onto the windscreen. Later he bought some popcorn which they shared. It was a delightful evening and altogether a new experience, watching a film from the inside of a car. It was in the tradition of the American 'sixties, he thought, when it was customary to take one's girlfriend to a Drive-In movie: one enjoyed the evening precisely because one saw so little of the film. But they saw a great deal of the plot action and dutifully watched as a brazen older woman in a flounced dress challenged her lover to seduce the tearful heroine, also in fancy dress.

It made him think of his relations with Anne and Eleanor. He still felt twinges of guilt since it was he, not Anne, who had made a play for Eleanor. His mind drifted back to Eleanor who seemed tearful when he last saw her that evening in the little Borders cottage. He saw her now, seated on the carpet by his feet, apologising for her behaviour. She had looked pale and drawn, yet told him to follow his dreams. Tears pricked his eyes. He ought to have apologised to *her*.

'What are you thinking, Harry?' Zola asked when the film had ended, detecting that he had become quieter.

'I'm sorry, Zola,' he said. 'The truth is, I was thinking of a girl I once knew in Scotland. I fell in love with her, I suppose—but she was married. That film triggered off some of my old feelings.'

Zola touched his hand. 'Tell me,' she said.

His words came in a torrent, releasing his need to tell someone about Eleanor and the effect she had produced on him. Zola was a patient and gentle listener and he found himself telling her all about the dreadful way in which he forced himself on her. 'It's just that I miss her so much, Zola. But I've put it all behind me now.'

'That's the best, yes.' She placed her hand on his and dropped her voice. 'I know what it's like to miss someone.'

'You miss your late husband, of course.'

'No, I don't.' She turned her eyes towards the unlit screen. 'I miss my son. I miss him dreadfully.'

'You have a son?'

'I had a son. He committed suicide.'

'Oh my goodness, Zola.' Harry was shocked. 'How did it happen?'

'He was in the army, the permanent force. His wife—a selfish uncaring thing—was having an affair and Andries, my son, found out. He couldn't take it so he left a note.' She paused and her voice trembled. 'He shot himself with his service revolver.'

'How dreadful, Zola.' Harry took her hand in his. 'I...I've never suffered a loss like that. I'm so sorry.' He hardly knew what to say.

She pulled her hand away, patted his shoulder and smiled. 'It's okay, Harry. I think I should go home now.'

He turned the key and the engine spluttered into life. 'Now we'll have some fun,' he said, changing the mood. He swung the little car around and sped over the humps of the crinkled terrain, taking care to miss the poles bearing the speakers. The car humped down and up, lurching, leaving a dizzy sensation in their stomachs.

'Harry, you're crazy!' she laughed, pressing her hands against the dashboard to steady herself. 'Be careful!'

'I thought I could make you laugh!' he grinned.

When he walked her up to her daughter's door in Blesbok Avenue, he made to kiss her cheek but she turned away. 'It's not that I don't want to,' she drawled kindly, squeezing his hand. 'Thank you for a lovely evening, Harry.'

'Thank you, too, Zola. Especially for listening to me. I needed to talk to someone.'

She smiled. 'Perhaps you'd like to come to our Cripplecare party on Saturday? You may find it an interesting experience.'

CHAPTER 41

Curry and Courtly Love

'**I**'M A CURRY ADDICT, REALLY,' shouted Harry. 'I need a fix at least once a week.'

'Then let me make you a curry,' Zola said as stridently as she could manage to make herself heard above the din.

The music flared and Sandie Shaw's voice blared, distorted by the large black speakers as she belted out her predicament about being a puppet on a string. Marie with her double chins squatted on her wheelchair, leaning backwards and working the wheels furiously with her strong arms, making the wheelchair rear upwards and jerk backwards and forwards in time to the music. Her partner opposite her, the diminutive Willie, worked his arms and legs like a methodical puppet trampling grapes, spinning round sporadically, then unspinning to untwist the invisible strings above him. The graceful Tiresa allowed her dutiful boyfriend to trundle her wheelchair in tight circles; he pranced and splayed his legs in token recognition to the beat of the music. She, in the meantime, sat smiling, her long blonde hair flowing, her hand propped up in a regal wave. Ulrika relaxed her lopsided grin into a crooked grimace, her abbreviated body perched precariously on her wheelchair while she intermittently shouted reprimands to her partner who tipped the chair precariously when his shorter leg landed harder than its companion. A stout lad with oriental eyes sat in the corner clapping and laughing with abandon, while a tall striking young woman with golden curls and wearing a flowing white dress perambulated around the room, arm in arm with her visiting parents, smiling and bowing.

Harry was honoured to accept Zola's invitation to attend the Cripplecare party and meet some of the inmates of the home. It was in keeping with her caring personality and instant friendliness that she should be there, eminently approachable by the afflicted residents and by staff.

'I'd love you to make me a curry!' Harry bent forward. 'But let me provide the ingredients.'

'I'll get them from Checkers and bring them with me,' she shouted, smiling. 'You provide the chicken. I'll bring Joey to help.'

'Then I'll refund the cost! That would be lovely, Zola. Dick will love it, too.'

'If he doesn't fall asleep!'

'No, he'll fall asleep afterwards!'

She laughed, nodding her head.

Ulrika broke away from the dancers and wheeled up to them with a lopsided grin. '*Yislaaik*, Zola, why aren't you dancing?' Her dress concealed her withered legs but was low cut on top to reveal an impressive cleavage between two rounded budding white breasts.

'We were just talking,' said Zola.

'*Haai*, what's wrong with you?' she accused Harry cheekily. 'Are you scared to ask the lady to dance, man?'

'Ulrika, *moenie!*' Zola chided, smiling.

Ulrika swung her chair round to face Zola. 'You know, I like *this* one. He's kind of cute!'

'Go away with you!' Zola said, pretending to be cross.

Ulrika gave a shrill laugh and winked at Harry, then trundled off to persecute the dwarf. 'Hey, shortie!' she shouted.

'Shortie yourself!' the dwarf returned, the unseen strings still jerking his hands and feet while he circled in front of his partner's rearing wheelchair.

'You shortarse, come here!' she shrieked merrily just as the music stopped.

Zola smiled apologetically. 'They can be a little indiscreet,' she said.

The lovely tall girl with her parents came up to them. The girl bowed to them, smiling. 'Hi,' she said, putting out her hand to Zola.

'Hello, Victoria,' Zola said sedately, smiling at her and at her parents. She took the young woman's hand lovingly into her own.

Victoria's father bowed. 'Vicky speaks about you all the time. Thank you for your kindness,' he said. Her mother said: *'Dis baie lekker hier by jou. Dankie vir al jou vriendlikheid, hoor!'*

'What a lovely girl,' said Harry after they had moved on.

'Yes,' Zola said. 'Everyone loves her, especially the men. It's so sad. She had to have a hysterectomy, in case ... you know, she only has a mental age of ten.'

After the party Harry walked Zola back to her room in the main residential building and she offered to show him where she lived. It was a spacious *en suite* room with a sitting area where she kept her own settee and writing desk. There were large windows with sumptuous velvet curtains drawn shut against the moonlit night.

She smiled, pointing to her phone on a bedside table. 'I nearly fell off the bed when I heard your voice! I even dropped the phone.'

'Really?'

'Yes,' she laughed, then added seriously. 'But we better say goodnight now, Harry. There'll be talk if they thought I brought a man into my room.'

'But you did bring him in,' he said, grinning.

'That's why it's time to leave,' she said, smiling and taking his hand. 'It was nice of you to come, Harry. I hope it didn't seem too strange for you, all these handicapped people ...'

'It was a pleasure, Zola. And don't forget the curry evening with Dick and me. You're the main cook!' He was still holding her hand and he pulled her closer, planting a kiss on her lips. She turned away and he tried again, succeeding only to press his lips on her cheek.

'Harry, don't,' she drawled. 'I'm quite a few years older than you, you know.'

But her sweet perfume and presence went suddenly to his head and he drew her close, kissing her again on her mouth. She melted and he felt the weight of her limp body, wrapped in her long black dress, press lightly against him. Her lips opened and his hands ran down her slender back, gently cupping the tight cheeks of her bottom. Her pelvis pressed against his stirring manhood when all at once she drew away.

'*Harry*! What are we *doing*?' she whispered urgently, eyes wide with horror.

He blinked, coming back to reality, not smiling. 'I don't know. I think ... perhaps I'm falling in love with you.'

She placed her long fingers on his chest, spread out like the legs of a daddy-longlegs spider. 'Harry, *goodnight* now!'

'It's still okay for the curry evening?' he asked, grinning sheepishly.

'*Yes*!' Her whisper was like a hiss. 'But *go* now!'

It was a hot and desolate Saturday afternoon when Harry returned to Dick's house with two Checkers chickens for the curry. A silver sun shone out of the sky like a great magnifying glass. A stunted banana tree wilted in the back courtyard and flies crawled languidly on the fly screen door of the kitchen. Occasionally one of the flies would come across one of the two tears in the screen and infiltrate triumphantly, rejuvenated, into the cool recesses of the kitchen.

Jonas and Amos were lying under a battered and rusted Toyota minibus parked in an abandoned fashion outside the kitchen door, working chewing gum into a hole in the petrol tank. Petrol fumes hung in the air like a toxic drug. Though Dick didn't drive, his two black friends had persuaded him to invest twenty thousand rand for the acquisition of the minibus as a business venture. The two makeshift mechanics were preparing the vehicle for its maiden excursion to Seshego, the local township, to serve as a taxi for the Saturday-night revellers.

Harry gave the minibus a wide berth, avoiding Jonas's legs and bare feet that stuck out lugubriously from beneath the tatty vehicle. He shooed the flies off the kitchen fly screen, opening it and entering quickly to avoid further incursions by the persistent insects. Even so, one or two black impis swirled ahead of him, leading the way to the kitchen table where he placed the Checkers bag.

He poured himself a glass of wine and set about slicing the chicken meat into thin strips when the doorbell rang. He negotiated the passage which had loose floorboards under the carpet and found Zola and a large woman smiling at the front door. Zola was holding a bag full of groceries, but Harry was surprised to see the grand size of her companion. He smiled at

Zola who had obviously made an effort to look striking, dressed in a sky-blue trouser suit and bandeau top that gave just a hint of something more.

'This is Joey,' she smiled. 'She's the Cripplecare cook.'

Harry took in the rotund figure, noticing the stout legs dropping from an ample skirt into sensible shoes. 'Hello, Joey,' he said, looking into the small eyes lost in a rugged face.

'Hi, Harry! We're going to make some *lekker* curry, hey!'

Harry led the way down the passage, stressing the importance of avoiding certain planks in the middle. Joey stepped on one that made the carpet bulge more than usual some distance away.

'*Haai*!' she exclaimed. 'You want to make me fall in your booby trap!'

They laughed, filing into the kitchen. Harry said: 'Dick calls it the floating passage. Jonas has promised to fix it.'

'Jonas?' Joey said in her loud voice. 'The garden boy?' Then she stopped short, seeing the flies in the kitchen. '*Yislaaik*, Harry, you can't have flies like this in a kitchen! *Dis mos 'n skanda!* Where is your fly-squatter?'

'No, I...' Harry laughed, picking up a tatty and bent fly-swatter and aiming at a fly just settling on the table.

'Here, *gee dit vir my*!' she said, wrenching it out of his hand and expertly smacking various points on the table and cupboards in quick succession. 'You can't have this *vuilgoed*, they will make you sick, you *know*!' Smack! she terminated another moving dot on the wall.

Zola said, 'Where is your cooking pot, Harry?'

'I was going to use the pressure cooker. It's the biggest pot Dick has.' He brought it out of the cupboard.

'This will do,' she said. 'We won't need the lid. We'll just put the pot on the stove. Yes, it's a nice big one, isn't it?'

Zola was in her element. Harry watched with surprise as she emptied all the shredded bits of his chicken into the pot and immediately emptied the entire contents of three bottles of chutney which she took out of the bag she brought. Then she opened two large bottles of curry paste and spooned the contents into the pot as well, pouring in hot water from the kettle and stirring the lot with a big wooden spoon.

'Joey,' she said, turning, *'Sny vir my hierdie wortels en eiers.'*

Joey smacked two more flies and reached for a carving knife. It was getting hot in the kitchen and Harry felt the heat prick his temples and run down his forehead. Dick drifted into the kitchen, blinking and smiling.

'Hi, Dick,' said Harry, wiping his forehead. 'The curry's underway. We've got two professional cooks this evening! This is Joey, by the way.' He nodded to Joey who was slapping a knife through carrots at high speed, her ample breasts shaking in rhythm with the flabby flesh of her arm.

'Hi, Dick. Why don't you fix up your house, man! The fly screen and the passage. It's *lekker* to meet you.!' She wiped her beefy hand on a dishcloth and stuck it out towards Dick.

'Yes,' Dick blinked, taking the large hand and still recovering from his afternoon nap. 'I've complained to the landlord about the passage many times. Anyway, Jonas said he would fix it.'

'You can't trust these boys, man!' she proclaimed vociferously. 'They're lazy devils, *jy weet*! They're *onosil*! You gotta do things yourself!'

Dick smiled, putting on the kettle. Tea was one of his main pleasures.

There was a tap on the fly screen. It opened and Jonas crept in, cringing with long teeth.

'Hello, Jonas,' said Dick. 'I'm making some tea.'

'No,' Jonas bowed. 'I ...'

'Jonas, *jou skelm*!' shouted Joey, inflating herself to her full proportions. 'You're the *vabond* that doesn't want to fix the *gangvloer*!

'Ja missies,' he cringed instinctively, bowing lower and showing more teeth.

'Well, don't just stand there. *Sny* these *aartappels*!'

'Nee, missies, ek...'

'Kom, kom, kom, jou luisak!'

'Maar, missies ...' he grinned.

'What is it, Jonas?' Harry asked.

'The van,' he smiled, lifting big smiling eyes to Harry. 'It's blocked. There's a Mercedes ...'

'Oh, I parked my car behind a Kombi,' said Zola, shaking the contents of a bottle of tomato sauce into the swelling mixture.

'That's *your* Kombi?' shouted Joey. 'That piece of tin?'

Dick looked at her, raising his eyebrows with a polite laugh and pouring a cup of tea. 'I paid twenty thousand rand for that piece of tin.'

'Ag, you're having me on, hey!' she laughed.

'I'll move the car,' Zola smiled, wiping her hands on a cloth.

Jonas cringed again. 'I also am needing a push. I think the engine is being flooded.'

'I'll provide the push,' Harry smiled. 'Come along, Jonas, before you get involved in peeling potatoes and fixing the passage.'

Zola reversed her Mercedes out of the gate while Harry and Amos pushed the minibus backwards with much sweating and huffing into the street. When they pushed it forward two other black men on the opposite side of the street rushed over and joined them. The minibus resisted, lurched and sprang into life with a roar. Harry was enveloped by black smoke and before long Dick's new business venture was underway. Harry thanked the men who resumed their walk amidst much barking of dogs. He returned to the house, feeling that something had been wrenched out of place in his back.

Zola slid the Mercedes back into the driveway, and a white Golf pulled up behind her. Bob Rimmer was at the wheel, smiling, his eyes magnified by the owlish lenses of his glasses.

'This is Bob Rimmer,' said Harry to Zola, rubbing his back with one hand.

'How do you do?' Zola smiled.

'Oh, hello,' Bob smiled, obviously taken aback by Zola's glamorous trouser suit, matching blue eye shadow and pink lips. 'You look like a shiny-suited space-girl. You must be famous.'

She smiled. 'No. But I like the 'sixties.'

She clearly enjoyed the impression she made as well as the compliment and Harry liked her all the more for being able to laugh at herself. He thought she looked quite stunning and he wondered what her enigmatic hazel eyes hid as they took in Bob with his unruly hair and thick lenses. In spite of the hot afternoon and her recent cooking, she looked cool and graceful, wearing her hair bouffant and held in place by a blue hair band.

'I've just popped in to return Dick's chequebook,' he said. 'He left it in my office, as is his want!'

Harry laughed. 'Things are constantly tumbling out of his pocket. I don't think he's missed it yet. Come in and have some curry with us.'

'No, I can't stay, but I *will* have some tea,' he said, smiling at Zola.

Before long they were all seated at the kitchen table, drinking tea while Zola stirred the curry and Joey boiled the rice. The curry aroma made Harry's stomach somersault and his mouth water. Bob said he might stay for a bite after all, but couldn't stay long because of an appointment with a young teacher from Lebowa.

'Of the female persuasion?' winked Harry.

'Well, yes, as a matter of fact,' said Bob. 'It's about a new poetry publication.'

Soon he and Harry were chatting about the relevance of modern love poetry and Bob said it was vital that it made sense to the life-world experience of the student.

'I agree,' said Harry. 'The other day I was lecturing about romantic love poetry. My students can hardly be expected to relate to the concept of courtly love. They laughed when I told them English poets more or less worshipped feminine beauty.

'Exactly!' stated Bob.

'I asked the male students how they would express their love for a girlfriend. One said he wouldn't, because then she wouldn't work hard.' He put down his cup of tea. 'So I said, "But how would you show your love for her?" He replied, "By giving her a gift, like a watermelon!"'

'What, a *waterlemoen*!' laughed Joey. 'Give me a diamond ring any day!'

Zola smiled at Harry from the stove, beginning to dish out the steaming hot curry. 'You've written some poems, haven't you?' she said sweetly. 'Won't you read us one?'

'Well,' laughed Harry, 'I'll read you one totally within the courtly love tradition. I wrote it on a train after seeing a girl coming down an escalator at Waterloo station.'

Harry fished out the poem from his room. 'I called it *Sliced Meeting*, he said. They listened respectfully while he read about going up on an escalator and seeing a girl coming down towards him 'along a line of destiny'; he was moved by her delicate beauty:

A black coat hugged her chin
golden curls fell around
her white Dresden face

The poem related how his world centred on her blue brilliant eyes that came closer, nearer and nearer. And seeing their 'eyes together', his eyes flashed away embarrassed, she descending, he ascending; but his eyes crept back to capture a farewell impression and 'caught the full gaze of her diamond brilliance'; their eyes held, surprised and pleased, then flashed away never to meet again. The flicker of their smiles, Harry read, was 'sliced clean' by destiny.

Bob cheered and clapped in genuine appreciation, but Zola looked sad and said nothing. She remained very quiet during the meal.

Harry looked to see what Dick thought but he had fallen asleep in his chair.

CHAPTER 42

Reflexology

'**H**EY DICK!' shouted Joey. 'You like to sleep, hey?'

Dick looked accusingly at everyone, blinking. 'No, no, I was listening...'

'Dick concentrates better with his eyes closed,' put in Harry, defending him.

'Like when you dream?' laughed Joey.

Bob burst into laughter. *'Exactly!'* he said.

Dick glared at Joey but replied with good humour: 'I'll box your ears.'

Harry grinned. 'I wouldn't box the lady from Boksburg.' He'd no sooner said it than he wished he hadn't. He looked apprehensively at Bob.

'*Boksburg*!' Bob duly exploded. '*That* bloody place!'

'So what's wrong with Boksburg, hey?' Joey swelled, taking the bait.

Harry could have bitten off his tongue. Zola had mentioned Joey hailed from Boksburg and he should have known better than to mention it in Bob's presence to whom the name of that town, recently much in the news, was like a red rag to a bull.

'What's *wrong* with it!' Bob's eyes looked larger than ever through his thick lenses. 'The Boers have put a fence around the park to keep out the black people! Surely you know that!'

'So *why* not?' Joey's hackles rose. 'They leaves all their rubbish in the park *mos*!'

'So where else can they have their lunch?' demanded Bob.

'*Ja,* you English know everything!' she accused. 'The *blecks* mess up all the lavatories. They're such dirty...'

'No, no!' shouted Bob, sweeping his hand towards her and pointing accusingly. 'They're human-beings like you! They have to go *somewhere*!'

'But not in the blerry park!' she insisted volubly.

350

'There's *NOWHERE* else they can go!' he shouted, standing and raking his fingers through his uncontrollable hair. 'It's people like *YOU* that's holding this country back! You're in the dark ages!'

Joey's rocky face turned red. *'Ja*, you English peoples come here and thinks you know everything, hey! You just come here to blinking criticise us all the blerry time!'

Bob sank back in his chair, white faced and looking wildly at the others.

Dick cleared his throat. Zola sat quietly, smiling sweetly.

Harry emulated Dick and cleared his throat. 'Yes, well...'

Bob looked at his watch. 'I have to go,' he said sullenly and stood up.

'Hey, you *rooinek*!' shouted Joey. 'You can give me a lift.'

'What?' Dick looked at her in disbelief.

'The Cripplecare Home's not far, you know.' Her voice suddenly modulated. 'I must be back, too, and Zola can stay longer and listen to Harry's nice poems about girls.' She laughed, picking up her handbag. 'We can go on with our *lekker* argument in the car!' She nearly pushed Bob's slight figure out of the door and, turning, said to Zola: *'Ek gaan hierdie blikskottel donner!'*

'I'm not going your way!' protested Bob.

Joey placed her hands on her huge hips. 'So you can't be nice to a lady, hey?'

Bob relaxed his glare fractionally. 'You expect *me* ...?'

'You can take her to the park, Bob,' said Harry, trying to turn off the tension. 'No, no,' he laughed awkwardly, seeing his look of horror. 'Joey, I'll take you home. I can do with some cooling off after that delicious curry.'

'No, no, that's all right,' said Bob, suddenly calm. 'I might talk some sense into Mountain Woman.'

'Hey, *who* you blerry calling a mountain!' she chased Bob down the passage, swinging her handbag. *'Jesus*, why doesn't Jonas fix this blerry floor...'

They heard Bob's voice disappear beyond the passage: 'It's hardly Jonas's job to fix...'

Dick stretched one arm forward in a half yawn. He was quite unruffled by the preceding storm. 'I don't know what got into Bob,' he said. 'I've never seem him so intense.'

Zola, still smiling, had maintained her calm composure throughout the explosion. She said slowly, 'Bob's new to the problems of the country. And Joey never thinks before she speaks. I think they both mean well.'

'Yes,' said Dick, clearing his throat and dropping into lecturing mode. 'She's very colourful. Especially her use of language. I detected quite a bit of mother-tongue interference.'

Zola laughed. 'Do you know what she said the other day, when we were speaking about people mixing Afrikaans and English? She said, "*Ek haat die* peoples *wat hulle* languages *so op*mix!*"* '

Dick burst into a torrent of giggles. 'She was being ironic, I hope?'

'No,' smiled Zola. 'She always says exactly what she means. But she also wears her heart on her sleeve. They all love her at Cripplecare. She wouldn't hurt a fly, you know.'

'Well,' Harry said, 'she got a few tonight! Flies, I mean!'

They all laughed.

Dick looked at the wall clock. 'I have choir practice in half an hour.'

'Can I give you a lift?' enquired Zola.

'No, the church is just a block away,' he replied, standing up.

When they were alone Harry said, 'Dick's a Bahai, but he's happy to sing in the Methodist choir.'

'What's a Bahai?'

'I'm not sure, but the way Dick explained it, it's a sort of recycled Christianity. A new Messiah comes around more or less every thousand years and revitalises faith. But Dick likes to sing in the Methodist choir, he says, because so much of the greatest music happens to be part of the Christian tradition. Jonas and Amos are Bahais, too. An old lady comes around occasionally and they have a prayer meeting together. They invited me to join in last time. The old lady said "Prayer is for everyone." She was quite a sweet old thing. Dick gives her mealie meal and some old clothes.'

Zola's smile was sad. 'You believe in prayer then, Harry?'

'I used to. I still believe in providence, I suppose.'

'Then you're a Christian?'

Harry felt awkward. 'I once surrendered myself to Christ, as they say, but I don't know anymore. The world's so confusing, isn't it?'

'I wonder about my son,' she said quietly. 'About where he's gone. I drove over to Potgietersrus the other day and spent a long time praying at his grave.'

'Did that help?' he said softly.

She shook her head. 'I just sat there and cried and cried.'

'One should never have to bury one's own children, Zola. I'm really sorry.'

She went on. 'Someone came up behind me. I didn't see her until she touched my shoulder. She said, "You mustn't cry, my dear?"'

Harry smiled. 'It might have been an angel.'

She smiled. 'Yes.' Her eyes were damp.

Harry got up and stretched out his hand to her. 'Let's sit in the lounge. It will be more comfortable there and I can bring you some coffee.'

She took his hand and stood up. He kissed her on her lips and this time she didn't turn away.

'Come along,' he said tenderly, taking her hand. 'We'll go to the lounge.' He laughed. 'We've got the house to ourselves tonight.'

'Where's Dick's girl?' she asked, avoiding the loose planks in the passage.

'You know, I haven't seen her for some time.' Harry laughed but still felt a twinge of discomfort in his back. 'I think Dick's going through a celibate phase.'

She paused in horror. 'You mean he *sleeps* with her?'

'Well, yes,' said Harry, wondering if he'd betrayed Dick. But he felt no doubt that he could trust Zola. He laughed. 'Now I've let the cat out of the bag.'

She shrugged, smiling, taking off her jacket and sitting down primly on the sofa. She wore a white V-neck blouse that revealed a suggestion of cleavage. 'I don't like to judge people for the way they live, Harry. Dick just seems very mixed up.'

'Oh well, to be honest,' he said, grimacing from a sharp pain in his back as he sat down beside her, 'I think Amos and Jonas are basically using Dick. Sivongila is probably Amos's sister or maybe even his girlfriend, and ...'

'And the poor girl has to sleep with Dick!' her eyes grew large. 'So *they're* using Dick!'

'Well, I wouldn't like to say for sure...'

'Oh, the poor girl,' she said, shaking her head. 'It's so sad when people use people. You see it, even with the poor handicapped patients at the Cripplecare Home. Even Ulrika who's very sweet, really.'

'Which one's Ulrika?' asked Harry.

'She's the girl with the withered legs. The cheeky one in the wheelchair.' She smiled. 'Harry,' she said, 'I'm going to do something very naughty, now.'

'Oh?' he smiled quizzically.

'I'm going to have a cigarette. I know it's a very bad habit. I know it's not the proper way of being at one with a plant, of reaching my soul-level. I just feel very relaxed and...'

Harry laughed. 'Zola, you don't have to make excuses to me. It's not a cardinal sin, I'm sure!' He leant over to reach an ashtray. 'Ouch!' he said, grimacing.

'What's the matter?' she said, lighting a cigarette with a delicate gold-plated lighter.

'Oh, just my back—pushing that Kombi, you know. It's nothing.'

She smiled as she drew in the soothing tobacco. 'I can help you there with reflexology.' She deftly kicked off her shoes and pulled up her legs, tucking in her feet on the sofa to one side of her. 'Now give me your hands, both of them.'

'My hands?' he smiled.

'Yes.' She leaned over and stubbed out her cigarette in the ashtray and took his hands in hers. She spoke soothingly. 'There are pressure points on your hands and feet. By touching them I can release energy channels. Now I'll find the points that relieve back pain.'

'On my hands?' he laughed.

She nodded. 'Your feet, mainly, but your hands will do for now. You have nice hands, Harry.' Her thumb took on a life of its own, walking along the sides and the palms of his hands like a caterpillar inching its way along. It relaxed him and he forgot about his back. Her closeness was comforting and exciting at the same time.

'That's nice,' he said sleepily. 'You were telling me about Ulrika.'

'Oh, she's such a naughty girl.' Her voice was slow and soothing, just like her fingers. 'It's awful the way she uses little Willem, the dwarf. Just about whenever I go into her room she has him on her chair or on her bed, more or less on top of her.'

'You mean, making love?' He was incredulous.

'Yes,' she grinned. 'I know it's not a laughing matter, but it does look so ridiculous. She's terrible. They look like a couple of frogs, with their clothes off. It's sad, really. One shouldn't laugh, poor things.'

'I'm sure he doesn't mind being used,' said Harry. 'You know, I wouldn't think she was capable of doing it.'

She smiled with a sidelong glance. 'Oh yes, she is.' She stopped and returned his hands to him. 'Does that feel better now?'

'No,' he lied. 'You'll have to do my feet now!' He laughed, seeing her gentle reprimanding smile. 'Yes, you do have a magic touch, Zola.' He placed his hand instinctively on the soft fullness of her upper arm, running it gently to feel the delicate texture of her skin. 'I wonder where your pressure points are?'

'You'll put me to sleep,' she joked languidly.

'But you know,' he said, thinking again of Ulrika and Willem, 'at least Ulrika, and her friend too, are getting something out of life. My friend Bob says there's no such thing as a misspent youth! Most of us work hard for a future full of illness and then we die, like the rich man in the parable who never gets to enjoy his full barn!'

She sighed. 'You're probably right, Harry. I mean, if you don't make love to the person you like, you'll never know what you're missing.'

'Or what you've missed?' said Harry. 'Better to have loved and lost ...'

'Yes.'

Her reply all of a sudden drove home the realisation that she was saying, in effect, that she would not refuse him if he wished to make love to her. It was like a seduction, and the feeling was like the empty and dizzy sensation in the pit of the stomach just before a roller coaster plunges down an almost vertical slope. The excitement made his mouth go dry. He caressed her arm and whispered, trying to sound casual: 'I'd love to make love to you, Zola.' Then he couldn't believe he'd said it.

She turned towards him and their lips met and melted in a deep, lingering kiss.

He was out of breath when their lips parted and his heart beat high in his chest. He took a breath before he could speak. 'You know, we'd be much more comfortable in my bedroom.' He stood up and took her hand.

'Are you sure?' she said, holding his hand and standing up willingly, her smile slow and steady.

Almost in a dream he led her along the floating passage. In the narrow little bedroom they snuggled up together on the single bed. They kissed again in deep, loving kisses while he stroked the softness of her arms. His hunger for her fed upon the very kisses and touches whereby he sought to quench it.

'Perhaps it will be nicer if some of this came off,' he said, running his hands over the delicate silk of her blouse and smooth trousers. Her body felt well upholstered and inaccessible beneath the material. 'This won't come off easily,' he joked, trying to sound casual again.

'Not really,' she said. She stood up and then began the businesslike and unglamorous process of undressing, but she did it methodically. She unbuttoned and removed her blouse. She unrolled the trousers off her, bending down, then stood before him in yet another layer of clothing. But it was an elegant and very feminine deep blue basque that held together the entire torso except for the plunging neckline that revealed a deep cleavage between full sensuous breasts. She smiled enigmatically at him, let the silk straps slip from her shoulders and peeled the basque off her, stepping out of it and standing before him in the full glory of her naked body.

He was moved by her nakedness, by the swelling breasts crested by the pink nipples that matched her lips, by the curves of her legs and by the dense bush that flourished provocatively over her mound of Venus. Yet he was surprised by the slight droop of her full breasts and by the lines of red scar tissue over a stomach which, freed from the undergarment, relaxed into a fulsome softness laced with silver stretch marks.

Still in a daze of unbelief, he got up and undressed quickly, feeling shy yet unable to abate his rising excitement. He lay down beside her, kissed her, and let his hands run down her waist, her flaccid stomach and the flanks of her thighs. He placed a hand over one breast which had collapsed into a shallow volcano and compressed it gently.

'That turns me on,' she sighed.

He recalled that Liz had said that and the echo jolted him. He continued to massage her breasts.

'*You're* the one with the magic touch,' she sighed. Then she touched his cheek with her hand. 'Harry, are you sure you're not just using me? Are you sure you're not just missing your friend in Scotland?'

For a moment it broke the magic of the moment. The thought of using Zola as he had Eleanor disturbed him. He lay back, wanting to be honest. 'Am I?' he asked the ceiling. He lifted himself onto his elbow and spoke gently. 'Zola, dear, we don't have to do this.'

But her eyes sought his pleadingly. 'I *want* you!' she whispered, fiercely.

Her hand closed on his manhood, repeatedly squeezing so hard it felt uncomfortable. 'Am I squeezing too hard?' she said breathlessly.

'No,' he lied, sliding his fingers up her thighs and into the liquid crevice between them. He was taken aback by the sopping contact and her open readiness for him.

'I'm so ready for you,' she murmured.

He mounted her and slid effortlessly into her. He heard her gasp, feeling her stretch to take him. He began to thrust involuntarily, sensing the shock waves of pent-up shivers through her body. His heart beat uncontrollably and suddenly he panicked, thinking he would lose his stamina if he delayed. He thrust more quickly and his orgasm started instantly. All at once he convulsed as the fierce climax erupted. She whimpered with pleasure and he was still gazing into her eyes when everything became a blur. When she came back into focus her smiling eyes made him feel self-conscious and he giggled. She giggled in return and he rolled off her, panting. She was flushed and her eyes shone.

'Did you actually come?' he asked shyly.

She held up three fingers. 'Three times!' she grinned.

'I didn't hear you,' he smiled. He was still thinking of Eleanor.

'Couldn't you tell from my breathing?' She giggled again.

They lay together in the afterglow and Harry drifted off to sleep. He dreamt that he and Zola were in a holiday rondavel together and for some reason he had just decapitated a black man whose truncated body lay covered by a sheet on one of the single beds. The man's naked feet stuck out from under the sheet comically. Harry felt no malice towards the man but wondered what to do with the head. He put it into a plastic bucket that had a lid on and put it in the little hallway between the inner door and the outer door. He would dispose of it in the morning, he thought. Zola lay in the other bed, half asleep, and seemed relatively indifferent. While the door was still open he shouted back to Zola: 'No one will believe this!' Then from across a pond came a voice: 'Yes, I do! I believe in you!' He looked up and saw that it was a young woman with black hair. He woke up with a start, his heart thumping.

Zola spoke comfortingly. 'It's all right, Harry. You were dreaming.' She kissed him on his forehead. 'I better leave before Dick comes home and finds us like this!'

She got up and began to pull on her clothes. Harry watched, somewhat bewildered by his own feelings. She was bending over, pulling up the basque, her breasts swinging forward loosely and her stomach in a correspondingly loose bulge. His orgasm had been so deep and satisfying that it seemed to have left him without desire or any further interest in Zola. He wondered whatever had driven him so uncontrollably to make love to her. She was a sagging, middle-aged woman with stretch marks and he, Harry, had just shagged her. The loss of desire had evaporated the glamour. He felt empty and drained.

But she was all excitement and chattered on like a schoolgirl, pointing a finger at herself. 'This is *me*!' she said, giggling. '*Me, Zola Skepper, the Matron. Fancy this happening to *me*!'

She straightened, facing him again in her trousers and blouse, lifting her arms to fix her hair band in place. She smiled and for the first time he was aware of the network of crows' feet at the corners of her eyes.

'How's your back now, Harry?' she drawled.

'Oh,' he said, remembering. 'I'd completely forgotten about it.'

CHAPTER 43

Chameleon Heart

WHEN ZOLA CALLED for tea the following week, dressed in a fresh white dress with pleated skirt, Harry was surprised by the pleasure he took in seeing her again. In the hot weather there was something cool and refreshing about her, and her eyes shone with a new brightness that lightened his spirits.

But the memory of the poem he had read on their previous meeting seemed to disturb her. 'I didn't think,' she said with a touch of the old sadness, 'that you thought of girls, or other women, like that.'

He laughed. 'I wrote that long ago. What if you had been the girl on the escalator?'

She touched his hand and said with feeling. 'Oh Harry, it was a *lovely* poem!' She smiled wanly. 'Harry,' she asked, lowering her voice, 'won't you write a poem for me?'

'Certainly,' he said.

'Promise me,' she replied, touching his hand.

'I promise, Zola.' His eyes crinkled, smiling. 'I really mean it.' And he really did.

They had been drinking tea in Dick's kitchen and she stood up to leave.

He stood up. 'Zola, I haven't paid you for the curry ingredients. It was a really delicious curry.'

'It's on the house,' she said.

'Well, thank you, Zola. My treat next time.' He kissed her and her lips lingered on his. He smiled. 'Do you have to go so soon?'

'Harry, it's the middle of the afternoon.' It was like the reply of a tolerant mother to a spoilt child making an unreasonable request.

'And we're all alone here,' he said, touching the soft skin of her naked shoulders. The cool and fresh texture of her skin aroused him and his desire for her was strong and urgent again. 'As the spider said to the fly, won't you come into my bedroom?'

'All right, then,' she dropped her eyes, acquiescing.

He took her hand and took a short-cut to his bedroom, opening the kitchen door to the back porch and entering the bedroom through another gauze door. It was bright outside and like a cool cave inside. He pulled the curtains shut and the room went even darker. This time he felt more pleasure than surprise when he saw her naked and he drew her close, feeling her soft cool flesh down the length of his own body. He held her tighter, kissing her and feeling his manhood hard and taught against her. Her lips slithered wetly over his, her tongue insinuating and dipping into his mouth until his desire became a frenzy.

'Come,' she said, sitting on the bed and pulling him by the hand. 'Come, my darling.'

She swung her feet up and lay down, opening her thighs and offering herself to him. He straddled her, but paused, smiling into her eyes. 'I want to appreciate your charms first, Zola dear,' he said, then took her nipples in his mouth. He teased them with his tongue and lips until they were hard, red and shiny.

She sighed. 'Come on, Harry, *come*,' she urged.

He slipped into her effortlessly. Again he was surprised by the ease of his entry and by the warm, sodden dampness with which she received him. It felt like heaven.

'I'm always so ready for you,' she chuckled, a little embarrassed, looking up at him with dreamy eyes. 'I wish I could keep you there.'

He kissed her. 'It's heaven to be there, Zola.'

He couldn't hold himself back anymore and his pent-up desire demanded satisfaction. He thrust hard and quickly and his orgasm took him by surprise, ripping through him, draining him in spasms of thankful release. He felt Zola's back arch and the shudder of her own climax coming. By an effort of will he forced himself to continue until she shuddered and sighed.

He lay back, laughing. 'You come so quietly,' he panted. 'The girl in my hotel in Scotland used to cry out like an opera singer. She and her husband kept me awake.' It was close enough to the truth, he thought.

She looked at him, relaxed with deep contentment. She spoke languidly. 'I told you, Harry, you have to listen to my breathing.'

The following day, when Bob Rimmer saw Harry crossing the hot university courtyard which the students called Red Square, he hailed him.

'Where did you meet that mountain woman?' he said with puzzled eyes. 'She was the most bizarre person I've ever met!'

The heat of the sun burned down. They were not wearing hats and Harry blinked the sweat from his eyes. 'I hope she treated you delicately,' he laughed.

'Perish the thought!' his eyes widened. 'Do you know, she had the cheek to invite me in for coffee!'

Harry smiled. 'She likes a good fight. Also, I think she took a fancy to you.'

He looked scandalised. 'Harry, I'm surprised by the people you mix with!'

He felt awkward. 'Sorry, Bob. I didn't mean to inflict her on you.' He felt dazed by the heat. 'Shall we go to the canteen for a cold Coke?'

'No, no, it wasn't your fault,' he said. 'No thank you. I have a meeting with the new Director of the Language Bureau.' He passed his right hand across his forehead above his right eye, wiping away perspiration. He added: 'Mind you, the other woman was nice.'

'You mean Zola?'

'Yes.' He smiled. 'It was so strange. The one was so gross and noisy. The other was so sweet and quiet.'

'It's a strange country,' Harry smiled. 'As you said, it's a twilight world. It's phasing out while we speak.' He pushed his wet forelock out of his eyes. 'Damn, it's hot.'

'Damn right it is.' He blinked, shielding his eyes from the sun. 'But *you're* not part of it, thank God. It's important that we don't adopt the prejudices of this place, Harry. At least you don't blend in.'

'I hope not,' smiled Harry.

'Come around for dinner over the long weekend—on Saturday or Sunday. I'll show you what a real curry is like. A Madras curry—not just a conglomeration of tomato sauce and curry powder! I've invited Dick and Liz, your new secretary. And Derek, your new colleague. They seem normal, like you and me. Not like these ...' He swept his hand contemptuously. 'Like these damn loud-mouthed Boers.'

Harry gave a half smile. 'Thanks, Bob. But I've already made plans to spend the weekend with a friend.' He didn't want to say the friend was Zola whom Bob might consider to belong to the enemy camp.

They parted and Harry walked on in the dazzling heat. Large black ants scuttled over the hot stones. He stopped, suddenly, seeing a leathery chameleon, petrified on a stone. It rotated little round eyes like independent turrets, one eye scrutinising him impassionedly. It swayed, one alien arm poised in mid-step, wavering. Then it jerked forward in a spastic jolt, retrieving an ant with calculated precision.

'No, I *won't* blend in,' Harry mused, wiping his forehead and feeling dizzy in the heat.

The next meeting with Zola was at her daughter's house in Blesbok Avenue. She had phoned him at work in the morning.

'I'll make you lunch,' she said. 'We'll have the house to ourselves.'

'I'd love to have lunch with you,' he said, and added casually: 'Then I'll make love to you.'

When he arrived at the house in Blesbok Avenue he heard her again, playing the organ. The music was slow and sad and her voice was shrill when it touched the high notes: *I'll be loving you, al-wa-ays...* She played beautifully, he thought, but her normally slow and mellow voice went shrill and broke when singing. He entered quietly and touched her neck with his lips, as before.

'Hello, Harry,' she said slowly and warmly. But her eyes remained sad.

He sat on the sumptuous settee in the lounge while she busied herself preparing lunch. It was an open-plan kitchen. A breakfast counter with bar stools divided the kitchen from the lounge. She made him comfortable with a whisky and the morning paper.

'You haven't written me a poem, yet, Harry?' she asked, serving a steaming helping of beef and baked potatoes onto a plate.

He put the paper down and came over, sitting on one of the stools at the breakfast bar. 'No,' he said, 'but I will.'

She put a large serving of carrots and hot mashed pumpkin onto his plate, adding lumps of butter that immediately melted, collapsing and sliding over the vegetables like dissolving yellow snails.

She put the steaming plate before him with a large glass of cold Coke. She knew just what he liked. 'You did promise, Harry,' she said softly.

'Of course I did,' he said, forking the delicious hot pumpkin that dissolved in his mouth. But he detected her sadness and remembered the little heart he was given at church. He put his hand in his top pocket. Yes, it was still there. He took it out and picked up a pencil that lay nearby next to the telephone. 'In the meantime I'm going to give you this.' He wrote on the back of the heart: 'To Zola, so lovely to know, so easy to love.'

'Thank you, Harry,' she smiled, reading his lines. 'This will do for now. I'll keep it in my handbag.' She sat down, sipping some tea and watched him eating. She took a vicarious pleasure in watching him eat. He was obviously hungry and enjoying the meal she had cooked for him.

'You're a fantastic cook, Zola. What about you?'

'Oh, I'm a member of weight-watchers,' she smiled. 'The lady in charge of weight-watchers said I have small bones, so I can't afford too much weight.'

'Well, you look wonderful, Zola,' he said, pouring some more of the hot gravy on his beef and potatoes. 'These potatoes are scrumptious.'

She was gazing at him, cupping her chin in her hand. 'Did you know that I was once a model?' she said slowly, smiling. 'That's nice for you, isn't it?'

'Yes, it is,' he said with his mouth full, smiling. The thought of Eleanor, looking for a modelling job, came back to mind. Life seemed to be stitched together with fine threads of coincidences.

'I've got something for you, too,' she said, still smiling. 'I need you to try them on to see if they fit.'

'Really?' he said, surprised.

When he had finished eating, wiping his plate clean with the last forkful of potato, she opened a large parcel and brought out two long-sleeved cardigans. 'These are for you,' she said sweetly. 'They were on a sale.'

'You really shouldn't spoil me like this,' he laughed awkwardly. He felt alarmed by her generosity. He tried them on. They were on the tight side, but he said they were lovely.

'Keep them for winter,' she said. 'Every time you put one on, it will be like me giving you a hug. My love keeping you warm.'

She sat there for a while, smiling at him. Then she said, 'Shall we?'

She got up and he followed her to a bedroom, meekly. She said, 'This is where I sleep when I visit Nettie and her family. It's my granddaughter's room. I sleep on the other bed.'

'That's nice,' he said, wondering what to say. 'What's her name?'

'Johanna,' she replied, and kissed him. 'You can get undressed while I go to the bathroom.'

She went out and he took off his clothes, laying them on Johanna's bed. It felt like a violation of privacy.

She came back, smooth and dimpled in her nakedness, carrying a damp face cloth. 'I'll make it nice for you,' she said coyly, laying the cloth carefully on the bedside table.

He came up to her and held her close to him, standing, running his hands down the curve of her back and onto the soft cheeks of her bottom. He felt full from the cooked lunch, but the close contact made his desire rise. He kissed her and his desire firmed. He bent his knees, trying to enter her while still kissing and standing, but she wasn't tall enough. He remembered attempting the same position with Eleanor in the pool in Malta.

'I'll get on the bed,' she said, drawing away.

He squeezed next to her. Her breasts had fallen back into shallow volcanoes, again, and he pressed them together so the flesh billowed forward, creating a tunnel of cleavage. He ran his hand down and between her legs. Once again she was very wet, and as he parted her folds he felt her get even more moist.

'Come, Harry,' she whispered.

He slipped into her again. His full stomach worked against him and he began to lose his desire. Her full bush felt wiry, like sandpaper. He paused, panting. She looked into his eyes, searchingly and sadly. He felt obliged to say something. He smiled. 'I love you, Zola,' he said.

He heard the sound of cars whooshing past in the hot street outside. All of a sudden the absurdity of the situation, in the bedroom of an anonymous little girl, gave him a *frisson* of excitement. It was almost illicit, like forbidden fruit, shagging granny on a full stomach on a hot weekday afternoon. His resolution firmed and he thrust again, lashing his desire which rose and thankfully burst in a shudder of relief.

He lay back and Zola picked up the damp cloth, still warm, and bent over him, her breasts swinging forward limply. She wiped him carefully and tenderly, milking the last ounce of juice out of him.

'That's very nice of you,' he said kindly, but once again he felt empty. He felt cheated by a desire that, when satiated, drained away love. He remembered he needed to visit the bank and felt impatient to leave. He looked at Zola and saw that her eyes were damp.

'What's the matter, Zola,' he asked.

She folded the little face cloth and sat on the bed with her arms covering her breasts. 'It...', she hesitated. 'It's just that I feel like a dog.'

'Whatever do you mean?'

She was looking away from him and her voice was sad. 'Whenever we get together, we make love. I feel like a dog.'

She said dog, but she meant bitch, Harry realised.

She went on. 'I don't think you really love me. Aren't you just using me? I think you're really just missing your friend in Scotland. The girl you told me about.'

'Don't be silly, Zola,' he said.

He sat up next to her and tried to be cheerful. He pushed her arms away from her breasts, gently, and twitched her two nipples one after the other. 'Which is the on-button, and which is the off-button?' He smiled and kissed the nipple nearest to him.

She kissed his forehead and cradled his head against her breasts, trapping it in her long fingers. She spoke in her slow and relaxed drawl again. 'You're funny, Harry. I never thought you would be so much fun. I thought you were so ...' She laughed. 'So respectable.'

'What do you mean!' he said in mock horror.

She smiled. 'Are all university professors "respectable" like you?'

CHAPTER 44

Love is a Gypsy Child

HARRY'S NEW MAZDA purred to a stop next to a stunted apple tree just off the little driveway of the house in Blesbok Avenue. He got out and stretched. He was pleased with the new car, having sold the Beetle to his colleague, Derek Mann. It was a bright Saturday morning and Zola was taking him to spend the night with her brother and family who lived in the south-east Transvaal. He locked the car and a flock of pigeons swept above him, their wings whistling in unison as they flew in formation. He clutched his little overnight bag and made his way to the front door, jumping aside just in time to avoid a swirl of water spinning past him, drenching the lawn as well as the footpath. It was from the sprinkler attached to the borehole in the front lawn. A concealed electric pump submerged inside the hole spewed gallons of water every Saturday, soaking the lawn which was nevertheless blotched with large brown patches where subterranean ants had attacked the roots.

'Hello, Harry.' Zola greeted him in the doorway, her eyes twinkling. 'I told Nettie she should switch off the sprinkler. Come and meet the family.'

Harry entered the immaculate lounge, seeing a young man with a spreading beer belly settled frog-like on the settee. He lifted himself slowly, smiling toothily.

'This is Sarel, Nettie's husband,' said Zola. 'Sarel, this is Harry,' she said proudly, presenting Harry.

They shook hands. 'This is a lovely house, Sarel,' said Harry. He knew the house well, by now, since it had become a rendezvous for lunch and lovemaking with Zola on more than one occasion. But it was the first time he had been introduced to its owner.

'And this is Nettie,' Zola said, looking across the breakfast counter.

Nettie smiled a wide smile and came forward, shaking Harry's hand. 'Ag, I'm so very pleased to meet you, Harry.' She didn't look much like Zola apart from the heart-shaped face and the upward swing of the eyebrows. She was shorter and plump, but remarkably attractive with her rich auburn hair and short white skirt that revealed the shapely curve of her thighs. Harry's smile concealed the fleeting recognition that Zola must be a lot older than he first thought her to be, to have such a mature and attractive daughter.

Nettie's eyes were bright and appreciative. 'Mother speaks so much about you, Harry. She's been so different and happy since you two got together. You must be a real tonic!' She held his hand a little longer, her blue eyes looking candidly into his own. Harry crushed the unseemly regret that Zola didn't share more of the youthful radiance of her daughter.

Sarel came up to Harry. 'Can I get you a beer, Harry?'

'Not just yet, thank you Sarel,' he replied. 'But you go ahead.'

'Ja, it's going to be hot soon.' He went over to the fridge and took out a Castle Lager, opening it with a deft flick of the thumb. He padded back to the settee on his bare feet. He wore blue shorts that hugged his stout little legs. 'I'm waiting for the rugby, you know.' He laughed. 'Transvaal's going to *donner* the hell out of the Vrystaat!'

'I'm sure you're right,' he said.

'Ja, man,' Sarel took a swig from the tin, sinking back into the settee. 'Did you hear what happened to Uys van der Spuy, Nettie's boss?'

'He's the manager of the UBS?'

'*Was*, man, *was*, the poor 'oke.' He took another swig. 'He was burnt to a cinder yesterday.'

'Good heavens.'

'Ja! Didn't you know? A petrol can in his car exploded. He was bringing it home for his lawnmower, they say. You see, the tin of petrol was in his car all day and it was hot, you remember?'

'Yes it was. Gosh. So it just exploded?'

'No, he must have lit a cigarette while driving, and the fumes, you know.' He laughed ironically. 'Until we heard the report on the TV we thought it was another terrorist attack. We all thought an ANC terrorist threw a molotov cocktail onto the car from a bus.'

Harry shook his head. 'That's very sad indeed.'

'Ja! You should have seen the skid marks on the tar. The poor bloke even had time to stop the car before he burnt up. They say when they took him out his feet broke off, like charcoal, still sticking to the floor.'

'Good heavens.' Harry felt quite depressed at the news. He remembered the man who had a strong face. He had been a well-known Pietersburg personality. 'At least it wasn't a terrorist attack, then.'

'No,' Sarel smiled blandly. 'Not like the bomb in Mamelodi. There was one black guy whose foot was blasted off. The foot was still in the shoe. He sat there, dazed-like, trying to fit his foot back on!' He shook his head. 'These are terrible times, hey!'

'Ag Sarel, don't be so depressing, man!' Nettie chided. She came forward, smiling and holding a brown paper bag. 'Harry, I've packed you and ma some *padkos*. There's some *biltong* here and sandwiches. Now listen,' she said, looking at Harry, 'You and ma mustn't rush back. Monday's a holiday, *mos,* so stay overnight if you want to.'

Zola came up, smiling, having put on a smart double-breasted waistcoat. Her hair was done up in a beehive fashion and she looked exceptionally tall, especially in her high-heeled shoes. 'Ready?' she smiled.

Nettie planted a kiss on her mother's cheek. *'Totsiens, moedertjie.* Now don't do anything I wouldn't do, hear?'

The well-worn cliché jarred on Harry's nerves, recalling Anne. But the wink Nettie gave to Harry made her face look prettier than ever. She had her mother's Chinese eyes.

'I'll take good care of her,' he smiled.

'But don't be *too* good,' she squeezed his hand, smiling coyly. 'You're so good for my mother!' Turning to Zola she added, seriously. 'Listen, watch out for landmines, hey? Don't go on any dirt roads. Stay on the tar.'

'Ja!' put in Sarel, accompanying them to the door with his beer and ample stomach. 'Last week near the border a farmer in his bakkie hit a landmine. One of his little girls at the back was killed. They found the other one hours later, walking around and crying, poor little thing.'

'Ag Sarel man!' Nettie chided. '*Shetup* now, you're such a Job's comforter. Ma and Harry are going to have a nice time, *mos*.' She kissed her mother again.

'Ja, but it's the *truth* man!' protested Sarel, looking hurt. 'Everybody wants to hide away from the truth these days, like ostriches.' He shook Harry's hand. 'The border's not out there, anymore. It's everywhere, even amongst us.'

'Yes,' said Harry, shaking his hand.

Zola walked up to her Mercedes but paused at the door. '*Waar is Johanna*?' she asked in Afrikaans, looking at Nettie.

'*Johanna!*' Nettie shrilled, looking towards the back of the house. 'I think she's playing with the chickens again.'

As if on cue, a little girl, about seven, ran from the corner of the house. She too had Zola's oriental eyes and smiled cheekily, clutching a little yellow chicken in her hand. Her dress and knees were dirty. She offered the chicken to Zola. '*Kyk, ouma.*'

'Johanna,' scolded her mother. 'Look at you! You look like a gypsy child!'

Suddenly a swathe of water sprayed past them in a moving arc and caught Johanna who squealed in delight. Her chicken escaped, fluttering and running across the wet lawn. She ran after it, scooping it up again, coming back to them with a wide toothless smile.

'Sarel man!' Nettie said crossly. 'Turn off the sprinkler or we'll all be soaked.'

They laughed and Zola bent over, kissing Johanna. '*Soet wees, hoor*!'

Harry and Zola got into the Mercedes and she reversed it out of the driveway in a smooth movement. Once in the street, she waved as the automatic gearbox engaged first gear. Her bangles fell loosely around her elegant wrist. 'So,' she said, settling back and relaxing. 'Now we're alone again, darling.'

She was certainly in the driving seat, Harry thought, and took a deep breath to dispel his growing sense of unease. He sat back to enjoy the smooth ride of the car, determined to enjoy the outing. Zola had been looking forward to an opportunity of showing him off to her brother, the manager of a coal mine somewhere between Middelburg and Witbank in the south-east Transvaal. At least it would be a break away from the university and the recurring tensions of student strikes and marking overloads.

'We'll go through Potties,' Zola said, using the popular abbreviated name for Potgietersrus. 'I want to put some flowers on Andries's grave, too.'

The air-conditioning made the drive cool and pleasant. Zola opened the glove box, stretching out her bangled wrist in front of him. 'I bought some *biltong* for you, too, darling,' she smiled. 'It's not just Nettie that thinks of you!'

He took the packet from her. 'You spoil me awfully, Zola,' he smiled meekly. She seemed to know all his weaknesses. It was as though she were spinning a kind and loving web of silk around him and he'd not yet decided if he'd wanted to be caught.

But the *biltong* tasted good, dry and brittle, crumbling readily between his teeth and creating an instant addiction by its tart spicy flavour. The car purred as it wound uphill, the hot flat-topped kopjes distanced by the tinted windscreen. Weaver bird nests hung like bloated marrows, swollen at the bottom ends, from the Mimosa trees that grew sporadically by the roadside. The leaves were a fresh green but barely hid the long white thorns that grew amongst them. The little yellow birds flickered between the nests and rushed off in a swarm when the car drove by

'They're clever little birds,' Zola said, smiling sidelong at him through her slanting eyes. The black mascara on her eyelashes exaggerated the slanting effect. 'Did you know the female is very fussy? She supervisors her husband when he builds the nest. Then she inspects the nest. If it's not to her standard, she breaks it up and he has to start again.'

'Good heavens,' said Harry, frowning and swallowing a piece of *biltong*.

Zola laughed. 'Don't worry, darling. I'm not like that. Anyway, I already have a nice house. I'll show it to you in Potties.'

'You have a house in Potgietersrus?'

She nodded, slowing down behind a lorry hugging the centre of the road. 'I do miss my garden.'

372

'You haven't thought of selling it?'

She sighed. 'I suppose I still think of Potties as my home. So many old memories are there. Anyway, I want to stay in the property market.' She became impatient, trying to overtake the lorry. 'Why doesn't he move over!' she said crossly.

She put her foot to the floor and the car surged forward, spewing dust as the right-hand tyres momentarily slipped off the tar. She overtook and swung back to the left-hand side of the road. *'Gaan af!'* she said crossly, holding up her bangled wrist in front of the mirror for the benefit of the black driver in the lorry. She jerked her hand to the left, indicating that he should move over. For the first time Harry seemed to see the sinewy strength of her wrist as well as the scattering of grave spots.

The heat fell over them like a blanket as they stepped out of the car in the cemetery with its prosperous rows of white marble and polished blue granite stones. Each grave had a rectangular stone border filled with stone chips, or covered entirely by a stone slab. A few fresh flowers bravely withstood the heat amongst the sun-bleached artificial ones. They came to a substantial grave the size of a double bed with a heavy granite headstone like an expensively carved headrest. The name of Zola's late husband was blazoned on the right: 'MAJ. WYNAND JOHANNES SKEPPER, g. 1935, oor.1983.' What surprised Harry was seeing Zola's own name, but without any dates, on the left-hand side of the headboard: 'ZOLA MARIE SKEPPER, geb. DU TOIT.'

'You're going to put flowers on your own grave,' said Harry, bemused. He felt strange, seeing her name there. It was like the grave was waiting to receive her.

'No,' she said slowly, still holding her flowers. 'These are for Andries.'

He followed her to a newer part of the cemetery with rows of single graves. Many of the graves had headstones in the shape of aeroplanes or tanks, elaborately sculptured in stone. Others were truncated marble pillars guarded by serene angels with downcast eyes. 'Andries is here,' she said, dropping to her knees next to one of the weeping angels. Andries's name and rank was on the stone, like the others in his row and the rows around him.

'There's a lot of young men here,' said Harry quietly.

'Yes,' said Zola. She paused, still holding the flowers. Then she said in a voice nearly inaudible, 'But my poor boy wasn't killed in action.'

There was nothing Harry could say or do for her. He stood there, watching her quietly place the stems of the flowers into a small granite vase. She opened a plastic bottle and topped it up with water. In the distance a Piet-my-vrou bird called elusively and plaintively.

Afterwards Zola drove into one of the suburbs of Potgietersrus, pointing out her modern flat-roofed bungalow in attractive black facia brickwork. Rubber tree plants flourished, spreading elephantine leaves against the walls, and a wide manicured lawn with assorted shrubs encompassed the house.

Harry admired the house from the car. 'It looks wonderful, Zola. What a grotty place you must think Dick's house is, after living in this.'

She put her hand on his and smiled. 'But it's where I found you, darling. I'd do anything—and go anywhere—for you.'

He smiled, but he felt uneasy every time she called him darling. It implied a commitment he didn't feel he was ready to make.

She squeezed his hand gently. 'Wouldn't it be nice, if we could live together in my house? You would want for nothing.'

'You're very sweet,' he said.

'You don't know me,' she said, looking sad again. 'I can be very generous, darling. We could be very happy.''

'In your nest?' he said, laughing awkwardly.

'Yes,' she said, her eyes misting. 'My nest. But before Wynand died, I was more like a bird in a gilded cage.'

He looked at the house and noticed the bars on the window. But then most houses in white suburbs had burglar bars.

Soon they were underway again, travelling south-east towards Middelburg past an orange plantation. Then they were climbing through a desolate landscape, steeply up a mountain pass overlooking a shrinking lake. Barren ground, dried mud with wide cracks, rimmed the brown turgid water. Close to the top of the pass Zola pulled over into some deep shade where there was a bench and a chipped concrete table under some Pepper trees with interlocking branches. Desiccated red pepper seeds and discoloured bits of paper were scattered on the ground while squat bluebottle flies crawled lazily on the table. Monkeys rustled in the greenery and there was an occasional shout from a baboon across the narrow valley.

'This is a nice spot,' said Zola. 'I like to stop here for a picnic lunch.'

She sat primly on the little bench eating her sandwiches. She looked too formally dressed for a picnic in her smart waistcoat and beehive hairdo.

'You look very smart, Zola,' said Harry. 'Your hair always looks immaculate.'

'Thank you, Harry.' She smiled at him. 'I like to look nice. I feel terrible if I don't go to the hairdresser every day.' She touched her hair. 'I couldn't go today, of course. I had to sleep in a net!'

'Well, you look great.' He washed down a bite from an egg sandwich with tea from the thermos flask. He took another bite when a chattering monkey scuttled across the concrete table next to them and swiped away the sandwiches. 'Bloody hell!' Harry shouted, his mouth still full.

Zola stiffened with alarm but reacted with humour. 'They're so *naughty*!' she said. 'They think they can just take everything!' She looked at the monkey which was calmly eating a sandwich in a tree close by. 'You terrorist!' she laughed. 'I think we better move on, darling, before they all descend on us.'

They stood up and Harry noticed a nearby road sign indicating sharp bends ahead. The light shone through it in a peppering of holes. He walked up to the sign to examine it. On the opposite side the holes were torn, the metal sticking up in little jagged points. 'These are bullet holes,' he said, frowning.

'Harry,' her voice was suddenly urgent. 'I think we better go.'

They drove on for a long time in silence.

When she spoke her voice was sad. 'What are you thinking, darling?'

'Oh, nothing,' he said, smiling.

'You haven't written that poem for me yet.'

'No,' he said uneasily. 'But I will, Zola.'

'All I've got is that little heart you gave me, with a message in pencil. Sometimes I think its like your love for me. It will fade.' She sounded tearful. 'What's the matter, Harry?'

'Nothing's the matter, Zola.'

The road ahead continued to unwind. She spoke quietly. 'You know, Harry, I won't be around much longer.'

'What do you mean? Are you going away?'

She was silent. Then she said, 'I can't say. But make the best of me while you can.'

'I don't know what you mean!' he looked at her, alarmed.

'Well, I don't want to talk about it.' She sounded immensely sad and it made him feel sad, too. 'Look,' she said, pointing, 'I can see some coal minedumps. Over there.'

Slag heaps came into view. They did nothing to improve the already bleak aspect of the burnt barren veldt.

The car turned off the main road, kicking up dust as it ripped along a stretch of corrugated road.

Harry laughed. 'Sarel wasn't serious about landmines, was he?'

She spoke sadly. 'You're quite safe with me, Harry.'

The road ran alongside a row of Bluegum trees that looked tatty with their peeling bark and dusty drooping leaves. At length the road dipped to reveal a sprawling settlement of houses with red tin roofs and dry gardens cordoned off with wire fences. They met the tar again as they entered the town that was more like a suburb than a town. They turned into a driveway of a house that exactly resembled all the others.

Zola's brother, Freddie, was lean and wiry and welcomed them with a cheery smile. 'Hello, sis!' he said, kissing Zola. 'Man, you look like a fashion plate!'

Freddie and his wife Clara treated Harry like royalty. Zola smiled proudly, appreciating their attention to Harry, and pleased that Harry was seeing a more English side to her family. Wynand, her late husband, had been brought up in a thoroughly Afrikaans and right-wing tradition, and had given his predominating stamp to Zola's children. But Zola, like Freddie, was English-speaking since birth and Harry found himself relaxing more easily in the company of Freddie and Clara.

'You know,' said Freddie, becoming expansive over his sundowner that evening, 'Zola really needs a break. A visit overseas, perhaps.' He turned to Zola. 'Sis, why don't you take a holiday to England? Harry can fill you in about where to go.' He winked at Harry. 'You might even go together.'

They slept in separate rooms. Harry's room was next to the bathroom and his sleep was disturbed by banging pipes. When at last he drifted into sleep he dreamt he was back in the language academy in London. The students were laughing at him and making their desks bang, slamming the tops down hard every time he tried to speak. The Assistant Director of Studies ran in, looking alarmed. 'Please, please, please!' she reprimanded, lifting a warning finger. She turned and glared at Harry. 'Please control your students! Wake up to reality!' she said, suddenly smiling sweetly with her head cocked to one side. The Dutch girl at the back banged her desk petulantly, again and again, and Harry awoke to the throbbing noise of the pipes. It was as though the banging had got into his head. Someone, he realised, was running the bath next door and it was time to get up.

It was an interesting morning, in spite of his headache. Freddie took him to an open-cast mine to see the huge earth-moving trucks. He climbed up the permanently-fixed ladder beside a giant wheel that towered above him. In the cockpit high above the churned-up earth he felt as if he were in a galaxy-class spaceship in orbit around a planet torn and devastated by a nuclear war.

After lunch Harry and Zola set off on their return journey. This time they chose a more scenic route through the tropical lowveld via Tzaneen. Each of the houses in Tzaneen had a rectangular metal box protruding from a window—air-conditioning units to combat the high humidity. They suffered the humidity for a little while, drinking tea and sweating in a Tzaneen restaurant, then set off towards Magoebaskloof. Banana plantations with large spiralling leaves gave way to the immaculately cultivated, fresh green rows of tea bushes as they climbed up the escarpment.

'Perhaps we should stay the night at the Magoebaskloof hotel?' suggested Harry. 'Or are you keen to get back?'

'I really don't mind,' Zola said sweetly. 'It's up to you entirely. I only have to phone Nettie to tell her I'll be late.'

'Well,' said Harry, thinking it would be a pity to end the weekend so soon. It would be the first opportunity of spending an entire night with Zola. It would be cheaper to get back to Dick's house, of course, and he did a bit of mental arithmetic, estimating the probable cost of the overnight stay. Yes, he thought, it would be a pity to miss the opportunity.

'We could ask for one of their *en-suite* rondavels overlooking the valley,' he said.

'That would be nice, darling,' she said softly.

They were delighted to find a rondavel available and enjoyed an intimate dinner in the restaurant overlooking the thickly-wooded valley as the mists of the night drew in. The nearer trees, festooned with monkey vines, blurred as the mist enveloped them. Harry ordered a bottle of house wine but Zola, as usual, kept to her lemonade. Afterwards they sat on the balcony while Zola allowed herself one of her rare cigarettes.

'It's a lovely country, darling,' she said.

'Yes,' he agreed. 'You wouldn't think there could be so much bloodshed.'

They listened to the finches chattering, competing with the persistent screech of a cricket out of sight somewhere.

'The farmhouses in this area all have radio transmitters,' she said. 'Just in case there's an attack from terrorists.'

'Terrorists, or freedom fighters. Depends on your point of view. It's their country too, I suppose. They were here first.'

She looked at him sadly. 'Not really.'

'How do you mean?'

'When Jan van Riebeeck landed at the Cape there were only the Hottentots.'

'And they're extinct now.' He laughed ironically. 'But what about the races to the north?'

'They were moving south, of course. Our people started trekking north.'

'Our people?'

'Well, the Afrikaners, then. Two immovable forces. And what happens when two immovable forces meet?'

'Doesn't bear thinking of,' he smiled, taking her hand. 'Zola, let's not get into this.'

'No,' she said calmly. 'But just think, Harry. How would you have felt if your children were being attacked? Your wagons set on fire? This land was purchased with blood.'

He shook his head. 'I'd rather not think about it. Not tonight, anyway.'

They sat there in silence, enjoying the peace and listening to the night sounds. Somewhere a baboon shouted, proclaiming his territorial rights.

They retired to the rondavel, Harry taking with him the remnants of his bottle of house wine. Zola ran herself a bath while he put on his shortie pyjamas and settled into the low double bed, watching the television. He watched a performance of Bizet's *Carmen*, relaxing to the lilting flow of the soprano proclaiming that love knows no law. She sang plaintively of the waywardness and elusiveness of love, love like a capricious bird that won't be captured: when you think you've got it, it's gone; when you think it's escaped, it's got you. He was still listening, succumbing to the seductive sadness of the music, when Zola came in from the bathroom.

'How lovely, darling,' she said, smiling. 'It's *Carmen*.'

'Yes,' he said, looking up at her.

She was wearing her night-gown. She had put her hair down now, the blonde locks falling once again over her shoulders. Then she undid her night-gown, letting it slip to the floor while she stood there, smiling at him.

'I'm all yours, darling.'

He smiled up at her, taking in her soft nakedness. But somehow her breasts seemed to droop more than he remembered, and the scar tissue after her hot bath was a brighter red than it had seemed before.

'You look lovely, Zola,' he lied, feeling that she looked more like Lo-Tsen after she left Shangri-La than the eternally young girl she first appeared to be. She was so sweet and kind to him, but it was that very sweetness in her sadness that made him love her. Or was it pity rather than love he felt?

She lay down beside him and together they watched and listened to the enchanting performance of Carmen.

Yes, he thought again, Zola was so sweet. But the realisation began to dawn on him that he was being cruel to her, allowing her to lead him on. Why had he become so involved? Somehow he had just drifted into the relationship because of his rudderless condition, spiritually and emotionally.

He felt immense sadness, listening to the music. Eleanor's petite and provocative face swam before him, smiling, but then he remembered the tears in her eyes on that last night he saw her and he longed for her. How he had wished to take her in his arms and comfort her after Max's cruel outburst. Tears pricked his eyes and he tried to swallow the lump in his throat. Oh God, he thought, I wish I were a million miles away—or seven thousand, to be exact. He felt miserable and lost, and now had to make love to a woman more out of pity than love—a woman who was equally sad yet under the illusion that he loved her.

'What's the matter, darling?' Zola said sweetly. 'You look sad tonight.'

'No,' he said, touching her breasts. 'Come here. Come here and lie on top of me for a change.'

She slid over him and relaxed her weight on him, kissing him tenderly. But she was heavier than he expected and he felt crushed, suffocated, drawing breath with difficulty. He placed his hands on her buttocks that felt spongy and he tried to enter her, hoping to revitalise his desire with the new position. It was no use. He panicked and felt his desire fade and go limp.

Zola lifted herself on her elbows, smiling down at him, her hair brushing his cheek. 'I think the old way's better,' she said sweetly.

They reversed positions, but he had become too slack to enter her. He rolled back, panting from the effort, frustrated.

She propped herself up on one elbow, concern touching her eyes. The little pendant she wore round her neck swung forward, touching him. 'My poor darling, you're tired. You need some of my reflexology, don't you?'

She sat up and poured a little of the wine he had brought back with him into a glass. 'Here, she said, 'take a little more of this.' Her voice was calm and reassuring.

He felt the wine go down, warm and restive, like her voice. He lay back.

'Now close your eyes,' she soothed. She watched him, sadness and amusement playing together at the corners of her mouth. Her tapering fingers touched his thigh and ran up, touching his sensitive parts. Her fingers were gentle, insinuating and coaxing. Warm sensations of detached pleasure began to build up inside him, suffusing him, like the detached pain one feels under an anaesthetic. Once again he felt hard with desire and he mounted her quickly, entered her and threw himself into lust, body and soul. He struggled, panting and thrusting, thinking he was losing it; then, just when he had given up hope his orgasm rose, crested and broke, releasing him in spurts of relief.

He collapsed, panting.

'Oh, darling,' she said, smiling with her sad eyes. 'I would never have forgiven myself if I'd failed you.'

'You're so sweet and kind.'

'All it took was a little wine and ...,' she smiled shyly, 'and a little magic.'

They were silent and Carmen still sang her sad song. Zola held his hand and played tenderly with his fingers.

'You don't have a ring,' she said. 'If you were mine, I would make you wear one.'

Somewhere in the night an owl hooted.

Harry drifted off to sleep, exhausted. He dreamt they were still sitting on the balcony and he was methodically taking out his internal organs, placing them on a wooden table.

'What will you do with them?' Zola asked, drawing on her cigarette.

'I don't need them anymore,' he replied. Then he threw them down into the valley below. A dog—or was it a baboon?—caught his heart smartly between its teeth and ran off into the undergrowth.

The next morning, driving back to Pietersburg, Zola said, 'That must have been expensive for you.'

Harry was indeed surprised when the receptionist presented him with the bill after breakfast. It was easily twice as much as he had expected.

'You're worth it, Zola,' he smiled, looking at the road ahead.

She was the last person he'd want to hurt.

CHAPTER 45

Aftershock

MALE VOICES resonated in rich unison, stirring the deep throb of Africa and distilling fear in Harry's heart.

They came from the bands of students carrying placards around the campus while the staff, mainly white, peered nervously from their windows. The swelling tide approached the Arts Block. It was like a blood dance foretelling thunder.

Harry saw the Head of the Sotho Department walking down the corridor. 'It's beautiful, Professor Mphahlele. What are they singing?'

Professor Mphahlele chuckled and replied almost apologetically. 'They're revolutionary songs!'

From their window in the English Department the band of staff watched the chanting forms. When the students reached a line of press cars they broke up, black locusts hopping, bouncing one car backwards and banging their feet against the baked enamel that collapsed like tin.

'I can't stand this!' spat Pieter van Niekerk, one of the lecturers. 'They're dismantling the press cars!' He grabbed a phone and spoke to someone in the Administration Block.

But nobody dared to emerge from the Administration Block. Then a blunderbuss burst, pattering the window and burst again. They all dived for the floor, the women staff screaming. Outside, screeching students scuttled across the sun-baked campus while others brandished stones in clubbed fists. The staff got back to their feet and ventured to peer out again. They saw an old man, a white-bearded professor of law, ambushed by thronging students. A girl lunged forward, throwing acid on his suit. Pieter van Niekerk swung round, glaring at Harry who stood transfixed, fingering his chin. 'Send the women home!' he hissed.

A new commotion of students scattering shattered their minds. They looked out and saw alsations pursuing girls. One girl stumbled, shrieking, her hand lacerated by the teeth of a dog. Other dogs were chained to police in blue uniforms. Order restored, the police paraded the campus while towering elephant-like vehicles with guns moved in.

'God, they're intimidating!' said Harry.

'Nonsense!' replied Pieter. 'They're soothing. Peace at last.'

The armoured cars rumbled about the campus in queues, like rhino lumbering for a fight.

An eerie silence ruled. Apart from the police and army vehicles the campus was deserted. The lecture theatres were empty.

Harry returned to his office. This was one of many student protests and, as usual, the reason for the protest wasn't clear, though rumour had it that it was because Andries Coetzee in Animal Husbandry had unthinkingly said white hens laid better eggs than black hens. A more plausible theory was that it was 'Heroes Day'—the anniversary of Semora Machelle's death. Some said it was because Reagen had bombed Gedaffi.

Harry was particularly concerned since two members of his staff hadn't turned up that morning: Liz Evans, whom he had recently appointed as secretary, and the newly-appointed lecturer Derek Mann. The Head of the Linguistics Department had also come down to see him from the floor above to say that Dick hadn't turned up. Since Harry had now moved into his university house he was no longer aware of Dick's movements, though he was aware that all three persons—Derek, Dick and Liz—had been invited by Bob Rimmer for a curry evening over the weekend. Harry had also been invited but declined since it had clashed with his little trip with Zola.

He was relieved when Liz came in an hour later. She burst into his office and slumped into one of the chairs in front of his desk.

'Oh *Gawd*, Harry!' she exclaimed, out of breath. 'You won't believe this!'

Harry detected the familiar strong smell of stale alcohol. 'Liz,' he said, concerned and trying to sound severe. 'I told you, you can't come to work after hitting the bottle. It's the one condition I made for your appointment.'

'Oh, shit, Harry, give me a break,' she breathed stentoriously. 'I've come to tell you Bob's dead. Sophie, too. Dick and Derek are still with the police.'

He looked at her, aghast. 'What?'

She dug a cigarette out of a packet and a match flared. Her hands were shaking. 'I need another bloody drink, Harry.' She stood up and opened a filing cabinet. 'Where do you keep your Scotch?'

'Liz, I don't have any. What do you mean ... about Bob? You mean Bob Rimmer?'

She nodded, slumping back into the chair and drawing heavily on the cigarette. 'Christ, it was a nightmare. Derek and I just escaped ourselves.'

Harry was alarmed. He couldn't take in what she was saying. 'Bob's dead? My God, Liz, how? What happened? Did Sophie go bezerk? But you said Sophie was dead too?'

She nodded. 'Landmine. Early this morning. Bob was taking Sophie for a driving lesson. The landmine was in the dirt track from Bob's plot. Derek and I found them when we followed in the Beetle. Oh Gawd, it was horrible. Blood was spattered all over the windows.' She sucked her cigarette again. Her hooded eyes were black with smudged mascara. 'Derek dashed out and opened Bob's door, and he fell onto him. His legs had been blown off.'

A rush of ice froze Harry's backbone. 'Was he already dead?'

She nodded. 'Stone dead, with his eyes still open. Derek's shirt was covered with his blood.'

'And Sophie?'

'She was sprawled half out of the car, her head on the ground. Flies were crawling all over her face.'

'I thought you said you were right behind them?'

She shook her head. 'No, we followed at least an hour or more later. We didn't know what had happened until we found the car. It was all twisted with the door hanging open.'

'Jesus, Liz. Are you all right?'

She shrugged. 'Nothing that a stiff drink wouldn't fix. Look, I can fetch a bottle from the canteen bar, Harry. Do you mind?'

He ignored her question. 'What were you and Derek doing there? Did you stay the night?' He remembered the night he spent with Liz in Bob's rondavel and wondered if Derek had suffered the same fate as he had done.

'We had a curry evening and spent the night.' She nodded. 'Dick and I dropped off in the house and Derek slept in the rondavel. Derek said he thought he heard something after Bob and Sophie left, like a sort of pop in the distance. And the birds flew up from the trees, he said. Dick and I were still out for the count. We had no idea what happened until we came up with the Beetle. Oh Gawd, it was terrible.'

'What about Dick?'

'Oh, all he could do was stare and mumble "bully-beef!" He doesn't live in this world, you know. It's Derek I felt sorry for. He was really shaken. God, he tried to drive round Bob's car but I stopped him in time. Shit, Harry, there was another unexploded landmine just ahead of it! If we'd driven on we'd have had it! We drove back to the house and phoned the police. We waited there until the police searched and found the other mine. I heard that explode, all right.' She lit a new cigarette from the stub of the old one. 'I really need a drink, Harry. Can we go to the canteen? There's another strike on so there won't be any classes today. Thank God.' She drew on the cigarette. The smell of smoke mingled with the smell of stale alcohol. 'God, all three of us were nearly killed.'

'Who the hell landmined Bob's road?'

'ANC, the police said. But I can't think why the ANC wanted Bob dead. He was an ANC sympathiser.'

'The ANC is a handy scapegoat, I guess, Liz.' The whole country was a landmine, he thought, waiting to explode. He was mad to come here. 'This country is in a hell of a mess.' His eyes met hers. 'God, Liz, the minute I arrived I was mugged!'

'Quite,' she said, smiling ruefully. 'You did look a sight when I met you on the train. Poor thing.'

'Thank you for being there, Liz,' he said sincerely.

She smiled tearfully. 'You've been very nice to me, Harry. You even got me this job. I'd miss you if you left, you know.' She was beginning to feel maudlin.

When Harry returned home that evening the phone was ringing. He dropped his briefcase and picked up the receiver.

'Hello Harry,' came Zola's slow voice. 'I'm so worried about you. I heard about Bob Rimmer.'

'I'm all right, Zola. It gave me quite a shock, I must admit. If you hadn't invited me to see your brother I might have been there too. Bob had invited me too, you know.'

'You poor darling,' she drawled. 'Can I come and see you?'

'Sure, Zola.'

Her voice sounded sadder than usual, but he was pleased to see her, to have someone to talk to about the experience. His university bungalow, which was provided fully furnished, was in the same suburb as Zola's daughter's house and it wasn't long before he heard her Mercedes pull up. He went outside to meet her. She looked elegant as ever, showing long legs as she got out of the car. She always looked so immaculate, this time in a green trim jacket and eyes highlighted with green mascara. She smiled tenderly, putting out her hand and drawing him closer. He kissed her briefly on the lips.

'Come, let's go inside,' she said.

They went through the lounge towards the kitchen. 'Oh, this is lovely, Harry,' she said, taking in the neat modern furniture. 'This is an improvement on Dick's place. You don't have a floating passage, either!'

Once in the kitchen she put her arms around him and kissed him again. He returned the kiss and drew away.

'Would you like some tea, Zola?'

'What's the matter, Harry?' She looked anxious. 'Why don't you want to kiss me?'

'Oh, but I do,' he smiled, and kissed her again, making himself endure the kiss a little longer. 'Now we'll have some tea.'

'Yes,' she said sadly. 'I'm glad you're safe, Harry.'

He shook his head. 'This country's in a terrible state, Zola. You know it can't go on like this. What will you do when the government collapses? I sense there will be a great deal of lawlessness. Too many have been deprived for too long.'

'You think it will collapse?' She smiled sadly.

'Unquestionably, Zola. I work at a predominantly black university. One's got one's ear to the ground there, you know. Unlike the whites in their lager jobs and businesses and white suburbs, like ostriches with their heads under the ground.' He laughed at his own use of the two metaphors. 'You'd think they could hear the subterranean rumbling. There's got to be some sort of earthquake coming.'

They took their tea into the lounge where they sat in silence. When Zola spoke her voice sounded far away. 'Some of our right-wing people want their own homeland. They want a portion of the country they can call their own. There's talk of the Orange River basin. Or a portion of the Transvaal. But there's also some who want to buy an island. They've even found an island for sale.'

'An island!' Harry pricked up his ears. 'So they can have an independent racist society?'

She shook her head. 'A place where they can continue their own culture and speak their own language. Others will be able to join them—from other countries, if they have enough money. It will be a farming community, like the old days in the Transvaal and Orange River Republics. The main thing is to develop a safe community.'

'Where their children can grow up in safety, without the fear of landmines?'

'Yes.' She smiled.

'And the other people who join them? I suppose they'd have to be white?'

She gave a half smile. 'I suppose so.'

They drank their tea in silence.

'You know,' Harry said ruminatively. 'Buying an island's not a bad idea. I've always liked the notion of an island. Maybe it's not such an implausible dream. It could be a unique community of like-minded people where children can play safely and families can flourish free of the stresses of modern life. A tropical island paradise!' He drank some more tea. 'What you want is to build a safe, caring, family-oriented, non-racist community that will be as self-reliant and self-sufficient as possible. You want a tolerant community, rejecting extreme political or religious dogmas in favour of a democratic approach.' His eyes took on a faraway look. 'The community could be based on agriculture, tourism and—' He smiled. 'Self-sufficient people like writers and artists. People who are centred! People who have a heightened sensitivity to beauty and can develop their own sense of purpose in becoming part of a new spiritual awakening. A place where everyone has access to a universe of dynamic energy. Where no single group dominates and exploits the energy of another, where there's no ongoing struggle for power.' His eyes shone as he put down his cup of tea. 'By God, Zola, it's a *wonderful* idea! Once the people become alert and connected to the source of universal energy, chance encounters and coincidences will begin that will promote their personal evolution. The island would become a beacon of love and goodwill in a world still emerging from the travail of change. Zola, where is this island that's for sale?'

She laughed. 'Harry, you can't be serious. Where did you get all those strange ideas about energy? And you want to know the price of the island?' She shook her head. 'The price of the island is twenty-five million American dollars!'

Harry blinked. '*That* much? But then, if you have a dream, anything is possible, Zola. To what extent do our expectations create all the things that happen to us? You can have anything you want, you know. All you have to do is find the right vehicle.' He felt quite flushed with excitement. He looked intensely at her. 'Zola, you said yourself you believed in spiritual healing. You could find your soul-level on that island. You said yourself you believed in the power of the earth to hold you safe and secure. You could help others to become fully realised beings. Look!' He stretched out his hand and touched the little pendant round her neck. 'You're still wearing your birthstone! You said it had healing properties. Zola, don't you think we were meant to meet? You've made me feel alive again, with this idea! Just where is this island, Zola?'

She smiled indulgently at him, her eyes still touched with sadness. 'It's in the Gulf of Panama. It's a small island, but as big as Bermuda.' She shook her head and touched his cheek. 'It's a lovely idea, Harry, but it's an impossible dream. You'd be running after rainbows, like the *Broederbond* people who are talking about it. How on earth could you raise all that money?

Not even the *Broederbond* can get enough people interested to go in with them.'

'But you could help me, Zola! We'd need to advertise for a community. I don't have much money but I—and you too—we could be the driving force behind it. Each person or family would have to contribute a certain amount of capital. We just have to work out the logistics.' He stared at her intently.

Her eyelids drooped, her lashes fanned against her cheeks. Then she raised her eyes to his—eyes that uncannily matched her green mascara and made them look larger than usual. She shook her head again. *'Ag,* darling, I'm sorry to be such a wet blanket, but it's a pipe dream. Think about it in the morning again and you'll see.' She laughed sadly. 'I'm a matron of a Cripplecare Home. What could I do on a paradise island?'

That night Harry's sleep was restless. The idea of the island had gripped him and it was a long time before he fell asleep. Then he dreamt of a blackbird that he had caught. It squirmed and twisted in his hands, trying to escape. It had jade eyes and a long beak that closed on his fingers and tried in vain to hurt him. At length he reached his house where he placed the blackbird on a table next to a pet monkey that had a funny face with big eyes. The monkey reached out and touched the blackbird. The bird fluttered, then settled, contentedly, next to the monkey.

When he woke up the dream of the blackbird and the previous evening's conscious dream of the island seemed oddly connected.

When he drove to work in the fresh champagne air of the morning he could see steam curling up from the hot water pipes in suburban Pietersburg. He had joined a lift club and it was his turn to drive. Just outside the town he and his companions saw a stiff body being removed by police from a lone stationary car: the man had gassed himself during the night and his body was frozen in a sitting position. When they drove past the small black township called Nobody the bare thorn bushes were sprouting white plastic bags and other assorted rubbish driven by a forgotten wind storm. 'This is the future Azania!' scoffed one of the party. The Naboom trees that were really cactus bushes imitating trees congregated in scattered clumps. Their uplifted fingers appealed in vain to the steel-blue sky that overarched the desiccated veldt. The flat-topped kopjes stood like sentries, and great boulders piled high came into view as the Mazda purred down the final mile towards the university. In the distance Sheba's Breasts, Rider Haggard's Mountains of the Moon, conjured up a suggestion of mystery and romance: blue paps shimmered like a mirage, a hollow promise of wealth and adventure in an Africa that had once made white men dream dreams.

When he reached his office he sat down and calculated the value of twenty-five million dollars in British sterling. It was a touch over fifteen million pounds. He would need to advertise for a community, he thought, and considered Britain a better recruiting ground than South Africa. But he would need someone in Britain to help him—to correlate the responses and to interview candidates. It would be an immense task, but worth it in the end.

He returned his calculator to his drawer, but noticed Karen's little compliment slip that had accompanied the bank draft she'd sent. He picked it up and read the little note she had scrawled. Her handwriting was neat, but sprawled a little towards the end. 'Congratulations on your new post,' it read. 'Look me up if you ever return to the U.K. God bless—Karen Elgin.'

He nearly dropped it. He'd never noticed her surname before. Now it hit him between the eyes. And he recalled that she'd said she was born in Durban! His flesh crawled with goosebumps. Was it just a coincidence? Was it possible she was under his nose all the time and that he had hardly noticed her?

He sat back, trying to remember what she was like. He remembered how depressed he was when she called him into the empty room, when Keith told him they would have to let him go. But she had looked at him sympathetically. He remembered the way she had crept closer and put her head to one side and smiled, a bit like Eleanor. It was as though she wanted to say more, but didn't. He had liked her, but she was linked with Keith who had dismissed him. In effect, *she* had dismissed him. She and Keith were a team.

He picked up the phone and asked for an outside line.

CHAPTER 46

Engaging the Flow

HARRY DIALLED and held his breath, listening to the ringing tone. When she answered he immediately recognised her soft, crisp English accent: 'Karen Elgin. How may I help you?'

He swallowed and took a deep breath. 'Karen? This is Harry. It seems I've forgotten how small English distances are.' He gave a nervous laugh. 'So I'm here already. Could I see you this evening?'

She was silent a moment. 'Good Lord, Harry, where are you?'

'In Harrogate—at the Beech Hotel, just opposite the road from you. I can see the mauve door of your flat from here—as I speak!' He laughed.

Her laughter bubbled spontaneously. 'Harry, I can't *possibly* see you tonight! I'm in the middle of washing my hair!'

'Later on then?'

She laughed again. 'Out of the question! Can't we stick to our appointment for tomorrow?'

'Yes, all right, then.' He felt disappointed. He was a day early and impatient to see her again.

'All right?' Her voice was kind with a suggestion of laughter held back. 'Can you cope?'

'Yes. Just one thing—did you receive the details from the Panama Government? And has there been any response to the ad?'

Her laughter bubbled. 'Oh God, Harry, half my bedroom's *inundated* with letters. It's going to take weeks just to read through them. And yes, a large envelope arrived from Panama. It's full of maps and photographs of the island. Also an offer from the President to have someone show you the island. He's made a helicopter and his own private plane available for the purpose. At least he's taking your interest seriously. And that's not all.'

'What do you mean?'

'I've been inundated with newspaper reporters, wanting to interview you. And Channel 4 wants to make a TV documentary of your plans. They've offered to sponsor your initial trip to the island. You'd have to put up with their reporters and cameramen, of course, but the publicity will quadruple your recruiting drive. And ITV wants you for a chat show.'

'Good grief, Karen. You've done a great job.'

Her laughter bubbled again. 'All I did was place your ad— and provide a U.K. address for you! Look Harry, my hair's dripping all over the place. Can we talk about this tomorrow evening?'

'Yes. Shall we have dinner together?'

'That'll be great. See you at 7.30 Harry.'

'See you then.' He put the phone down. He was elated by the news of the response to his advertisement as well as the response from Panama. But he wondered why he had to wait another 24-hours to see her because she was washing her hair. He'd never understand women, he decided.

He went back into the cosy lounge of the Beech Hotel where he had spent most of the afternoon watching the girls go by in Montpellier Parade, wondering which of them was Karen. None of the dark-haired girls he saw resembled the tall, elegant girl he last saw in London.

He sat down next to an elderly gentleman who was glaring at the silent TV screen. He noticed it was Top of the Pops, and some long-haired youths and busty girls in T-shirts were belting out a silent rhythm. The old man waved his arm contemptuously at the screen. 'It's a load o' roobish!' he declared. 'So I turned the sound off!'

'Right,' Harry smiled, nodding. He settled for admiring the way the full T-shirts of the girls jiggled to the silent melody. Their pretty young faces mouthed expressively. None of them looked like Karen, he thought, who had a soft and kind face. At least that's how he remembered her. She had reminded him a little of Eleanor and he wondered how she was. Since he was caught up in the notion of a tropical island community he barely thought of Eleanor again, though he thought much of the sort of philosophy she had presented about realising one's destiny or personal mission by engaging the energy flow of the universe.

'Aye, it's a load o' roobish!' repeated the man, glaring.

'Quite,' Harry nodded.

'I turned the sound off!' the man repeated.

'Quite right.' Harry smiled. He wondered how he was going to get through the next 24-hours waiting to see Karen. The next day was Friday and first she would have to go to work at the newly established Harrogate English Centre. When he first tried to phone her from South Africa he had dialled the number of the language academy in London. He was told she had taken a new position as Assistant Director of Studies in Harrogate. When he phoned her there she was delighted to hear from him. She even suggested he might be interested in applying for the vacant position of Director of Studies—though ideally he'd need a TEFL diploma. 'But you're such a big shot now,' she laughed. 'I don't suppose you'd be interested in small fries like us!'

He was amazed, seeing she and Keith had dismissed him from his previous academy job. 'The thing is, Karen,' he went on, 'I've got plans of my own. Something that seems rather fantastical, and I need someone to help me implicate them in the U.K. So I thought of you, with your organising abilities.'

'What are your plans?' Her quiet, steady voice was relaxed but intrigued.

'I want to buy a tropical island. I need to advertise for a community—and screen applicants. I'd like you to help me.'

She was silent. Then her bubbly laughter came down the line. 'That's funny, Harry. I could have *sworn* you said you wanted to buy a tropical island!'

'That's what I said. The price is fifteen million pounds.'

'Come again?' Her voice held back the laughter.

He had felt she had treated the whole idea with a sense of amused tolerance—but she was quite willing to place his advertisement in *The Sunday Times* and receive post on his behalf. As instructed by him, she had opened the post, especially the replies from Panama, in order to familiarise herself with the scheme. In the meantime he had written her a long letter setting out his objectives to establish a safe, family-oriented society that will be responsibly self-reliant, self-financing and as self-sufficient as possible—a society that will never be plagued by crime, and where the mission of the community would be the uplifting of every person that came into their lives. It was to be a future-oriented community that would grow peacefully into the next millennium as an Utopia of care and conscious serendipity, where each person's growth was the result of an enriched educational environment in the context of the universal flow of psychic energy.

Time lay heavily on his hands the next day. He walked in the Valley Gardens, sensing the beauty of the autumnal colours. He kicked his feet through the heaps of fallen leaves on the winding path. He was restless, wanting to get on to the next phase of his life. He was also nervous and excited at the same time about meeting Karen again. He followed an avenue of pines and found himself in a small wood. Shafts of light illuminated the ground with a patchwork of light and shade. The light dappled over him. A plague set in a stone caught his attention and he drew closer. 'Sing to God, sing praise to his name. Extol him who rides on the clouds.' He stood transfixed. There were glimpses of the clouds floating above. He walked away from the shade where he could see them clearly. They were rimmed with light and seemed close, hanging in the clear blue of the autumn sky.

He found a bench and soaked up the quiet beauty of the trees and rolling lawns, focusing his mind on the peace and calm. He remembered Eleanor telling him to focus on natural beauty to absorb the energy inherent in forests or mountain peaks. He smiled, remembering Zola's talk in Magoebaskloof about finding the plant-level of one's being. He saw swallows gathering in the branches above him. The feeling of bursting joy took him by surprise, welling up in his chest, then subsiding into a deep calming in his soul. He was embarking on a great new adventure which required both courage and confidence.

'A full professor doesn't just resign!' the Dean's secretary had said to him. But he *knew* he would succeed. He knew, too, that Karen, who at that moment was teaching just around the corner, was to provide a vital role in his destiny. He knew intuitively that somehow she was the Golden Key he sought. Everything he had experienced, even his infatuation for Eleanor and his passing love for Zola, had brought him to this moment. When he walked out of the gates of the gardens he saw the ivy-covered front of an impressive stone-built hotel. Two Rolls-Royce cars were parked in front of it. He walked over and booked dinner for two at 7.30.

He had identified the door of her flat the day before from the directions she'd given in a letter she sent him while he was still in South Africa. 'It's a mauve door between a travel agent and a souvenir shop—you know, one of those curiosity shops that sell silver bowls and compasses! It's easy to find because it's directly across the road opposite a large Beech tree. Find the tree and you've found me!' The Beech Hotel he found obviously took its name from the tree. In any case, she had given him her full address—31 Montpellier Parade, so he knew exactly where to find her when he knocked on her door. It was a coincidence, he thought, that she was also 31 years of age.

While he waited, he noticed a huge cutaway model of a ship in the travel agent's window. It showed the various levels and decks. It reminded him that he was bound for a destination beyond the shores of Britain. Thank God, he thought, those two old ladies had stopped to talk to him that night on the ferry.

When the door opened his heart missed a beat.

'Harry!' she said with a wide, fleeting smile.

She was just as he had remembered her—a tall girl with dark hair cut short, soft curls fluffed around her face. He couldn't see her face clearly in the dying light for she fiddled in her handbag, putting away her key. When she looked up her smile was engaging but businesslike. 'Do you like curry?' she said, already walking up Montpellier Parade.

'Actually, I've booked a table at the Old Swan,' he said, sprinting to catch up with her.

'Oh!' Her eyes registered surprise. She swung round, walking in her long, loose strides in the opposite direction. Harry had to breathe deeply and increase his normal pace to keep up with her. She wore a flowing black floral dress that swirled around her long legs as she walked.

They had a drink in the bar before ordering the meal. 'I hope you know what you're doing,' she smiled broadly at him. Her jade green eyes sparkled. 'And I hope your island venture doesn't turn out to be a Pandora's Box. It's certainly unleashed an incredible amount of interest. But the idea is wonderful, I'll give you that. You're not thinking of some kind of commune though, are you?'

He smiled, feeling relaxed by her calm, happy face that studied him mischievously, her eyes twinkling beneath her arched eyebrows. 'It will be idyllic as far as possible,' he said enthusiastically. 'But my dream is not a result of hippie-style wishful thinking, Karen.' He laughed. 'There'll be no communes, no free love, no healing temples. The community will not be religiously or politically motivated. The main thrust of the project is pragmatic: prospective islanders will need to pay up to £150,000 each. This will cover the cost of buying the island and creating farms and an infrastructure in order to make it viable.'

'You said the economy would be largely agrarian? A sort of eco-culture?'

He nodded. 'It would be family oriented. Each family would have their own private plot with a central farm to help support the community. One part of the island could be set aside for commercial purposes, of course, so inhabitants can make enough money to enjoy the sun without cash worries. A hotel would be built to generate tourist income, and possibly a water sports centre.'

She tilted her head in that characteristically sympathetic way of hers, a smile playing at the corners of her mouth. 'Some people have said it sounds cranky.'

He shook his head. 'All I want to do is create a safe and perhaps old-fashioned lifestyle where people care for each other and live together in harmony. It will be a model society in touch with ecological principles and the universal flow of energy. A society where intuition will show the way for a higher personal and social evolution.' He smiled, seeing her perplexed smile. 'It will be a place where each person is free to explore "the road not taken," as Frost calls it in his poem—you know, the road that leads to what might have been. Where people can respond to the coincidences and chance events that normally help them discover their true missions in life and help them grow.'

She smiled generously. 'A society of meaningful coincidences,' she said. 'What Freud called synchronicity. Coincidences are a primary way that the universe evolves, like natural selection. You want to build a society where your environment responds to the peoples' consciousness and expectations. Yes, I know what you mean. The education of the children would need to take account of this. Taking their lessons from nature.'

'Exactly.' He gave her a full smile, looking into her eyes. 'Where opportunities to realise dreams arise naturally because you're alert and connected to the energy of your environment. The challenge will be to see the silver lining in every event, and to move forward in an environment where there is no exploitation or manipulation of other people.'

She gave way to a burst of laughter, her eyes twinkling merrily. 'Oh, Harry, you'll have to crystallise your thinking a lot more if you want people to develop like that! But if you selected the right type of people, then you might have a chance.'

'That's where you could help me.'

They chatted pleasantly throughout the dinner. Karen announced that she was a vegetarian and Harry felt guilty asking for pheasant. She smiled, saying she didn't like the idea of eating anything that had a face. He liked her immensely, though doubted anyone so elegant and easy-going would be attracted to a burnt-out case like himself. But he felt more alive than ever in her company. Then he remembered that she and Keith had dismissed him from the language academy in London.

'I'm surprised you thought I might be eligible for the Directorship at the English Centre here,' he ventured. 'You weren't all that impressed with me in London.'

She coloured and dropped her eyes. 'I felt very awkward about that, Harry. The truth is there was a lot of favourable feedback about you from the third-world students. They thought you were marvellous.'

'But not the Dutch girl, if I remember correctly.' He smiled.

She looked up at him. 'The truth is, Harry, Keith and the Dutch girl were having a relationship. She was boarding with him. You might remember we asked staff members to help accommodate the students. Keith had the Dutch girl—in more ways than one.' She smiled coyly at him. 'I suspect she was giving him a great deal of favourable feedback about you and he didn't like it. He saw you as a competitor for his job.'

'Good heavens, Karen.' He looked at her, amazed. 'Then in a sense, *he* was a Toucher, too?'

Her laughter bubbled. 'But in all honesty, Harry, I did think your teaching suffered from tunnel vision. You seemed to be relying too much on textbooks. That's why I felt you'd benefit from a TEFL course at Pilgrims.'

'Yes,' he said quietly. 'I'm sure you're right.'

'A TEFL diploma would also have put you in a better position for Keith's job!' She laughed. 'You've got that little boy lost look again. I felt so awful when I was brought in to witness your dismissal. It was so unjust. I wanted desperately to speak to you. I'm sorry, Harry.'

'I remembered your look,' he smiled.

They went back to her flat for coffee and sat by an open fire. The fireplace had piles of wood next to it. They watched the flames flicker as they talked. He felt relaxed and tried not to be too aware of her cleavage and the swellings of her rounded breasts, like firm apples just peeping from the top of her black blouse. After an hour they arranged to meet the next day.

'It's been lovely talking to you, Karen,' he said, looking into her smiling green eyes. On impulse, he said: 'May I have your permission to kiss you.'

'All right then,' she said simply, smiling.

He placed his lips on hers, which were soft and delicate. All at once the floor dissolved under his feet and he felt himself tumbling through space. He was dimly aware of the gentle touch of her fingers on the back of his neck. He drew back with a deep breath, still dazed. 'Good night, Karen. You have C-category lips. I didn't know there was a C-category.'

'I'm sure I don't know what you mean!' she laughed. 'Good night, Harry.'

That night he was almost too excited to sleep. He had drunk nearly a full bottle of wine at dinner and during the night got up twice to relieve himself, feeling incredibly excited all the time. When he did sleep his dreams were full of impressions of Karen—her windswept curls, her slight provocative smile, her brilliant jade eyes laughing at him. When he awoke he recalled her cleavage and the swellings of her rounded breasts. But it wasn't merely her youthful beauty that stunned him. It was some quality ... a vitality. Being with her was like coming home.

The next day they met again and discussed the island project. In the evening she picked him up at his hotel in her little mini and took him for a drive to Fountains Abbey. The Gothic arches and colonnades were floodlit and Gregorian chants hummed in harmony from hidden speakers. Karen was dressed in a polo-neck sweater, jeans and red sneakers. A typical girl next door, he thought, looking appraisingly at her slim figure.

'This must be another energy centre,' he said, smiling. 'A girl I knew in Scotland spoke of energy centres and the importance of being centred. There's an Abbey in Jedburgh where I had a small hotel. Once I felt a strange sense of power there. I'd like to show it to you. I'd like the island to be an energy centre where people can come and energise themselves.'

'It sounds incredibly romantic and idealistic, Harry.' She stopped under one of the Gothic arches, smiling with her head coquettishly tilted. 'I really hope you can make it work. You'll need a lot of help.'

He took her hand. 'I was hoping you would help. Not just with my administration work here.' He looked intensely into her eyes. 'Come with me, Karen.'

Her laughter bubbled. 'Don't be silly, Harry. I'm a language teacher, not a pioneer!'

'But you're also so sensible, so capable of recognising genuine people and seeing through frauds. It's something I feel instinctively.' He smiled. 'I need someone who can help me select capable people. People who cope better because they're positive.' He squeezed her hand. 'And the better people cope, the more positive they become. I want to avoid the pathetic, spoilt people I sometimes used to serve at my old hotel—people who cancelled their bookings because the shower temperature wasn't exactly to their liking; who were paranoid about their material assets, like a man who made me stand guard over his Ford Escort all night, and others who complained about the car-park being too small or the attic rooms too small. People who complained the radio wasn't working because they couldn't see it wasn't plugged in.' He shook his head. 'No, I want positive, go-ahead people who aren't the product of a spoilt and pampered society. I'm sure you have a nose for people like that!'

'You hardly know me, yet you have a lot of confidence in me, Harry.' Her eyes crinkled. 'But it's true, I know a con person when I see one.'

He squeezed her hand. 'You can help me sift through the applicants. I need to eliminate wingers as well as brash materialists that glorify in their wealth, like people who brag about their success to recruit members in network marketing.' He looked at her intensely again. 'It will be worth it in the end. Just think of all the evils we'll be free from. We want to get away from loutish hooliganism, graffiti, drunken behaviour, joy riding, sexual abuse, and all the other dreadful crimes against humanity: landmines, muggings, robberies, senseless murders, political upheaval. We need to begin a new healthy society. One that will be a beacon for the world as it enters the new millennium.'

The Gregorian chants resonated in the silence. Karen laughed. *'Almost thou persuadest me*, Harry! You certainly have a sense of mission. I'll give you that.'

The following weekend she accepted his invitation to visit Jedburgh and they drove up together in her mini. They booked two rooms in the very hotel Harry used to own. The evening was cool and Harry put on a cardigan which felt tight around his waist. Then he remembered it was a cardigan given him by Zola. He looked at the reflection of the cardigan in the mirror, seeing his own face wistful with memory, and the sweetness and sadness of her smile came back to mind. He wondered how she was and made his way down to the payphone in the lobby. He dialled the South African code followed by Sarel's number in Pietersburg.

It was Johanna who answered the phone, her little voice trickling across the world from the southern hemisphere: *'Johanna hier!'*

'Johanna?' he smiled down the line. 'Can I speak to your Grannie please?'

There was silence. Then she said, in Afrikaans, *'Sy's dood, Oom.'*

Dead? He must have heard incorrectly. 'Your Grannie Zola,' he explained.

'*Wag, ek roep my ma*!' she said, running to call her mother.

Nettie's voice came clearly on the line. 'Harry? Is that you? Look, I'm sorry, Harry, but ma's dead. She died last week. I thought you knew. I left a message with the English Department. With the Secretary.'

A sense of unreality swept through him. Zola's sweet sad smile still lingered in his mind. The thought of her grave next to her husband in Potgietersrus swam before him. He saw the blank space on the wide granite headstone filled with her name, the date of her death newly chiselled in.

'Why? Why?' he heard himself saying automatically.

'She had an operation, you know. It was an emergency. It was kidney failure.'

It just didn't make sense. But he remembered the silvered scar tissue across her middle. She'd certainly had operations before. He had known so little about her, he realised.

Nettie said: 'I'm sorry, Harry. It's one of those things.'

'Yes,' he said. 'I'm sorry.'

'Goodbye, Harry.'

'Goodbye.'

He replaced the phone on its cradle and stared at it. It was like saying goodbye to his past. But he remembered her words, about leaving soon. Had she known her life was so soon to be extinguished? No wonder, then, she had not been interested in his new venture, though it was she who had opened those doors for him. He touched the sleeve of his cardigan. It was the closest he would ever be to her now. The cardigan was so tight-fitting it was almost uncomfortable. It was the closest she would ever come to hugging him. 'Every time you wear it, it's a hug from me.' It was difficult to think of her dead. There were many moments when he felt happy in her company. He smiled wistfully, counting the moments. Yes, he had made love to her thirteen times. He had meant to send her a bunch of thirteen roses when he left, but thought she wouldn't have appreciated the gesture. After all, there were times when their lovemaking made her feel like a 'dog,' as she said. Had she really felt so debased? Oddly enough, those first orgasms with her—in Dick's house and in her daughter's house—were amongst the most powerful and satisfying he had ever experienced. They had drained him so completely of lust, even of love, that they eradicated his need for her. In the end he couldn't even make the effort to write that poem she wanted him to write. He had just lost the motivation, he thought sadly—and now it was forever too late.

'Penny for them!' Karen's voice broke in on his reverie.

She looked fresh and alert, her smile wide and sincere, as she stood at the foot of the stairs. She seemed so self-possessed and confident, yet she evoked in him a warm, caring love that increased his desire to be with her. Her natural energy added to his own sense of confidence and well-being.

He smiled reassuringly. 'Oh, just musing about the past. Everything we do seems to be controlled by the past. Shall we visit the Abbey now? It's a monument to the past. After that we can move on—to the future.'

They walked through the grounds of the Abbey. Karen moved with a fluid grace, looking like a vision of beauty in a flowing white dress. Harry found the altar stone where he had once sat with Eleanor, and they sat down together with a clear view of the rose window down the length of the nave. The giant cylindrical columns that carried the arches produced the same sense of awe and power they had produced when he sat there with Eleanor. The same patchwork of light and shade lay across the floor of the nave he had seen in the tree-lined arcade in Harrogate. Light fell in shafts between the rows of pillars.

'This place produces a kind of cosmic resonance,' Harry said, looking at the rose window through the shafts of light. 'Like the time when I was a boy. There was a moment at school when I was drinking milk in the open. I had a sudden awareness, a sort of epiphany, of the strangeness of existence. Why do the stars exist, the planets and the earth? Why do we exist at all?'

'I know what you mean,' she whispered. Her fingers tightened on his.

He was struck by a sudden sense of *déjà vu*, and the sensation thrilled him, filled him with a sense of overflowing love for Karen. His words slipped out naturally: 'I love you, Karen.'

'I love you too,' she said, her fingers tightening on his once more.

He turned and looked at her. Her head was almost on the same level as his and he gazed into her smiling eyes. 'You're still here?'

'Did you expect me to disappear?' Her eyes twinkled.

'Did you really say what you said?'

Her smile broadened. 'I know it's crazy, but yes—I did.'

'Will you help me set up the island?'

She squeezed his hand. 'Try and stop me!'

THE END